CRAZY FOR YOU

Jennifer Crusie is the author of *Tell Me Lies*, as well as
the award-winning author of nine romances. She teaches
writing and literature at Ohio State University

Also by Jennifer Crusie

TELL ME LIES

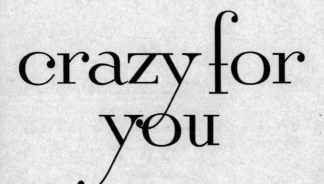

crazy for you

Jennifer Crusie

PAN BOOKS

First published 1999 by St. Martin's Press,
175 Fifth Avenue, New York, N.Y. 10010

First published in Great Britain 2000 by Pan Books
an imprint of Macmillan Publishers Ltd
25 Eccleston Place, London SW1W 9NF
Basingstoke and Oxford
Associated companies throughout the world
www.macmillan.co.uk

ISBN 0 330 39015 5

A CIP catalogue record for this book is available
from the British Library.

Printed and bound in Great Britain by
Mackays of Chatham plc, Chatham, Kent

For
Lee K. Abbott,
a god among men

acknowledgments

THIS IS MY chance to show my long-overdue gratitude to the faculty of the Ohio State University Creative Writing Department, in particular Lee K. Abbott, Melanie Rae Thon, Lore Segal, Michelle Herman, and Bill Roorbach, for their support, guidance, and wisdom. I'd also like to thank Ron Carlson and Alice MacDermott, visiting professors who taught me so much in such a short time, and Christopher Griffin and Cartha Sexton for keeping the administrative part of my education on track so that I actually graduated. Finally, I must thank my fellow students in the Creative Writing Program, who did me the ultimate honor of treating my work with respect and attention, for their encouragement and companionship. In particular, I am grateful to Will Allison, Richard Ashbrook, Michael Azre, Michael Charlton, Jennifer Cognard-Black, Kristina Emick, Polly Farquhar, David Ferguson, Kathryn Flewelling, Steve Guinan, Vicki Henriksen, Michael Lohre, Jeff MacGregor, Bruce Machart, Susan McGowan, Susan Metcalfe, Tom Moss, Jason Nunemaker, Dan O'Dair, Bruce Ortquist, Todd Renger, Bonnie Riedinger, Vicki Schwab, John Shamlou, Deborah Sobeloff, Tamara Stevens, Laura Swenson, Mary Tabor, Rick Vartorella, and Deborah Way. I apologize to anyone I may have missed.

one

ON A gloomy March afternoon, sitting in the same high school classroom she'd been sitting in for thirteen years, gritting her teeth as she told her significant other for the seventy-second time since they'd met that she'd be home at six because it was Wednesday and she was always home at six on Wednesdays, Quinn McKenzie lifted her eyes from the watercolor assignments on the desk in front of her and met her destiny.

Her destiny was a small black dog with desperate eyes, so she missed the significance at first.

She didn't miss anything else. The dog that her favorite art student held out to her was the canine equivalent of an exposed nerve: wiry black body, skinny white legs, narrow black head, all of it held together with so much tension that the poor baby shuddered with it. It looked cold and scared and hungry and anxious as it struggled in Thea's arms, and Quinn's heart broke. No animal should ever look like that.

"Oh." Quinn rose on the word and went toward Thea while Bill groaned and said, "Not another one."

"I found it in the parking lot." Thea put the dog down on the floor in front of Quinn. "I knew you'd know what to do."

"Come on, baby." Quinn crouched in front of it, not too near, not too far, and patted the floor. "Come here, sweetie. Don't be scared. It's all right now. I'll take care of you."

The dog trembled even harder, jerking its head from side to side. Then it made a dash for the nearest door, which, unfortunately for it, was the storeroom.

"Well, that'll make it easier to trap and catch," Bill said, his tone as cheerful and sure as always. It was always a beautiful day in the neighborhood for Bill, a man who'd taken the Tibbett High football team to five consecutive championships and the baseball team to four—fifth one coming right up—almost solely, Quinn believed, by never considering the possibility of defeat. "Know where you want to be and go there," he'd tell the boys, and they would.

Quinn decided she wanted to be someplace else, with a pizza, but she had to comfort this dog and get rid of Bill before she could go there. She crawled on her hands and knees to the door, trying to look nonthreatening. "Now look, dogs like me," she said in her best come-to-mama voice as the dog cowered against a carton of oaktag at the back of the narrow storeroom. "You're missing a good deal here. Really, I'm famous for this. Come on." She moved a little closer, still on her hands and knees, and the dog peeled its eyes back.

"I suppose you had to do this," Bill said to Thea good-naturedly, and Quinn felt equally annoyed with him and guilty about misleading him. "No more dogs," he'd said the last time she'd rescued a stray. "You don't have to save them all." And she'd nodded at him to acknowledge that she'd heard him, and he'd taken it as agreement, and she'd let him take it that way because it was easier, no point in creating a problem she'd just have to turn around and fix.

And now here she was, cheating on him with a mixed breed.

She looked into the dog's eyes again. *It's going to be all right. Ignore what the big blond guy says.* The dog relaxed away from the box a little and looked at her with caution instead of terror in its worried little eyes. Progress. If she had another ten hours and a ham sandwich, it might even come to her on its own.

"You're not bringing it home with you, right?" Bill loomed behind her, cutting off the afternoon light that came dimly through the wall of windows and casting a shadow over her so that the dog shrank back again, anxious at the darkness. It wasn't Bill's fault that he was huge, but he could at least notice that he cast considerable shade wherever he went.

"Because we're not allowed to have dogs in our apartment." Bill's voice was patient as he went on, a teacher's voice, telling her what she already knew, guiding her to form the correct conclusion.

My conclusion is that you're patronizing me. "Somebody has to rescue strays and find them homes," Quinn said without looking behind her.

"Exactly," Bill said. "Which is why we pay taxes to support Animal Control. Why don't I go call them—"

"The pound?" Thea's voice was full of horror.

"They don't kill them all," Bill said. "Just the sick ones."

Quinn looked behind her and met Thea's disbelieving eyes. *Yep,* Quinn wanted to tell her, *he really believes that.* Instead, she patted the floor again. "Come here, baby. Come on."

"Honey." Bill put his hand on her shoulder. "Come on, get up."

If she shrugged his hand off her shoulder, he'd be hurt, and that wasn't fair. "I'm okay," Quinn said.

Bill moved his hand, and Quinn let out a breath she didn't know she'd been holding.

"I'll just call—"

"Bill." Quinn kept her voice as friendly as she could. "Go finish in the weight room so I can do this. I'll be home at six."

Bill nodded, radiating tolerance and support in spite of her illogical resistance to Animal Control. "Sure. I'll go warm up the car for you and bring it to the door first." He patted her shoulder and said, "You stay here," as if she'd been planning to follow him, and after he left, she could picture him crunching his way across the icy parking lot toward her CRX as if slipping weren't a possibility. It probably wasn't for him; Vikings loved ice, and at six foot five, two hundred and forty-three healthy blond pounds, Bill was a Viking's Viking. All of Tibbett adored Bill, a coach in a million, but Quinn was beginning to have doubts.

And it was so unfair of her to have doubts. She knew he'd warm the car for her, first opening the door with his key instead of hers, which was another thing about him that bothered her, that he'd had that key cut without her permission two years ago when they'd first begun to date. But since he'd had the key cut so he could keep her gas tank filled, it was completely illogical that she should be annoyed. It was wrong to complain about a man who was unfailingly clean, generous, considerate, protective, understanding, and successful, and who'd shelled out hundreds of dollars in fossil fuel for her since 1997. Really, the dumbass was the perfect man.

Quinn looked at the dog again and said, "As soon as I get you out of this storeroom, I'm taking a serious look at my love life."

Thea said, "What?" but even before she finished the word, Quinn was shaking her head.

"Never mind. You don't have any food in that bag, do you? I know I could just go in and grab it, but it's so scared, I'd rather it came to me on its own."

"Wait." Thea fished around in the huge leather bag she carried everywhere and came up with half a granola bar.

"Granola," Quinn said. "What the hell." She unwrapped it and broke off a piece and slid it across the floor to the dog. It shrank back and then edged forward, its little black nose quivering. "It's good," Quinn whispered, and the dog took it delicately.

"What a nice little dog," Thea whispered beside her, and Quinn nodded and put another piece on the floor, this one closer to them. The dog edged forward to take it, keeping its eyes on them just in case they did anything anti-dog, big dark liquid eyes that said to Quinn, *Help me, save me, fix my life*.

"Come on, sweetie," Quinn whispered, and the dog came closer for the next piece.

"Almost," Thea breathed, and the dog sat down in front of them, still wary but calmer as it chewed the granola.

"Hi," Quinn said. "Welcome to my world."

The dog tilted its head, and its little black whip of a tail began to dust the floor. It had one white eyebrow, Quinn noticed, and four white socks, and the tip of its tail was white, too, as if it had been dipped in paint.

"I'm going to pick you up," Quinn told it. "No fast moves." She reached out and picked it up gently as it cowered back a little, and then she sat down so she could hold it in her lap. She gave it the last of the granola, and it relaxed and chewed again as she stroked its back. "Really a sweet little dog," she told Thea and smiled for the first time since Bill had walked in the room. Another problem solved.

"Car's here," Bill said from the doorway, making the dog jump. "Now you can take it to Animal Control on your way to pizza."

Quinn patted the dog and counted her blessings. She was *lucky* to have Bill; after all, she could have ended up with somebody difficult to live with, somebody like her father, who lived for ESPN, or her ex-brother-in-law, who was congenitally incapable of commitment. Nick would have dumped her after a year and moved on from boredom, which was a lousy reason to dump anybody. If it hadn't been, she would have left Bill long ago.

"It's out on the old highway," Bill said. "Past the old drive-in."

Quinn smiled at Thea. "You did good, thanks for the granola." She stood up, still cuddling the dog, and Bill picked up her coat.

"Put that thing down," he said and held her coat for her.

Quinn passed the dog over to Thea and let Bill help her shrug into her coat.

"Don't stay too long with Darla," he said and kissed her cheek again, and she moved past him to take the dog back, wanting the warmth of its wiry little body in her arms. It looked up at her anxiously, and she said, "We're fine, don't worry."

Bill walked them to the door and then outside into the cold March wind, holding Quinn's car door open for her while she asked Thea, "You need a ride?"

Thea said, "Nope. See you tomorrow." She hesitated, casting a wary eye at Bill and added, "Thanks, McKenzie."

"My pleasure," Quinn said, and Thea started off across the ice to the student lot as Quinn slid into the driver's seat.

"You are going to take it to Animal Control, right?" Bill said as he held her door open.

Quinn turned away. "I'll see you later." She pulled the door shut and Bill sighed as if his worst suspicions had been confirmed. She looked down at the dog now standing tensely on her lap, and said, "You know, you're messing up my day," in her most friendly voice. *Nothing wrong here, nothing at all, everything's fine in this car, especially if you're a dog.* "I was supposed to meet Darla for pizza at three-thirty, and now I'm late. You weren't part of my plan."

The dog's eyes were bright, almost interested, and Quinn smiled because it looked so smart. "I bet you are smart," she said. "I bet you're the smartest dog around."

The dog folded its bony little butt onto her lap, wrapping its white-tipped tail around it as it cocked its head at her.

"Very cute." She stroked its shiny smooth coat, feeling how cold it was, no insulation to keep a body warm, and the dog shuddered under her hand, all sinew and muscle and tension.

Quinn unbuttoned her coat and wrapped it around the trembling little body until only its head poked out, and it sighed against her and snuggled into her heat. The snuggle was immensely gratifying—a solid, simple, physical *thank you,* no strings attached—and Quinn let herself enjoy the pleasure of the moment even though she knew it wasn't hers to have. Bill would be upset if he saw her, telling her she could get bit or fleas or God knew what, but Quinn knew this dog wouldn't bite, and it was too cold for fleas. Probably.

"It's okay," she said, looking down into the dog's dark, grateful eyes. It pushed its head under her coat, looking for more warmth and safety, and Quinn felt herself relax completely for the first time that day. Teaching art was never easy—days full of X-Acto knife cuts and spilled paint and officious principals and artistic despair—and lately she'd been tenser than usual, a little depressed, as if something was *wrong* and she wasn't fixing it. But now as she cuddled the dog closer and it dug one of its bony little knees into her stomach, she felt better.

"What a sweetie you are," she whispered into her coat.

Bill rapped on the window, making the dog jerk its head out, and Quinn exhaled through her teeth before she rolled it down. "What?"

"I was just thinking," Bill said, and then he looked down and saw the dog inside her coat. "Is that a good idea?"

"Yes," Quinn said. "What were you just thinking?"

"You're going to be late for pizza with Darla anyway," Bill said, "so it makes sense to take it to Animal Control now so that a lot of people will see it sooner. It'll find a home faster that way."

Quinn imagined the little dog shivering on a cold concrete floor, trapped and alone and afraid behind thick steel bars, doubly betrayed because she'd promised it warmth. She looked down into its dark, dark eyes again. Somebody had thrown this darling little dog away. It wasn't going to happen again. *I will not betray you.*

"Be practical, Quinn." Bill sounded sympathetic but firm. "Animal Control is a clean, warm place."

Her coat was a clean, warm place, too, but that would be a childish thing to say. Okay, she couldn't keep the dog, that wouldn't be practical, she had to give it to somebody, but there was no way in hell it was going to Animal Control. So who?

The dog looked at her with trusting eyes. Almost adoring eyes, really. Quinn smiled down at it. She needed to find somebody kind, somebody calm, somebody she trusted absolutely. "I'll give it to Nick," she told Bill.

"Nick does not want a dog," Bill said. "Animal Control—"

"We don't know that." Quinn cuddled the dog closer. "He owns his apartment over the service station so he won't have a landlord problem. I bet he'd like this dog."

"Nick is not going to take this dog," Bill said firmly, and Quinn knew he was right. As Darla had once pointed out, the best way to describe Nick was tall, dark, and detached from humanity. She was grasping at a particularly weak straw if she thought Nick was going to put himself out for a dog.

"Take it to Animal Control," Bill said, and Quinn shook her head.

"Why?" Bill said and Quinn almost said, *Because I want her.*

The thought was so completely selfish and felt so completely right that Quinn looked at the dog with new eyes.

Maybe she was meant to keep this dog.

The thrill that ran through her at the thought of doing something that impractical was almost sexual, it was so intense. *I don't care that it's not sensible,* she could say. *I want her.* How selfish. How exciting. Quinn's heart beat faster thinking about it.

Just a little selfish. A dog was such a small thing to want, not a change of life or a change of lover or really a change of anything much. Just a little change. Just a little dog. Something new in her life. Something different.

She held the dog closer.

Her mother's best friend, Edie, had been telling her for years to stop settling, to stop being so practical, to stop fixing everybody else and fix herself. "I'm not broken," she'd told Edie, but maybe Edie was right. Maybe she'd start small, with a dog, with *this* dog, with a little change, a little fix, and then she could move on to bigger things. Maybe this dog was a Sign, her destiny. You couldn't argue with destiny. Look what happened to all the Greek heroes who'd tried.

"You can't keep the dog," Bill said, and Quinn said, "Let me talk to Edie."

Bill smiled, his handsome face flooding with relief and goodwill. One happy Viking. "Great idea. Edie's all alone. She could use this dog for company. Now you're thinking."

That's not what I meant, Quinn wanted to say, but there was no point in starting a fight, so she said, "Thank you, good-bye," instead. She rolled the window up, looking into the dog's dark eyes. "You're going to be just fine." The dog sighed a little and rested her head on Quinn's chest, keeping eye contact as if her life depended on it, trembling a little bit in her intensity. Smart, smart dog. Quinn patted her to slow her quivering and smiled. "You look like a Katie. K-K-K-Katie, just like the song. A pretty, skinny K-K-K-Katie." She bent closer and whispered, "My Katie," and the dog sighed her agreement and burrowed back to shiver into the dark warmth of Quinn's coat.

Outside the window, Bill waved at her, clearly pleased she was being so practical, and she waved back. She could deal with him later, but now she was late to eat pizza.

With her dog.

———

ACROSS TOWN, IN the brightly lit second bay of Ziegler Brothers' Garage and Service Station, Nick Ziegler leaned under the hood of Barbara Niedemeyer's Camry and scowled at the engine. As far as he could tell, there was nothing wrong with it, which meant Barbara had an ulterior motive, and he had a pretty good idea what it was, given Barbara's taste for married blue-collar men. His brother Max's number must have come up. This was going to be a problem for Max, but nothing for Nick to worry about in general. People needed to go to hell in their own way, he'd decided long ago when he'd gone to hell in his, and if he had some scars from past screwups, he had some interesting memories, too. No point in getting in the way of Max's memories.

He slammed the hood shut on Barbara's Trojan horse, pulled a rag out of his back pocket, and wiped the gleaming paint to make sure he hadn't left fingerprints. Then he walked over to the third garage bay to inspect his next problem, Bucky Manchester's muffler.

"Did you find a leak in the Toyota?" Max asked Nick from the door to the office.

"There is no oil leak." Nick stood under Bucky's Chevy, wiping his hands on the rag, surveying the damage. The b-pipe looked like brown lace. He'd have to call Bucky and tell him there would be significant money involved. Bucky wouldn't be happy, but he'd trust him.

"That's what I told Barbara," Max said. "But she said, 'Look again, please.' That woman is just overcautious."

Nick considered warning Max that Barbara was not interested in a phantom oil leak, but he didn't consider it for long. Max wasn't a cheater, and even if he lost his mind and actually contemplated it, there was Darla. Darla was not the kind of wife a man messed around on and lived to tell the tale. Barbara was a nonproblem.

"She's never been that fussy about her car before," Max groused on as he came out of the office. "You'd think she didn't trust us anymore." He stopped to squint out one of the windows in the door of the first bay. "Did Bill knock Quinn up when we weren't looking?"

Nick's hand tightened on the rag, and he stared at the b-pipe for a couple of seconds before he answered. "Doesn't seem like something Bill would do."

"She's going into the Upper Cut." Max squinted through the window. "And she looks like she's holding her stomach. Maybe she's sick."

The door was on Nick's way to the office anyway, so he walked over and ducked his head to look past Max's ear. Quinn did look awkward as she struggled with the door to the beauty parlor, her navy peacoat bunched bulky around her stomach, her long, strong, jeans-clad legs braced against the wind, the auburn swash of her pageboy swinging forward as she bent over. Then she turned to lean into the door, and he saw a dog poke its head up from the neck of her coat. "Forget it," he told Max. "It's a dog."

"I am not adopting another dog," Max said. "Two is more than enough."

Nick stopped at the sink to get the last of the oil off his hands. "Maybe she's going to give it to Lois."

"It's Wednesday," Max said gloomily. "She's meeting Darla over there for pizza. She'll talk her into it, and then we'll have to get used to another one." Then he brightened. "Unless Lois kicks her out for bringing the dog in. She's awful particular about that beauty parlor."

Nick nudged the tap with his wrist. "If Quinn wants to take the dog in, Lois will let her." The hot water splashed over his hands, and he scrubbed gritty soap into them, paying more attention than usual because he was irritated with Max and he didn't like being irritated with Max. Nick turned the taps off and dried his hands and heard Max finish a sentence he'd missed the beginning of. "What?"

"I said, Lois would have to be in an awful good mood to let that happen."

"She probably is." Nick's annoyance made him go on to add a little grief to Max's life. "She's probably heard that Barbara dumped Matthew."

Max looked as startled as possible for somebody with a permanently placid face. "What?"

"Barbara Niedemeyer set Lois's husband free," Nick said. "Pete Cantor told me this morning."

Max pointed a finger at Nick. "Anything else Barbara wants checked, you're doing."

"Why don't you just run a full check on the damn car now so she doesn't have to come back?" Nick walked over to the office to call Bucky. "Save us both a lot of trouble."

"She's a good-looking woman," Max said. "Good job at the bank. You check the car."

"I don't need a woman with a good job. Barbara's car is all yours and so is Barbara."

"You own half the garage," Max said. "Hell, you're single. Why isn't she asking you to check her oil leak?"

"Because she likes you better, thank God." As Nick went in the office, he heard Max let out a sigh behind him, and then, a couple of minutes later, from where he stood dialing Bucky, he heard the hood go up on Barbara's Toyota.

"Nick?" Max said from under the hood.

"Yeah?"

"Sorry about that crack about Quinn. I didn't mean it the way it came out."

Nick listened to the busy signal at the Manchesters' and thought of Quinn, warm and determined and dependable, the complete opposite of her scatty sister, Zoë. Quinn in trouble wasn't funny. "Doesn't matter."

"I know you're close."

Nick hung up. "Not that close."

When Max didn't say anything else, Nick went back into the garage and put his mind where it belonged, on the Chevy. Cars were understandable. They took a little patience and a lot of knowledge, but they always worked the same way. They were fixable. Which was more than he could say for people. Nothing a good mechanic could have done about him and Zoë, for instance. He didn't think about Zoë much any more; even the news she'd gotten married again ten years ago hadn't made much more than a crease in his concentration. Nothing like the crease Max had just made with that crack about Quinn.

"Nick?"

Max's voice was still a little worried, so Nick said, "You don't suppose Barbara has two cars, do you? You could be spending some significant time with her."

"Funny," Max said, but he went back to work and let Nick concentrate on the muffler. It was the only real problem he had, anyway, since Max would never cheat on Darla, and Quinn was always rescuing strays and giving them away. Nothing in his world was going to change.

Except Bucky Manchester's b-pipe.

ACROSS THE STREET, Darla Ziegler plopped herself onto the beat-up tweed couch in the tiny break room of the Upper Cut just as Lois Ferguson came in scowling, her impossibly orange upsweep making her look like a small torch. Lois had been trying to establish her authority over Darla ever since she'd taken over the Upper Cut six years before, but Darla had watched Lois eat paste in kindergarten. After that, there was no turning back.

"You done for the day?" Lois snapped. "It's only four."

"It's pizza day," Darla said. "I'm done."

"Well, you made that Ginny Spade looked good, I'll give you that." Lois folding her arms so tightly that her gray smock stretched flat over her bony little chest. "Better'n she has in years."

"Yeah, maybe now she'll meet somebody and get over that worthless, cheating Roy," Darla said, and then kicked herself for forgetting that it had only been a year since Lois had lost a worthless, cheating Matthew.

"Matthew wants to come back," Lois said, and Darla sat up a little to pay attention to Lois for a change just as Quinn came breezing in the door from the shop with her copper hair flying and a dog tucked inside her peacoat.

"I know I'm late," she said. "I'm sorry—"

Darla blinked her surprise at the dog and then held up her hand. "Wait a minute." She looked at Lois. "You are kidding me. He left her?"

"Who left who?" Quinn struggled to shrug her coat off one arm at a time. The dog looked fairly ratty, Darla noticed. But rescuing ugly dogs was business as usual for Quinn and not nearly as interesting as the bomb Lois had just dropped, so she kept her attention on Lois.

"That's a dog," Lois said.

"Good call." Quinn draped her coat over the back of one of the avocado armchairs. "I'll hold on to her. She'll never touch the floor, I swear. Who left who?"

"Ha." Lois's lips curved in a tight little smile as she returned to her triumph. "Barbara left Matthew. The Bank Slut dumped him good yesterday."

"Wow." Quinn sank into her chair with the dog cradled in her arms.

"Jeez." Darla sat back, exhaling as she considered the development. "They've been tighter than ticks for a whole year. What happened?"

"Something on that damn trip to Florida they took." Lois's lips pressed together harder. "He never took me on any damn trip to Florida."

Darla ran down the possibilities in her mind. "Another man?"

"If it was, he's gone, too. She's in town, and she's living alone in that little house of hers, and Matthew's down at the Anchor." Lois sat down in the other rump-sprung armchair across from Darla. "He wants to move back."

Darla shrugged. "That makes sense. What guy wants to live in a motel?"

"You going to take him back?" Quinn asked.

Lois shrugged. "Why should I? I got the house to myself and this place. What do I need him for?"

Darla thought about Max. "Friendship. Fun. Sex. Memories. Somebody to kiss on New Year's Eve."

"He left me for a Bank Slut," Lois said. "How much friendship do you think we got at this point?"

Something about the way Lois rolled the words *Bank Slut* off her tongue made Darla fairly sure Lois wasn't focusing her anger on Matthew. Maybe this marriage could be saved. Lois would sure be easier to work for if it could. "You married him the day after we graduated. You were with him for sixteen years. He only spent a year with Barbara Niedemeyer, and now he's sorry. That's something." At least, Darla assumed he was sorry. If he wanted to come back to Lois knowing how bitchy she could be even before he left her for a younger woman, he must be *really* sorry now. "And he makes good money." She thought back to the last time Matthew had fixed their sink. "He makes damn good money."

"I make good money, too," Lois said. "Who needs him?"

"Well, you do," Quinn said, practical as always, "or you wouldn't be talking about it."

"It just makes me mad, that's all." Lois's jaw clenched tighter before she went on. "We were doing just fine, and then she comes in with her broken bathtub drain and stopped-up sink and plans for a second bath downstairs, like she needed a second bathroom, living there all alone, if you ask me, she had it planned—"

Darla tuned her out, having heard this rant before, several times, in fact, since Barbara Niedemeyer had walked off with Matthew the previous April. As far as Barbara planning it, well, it wasn't as if Matthew had been her first married man. Really, Lois should have caught on when Barbara had started talking about the second bathroom. Darla would have caught on with the second service call. The woman had a track record. Matthew was number three, for heaven's sake.

"—and now he thinks he's going to come waltzing back in," Lois finished. "Well, the hell with him."

"I'd think about it some more," Darla said. "Barbara's sort of like the flu. Men catch her, but then they get over her. Gil and Louis don't seem to have any warm feelings for her. Last I heard, Louis was getting married again. I mean, obviously, Barbara's men recover. And Matthew makes damn good money, so he's going to have his chances if you don't take him back."

Lois glared at her.

"She has a point," Quinn said. "If you want him back."

Darla spread her hands and tried to look innocent. "All I'm saying is, if you really didn't care, you wouldn't be this mad. Take him back. Make him pay. You work it right, he'll take you on a damn trip to Florida."

"You don't get it," Lois said. "What if it was Max?"

The thought of Max cheating was so ridiculous, Darla almost snickered. Max was gorgeous and about as nice as a human male could be, but women didn't even flirt with him because he was so clearly Happily Married. Or at least, if she were honest, clearly uninterested in any change in his life. That wasn't quite the same thing, really. Darla's urge to snicker faded, and she told herself she was lucky to have a guy who was so content. "I'd say, 'Max, you jackass, what the hell were you *thinking?*'" she told Lois. "And then I'd take him back. He's your husband, Lois. He fucked up and he should pay, but you shouldn't just give up on him."

Lois still looked mad, but there was some thoughtful mixed in with the mad.

"Unless you don't love him anymore," Quinn said. "Unless you really want to be free to do what you want."

"Hello?" Darla said to her. This wasn't like Quinn, the fixer. "Of course she wants him back."

Lois stood up. "That's ridiculous," she said and went back out to the shop, slamming the door behind her.

"You know, I don't understand Barbara," Quinn said, frowning as she patted the dog in her lap. "She's a nice woman. Why does she keep snagging other women's husbands?"

"Because she's not a nice woman," Darla said flatly. "What's with you telling Lois to be free? Lois wants to be free like she wants to be middle-aged."

"I just thought she should think about it," Quinn said, settling back in her chair, not meeting Darla's eyes at all. "There's nothing that says that life is always better if you have a man around."

"It is in Tibbett," Darla said. "You really think Lois wants to hang out at Bo's Bar & Grill and pick up divorced drunks for recreation?"

Quinn made a face. "Oh, come on. There has to be a middle ground between marriage and Bo's."

"Sure. There's Edie's life." Darla stretched out on the couch again. "Teaching all week, going to garage sales with your mom on her time off, reheating leftovers in a lonely house at night." It sounded like hell to Darla.

"Alone doesn't have to mean lonely," Quinn said. "I think Edie likes the solitude—she's always talking about how good it is to get home where it's quiet. And you can be with somebody and be lonely."

As far as Darla was concerned, being lonely with somebody was probably the way most people lived. Not that she was lonely with Max.

Quinn cuddled the runty little dog closer and did not look happy, and Darla narrowed her eyes. "Something wrong with you and Bill?"

Quinn stared down into the dog's eyes. "No."

"Okay," Darla said. "Out with it."

Quinn shifted in her chair again while the dog watched them both. "I'm going to keep this dog."

You have beige carpeting, Darla wanted to say, but it didn't seem supportive.

"Bill wants me to take her to Animal Control," Quinn went on. "But I'm keeping her. I don't care what he says."

"Jeez." Darla caught the lift of Quinn's chin and felt the first faint stirrings of alarm. Bill was being incredibly dumb about this. "He's known you for two years, and he doesn't know you any better than to think you'd take a dog to the pound?"

"It's the practical thing to do," Quinn said, her eyes still on the dog. "I'm a practical person."

"Yeah, you are." Darla felt definitely uneasy now. The one thing she'd always wanted for Quinn was a marriage as good as her own. All right, Bill was a little boring, but so was Max. You couldn't have everything. You compromised. That was what marriages were about. "What if he says, 'It's the dog or me'? Tell me you're not going to risk your relationship over a dog."

The dog looked over as she spoke, almost as if it were narrowing its eyes at her, and Darla noticed for the first time how sneaky it looked. Tempting. Almost devilish. Well, that made sense. If Quinn had been in Eden, Satan would have showed up as a cocker spaniel.

"Bill's not difficult like that." Quinn leaned back, obviously trying to sound nonchalant and only sounding tenser because of it. "We don't have problems. He wants every day to be the same, and since they always are, he's happy."

That could be Max. "Well, that's men for you."

"The thing is, I don't think that's enough for me." Quinn petted the dog, who leaned into her, gazing up at her with those hypnotic dark eyes, luring her into messing with a perfectly good relationship. "It's starting to get to me, knowing this is going to be my life forever. I mean, I love teaching, and Bill's a good guy—"

"Wait a minute." Darla sat up. "Bill's a *great* guy."

Quinn shrank back a little. "I know."

"He works his butt off for those kids on the team," Darla said. "And he stayed after school to coach Mark for the SATs—"

"I know."

"—and he's the first one in line every time there's a charity drive—"

"I *know*."

"—and he was teacher of the year last year, and that was long overdue—"

"Darla, I *know*."

"—and he treats you like a queen," Darla finished.

"Well, I'm tired of that," Quinn said, her chin sticking out again. "Look, Bill's nice—okay, he's great," she said, holding up her hands as Darla started to object again. "But what we have, it's not exciting. I've never had exciting. And with the way Bill plans things, I'm never going to have exciting."

I *did*, Darla wanted to say. She and Max had been hot as hell once. She could see him now—that look in his eye as he zeroed in on her, that grin that said, *I have plans for you*, the way they laughed together—but you couldn't expect that to last. They'd been married seventeen years. You couldn't keep exciting for seventeen years.

"It's not really Bill's fault," Quinn said. "I mean, I didn't have exciting before he showed up, either. I just don't think it's in the cards for me. I'm not an exciting person."

Darla opened her mouth and shut it again. Quinn was a darling, but—

"See?" Quinn finally met Darla's eyes, defeated. "You want to tell me I'm exciting and you can't. Zoë was exciting, I'm dull. Mama used to say, 'Some people are oil paintings and some people are watercolors,' but what she meant was, 'Zoë is interesting and you're sort of washed out.'"

"You're the dependable one," Darla said. "You're the one everybody leans on. If you were exciting, we'd all be screwed."

Quinn slumped back. "Well, I'm *tired* of that. And it's not like I'm going out Bungee-jumping or something stupid. I just want this dog." The dog looked up at her again, and Darla's uneasiness morphed into real dread. "That's not even exciting, adopting a dog. And it's not so much to want, is it?"

"Well, that depends." Darla glared at the dog. *This is all your fault.*

"Don't you ever want more?" Quinn leaned forward, her hazel eyes now fixed on Darla's with a passion that made her uncomfortable. "Don't you ever look at your life and say, 'Is this all there is?'"

"*No*," Darla said. "No, no, I don't. Look, sometimes you have to settle for less than you want to keep your relationship going."

"You've never settled with Max," Quinn said, and Darla bit her lip. "Well, now I'm going to be like you. Just this once, I'm not going to settle."

She cuddled the dog closer, and Darla thought, *Everybody settles*. The dog looked over at Darla, daring her to say it out loud, the devil in disguise. *Forget it*, Darla told it silently. *You're not getting* me *in trouble*. "So what do you want on your pizza?" Darla leaned across the table and picked up the phone. "The usual, right?"

"No," Quinn said. "I want something different."

two

BILL HAD gone back to the weight room slightly exasperated with Quinn but mostly amused, so when his principal, Robert Gloam, perspiring elegantly in royal blue sweats, caught the look on his face, he stopped mopping his face on a Ralph Lauren towel and said, "What's so funny, Big Guy?"

Of all the crosses Bill had to bear in life—parents and boosters, teenage athletes with hormones pinballing through their bodies, the struggle to make ideas like the Great Depression real and significant to a generation of mall credit junkies—the most irritating was his biggest fan, Bobby Gloam, the Boy Principal. Bill tried hard not to think of Robert as Bobby or the BP because it wasn't respectful, and Robert was a hardworking little man, if a bit obsessive about sports; but he was so young and so clueless that the nicknames were almost irresistible.

"Funny? Oh, Quinn found another dog," Bill said, and Bobby rolled his eyes in male sympathy.

"You got a lot of patience there, Big Guy," Bobby said.

"She's practical," Bill said. "She'll do the right thing." He began to do the last check on the weight room, which was pretty much unnecessary since he'd trained the boys well, and the BP had been in there while he was gone, nagging at every dropped towel or misplaced weight. The BP felt proprietary about the room since it had been renovated only the past month and was now almost embarrassingly plush, a symphony in scarlet and gray. "The teachers' lounge should look this good," Quinn had said, and Bobby had answered, "Hey, the athletes earned this. What have the teachers done for anybody?"

"I wish Greta would do the right thing," Bobby went on now. "Of course, she's due to retire after next year, but that's still a year and a half to go, and that's a long time to put up with a lousy secretary."

Bill heard him only peripherally, moving toward the light switch, ready to shut down and go home and make dinner for Quinn, just like every Wednesday. Quinn. He felt good just thinking about her.

"I mean, sometimes I think she's *defying* me," Bobby was saying.

"She's just a little tactless sometimes," Bill said. "She's a darn good art teacher, and that's all that matters."

"Not Quinn, Greta," the BP said. "Although I have doubts about Quinn, too."

"What's Greta doing exactly?" Bill asked, feeling a little guilty for tuning him out.

"Well, take my coffee," Bobby said. "I ask her to get me some, and she pours it and puts it on the corner of her desk. And then I have to ask her to bring it in to me."

"Why don't you get your own coffee?" Bill asked. "The pot's right there on the counter outside your door. You're probably closer to it than she is."

"Chain of command," Bobby said. "What kind of authority do I have if I get my own coffee?"

None, which is what you have now anyway.

"What would you do?" Bobby asked, and Bill repressed the urge to say, "I'd get my own coffee," and said, "Just make my expectations known, I guess, like I do with the boys."

Bobby looked confused, so Bill went on. "I make it clear what I want from them. I don't get upset, I just expect them to deliver. Expect Greta to give you what you want, and eventually she will."

"That seems pretty optimistic," Bobby said.

"No." Bill flipped off the lights and started for the door. "Take this thing with Quinn and the dog. She knows we can't have a dog, so I just kept reminding her of that until she agreed to give it to Edie."

"Edie's another one I'm not too sure about," Bobby said. "These older women do not understand authority."

"Look," Bill said, pretty sure he was fighting a losing battle. "People want to be thought well of, they want to live up to other people's good opinions of them. You let people know what they have to do to earn your approval, and they'll do that, as long as it's within their capabilities, of course. Never expect something from people that they can't deliver."

"Greta can bring me coffee," Bobby said.

"And Quinn can give the dog away to a good home." Bill opened the door as the last of the afternoon sunlight filtered into his weight room. "All it takes is patience."

"You're really something, Big Guy," the BP said. "A real master of people."

Bill drove home a contented man. Giving the dog to Edie had been a good idea, and so like Quinn, solving Edie's loneliness problem and finding the dog a home, too—two good deeds at once. Bill had lived alone a couple of times in between relationships, and he'd hated it, so he knew Edie must hate it, too. When he'd met Quinn, he'd known instantly that she was the one, the way she was so practical, the way she always made everything all right. There were no waves when Quinn was around; she calmed the waters. It had taken him a year to convince her to let him move in, and another six months to get her to move to the great apartment he'd found for them, but she'd understood in the end, and now his life was perfect.

So in June they'd get engaged, and they'd get married at Christmas. He had it all planned out so it wouldn't conflict with school or the athletic season, and he imagined the future with her while he parked the car at the apartment. They'd have children, of course. She'd sit in the stands while he coached their sons, she'd tuck them in at night, she'd do all those mother things. Whenever he saw mothers in stores yelling at their kids, he'd think of Quinn's round, serene, Madonna-like face and know she'd never do that to his kids. And she'd always be there for him, too, warm and understanding. She was everything he needed, the solid, sure center of his life.

So when Quinn came in the apartment door at six-fifteen with the dog smirking at him from her arms, he kept his voice calm, his tone warning her that this was not negotiable as he said, "Quinn, the dog goes to Edie."

Quinn's chin came up, and her jaw clenched, and suddenly her face didn't look as round as it usually did. Her hair slid back, and two bright spots stood out on her cheekbones. She looked awful, and the dog looked worse, feral, as if it had bitten and infected her.

"No," she said.

"HEY," DARLA SAID to Max as she came into the grimy, cluttered station office that was decorated in what Quinn called Early Clipboard. "Whose Toyota is that out there?"

"Barbara Niedemeyer's," Max said without lifting his head from the bill he was making out. "And we are not adopting another dog, so just forget about it."

Darla grinned at the back of his head and thought how sexy the curve of his neck was, rounding down into the back of his T-shirt. Max had put on a little weight in the seventeen years since they'd graduated, and his dark hair was a little thinner, but she could still see the best-looking boy in the senior class who'd invited her to be the first girl he took to the drive-in in the car he'd finally gotten running. They'd seen *The Empire Strikes Back*, or most of it. Looking at him now, she wanted to jump him all over again. Not bad for seventeen years, after all.

She peered out into the service bay. "Where's Nick?"

"Upstairs." Max pushed his chair back. "I mean it, no dog."

Darla sat on the edge of the desk and nudged his thigh with hers. "Not even if I asked real nice?"

"Not even then," Max said, but he'd caught the undertone in her voice; she could tell by the way his eyes crinkled. "You could try to persuade me, though."

Darla slid until her legs were on the outside of Max's and leaned over to put her hands on the arms of his desk chair. "Well, I want this dog pretty bad. What exactly would I have to do?"

"Come home and give me a back rub," Max said. "And a few other things. You're still not getting that dog, though. I got to be fair here."

He tried to look stern, and Darla laughed, leaning closer. "Forget about home," she whispered. "It's full of kids. You and me, right here, honey." He started to frown and she kissed him, and Max kissed her back, their good, solid, damn-I'm-glad-you're-here kiss, but tonight her blood rose faster because they weren't at home, they were in the office, windows all around, lights on, acting like dumb kids all over again. Sex with Max was never bad, but it wasn't always pulse-pounding, and lately it hadn't even been often.

Now her pulse was pounding.

"Wait a minute," Max said, coming up for air, and she slid down into his lap as best she could with the chair arms in her way, straddling his thighs but not tight against him the way she wanted to be.

"Come here," she said, and he said, "Jesus, the whole world can see us."

"So they'll learn something," Darla said, but Max was standing up, sliding tight against her for a lovely second before the straightening of his body nudged her back onto the desk.

"Let's go home," he said. "The kids'll be in bed by eleven. Then it's you and me, girl."

Darla felt the heat die out of her. "That's five hours."

Max grinned. "We can make it. Come on. Let's get out of here before somebody sees us necking."

"Yeah, that would be bad," Darla said flatly and followed him out the door. The white Toyota gleamed at her in the garage lights. "Whose car did you say this is?"

"Barbara Niedemeyer," Max said.

"She just dumped Matthew," Darla said, and stopped in her tracks. "Oh, my God, she's after Nick."

"Maybe she just thought there was something wrong with her car," Max said. "You don't really want another dog, do you?"

"No, and anyway, Quinn wants it." Darla's mind turned over the possibilities, sliding away from her own disappointment. "I'm telling you, if that Toyota comes back in here again within the week, she's gunning for Nick." She turned to look at Max. "Should we try to save him?"

"Nick doesn't need saved from anybody," Max said, and he looked so uncomfortable, Darla let the subject drop. Max and Nick were close, but they didn't interfere with each other, a relationship plan that had worked for the thirty-five years they'd been brothers. No need for her to go suggesting they change it now.

"All right," she said, and Max said, "What do you mean, Quinn's keeping it? That's not like her."

Darla followed him out into the dreary March dusk, trudging through the slush and thinking that Quinn would laugh when she found out Barbara was after Nick, and trying hard not to think about how much she'd wanted to make love back in the office, something different, just once after seventeen years.

"Maybe she wants something different," Darla said, and Max said, "Quinn? Not likely." He yanked open the truck door on the driver's side and climbed in. "She's got a good life, and if she plays her cards right, she can keep it forever. Why mess it up?"

Darla stood in the parking lot, the snow drifting around her, suddenly cold to the bone. "Because sometimes you need something new to feel alive again, Max. Sometimes what used to be good isn't enough."

"What are you talking about?" Max leaned over and opened the passenger door. "That's the dumbest thing I ever heard. Get in here before you freeze."

Darla walked around the truck, and climbed into her seat. She wasn't sure what she was talking about, but she was fairly sure she knew how she felt.

And if Max thought he was getting laid tonight after the kids were in bed, he didn't know her at all.

He patted her knee. "After the news, girl," he said. "You and me."

SAYING NO, FLAT-OUT no, went to Quinn's head like cheap wine—she felt dizzy and lightheaded and a little sick as Bill smiled at her, hi, lips together.

"Don't be silly," he said. His face was set in the benevolent Captain of the Universe look that had earned him the respect of all of Tibbett. A real man's man, her father had said when she'd brought him home the first time. Which would explain why she didn't want him now. Let the men have him.

Quinn bent to put Katie on the floor. As she stood, she looked past Bill to where pots simmered on the stove and flushed with annoyance. "You cooked again. I've told you over and over, on Wednesdays I eat with Darla—"

"You eat early," Bill said. "And pizza is not good food. You need good food." He opened a cupboard and took out a plate.

Quinn considered running down the food groups that pizza satisfied and gave up. It was easier to eat than to argue. She walked across the kitchen to rummage in the cupboard under the sink, Katie tiptoeing anxiously behind her, toenails clicking on the tile floor. "Where's the puppy chow from the last time?"

"Clear in the back." Bill's voice sounded flat, and Quinn pulled her head out in time to see him glaring at Katie.

Quinn stuck her head back into the cupboard and fished out the puppy chow. When she stood, Bill had his back to her, dishing up noodles and sauce.

"Our lease says no pets." Bill put the plate on the table and stood beside it, his arms folded, a nonjolly, nongreen giant.

Quinn poured chow into a bowl and put it on the floor. "Come on, baby. Dinner."

The dog sniffed the food and began to eat cautiously. Quinn filled a second bowl with water and put it beside the first. Katie bent to eat, and she looked so sweet that Quinn stroked her head.

Katie squatted and peed.

"Quinn!" Bill yelled, and the dog cringed away from his voice.

"I've got it." Quinn grabbed a paper towel from the roll beside the sink. Katie looked apologetic and distraught, and Quinn murmured her consolation as she mopped up the urine and then took a bottle of spray disinfectant out of the cupboard. "She's a submission pee-er," she told Bill as she scrubbed. "I didn't know because I've been holding her all day. She gets nervous when people pat her and—"

"Well, obviously it can't stay here," Bill said, triumph in his voice. "We can put paper down in the bathroom tonight, but tomorrow it goes."

Quinn finished mopping without saying anything. When she'd washed her hands, Bill extended his peace offering. "Your stroganoff's getting cold."

Quinn slid into her chair and picked up her fork.

Bill smiled at her, approving. "Now Edie will take the dog—"

"I'm keeping the dog." Quinn put her fork down.

"You can't," Bill said. "It'll ruin the carpet and there goes our damage deposit. Plus you're at school all day. Who's going to take care of it then?" He shook his head, calm in his own logic. "You'll give it to Edie."

"No."

"Then I will," Bill said, and began to eat.

Quinn felt cold. "That's a joke, right?"

"You're being irrational," Bill said when he'd chewed and swallowed. "This dog would drive you crazy in no time. Look at it. All it does is shake. And pee."

"She's cold," Quinn said, and Bill shook his head and kept on eating. "Are you listening to me?" she said, as she felt the heat rise in her.

"Yes, I'm listening," Bill said. "And I'm taking care of you by taking it to Edie."

Quinn went dizzy for a minute with rage and then bit back her anger because yelling would only create a problem she'd have to fix.

"It's the sensible thing to do," Bill told her. "Eat your dinner."

Looking at his smug, sure face, Quinn realized she'd created a monster. Bill thought she was going to give in because she always had; so why should he expect anything else? She'd *trained* him to be smug. She looked around. This wasn't even her apartment. Bill had picked it out and moved them in, and when she said, "It's too beige," he'd said, "It's five minutes from school," and that made so much sense she'd given up. And he'd bought furniture, everything in minimalist stripped pine, and when it was delivered and she said, "I don't like it, it looks cold and modern," he said, "I paid for it, and it's here. Give it a chance, and if you still hate it in a couple of months, we'll get something you like." And she'd said okay because it was just furniture, not worth fighting over.

Katie leaned against her leg, her butt rolling on the carpet. Katie was worth fighting for.

And maybe the furniture had been worth fighting over, too. All that damn beige.

Bill smiled at her across the table, equally beige.

In fact, right about now, *anything* was worth fighting over.

"Now, don't sit over there and sulk," Bill said. "Edie will be good to the dog."

"I hate this furniture." Quinn shoved herself away from the table and got up to get her coat.

"Quinn?" Bill sounded a little taken aback. "What are you talking about?"

"All of it." She shrugged into her peacoat. "I like old stuff. Warm stuff. I hate this apartment. I hate beige carpet."

"Quinn."

She turned her back to him to pick up Katie. "And right now, I'm not too crazy about you, either."

The last thing she heard as she went out the door was Bill saying, "Quinn, you're acting like a *child*."

NICK WAS JUST getting into Carl Hiaasen's latest when somebody knocked on his door. He'd only been home an hour, the cubes in his second Chivas hadn't started to melt yet, and now company. One of the many benefits of being single was that he got to be alone a lot in a quiet place, so he dropped the book on the floor and pushed himself out of his ancient leather armchair, determined to get rid of whoever it was.

But when he yanked the door open, it was Quinn, swathed to her nose in a thick, fuzzy blue scarf, her copper hair shining under the porch light, and shutting the door on Quinn was never a possibility. She was holding a skinny black dog that looked at him with imploring dog-orphan eyes, so he said, "I don't want a dog," but he stood back to let her in.

Quinn brushed by him and put the dog down as he shut the door. She pulled the scarf from her mouth and said, "That's good because you can't have her." She smiled down at the dog, who was cautiously surveying the apartment, and then she turned to him, all shining eyes and glossy hair, her cheeks glowing red in her round little-girl face. "I'm keeping her."

"Dumb idea," he said, but he said it without heat, smiling at her from habit and from pleasure because she was there. "Drink?"

"Yes, please." Quinn unwound her scarf and dropped it on the hardwood floor next to his mother's old braided rug, and the dog immediately curled up on it, looking at Nick as if it expected to stay. *Don't even think about it, dog.*

"Boy, what a day," Quinn said.

"So tell me." Nick went out to his tiny kitchen and she followed, taking a glass down from the pine shelves over his sink while he cracked ice from a tray in his ancient fridge.

"I don't even know where to start," she said.

The kitchen was a tight fit for two, but it was Quinn, so it didn't count. She held the glass to her chest because they were too close for her to hold it out, and he dropped the ice into it and then reached past her for the Chivas on the shelf, absent-mindedly enjoying her nearness. "Start with the worst stuff," he told her, as he poured about a quarter inch in the glass for her. She was driving home, so that was all she was going to get. "That way we'll end on an up note."

She grinned up at him and said, "Thank you. Can I have some more?"

"No." He nudged her toward the living room with his hip as he put the Chivas back. "You're too young to drink anyway."

"I'm thirty-five." Quinn dropped to the rug beside the dog, all long legs and bright hair above her paint-stained sweater and jeans. "I'm allowed to do anything I want." She stopped as if she'd just heard herself say something radical instead of sarcastic, and then she shrugged. "Okay, the worst is that I had a fight with Bill."

Nick appreciated the color for a moment, the copper in her hair, the honey of the oak floor, the soft blue of her sweater and the faded greens of the rug, and most of all Quinn herself, everything she was, glowing in the middle of all that warmth. Then he registered what she'd said. "What?"

"I had a fight with Bill. At least, I think it was a fight. It's hard to tell because he never gets mad. I told him I was keeping this dog and he said no. Like I was a little kid or something."

Quinn was so flustered, widening her big hazel eyes at him, that Nick grinned. "Well, you act like a little kid sometimes. You live in an apartment. Where are you going to keep a dog?"

She shook her head, her hair swinging like copper silk. "That's not the point. The point is that I want it, and he just said no."

"Well, he doesn't want it." Nick settled back into his armchair, determined not to get sucked into Quinn's fight but not worried about it. He could resist getting involved in Quinn's life. He just couldn't resist her company. "He shouldn't have to live with an animal if he doesn't want to." The dog looked at him reproachfully, so he ignored it.

Quinn shook her head. "And I shouldn't have to live without one."

"So one of you will give in," Nick said. "You'll work it out." He watched her stick her chin out and thought, *Bill, you just became a dog lover*. He'd known Quinn since she was fifteen, and when she dug her heels in like that, there was no moving her.

"I'm not working it out," Quinn said. "I'm keeping Katie."

"Who?"

"Katie. That's her name."

Quinn pulled the dog onto her lap and stroked its head, and Nick studied it, trying to see what Quinn saw in it. Slick and bony, it looked like a rat on stilts, and its huge dark eyes made him nervous. *Save me*, it seemed to be saying. *Take care of me. Be responsible for me forever.* He shook his head. "Couldn't you have named it something about a thousand times less cute than Katie?"

"You want to get a dog of your own and call her Killer, be my guest," Quinn said. "This is my dog, and her name's Katie." She looked at him, suddenly thoughtful. "You know, a dog would be good for you."

"No." Nick settled deeper in his chair. "An apartment is a lousy place for a dog. Also, I do not need another responsibility."

Quinn looked at him with affectionate contempt. "A dog wouldn't be another responsibility since you don't have a first responsibility. It would be your first responsibility. It'd be a sign you're maturing."

"I have enough signs I'm maturing," Nick growled. "I'm going gray."

"I know." Quinn sounded smug. "Just at the temples. It's very attractive, but it's probably going to cut down on those teeny-boppers you've been dating."

"I do not date teenagers." Nick glared at her. He did not date teenagers. He had some morals, for Christ's sake.

"Oh, please, how old is Lisa? Twelve?"

"Twenty-two," Nick said. "I think."

"An immature twenty-two," Quinn said. "And you're pushing forty."

"Thirty-eight." Nick thought about telling her he hadn't seen Lisa since Christmas and decided not to. It would open up a whole different conversation he didn't want to have, one they'd already had several times, the one about how he dated women who were too young for him so he wouldn't have to get involved. That was true, but it also worked, so why discuss it? Time to change the subject. "So what's new? I haven't seen anybody all day. I worked right up to six. Bucky Manchester's Chevy has a dead muffler."

"He can afford it," Quinn said. "Mama said Bucky's making money hand over fist at the real estate office." She took her first drink of Chivas, knocking back half of it at once.

"Well, that's good because Max and I are siphoning some of it off." Nick pointed his finger at her. "Don't chug that. You're driving."

"Just home to Bill." Quinn sipped her drink, tense all over again. "You know, if he doesn't give in on this dog, I'm moving out."

"Well, think about it first," Nick said, definitely not interested in discussing Bill. "How's school?"

"School?" Quinn blinked at him, readjusting subjects. "The same. Edie's got the school play again, and Bobby's giving her fits over it. If it isn't athletics, he doesn't care about it. She wants me to do the sets and costumes, but I said no. More headaches I don't need. And Bobby's driving Greta nuts, too, but all our money is on her since she's been school secretary forever, and he's just brand-new. He can't run the school without her."

"You call him Bobby to his face?"

"No. We don't even call him Bobby in the teachers' lounge. Edie started calling him the Boy Principal when he took over in November, and now everybody calls him the BP. I think that's one of the reasons he's so mad at her."

"That would do it," Nick said, mostly to keep her talking. Quinn talked with her entire body: arms, eyes, shoulders, mouth. She was performance art, so alive that sometimes he argued with her just so he could watch her flush and gesture.

Her smile was rich in her voice as she said, "Well, that, and

I think he overheard her one day after he'd been shooting his mouth off, and she said"—Quinn shifted tone to mimic Edie's blonde little soprano, the quasi-Southern lilt with the scorpion's sting—" 'You know, it's so much easier to like Robert when he's not in the building.' " Nick grinned, and Quinn finished, "Well, yeah, but the BP didn't think it was funny."

"No sense of humor," Nick said.

"No brains," Quinn said. "He thinks he knows it all. Smug little twit. I used to think Harvey was a mess, but now that he's gone and we've got the BP, I realize how lucky we were to have somebody that let Greta run the school. Bobby's obsessed with changing everything, and he's screwing things up right and left, and he won't listen when we tell him he's making mistakes. The only person he listens to at all is Bill, but then he thinks Bill hung the moon. All those championships. If Bill wins the baseball trophy this spring, the BP will probably ask Bill to adopt him. And as far as I'm concerned, they deserve each other."

The shadow was back in her face again, and Nick felt uneasy. "Look, Bill can't be dumb enough to risk losing you over a dog," he said finally, not wanting to get in the middle of the mess but wanting to give her some kind of comfort. "When he sees how much it means to you, he'll give in."

"I don't know," Quinn said. "Sometimes I don't think he sees me. I think he just sees the person he wants me to be. You know? The person he can cope with. Because the real me is too messy and difficult."

Nick shook his head. Bill couldn't possibly be stupid enough to miss who Quinn was and what she meant to him. She leaned forward to pull the dog into her lap, and her hair swung like copper silk, the lamplight making it gleam rich against the pale gold flush of her skin.

It would take a real moron to miss Quinn.

"So tell me about how you found this rat," he said, just to see her eyes flash, and when she jerked her head up and glared at him, he laughed.

Good old, safe, predictable Quinn.

WHEN BILL ROLLED over the next morning, Katie was stretched out between him and Quinn on the bedspread, a damn dog in bed with them in spite of his plans for newspaper in the bathroom. Quinn had just said, "No," and put a folded blanket beside the bed, and of course during the night the dog had jumped up. It was a miracle it hadn't peed in the bed. He felt his temper rise and calmed himself the way he always did, with deep breaths and clear thinking. Quinn was just confused. She'd come in late last night and shook her head when he tried to talk to her, refusing to eat the stroganoff he'd reheated for her, taking the dog into the bedroom with her. She was acting like a child, but he was used to dealing with children. He was a teacher. Patience was everything.

Besides, last night after she'd stomped out, he'd tried to figure out what was wrong and realized that she was probably just tense because she wanted to get married and have children like he did. Of course, he had plenty of time to have kids, but she was thirty-five and not getting any younger. And there he was, not telling her they were getting married because he was focused on the season. So all he had to do was get the dog out of the way and propose early, and then they'd get married and have the children she wanted, and he'd wake up and find Bill Junior snuggled between them. The thought warmed him. A little boy with all of his strength and honesty and intelligence and all of Quinn's sweetness. All he had to do was be patient and get rid of the dog and things would be fine.

The dog stretched, all skinny legs and body, and then curled closer to Quinn's back.

"Get down," Bill whispered as sternly as he could without waking Quinn.

The dog opened its eyes and glared at him.

Bill shoved at the dog's butt with his hand. *"Down."*

The dog curled a lip and growled low in its throat, viciously staking its claim to Quinn, and Bill pulled his hand back.

"What're you doin'?" Quinn mumbled sleepily over her shoulder.

"That dog growled at me."

"You prob'ly woke her up." Quinn yawned and patted the bed on the other side of her. "C'mere, Katie."

Katie stood up slowly, stretching, insolent, and then clambered over Quinn's waist to curl up victorious against her stomach. Quinn let her hand fall carelessly along the dog's back, patting a little as she drifted back to sleep.

Bill took some more deep breaths and then sneezed. Probably allergic to dog dander.

That dog was history.

"IS MAX HERE?" Nick straightened from under the hood of Mary Galbraith's ancient Civic and said, "Pardon?" but he'd recognized the voice even before he saw the slender blonde in the powder blue suit. First National Bank Barbie, Darla called her, which was a lot kinder than Lois Ferguson's nickname for her. She did have that plastic look that made it hard to believe she was stalking Max, but there she was. "Hi, Barbara. Nope, he's out right now. Your car's all right, I hope."

"Oh, he did a wonderful job." Barbara looked uncertain, out of place in the dingy garage, but then Barbara looked out of place anywhere but the bank. She gave Nick the creeps, but he knew that wasn't fair. For one thing, she was damn good at her job. Nobody's deposit ever got screwed up when Barbara took it.

"I don't know when he'll be back," Nick said, when Barbara seemed stalled out on the next thing to say.

"I just brought him these." She stuck a painted tin out toward him tentatively, and Nick felt sorry for her and wary for Max. The tin was plaid with a painted green bow and a painted white card that said THANK YOU! "They're cookies," Barbara said. "Because he did such a good job."

"Oh." What the hell was he going to do with cookies? "Why don't you put them in the office. I'll tell Max you left them."

"Thank you. That would be nice." Barbara stood there, perfectly dressed, stuck again.

"Right there in the office," Nick said, trying to be encouraging.

Barbara took a deep breath. "He's really good with cars, isn't he?"

"The best," Nick said. "The office is right there, through that door."

"Because my car is running much better. He even fixed the heater."

"It was just a loose switch," Nick said, not mentioning he was the one who'd fixed it. "Max is good at catching things like that."

"Well, that's what I *thought*." Barbara came a step closer, and Nick realized there was something different about her. She didn't look as flashy for some reason. Like her hair was darker or something. "I think paying attention to details is important, don't you?"

"Yeah." Nick gave up on remembering what color her hair had been before because he didn't care. "Well, you can just put those cookies in the office."

"Is he good around the house, too?" Barbara asked, and Nick decided she was weird.

"He does okay," Nick said. "Darla never complains. He debated saying more and decided against it. No point in getting involved.

"I know. She does wonderful hair." Barbara seemed guileless. "She's lucky to have Max."

"Right there in the office," Nick said. "That would be the place to put those cookies."

"You're busy." Barbara backed up a step. "It must be wonderful to work with Max."

"Makes my day," Nick said.

"I'm sure you're good, too," Barbara said politely.

"Not very," Nick said.

"I'll just put these in the office."

"That would be the place." Nick stuck his head back under the hood of the Honda and thought, *Max, you're going to have to handle this*.

And then he concentrated on the Honda because Max and Barbara were none of his business.

QUINN GOT HOME a little after three, faster than usual because she was so excited to see Katie. Katie would need to go out right away, so she'd take her out in back of the apartment the way she had that morning, watch her jump and skip across the frozen ground and then come running back, and she'd feel the exhilaration she'd felt then, the lift of having something that loved her without expecting anything from her. She'd pick Katie up as she pawed at her coat, shivering all over from anxiety and excitement cuddle her warm, and feel Katie's little head rest on her shoulder again. It was so amazing to have a dog of her own that she smiled as she opened the door to the apartment and called "Katie!", waiting to hear the newly wonderful clatter of dog toenails on the kitchen tile.

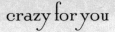

The apartment stayed silent.

"Katie?"

Still no toenails. Quinn shut the door behind her and began to look, her heart pounding, checking to make sure Katie wasn't locked in the bathroom or asleep on the pine poster bed. The apartment was small enough that she had the entire place searched in two minutes. No Katie.

She tortured herself with the thought that the dog might have gotten out somehow, but when she went to see how much dog food was left, evidence of how long Katie might have been in the apartment, both bowls were gone. Quinn found them in the dishwasher.

Bill was always tidy.

The blood rose in her face and all the irritation and frustration she'd been feeling coalesced into rage.

He'd taken her dog.

He'd *stolen* her dog.

It took her no time at all to cover the mile back to school.

three

ACROSS TOWN at the Upper Cut, Darla backcombed Susan Bridges and tried to talk herself out of being angry. There was no reason to be angry. Max had been right the night before. Having sex while all of Tibbett watched would probably have been bad for business. And anyway, she'd had all the payback she needed when she'd turned Max down at eleven. He'd put his arms around her in the empty kitchen after Mark and Mitch had finally gone off to bed, and she'd said, "Out of the mood." Max had dropped his arms and said, "Ooooh-kay," and wandered off to bed himself without another word to her. Not another word.

"Ouch," Susan said, and Darla apologized and put her mind back on Susan's hair.

"Did you ever think of changing your style?" she asked Susan, looking over her shoulder into the gray and scarlet–framed mirror. "You've been doing it this way for . . . a while now." Thirty years about, was Darla's guess. "You'd look good in one of those wedge cuts. Bring out your cheekbones."

Susan sucked in her cheeks and studied herself in the mirror. "Darryl wouldn't even know me."

"Well, that could be good," Darla said. "Give him something different. Make him look at you again. Make him think he was sleeping with a brand-new woman."

"I don't notice you changing your hair," Susan said.

Darla checked her light brown French twist in the mirror. "Max likes it long and this is the only way I can stand it during the day."

"Well, cut it off," Susan said. "Make him think he's cheating on you."

"That's not what I meant," Darla said. Actually, cutting her hair short was tempting. Except Max liked it long. It would be a crummy way to pay Max back for something he didn't even know he'd done, that she couldn't even explain to him. *I want something different*, she wanted to say to him. *I want us to be new again*. And there poor old Max would be, clueless as to how to give her what she wanted. Not his fault. "I couldn't do that to Max."

"Well, *see*," Susan said.

As Susan left, Darla's sister Debbie came back from the break room and plopped herself down on the scarlet seat at the next station.

"Mama said you haven't called her." Debbie checked her impossibly blonde hair in the mirror. "She said she raised you better than that and what are you thinking. Do you think I look like Princess Di with my hair this way? I thought it might be too long, but Ronnie says no. Was that Susan Bridges who just left? That woman hasn't changed her do since the Doobie Brothers broke up."

"Hi, Deb." Darla swept the last of Susan's trimmings from the scarlet and gray–tiled floor around her station and fought back the impulse to point out that since Princess Diana was no longer setting fashion, there was something slightly icky about trying to look like her.

Debbie straightened her Upper Cut smock in the mirror as she babbled on. "Do you know what I heard?" She craned her head to see if anybody at the other stations could overhear, but the only three people at work besides them were across the room. "Barbara Niedemeyer broke up with Matthew Ferguson. Dumped his butt good." Debbie nodded her head, a good-riddance nod.

Old news, Deb, Darla thought, but kept her mouth shut as she tidied her station. Let Debbie enjoy herself. She'd probably never wanted anything different in her life, just Ronnie, the Upper Cut, and the chance to be the first with good gossip.

"And do you know what that means? She's gonna be in here to get a new hairdo one of these days. And when she does, we'll know who the next one is."

Darla stopped tidying. "What are you talking about?"

"Well." Debbie leaned forward, waiting for Darla to join her.

Darla checked her watch. It was four o'clock. "I've got Marty Jacobsen now."

Debbie waved her hand. "Marty's always late. Probably out collecting gossip again. Some people."

"Right," Darla said and sat down. "Okay, I'm listening."

"Well, remember right before Barbara went after Matthew? She came in here and she had me do a henna rinse and put it all up on top of her head, only she said, 'Make it tasteful, Debbie, and soft, like Ivana's.' And I thought that was funny at the time, but then when Ronnie told me she'd dumped Matthew, I thought, 'I wonder if she'd come in for a new hairdo again,' and that's when it hit me."

"Hit me, too," Darla said. "I'm lost."

Debbie leaned closer, letting the arm of the chair dig into her soft middle. "She was trying to look like Lois."

Darla frowned at Debbie. "Barbara was?"

Debbie leaned back, satisfied. "Yep. Because I remembered that when she was after Janice's Gil, she wore that ponytail, just like Janice except she fluffed it out some and had me French-braid the top so she looked classy. And then with Bea's Louis, it was a knot on top of her head, except she had those wisps at the side that make it look so sexy, remember? Poor old Bea just looked like she had a bagel on her head, but Barbara looked great. And then she went strawberry-blonde Ivana for Matthew, and there's Lois with that orange beehive she will not give up even though she runs a beauty salon for heaven's sake, so"—

Debbie leaned forward again—"I figure sometime this month she'll be in for something different. And then we'll know who she's after, whoever's wife matches the new do. Isn't that the wildest?"

"She's after Nick," Darla said. "She brought the car in yesterday and it didn't have anything wrong with it."

"Nick." Debbie sat back, not frowning because that made wrinkles but clearly puzzled just the same. "Jeez. That could be anybody. Who's he seeing now? That Lisa girl?"

"No." Darla got up and began to tidy her station again. "That's been over a while. She wanted a ring for Christmas, and he got her the *Dusty Springfield Anthology*. She didn't even know who Dusty Springfield was. I don't think he's dating anybody."

"Well, it's not like any of them last long. A year tops." Debbie shook her head. "There's something wrong with a man who isn't over his divorce twenty years after it's over him."

"He was over that divorce twenty minutes after it was final," Darla said, trying to keep the tartness out of her voice. Nick might not be steady with women, but he was a damn good brother-in-law, a damn fine man. And he wasn't stuck in a rut a mile deep, either, not like some people. "He just doesn't like being tied down."

"A man should be married."

"Why?"

They stared at each other, annoyed at being crossed, the same stare they'd been giving each other since Darla had first looked over the edge of her newborn sister's bassinet and not been impressed by what she saw. There was no reason every man had to be married. Or every woman. No matter how contented Debbie was in her marriage to that fool Ronnie.

Or how contented she was with old stick-in-the-mud Max, damn it.

Something was going wrong with her train of thought. She

shouldn't be this upset. She particularly shouldn't be this upset with Max, who hadn't done anything wrong, who was worth twenty of that knucklehead Ronnie. She shouldn't be bored with him, she was ashamed to feel that way, it was wrong.

But she still felt that way.

"Why are you so touchy all of a sudden?" Debbie said, and Darla felt guilty again. Debbie wasn't a rocket scientist, but she was a good sister. Darla could have been stuck with Zoë the Exciting who left Quinn feeling gray and flat. Deb was just being Deb.

"Never mind," she said, and Debbie said, "You mark my words, Barbara'll be in here any day now. And if she wants to look like Lisa, she's going to have to grow some hair because it was clear down past that girl's butt last time I saw her."

"He's not dating Lisa." Darla stood up as Marty Jacobsen breezed in late. "Maybe Barbara's wised up and is going after unattached guys."

"That'll be the day," Debbie said. "People don't change. She's gonna be dating married guys forever. And I'm telling you now, she ever starts hanging around the hardware store and Ronnie, she's not going to have any hair to do, 'cause I'll pull it out for her."

"People change," Darla said. "If they have good enough reason, they—"

Marty plunked herself down in Darla's chair and said, "Hi. I'm not late am I? Are you talking about Barbara? Because she's definitely through with Matthew. I heard—"

BY FOUR, BILL had had a long day, made even longer by the BP's insistence on helping the boys lift, even though they knew more than he ever would. "Hey, Coach, you think Corey needs more weight?" Bobby called to him now, while Corey Mossert, Bill's thickest athlete in more ways than one, rolled his eyes.

"He's fine," Bill said, and moved on to the next lifter with Bobby close behind.

"That Greta is driving me crazy. She's old, you know." Bobby shook his head, and Bill almost said, "She's fifty, that's not old," but since the BP had just cracked twenty-eight, it was probably useless to point out the relative youth of his secretary.

"She thinks everything should be done the way that Harvey did it," Bobby went on. "Can you imagine?"

"Actually, the way Harvey did it was the way she did it," Bill said as he checked the form on the next lifter. "She's always pretty much run the school." She'd had to since Harvey had been mentally dead for the past twenty years, refusing to retire until he'd keeled over from a heart attack at the Pumpkin Festival four months earlier, finally really dead, although as Quinn had said, it was hard to tell since he'd looked a lot like he always had at the assemblies.

"Well, there, see?" Bobby said. "That's why the school's been going downhill; no leadership. Until now."

Bill checked Jason Barnes's weight stack, which was exactly the weight it was supposed to be. He could count on Jason. He nodded at the big blond senior Quinn called "Bill, the Next Generation." Their sons would grow up to be like Jason, tall and strong and dependable.

"You know what Carl Brookner told me?" Bobby was saying.

"What?" he said, mainly to humor Bobby.

"He said he thought the levy was a go for this year." Bobby's eyes glittered as he stared off into the distance. "He said he'd noticed the murals and he thought a new weight room wasn't really enough reward for what you were doing with the boys."

"Well, we've needed that levy for awhile," Bill said mildly.

"New textbooks, teacher raises—we're overdue." The murals were a touchy issue since he'd asked Quinn and the art department to do them, and she'd been against it. "Tell me again why the art kids should shill for the athletic department?" she'd said, but he'd been patient and she'd given in.

"Yeah, but here's the thing," Bobby said. "He said we shouldn't aim low. He said there should be a bond issue in the fall for new buildings." Bobby's voice hushed a little as he remembered. "A stadium and a new fieldhouse."

Bill straightened at that. "You're kidding."

"Nope." Bobby shook his head, staring into his future. "Bill Hilliard Stadium." He didn't add "Robert Gloam Fieldhouse," but Bill knew it was there.

"I don't care what they call it," Bill said. "But we need a stadium."

"I know, I know, Big Guy," the BP said, eager to bond again. "And we can get it. You get that tenth trophy, and it's ours."

He'd get the tenth trophy. He'd spent five years building a hell of a baseball team, and he'd get that trophy.

And then the stadium. Bill smiled at the thought.

"It's a beautiful future we're looking at," the BP said.

Before Bill could answer, he heard the door to the parking lot slam and Quinn's voice came from behind him. "I need to *talk* to you."

He swung around to see her breathing heavily, glaring at him. Some of the boys stopped lifting to watch until he frowned and they all went back to work except for Jason Barnes, who let his weight stack come to rest.

"Jason," Bill said, and waited until Jason gave up and the clink of his weight stack was rhythmic again. Then he turned to the BP, now glowering at Quinn, and said, "Take over, Robert."

Quinn stomped back toward the door, and Bill followed her,

figuring she was just a little upset about the dog. Nothing he couldn't reason her out of.

"Where is she?" Quinn demanded as soon as they were outside standing next to her car. Her hazel eyes snapped at him and color flooded her cheeks. She looked great.

"It's safe and warm." Bill patted her arm. "It's fine. Calm down."

Quinn shrugged his hand from her arm and took a step closer. "No, it is *not* fine. I want that dog back. Wherever you took her, we're going there now to get her back. And it better not be the pound, or I'm never speaking to you again."

"You're overreacting." Bill spoke calmly, but he was puzzled. Things weren't going right. She shouldn't be this mad. "The dog is fine. I told them not to put it to sleep. I told them to call us if nobody—"

"You took her to the pound." Quinn's voice shook. "You take me there *right now*."

"Quinn, be reasonable—"

"I am being reasonable." Quinn's voice was flat, deadly serious, her round face even paler than usual. "But I'm about this far away from throwing a fit you're not going to believe. Now you take me to get my *goddamned dog!*"

He handed her into the passenger seat of her car and got in the driver's seat, thinking that he really should get her new seat covers because hers were a mess. Once he had her calmed down, they could stop by Target and pick up some. "I'm sorry if you're upset."

"*If?*" Quinn's voice rose to a shriek. "You're listening to me and you're *not sure?* Well, *count on it! I'm upset!*"

"But we can't keep the dog anyway," Bill went on, flooding his voice with calm as he started the car and pulled out of the parking lot. "I checked with the apartment manager, and she said absolutely not."

"Then I'll move." Quinn folded her arms across her chest.

Bill took a deep breath. She was upset, but she'd calm down. "We can't leave the apartment. It's a great deal. And it's close to school. It's—"

"I said, *I'll* move," Quinn said. "You can stay there."

"Quinn—"

"It wasn't working out for us anyway," she said flatly, all emotion gone from her voice, only tightness there. "And now that you've stolen my dog, it never will."

Bill wanted to shout at her, but he didn't. No point in them both behaving badly. "Don't be ridiculous. You are not going to move out."

She looked at him then, and Bill wished she hadn't. "You just watch me," she said evenly. "You just watch me go."

Bill stopped arguing. It was futile with Quinn in this irrational state. She'd calm down and then she'd see reason. He switched over to thinking about the weight room—who was slacking, who was going to have to add weight, who was bulking up too much for agility—and he was so caught in his own plans that he almost missed the turnoff to Animal Control.

Once inside, Quinn was worse, practically leaping over the counter to grab the poor woman in the brown uniform by the throat. She was a nice woman, too, a real Tiger fan, she'd told him when he'd brought the dog in. "You're doing such a fine job, Coach," she'd said, and he'd thanked her because community support was vital to a good athletic program. Her name was Betty, he remembered now. He felt a little embarrassed when she led them back to the pens and Quinn sank to her knees on the concrete and reached her hand through the bars and called "Katie" as if she'd been parted from the mutt for centuries instead of just hours. The dog came tiptoeing up to her, shaking all over. It was acting, Bill knew. Dogs were manipulative like that, always looking at you with those calculating eyes, especially this sneaky, sly little rat. The pen was huge and the place was warm and there was a bowl of food and a water dispenser right there; clearly this dog was not suffering.

"Get her out of here," Quinn said without looking at him. She was stroking the dog through the bars, giving it all of her attention. "Get her out of here now."

Something in her voice, something strange and a little frightening, made Bill decide this was not the time to argue. "I brought the dog in this morning," he told Betty. "I'd like her back."

"Sorry, Coach, but that'll be thirty dollars plus the license fee." Betty was clearly apologetic. "That's the law."

Bill wanted to protest that since he was the one who'd brought the dog in, surely he should be able to take it back for free, but it was easier to pay the money. No point in annoying a Tiger fan, and besides, the sooner he got Quinn out of there, the sooner he could talk some sense into her and get rid of the dog for good. He'd have to find it a home, though. Animal Control was obviously not going to satisfy Quinn.

It was unlike her to be this unreasonable. Maybe it was PMS.

Out in the car, Quinn cuddled the dog to her, not speaking, while it looked over her shoulder at Bill and smirked. Bill ignored it. He might be stuck with the damn thing for awhile, but not for long. He and Quinn had a future, and it didn't have a dog in it, no matter how mad she was right now.

"So what are your plans for this afternoon?" he said heartily, trying to get them back to normal.

"I'm moving out," Quinn said in the same voice she might have used to say, "I'm having pizza with Darla."

"Oh, come on, Quinn." Bill took the turn to the road to the school a little too sharply in his annoyance. "Stop being childish. You are not moving out. We'll talk about this when I get home."

When she didn't say anything, he knew he'd made his point,

and he let his mind go back to the wrestlers. Some bad attitudes there, Corey Mossert's among them. Too bad Corey wasn't more like Jason Barnes. Corey and Jason were best friends, though. Maybe a word to Jason.

Beside him, Quinn rode in silence while the dog watched him over her shoulder.

"OKAY, JUST FOR the hell of it, let's try to be calm," Nick said from the other side of a Blazer, wondering why it was his day to deal with weirded-out women.

Quinn glared across at him as if she knew what he was thinking. "This is not the time to be calm."

She clutched Katie in her arms, and the dog rested its chin on Quinn's arm and stared at him reproachfully. They made quite a picture, and Nick decided not to let himself get sucked into pictures. "I can't help you till I know what's going on, and I won't know what's going on until you tell me."

Quinn took a deep breath. "I just need you to help me move my stuff out of the apartment and back to Mom's while Bill is finishing up at school. That's all."

That's all. Nick leaned against the car and wished he were someplace else. He liked Bill. He played poker with Bill. "Maybe if you talked to Bill—"

"He took my dog out to the pound and left her there in that cold cell all day. She could have *died*." Quinn clutched Katie closer, looking ill as she spoke. "They kill the ones they think are sick, and she shakes all the time. They could have killed her."

Nick shook his head. "Bill's a good guy. Maybe—"

"Did you hear a word I just said?" Quinn demanded. "He took Katie to the *pound*."

"Yeah, I know." Nick tried to think of the right thing to say, the thing that would make Quinn calm down and get him out of the middle of this mess. "But he's not a mean guy, Quinn. You know that. Before you do something you'll regret, you have to calm down."

"*No.*" Quinn began to pace up and down the garage bay, still clutching Katie in her arms. "I'm never going to calm down again. That's been my problem all along. Zoë got to break rules, and my mother got to pretend everything was fine, and my dad got to watch TV until the mess was over, and Darla got to insult people, and you got to be uninvolved, but I was always the calm one, the one who fixed things."

"Well, you're good at that," Nick said, wishing she'd stop pacing.

"But I'm not calm. It's all a lie." Quinn held Katie closer, breathing faster. "It's just that when everybody else is screaming, somebody has to be mature and unemotional, so I have these brain-dead moments where I don't react the way any sane human being would. I stay completely calm and ignore my feelings and compromise and make everything work again. And I'm not going to do that anymore. From now on, I'm going to be Zoë. Screw calm. Somebody else is going to have to do mature because I'm going to be selfish and get what I want."

Nick watched her while she talked, making no sense, scaring him a little because of the look in her eye. Quinn saying she wasn't going to be calm anymore was like Quinn saying she was going to stop breathing. When her mother had missed the turn down by the root beer stand and hit the big oak, Quinn had been the one who'd used her gym sock to stop Meggy's bleeding while Zoë yelled her head off. When Zoë had freaked halfway down the aisle at their wedding, Quinn had been the one who talked her into going back into the church. When Max had screwed up his history final, Quinn was the one who'd coached him through the retake she'd talked the teacher into giving him so he could graduate. Nick had known Quinn for twenty years, and in all that time, she'd been the one who fixed things, who never got upset, who made everything all right.

Now that he thought about it, that had to be getting old.

All she wanted was a dog.

And Quinn deserved to have anything she wanted.

Quinn stopped her harangue to take a breath, and Nick said, "Okay."

She blinked. "That's it? Okay?"

"What are we moving?"

"You're going to do it?"

The disbelief in her voice ticked him off. "When have I ever not done what you needed?"

"Never." She answered so promptly he wasn't mad anymore. "I just wanted to make sure this was what you really wanted."

Quinn nodded. "It's what I really want."

"I don't mean the dog. I mean leaving Bill."

"It's what I really want," Quinn repeated, and her voice was firm.

"Okay." Nick moved around the car to the coatrack. "You want to tell me why we have to do this while Bill is at school?"

"I don't want to see him again," Quinn said. "I told him in the car I was leaving, and he just smiled."

Nick stopped as he reached for his coat. "He what?"

"He just smiled." Quinn shook her head. "He wants to talk about it when he gets home, but he won't listen, and I don't want to talk to a brick wall anymore."

"He just smiled? Are you sure you told him?"

"I said, 'I'm leaving.' I said, 'You just watch me leave.' "

"And he smiled." Nick took down his coat. "You have a problem."

"Which is why I'm moving out." Quinn shifted on her feet, impatient, like a little kid. "Could you hurry? He's going to be late tonight because there's a baseball meeting, but that won't last forever."

"I'm coming. What are we moving?"

Quinn stopped shifting to think. "The pie safe and Grandpa's washstand and Grandma's silverware. And my books and my quilts and my pictures and my clothes. This is really great of you, Nick."

"You got boxes for the books?"

"No." Quinn's voice wavered.

"Okay, I'll round up some boxes tomorrow." Nick turned his back to get his gloves out of his pockets so he wouldn't have to watch her chin quiver. "In the meantime, we can get the furniture and the rest of the stuff so you can feel you've moved out. And then later we'll go back for the books and whatever else you've missed."

"Thank you." Quinn said from behind him.

"It's no big deal." He turned to see Quinn clutching that dog, her eyes huge and hazel and grateful and alive, more intense than he'd ever seen her before.

"It is a big deal," she said. "I know what you're doing, I know how hard it is for you to get involved with people. I know how much you hate it, and how you're going to hate facing Bill."

"It's okay," he said, and then to his horror, she came closer and hugged him, squashing the dog between them, her hair soft and smooth against his jaw. She was warm against him, and she smelled like soap, and his heart beat a lot faster, and he was suddenly conscious of every curve she had, of every breath she took, and he did not put his arms around her.

"It's not just okay," she whispered into his neck. "It's what I really need and what you hate doing. You're the best." Then, after a couple thousand years at least, she let him go and went to the door.

He breathed again. "Good. Remember that." He followed her out, a little confused from her heat, calling to Max to watch the pumps, determined not to do anything that would bring her that close again.

THE SHORT RIDE to Quinn's apartment seemed longer than usual and the cab of the truck smaller. Nick felt lousy that she was so upset, and guilty about betraying Bill, but mostly he just felt tense in general. She sat next to him, cuddling that damn dog, and the insane need to be close to all her warmth again grew stronger. This was why it was better when Quinn was involved with somebody. As long as Quinn was off limits, she was just Quinn, and he didn't think about her much. It was these times between her guys that made him uneasy, which didn't happen often, thank God, because Quinn wasn't flighty but—

"Why are you so quiet?" Quinn said. "It's because you don't want to do this, isn't it?"

"I want you to be happy," he said truthfully. "I don't want you to be alone."

"I won't be alone." Her voice sounded surprised, still a little shaky with emotion. "I'm never alone. I have a ton of people in my life."

"I mean a guy."

"I don't need a guy." Quinn turned away from him to look out the window. "Especially a guy who steals my dog."

"Right."

Nick pulled into the driveway to Quinn's apartment. "The dog stays in the truck," he said, and Quinn hugged the mutt one last time and then helped him lock it in the cab. Its eyes were accusing as they walked away. *What about me?* it seemed to say. *Who's taking care of me?*

Nick ignored it.

When they got upstairs, he found that Quinn was right, there wasn't much there that she wanted, and they loaded everything but her clothes into the truck in half an hour. "That's it?" Nick asked her. "You're not taking anything else?"

"I feel guilty enough about leaving him," Quinn said. "I mean, he stole my dog, so I can't stay, but I'm not going to leave him without furniture. This is the stuff that's important to my family. The rest was just garage sale stuff or stuff he bought new that I hated anyway. I'll put my clothes in garbage bags, and we'll be done. Is she warm enough?"

Nick looked at Katie watching them anxiously through the back window of the truck, her paws pressed against the glass. For a rat, she was kind of cute. Kind of. "She's fine. Let's get your clothes."

"I really appreciate this, Nick."

Nick kept his focus on Katie. "Let's get your clothes."

He followed her upstairs to help, which was a mistake. Watching her fold dresses into garbage bags wasn't a problem, but then she opened drawers and started tossing fistfuls of silky underwear into a bag, all of it in the weirdest colors like electric blue and hot pink and metallic gold, and in patterns like plaid and polka dots and leopard and zebra, and he couldn't help but imagine what it must look like on her—all that color next to her pale honey skin, all that silk filled out round and warm the way she'd felt with her arms around him.

"I'll carry this down," he said, grabbing the two nearest bags when she started pulling out nightgowns. "Be right back." He ran down the steps and threw the bags in the back of the truck, and then stood out in the cold trying to get his mind back so he could figure out what the hell was wrong with him while Katie stared at him reproachfully through the window.

Quinn was a friend, that's all.

Okay, so she was the best friend he had next to Max and he loved her, a friendship kind of love, but that was all. He was not having hot thoughts about Quinn. That would be crazy.

It isn't the first time, he told himself, and thought of nineteen years before, of the August he and Zoë had come home because things were going so wrong for them. In the three months since their wedding, they'd found out that all they had in common were bad tempers. But in the same three months, Quinn had changed. When he'd left, she'd been a perplexed sixteen-year-old drink of water in a blue chiffon bridesmaid dress, trying to put his wedding back together when her sister had balked half-way down the aisle. "I can fix this," she'd told him, and she had, while he'd sat and fumed and wondered if he really wanted to marry Zoë after all. But when he'd come back three months later, Quinn had run out to the car in her cutoffs and tank top to hug her sister—Zoë grabbing onto Quinn with more emotion than she'd ever grabbed onto him—and he'd gaped in surprise and guilty lust as Quinn laughed and rocked Zoë back and forth, confident and round and happy and suddenly sexy. *Shit, I got the wrong sister*, he'd thought then, with all the depth of a nineteen-year-old.

And that was when Zoë had looked over and caught him and glared at him so that he'd turned back to the car to get their things before she could say anything out loud. Later that night, she'd backed him up against her mother's white metal kitchen cabinet with a paring knife under his chin and said, "She's sixteen, you sonofabitch."

He winced at the memory now. Christ, sixteen and he'd been scoping her out. Of course, he'd only been nineteen, so it wasn't as if he were doing it now.

He thought of Quinn in that gold leopard bra she'd thrown in one of the bags. Yeah, he'd matured.

"If you ever cheat on me, Nick Ziegler," Zoë had said, "I'll just leave you flat. But if you ever touch my sister, I'll cut your liver out with my manicure scissors and *then* I'll leave you flat." Since Zoë never made idle threats, he'd pretty much stopped looking at Quinn entirely. His marriage had been in enough trouble at that point without Quinn and the manicure scissors. Zoë had bolted about three months later to his surprised but great relief, and he'd forgotten her and Quinn and all of Tibbett while he'd finished his four years with Uncle Sam and then used the GI Bill to collect a business degree with a minor in English poetry. The poetry was dynamite for seducing girls, the girls who had contributed to the ease with which he'd pushed the McKenzie sisters to the back of his mind. By the time he'd come back home, Quinn was teaching art and involved with Greg somebody, a good guy, and that was enough to make her safe again while he quoted Donne and Marvell to surprised but impressed Tibbett women, and the manicure scissors faded to a vague memory.

His mind went back to Quinn in that leopard bra. Somehow he didn't think Bill was going to feel the same relief about Quinn bolting that he'd felt about Zoë's leaving.

He sure wouldn't.

UPSTAIRS. QUINN TOOK notepaper out of the desk and sat down at the stripped pine dining-room table.

Dear Bill, she wrote.

Now what? All right, she was furious with him about the dog, but he deserved a note. After two years, he really deserved a note.

I'm moving out.

Well, that was good. To the point.

It's not just because of Katie

But a lot of it was. He'd just taken her dog, as if what she wanted didn't matter. He thought she'd get over it. He didn't know her at all.

but what happened with Katie has made me realize that we don't know each other at all.

Of course, that was probably her fault. She'd never really made him look at her, never said, "I don't agree," never said, "I really want a dog," while she was giving up all the ones she'd found. It really was her fault. She couldn't stay with him, she absolutely couldn't stay with him after the pound thing, but she didn't need to be nasty about it, create hard feelings, make things difficult for everybody.

This is all my fault for not being honest with you, but I know now we're too different and it would never have worked out for us.

That sounded good, reasonable. She really didn't have much more to say, so she just scribbled the end to her letter—*I'm moving in with Mom and Dad until I can find my own place. I'll be back to pick up my books later, and I'll leave the key then*. She almost signed it *Love, Quinn* from habit, but she stopped. She didn't love him. She'd never loved him. She'd liked him enough to stay with him because she hadn't disliked him enough to leave. How sad.

So she just signed it *Quinn* and left to go downstairs to Nick and Katie, a little guilty but mostly relieved because that part of her life was ended completely.

NICK HELPED QUINN unload her furniture into the McKenzies' garage, and then against his better judgment stayed for a beer to keep her company until her parents got home. "They'll be home any minute now," Quinn had said when she asked him to stay. "I can't wait to explain this one to them."

"They going to be upset?" He followed her into the kitchen, trying not to look at her rear end. Her jeans were too tight.

He'd never noticed it before, but her jeans were definitely too tight. It was a miracle she didn't have guys baying at her on the street.

"Well, they got used to seeing Bill and me together." Quinn dropped the last garbage bag of clothes on her mother's kitchen floor where Katie could sniff it the way she'd sniffed the other eight, evidently suspicious something threatening lurked within. "I'm not sure they can see me without him. After two years with him, I don't think anybody sees me anymore, not the way I really am. I mean, look at you."

Nick froze for a moment in the act of taking a beer out of the fridge. "Leave me out of it." He twisted off the cap and nudged the door closed with his shoulder.

Quinn leaned against the counter, folding her arms so her pink sweater pulled tighter against her breasts as she scowled her exasperation at him. "I bet your whole life you've thought of me as either Zoë's sister or somebody's girlfriend."

Nick shook his head. "You know better than that." He knew better than that, even if he didn't want to think about it.

"It was different when Zoë was around." Quinn went past him to the fridge. "I could understand that when Zoë was around, nobody saw me."

A gentleman would have told her that wasn't true, but it was. Zoë had been perfect, exotic, her little vixen face capped with wild naturally kinky hair that fell past her shoulders, the red of it so dark it was almost black out of the sunlight.

"I got used to it." Quinn got a beer from the fridge. "But you'd think somebody would notice me standing next to a *guy*."

She screwed the cap off her own bottle and drank, and he watched the curve of her neck as she leaned back and the movement of the muscles in her throat, willing his eyes not to drop farther down that curve to that damn pink sweater. Her hair fell back in the same smooth bell cut she'd worn since she was fifteen. No kink to Quinn at all, he thought, keeping his mind off curves. Just all that smooth silky red-gold hair, the kind that looked like it would fall like water through his fingers.

"I saw you." Nick put his beer down. "Listen, I have to go."

"You haven't finished your beer," Quinn said. "But I can take a hint. I'll stop whining."

She walked out of the kitchen through the wide archway into the dark little living room, Katie stepping nervously beside her, and detoured around the big red couch that had been in front of the arch for as long as he could remember. "Do you believe this?" Zoë had said when they were seniors. "My mother bought a Carnal-Red couch. Don't you just want to fuck every time you look at it?" Since he'd been eighteen and wanted to fuck anybody any time he looked at anything, the question was moot, but it came back to haunt him now because Quinn had plopped herself down in the center of it. Pink sweater, copper hair, orange-red couch: he could feel the heat from where he stood.

Get out of here, he told himself, but Quinn rolled her head to smile at him over the back of the couch. "Really, I'll stop whining. I truly am grateful you helped me move, and I'm sorry I've been such a grouch."

The light from the kitchen gleamed on her hair.

"Your mother should redecorate," he said and walked around the couch to sit beside her.

"There's a lot of things my mother should do." Quinn moved over to give him room while Katie sat anxiously at her feet. "Like get a life. I think that's one of the reasons I decided I had to have Katie." Quinn smiled down at the little dog. Then her smile faded. "And leave Bill. I don't want to end up settling like my mother, hitting the garage sales with my best friend while my husband watches TV instead of me, and that's the way I was heading with Bill. I want it all. Excitement. Passion."

Nick leaned against the cushions, his arm stretched along the back of the couch but not touching her—that would be bad, touching her, don't go there—and watched her soft lips part and close while she spoke, and felt his breath come a fraction faster. *This is dumb, get out,* he told himself, and yanked his mind away from her mouth in time to hear her say, "I want to be new, different, exciting. I want be Zoë."

"You can skip that part if you want," he said.

"I think maybe Katie was a sign. You know, like my destiny telling me to get a life." Quinn smiled at him and said, "You can't ignore your destiny," and he lost his place in the conversation again. Everything about Quinn was warm, he'd always known that, but for twenty years he'd been telling himself it was a puppy kind of warmth, cute and safe. But there was her mouth now, lush and smiling—

"Nick?" Quinn leaned forward a little and her hair spilled on the couch back. "Are you okay?"

Her voice came from far away. He only had to lift one finger to touch her hair. Just one finger. It was so easy, and the strands slid like silk, the way he'd thought they would, cool and slippery, and his breath snagged in his throat.

Her eyes widened, and he was caught, both of them caught, staring into each other's eyes for long seconds, too long, way too long, hours too long, frozen in each other's gaze, and the longer he looked the more he saw Quinn, her eyes huge and startled, Quinn, her soft lips parted, Quinn, hotter than he could have imagined, *Quinn*. He began to lean forward, sucked into her warmth, a little dizzy because he wanted her mouth so much. She closed her eyes and leaned forward, too, close and possible, too possible, *don't go there*, but he leaned anyway to take all of her heat, and then a car door slammed outside and Katie barked, and Nick jerked back.

"Oh, *hell*." He stood up, pulling away from her so that she fell forward a little, and Katie went under an end table in terror.

You have lost your fucking mind, he told himself. "Okay," he said to her briskly, betrayed only by how husky his voice came out. "Nothing happened. This is not you. You don't do this. I'm sorry. It's the couch. I have to go."

Quinn took a deep breath, and he tried not to watch her sweater rise and fall. *Manicure scissors,* he told himself. *Sister-in-law. Best friend. Bill's girl.*

None of it was helpful.

"Maybe it is me," Quinn said faintly. "Maybe I do this. I've changed some today." She swallowed and the movement of her throat made him nuts again.

"No, you haven't," Nick said. "I'm going now." He backed around the couch just as Quinn's mother came in the back door and screamed.

four

IT TOOK a couple of minutes to sort things out, especially since Nick's guilt made him babble. *"Nothing happened,"* he said, while Quinn straightened and said, "Mama, it's okay, it's just us."

"Us?" her mother said and Nick said, "No, there is no us, it's just Quinn. And me. Not together."

Then Quinn's father came in from the garage, and said, "What the *hell?*" and Nick thought, *Good question.*

"What are you doing here?" Meggy McKenzie looked at them and then at her garbage bag–strewn kitchen, the overhead light making her short curly auburn hair an improbably red-gold halo around her pretty, perplexed face. "What is this stuff? Why aren't the lights on?"

"Hello, Nick," her husband said, squinting into the dark living room, his voice a little slow with suspicion. Joe was a big guy, a little balding, a little paunch, but mostly solid blue-collar electrician bulk, all of it radiating disapproval of Nick.

Nick could relate. He wasn't any too pleased with himself at the moment. "Hey, Joe. Well, I got to go. Have a good night. Quinn will explain." He detoured around Meggy and was out the back door before she could ask him anything else, like *What were you doing on my couch with my daughter?* The second daughter of hers he'd been on that couch with. *Don't even think about that.*

Once he was in the truck, he realized he'd left his jacket behind, but he didn't care. The cold could get his head back for him, or at least some of the blood it needed to function. He sat for a minute, trying not to think about how stupid he'd just been, blowing twenty years of self-control like that.

"This did not happen," he said and started the truck.

It was all that damn dog's fault. If it hadn't been for the dog, Quinn would still have been with Bill. As long as Quinn had been with Bill, he'd known how the world worked. And before Bill it had been Alex and before that it had been Greg and before that—why in the hell hadn't she married any of those guys? Not that they were good enough for her, but why was she still rolling around town unattached, a loose cannon with a mouth that made men stupid?

Why did he care?

He put the truck in gear and backed out of the driveway and drove away from Quinn and confusion and trouble, and the farther away he got, the easier it was to deny anything had happened, that anything had changed.

Because nothing really had.

QUINN SAT POLEAXED on the big red couch while her mother stared at the garbage bags in the kitchen and her father moved around her to turn on the TV. ESPN kicked on with a guy in a blazer and a bad hairpiece talking about some team's loss as if it were a major tragedy.

"Hi, Daddy." Quinn moved over on the couch to make room for him, trying to get her mind back from heat and surprise. Nick had almost made a move on her. And she'd been all for it. Amazing.

"How you doing?" her father asked as he sat, never taking his eyes from the screen. Joe's question was the equivalent of "nice day," not a request for information. Quinn was fairly sure that whatever was going down with Nick, he didn't want to know.

"I've left Bill," Quinn said, to test the waters.

"Good," her father said, his eyes still on the TV, and then part of it must have registered.

"What?" He frowned at her a little, but Quinn knew he was bluffing.

"Never mind," Quinn said, and when he patted her knee and put his attention back on the TV, she put hers back on her own life, which was suddenly interesting.

Nick had almost made a move on her and she'd said yes. Not an hour after she moved out on one guy, she was sending signals to another one, feeling hotter than she had in her whole life and, stranger yet, feeling that way about *Nick*, and the more she thought about him now, the dizzier she got. *How long has this been going on?*

"What's going on?" Meggy said from the kitchen. "There are nine garbage bags here. Nine."

"Right." Quinn got up and moved away from the couch where she'd almost done something exciting and into the dim little kitchen of her childhood. "I'm staying with you for a little while, if that's okay."

"There's a *dog* in here," her father called from the living room.

"Don't pet her," Quinn said, and then Katie came clicking around the couch, casting worried looks over her shoulder in Joe's direction.

"Does she bite?" Meggy said.

"No, she pees." Quinn scooped her up. "Her name's Katie. I'm keeping her. I have a dog now."

It sounded wonderful. *I have a dog*. And then there was Nick. Such an interesting life she was getting. Finally.

"In your apartment?" Meggy frowned, her pretty, faded face crinkling with incomprehension. "Is this why you've left Bill? You couldn't be that frivolous—"

"Sure I could." Quinn hugged Katie closer. "I'm gone. It's over."

Meggy's frown bleached out into simpler worry. "Oh, dear, I

think this is a mistake. Relationships take compromise. Maybe if you go back—"

"He took my dog to the pound," Quinn said. "I told him I was keeping her, and he took her anyway while I was at school."

Meggy looked torn, probably between wanting to escape and wanting to save her daughter from being manless. "Quinn, dear, we're talking about a *dog*. This isn't like you. You're the—"

"No, I'm not," Quinn said. "Not anymore. I'm tired of being sensible and settling. I'm thirty-five. If I don't go after what I want now, I never will." Like Nick. She hadn't realized it until he'd looked at her like that, but she wanted him. He was excitement personified, the absolute worst person in the world for her. Perfect.

Of course, considering the way he'd left the house at a flat run, he was going to take some convincing. Maybe she should go after something easier first and work up to Nick.

"Life doesn't end at thirty-five," Meggy said. "I'm fifty-eight and I'm still doing fine. You just stop taking chances before you lose everything."

Quinn wondered if her mother had ever wanted anything much, ever felt the zing and the pull she'd just felt with Nick. Stop taking chances? It was the advice Meggy had given her all her life and suddenly Quinn was annoyed about that. "I don't want to be you," she told her mother. "You're doing exactly what you've always done. You get up, you go answer phones for Bucky at the real estate office, you go to a garage sale with Edie after school, you come home and fix dinner for Dad, and then you watch him watch TV." Quinn slowed a little as Meggy's face grew grim. "Look, if that's what makes you happy, fine, but it's not enough for me. If I stay with Bill, I'll end up the same way you have, no passion, no excitement, and no real reason to get up in the morning. I'm not going to live like that."

Meggy's words came out stiffly. "And this dog is going to give you that."

"No, this dog is just the beginning." Quinn put Katie down so she could re-explore the kitchen. "Katie is the canary in the mineshaft. I didn't know how stifling my life was until Bill wouldn't let me keep her." Quinn took a deep breath. "I'm not adapting anymore, Mama. From now on, people are going to have to adapt to me. I'm going after what I want." It was such a lovely selfish thing to say, Quinn felt lightheaded for a minute. There should be background music. Trumpets. Nick.

"Need a beer here," Joe called from the living room, and Meggy automatically went to the refrigerator and got it, frowning as she went. When she came back from the living room, she folded her arms, evidently still unconvinced and showing amazing staying power considering that her usual response to anything that upset her was, Well, all right. "Is this about Nick?"

Quinn felt herself flush. "No. This is about me."

"Because you and Nick would be terrible," Meggy said. "Bill—" The phone rang and Meggy turned her back to pick it up. "Hello? Just a minute." She held the phone out to Quinn. "It's Bill." Her tone added, *Be careful, dear.*

"Oh, hell." Quinn felt the pit of her stomach drop to her knees as she took the phone. "Hi, Bill."

"What's going on?" he asked. "Your clothes are gone."

"I know. I moved out. I left you a note." Quinn closed her eyes and leaned against the cabinets. "I'll come get my books later, but you can have the rest of the stuff."

"Your note makes no sense," Bill said. "And the silverware is missing."

"I know." Quinn tried again. "I took it. I moved out. You'll have to buy some more."

"But then we'll have two sets," Bill said, and Quinn stopped feeling guilty.

"Bill, I moved out. There isn't any 'we' anymore. I'm gone. It's over."

"Don't be ridiculous." The calm certainty in his voice kicked up Quinn's anger again.

"I'm not ridiculous. I'm *gone*." *I'm necking with other men.* Sort of. "It wasn't working for me, Bill."

"Of course it was. I'll come get you, and you'll come home, and we'll talk this out tomorrow after school."

"No."

Meggy turned around startled, and Quinn shook her head at her. "No, you will not come get me," she said to Bill with brutal firmness. "I've left you. It's over."

"I'll be there in five minutes," Bill said and hung up.

"I don't believe this." Quinn put the phone back. "He's coming over. I told him it's over, and he told me not to be ridiculous. He thinks I'm coming back." She turned to see Meggy still eyeing the bags littering her kitchen, as if they'd evaporate if she just stared at them long enough. "Forget it. I can go to a motel if you want, but I'm not going back to him."

"You really want this." Meggy sounded unhappy.

"I really want to be free," Quinn said. "It feels really good to be away from him."

"I need to talk to Edie about this," Meggy said. "This is so rash. I wish you—"

"Mama," Quinn said. "It's over. I'll find an apartment tomorrow, but if I could stay here tonight—"

"Of course you can stay tonight," Meggy said. "You're my daughter, and you can always stay here, even when you're making a big mistake."

"Mama—"

"I'll get you a list of apartments tomorrow. Stop by the office after school, I'll have a list off the computer if you haven't come to your senses by then." Meggy patted her shoulder, still looking doubtfully at Katie, who looked doubtfully back.

"Apartments that take dogs," Quinn said.

Meggy watched with patent disapproval as Katie returned to sniffing the garbage bags. "That dog is up to something. It's sneaky."

Katie looked up at her, dark eyes wide with anxious innocence.

"She is not," Quinn said. "Look at that sweet face."

"That dog has a secret," Meggy said.

"Mother—"

"All right, apartments that take dogs. Did you say Bill was coming over?"

"Yes," Quinn said. "He thinks he's coming to get me."

"Well, don't burn any bridges," Meggy said. "Bill is a good man with a good job and a good future. I'm sure it will all work out."

"Bill is another thirty years of stripped pine furniture, high school athletics, and ESPN," Quinn said, and Meggy glanced at the archway. The room glowed with the dim blue light from the TV and they could hear the faint cheers of some crowd enthused over some play.

"We got any Cheetos?" Joe called, and Quinn went to get them without saying anything else, feeling guilty about the damage she'd already inflicted on her mother. Her mother liked her boring life. Passion would probably have made her worry.

"I'm sorry, Mama," she said on her trip back from the living room. "I shouldn't have said that stuff. You live the way you want. What do I know about you?"

"Nothing," Meggy said shortly, but when Bill came to the front door while Quinn was hauling her clothes upstairs, Meggy opened the door, said, "She's staying here for a while, Bill, go home," and slammed it in his face.

"Way to go, Ma," Quinn said from the staircase.

"Was that Bill?" Joe said.

"Just watch the TV," Meggy said. "God knows if you paid attention to anything else, you might miss something important."

"What did I do?" Joe asked, but Meggy ignored him and went upstairs.

WHEN MEGGY WAS gone, Quinn went into the kitchen and punched "speed dial" and "one" and waited for Zoë to answer.

Quinn was "two" on the speed dial.

Zoë's husband answered instead. "Hello," Ben said, and Quinn pictured him leaning against their refrigerator, tall and unflappable, the only man who'd ever loved Zoë and not been driven crazy by her.

"This is your sister-in-law," she said. "How are the kids?"

"Hey, Q," Ben said. "They're fine. Harry got an A on his reading test and Jeannie got head lice at nursery school. What's new with you?"

"I left Bill," Quinn said.

"Oh. Well, you probably want to talk to Zoë then." He put his hand over the receiver and yelled, "Zo, it's Quinn."

"I guess this means you don't want to discuss my personal life, right?" Quinn said.

"Hell, no," Ben said. "Although I never did think he was good enough for you."

"Well, thank you," Quinn said. "And you couldn't have mentioned this to me two years ago?"

"Hell, no," Ben said. "Zo's coming. Hang on."

"What's up?" Zoë said, and Quinn said, "I left Bill." It was almost becoming a mantra; every time she said it, she got more cheerful. "I moved out. I'm at Mom and Dad's."

"You're kidding," Zoë said. "So you're going to live with them now?"

"Just for a little while." Quinn boosted herself up on the counter and began to swing her feet and bump the metal cabinet. Lovely déjà vu, talking to Zoë again and kicking cabinets. "I just got here. Nick helped me move some of my stuff, and he's going back for the rest on Monday, and by then maybe I'll know where I'm going." She waited for Zoë to say something about Nick, ask about him, anything.

"So what happened with you and Bill?"

"He stole my dog," Quinn said.

"What dog?" Zoë said, and Quinn told her the whole story.

"I'll be damned," Zoë said when she was through.

"So what do you think?" Quinn hunched a little on the cabinets. "Mom says it's a mistake."

"Yeah, and look at Mom's life." Zoë's scorn came cleanly over the line. "You got to do what you got to do, kid."

"Mom says I'm nuts to do this over a dog."

"It's not about the dog," Zoë said and then muffled she said, "*Later*, do you mind? I'm still getting this myself." She turned back to the receiver, her voice clear again and said, "Ben thinks Tibbett is like a soap opera. He keeps expecting to hear that somebody's married her cousin and had her uncle's baby. He wants dirt."

I just got turned on staring at your ex-husband, Quinn thought, but she said, "Barbara Niedemeyer dumped Matthew Ferguson." She opened the cabinet beside her and went rooting one-handed for graham crackers.

"Oh, big deal," Zoë said. "She's boring, she keeps doing the same thing over and over. Give me something good."

"Nick and Lisa broke up," Quinn said, pushing her luck as she fished a cracker out of the box.

"Who's Lisa?"

"You know, Lisa Webster."

"I used to baby-sit a Lisa Webster," Zoë said.

"That's the one."

"He was dating somebody I used to baby-sit?"

"She's twenty-two," Quinn said around a mouthful of graham cracker, trying to be fair.

"And he's twelve," Zoë said. "I swear, that man is never going to grow up."

"He's pretty dependable," Quinn said. "He and Max are doing great with the service station."

"I mean socially," Zoë said. "He still acts like he's in high school. But he's not my problem anymore, thank God."

"He's good to me."

"He always was," Zoë said. "I think you're the only thing he kept out of our marriage. He always said you were the best thing about it."

Quinn swallowed. "He did?"

"Yeah. He said he'd always wanted a little sister and then he got the perfect one in you. He thought you could do no wrong. Like everybody else thought."

"And he thought you were exciting," Quinn said. "Like everybody else thought."

"You don't sound so good," Zoë said. "Are you okay?"

"I'm just tired of being the practical one," Quinn said. "I don't want to be dependable anymore. I want exciting."

"Good call dumping Bill, then," Zoë said. "He always bored me to tears. Now go do something that'll shock everybody and be free for a change. You were the only one who thought you had to be good."

"Mom thinks so, too," Quinn said. "She always said I was the calm one like her, remember?"

"She's not calm, she's catatonic." Zoë's voice faded again. "In a minute," she said to Ben and then came back to Quinn. "I have to go, he's driving me crazy. Listen, I love you, Q. Don't let the 'rents make you nuts. If you need to get away, come stay with us for awhile."

"I love you, too, Zo. Sorry about the head lice."

"I'll take them over living with Mom and Dad any day," Zoë said. "Find a place fast."

When they'd hung up, Quinn sat on the counter and nibbled on a cracker, staring into space, trying to get her mind around the new wrinkles in her already corrugated life. She didn't feel guilty about Bill, she really didn't; well, she felt a little guilty, but not enough to move back, she was never going to go back. No, she'd find an apartment tomorrow, a place of her own—her pulse kicked up at the thought—and then she and Katie could move in. She looked down to see Katie waiting anxiously at her feet and fed her a graham cracker, watching as Katie took it delicately, no grabbing—and she could get some furniture of her own, and maybe Nick could move it for her—

Do something that'll shock everybody, Zoë said.

Dating her sister's ex-husband would do the trick. She shivered a little at the thought. Nick was the only exciting thing in her entire life; how could she have missed him up till now? He'd always been the wild Ziegler brother, but she'd never quite understood that part because she always felt so safe with him. Until he looked at her like that. Until she'd looked back and really seen him, dark and dangerous and full of infinitely impractical possibilities. Really, he was the perfect guy for her right now: a bad guy who would never hurt her. Excitement without risk. The more she thought about it, the better he sounded and the warmer she felt.

Now all she had to do was get him to stop screaming and running whenever he looked at her, and she'd be exciting, too.

Just like Zoë.

BILL STOOD IN the backyard of the McKenzies' little white frame house, cursing Quinn's mother for the nutcase she was. She probably hadn't even told Quinn he was there or Quinn would have come down and talked to him and come home with him. He stared up at the square of yellow light from Quinn's bedroom. He could see the wall and ceiling light clearly. The curtains weren't shut. That was dangerous, didn't she know that was dangerous? Men would try to look in. He'd had to think for a minute, trying to remember the layout of the upstairs, but he was sure that was Quinn's window, naked and vulnerable, and anyone could see in, and that was really dangerous.

Then she was there, standing by the window, her body round in her pink sweater, sharp against the yellow light in the room. She stretched to grab the top of the curtain—he could see the outward curve of her breast and the inward curve of her waist and the outward curve of her hip—and Bill felt his heart contract, felt the loss of her in every bone and muscle, and then refused the thought, she wasn't lost, they'd talk, it would be fine, they'd be together forever, have the sons and the dinners and the life he'd planned; she wasn't gone.

She began to pull the curtain closed, and then the curtain was across the window, and he was alone.

He stood watching for another half hour or so, not noticing the cold, and then the light went off behind the curtain and made the window blank, and he knew she'd gone to bed or downstairs, and wherever she was, there was nothing there for him anymore. He got in his car and drove home, knowing she'd come back to him tomorrow.

"SO YOU'RE JUST moving out," Darla said for about the for-
tieth time the next afternoon after school, and Quinn held on to
her patience. There was something wrong with Darla, and the
move was making whatever it was worse, so snapping at her
wasn't an option, especially since Darla had spent the last half
hour helping pack Quinn's books into boxes.

Quinn shoved the last of those boxes toward the door of the
apartment, making Katie skip back a step to avoid getting
squashed. "Yep, it's over. As soon as Nick picks these up on
Monday, I'm out completely." She glanced at the clock. "Let's
get going. Bill's only got another fifteen minutes of weightlifting." She shrugged on her coat and picked up Katie, who looked
over her shoulder, as suspicious of the world as ever.

"Okay, I know I'm being thick," Darla said when they were
in her car, waiting for the heater to thaw their blood, "but could
you please explain how you can just move out on a guy you've
been with for two years?"

"I wasn't with him." Quinn held on to Katie as the dog put
her paws on the window and anxiously surveyed the sidewalk
for enemies. "I was just sort of next to him. He asked me to go
to the third baseball championship party, and he was sweet and
we started dating, and then he started leaving things at my apartment a little at a time until he was all moved in, and then he
found this apartment and moved us here, and I never really said
yes to any of it. He's just patient and he never quits and eventually, there he is, right where he wants to be. And I don't want
to be there. I didn't realize it until he took Katie to the pound,
but I don't want to be where he is." She shivered a little, and
Katie transferred her attention, evidently sensing that the trouble
was inside the car, not outside. "He came to the art room today,
acting like nothing was wrong, like I was just visiting my mom

and dad, like he assumed I'd be back any time. He's sort of giving me the creeps." Quinn patted Katie for comfort, and the dog curled up her lap, keeping nervous eyes on her. "Could we please go somewhere else? I'm supposed to go to the real estate office to pick up a list of apartments from Mom. Let's go there."

Darla put the car in gear. "Well, once Nick gets the books, you'll be out of there, and even Bill will have to see you're not coming back. How'd you talk Nick into getting involved, anyway? I'd have thought he'd have headed for the hills to avoid being in the middle of this."

Quinn thought of Nick the night before, solid and warm next to her in the truck, solid and hot on the couch. "He's a good guy," she said, trying to make it sound offhand.

Darla slowed to make the turn onto Main Street. "Am I missing something?"

"I think Nick almost kissed me last night," Quinn blurted, and then felt stupid and relieved at the same time.

Darla pulled over and parked the car.

"The real estate office is another two blocks," Quinn said.

"Yes, but the interesting stuff is happening here." Darla looked more appalled than interested. "He *kissed* you?"

"I said *almost*." Quinn squirmed a little in the seat, to Katie's dismay. "We were on the couch talking and he stopped and we looked at each other for a long time, you know?"

"I think so," Darla said. "One of those long looks that starts out a regular Hello and then turns into *Hello?*"

Quinn nodded, patting the dog quiet. "But then he stood up and said, 'You aren't like this,' and left."

Darla slumped in her seat. "Oh, boy. I don't know. You and Nick?"

"There is no me and Nick." *But there could be.* "There was a nice little zing for that nanosecond between the time when I realized he was looking at me like he wanted me and the time when he got up and ran. But he got up and ran just the same."

Darla stared out the windshield. "Zing, huh?"

Quinn nodded. "There was more zing in him not kissing me than there was in the two years Bill *was* kissing me. Definite zing."

"The zing doesn't last," Darla said, and Quinn jerked around at the flatness in her voice. "Well, it doesn't. So if you're leaving Bill because of no zing—" She shook her head. "A good guy, one who's faithful and who loves you? That beats zing."

"No, it doesn't." Quinn eyed Darla cautiously. Darla would talk about her problem only when she was good and ready. Was she good and ready?

"You can't keep excitement forever," Darla said. "It goes. And then you have to settle for what you've got, and if you've got a really good guy, that's enough, that's more than enough, that's fine. Maybe Bill didn't understand about the dog. Maybe if you gave him another chance. He could give you a safe life, a—"

"I don't want that," Quinn said. "I've had a safe life for thirty-five years and I'm tired of it. I want to wake up every morning knowing that something good is coming, that there's a reason to get out of bed. The same damn thing over and over is not a reason."

Darla's eyes narrowed and her jaw grew tighter. "So you change it a little. You do something small, not this huge."

"I did," Quinn said. "I adopted Katie." Katie looked up at her, and she stroked her head to quiet her. "It was such a little thing, but now it's big because Bill couldn't see me any way but the way he wanted me. At least Nick sees me." She thought back to the couch the night before and felt warm again. "Last night he really saw me."

"He'll dump you in a year," Darla said, her voice flat again.

"Or he'll drive you so crazy that you'll dump him, only this time you'll lose him as your friend, and he's the best one you've got next to me. If you stay with Bill, you can have them both, but if you do anything about this, you're going to lose Nick, too. You really want that?"

"I want that feeling again," Quinn said, stubbornly. "I'm pretty sure Nick doesn't, but I do. What's going to happen next year, that's next year. This is now, and I'm not settling anymore."

Darla shook her head, looking close to tears. "Quinn—"

"Are things that bad with Max?" Quinn said and regretted it when she saw Darla's face twist. "Okay, I'm sorry. We'll talk about it later—"

"I love Max," Darla said.

"I know you do," Quinn said.

"I've got it all under control," Darla said. "I'm happy."

"Absolutely," Quinn said, nodding.

"I love my life," Darla said. "My kids are great, my house is beautiful, I enjoy my job, my husband is hardworking and faithful."

"These are good things," Quinn said.

"I'm so bored I could scream," Darla said.

"Right," Quinn said, relieved it was out. "So what are you going to do?"

"Nothing." Darla turned to look at her, accusation in her eyes. "I'm not messing up a great relationship just because I'm bored."

"I didn't have a great relationship," Quinn said. "Bill isn't Max."

"He sounds like Max," Darla said glumly. "Oh, hell, forget it, let's go get you an apartment."

"Maybe you just need a little change," Quinn said. "Nothing big, just a one-degree change to shift things a little, to make things new again." She looked down at Katie on her lap. "Never mind, forget I said that."

"A little change," Darla said.

"Little changes have a way of multiplying," Quinn said. "Maybe—"

"No, I like it." Darla gripped the steering wheel tighter. "A little change. Just something to make him look at me, like you said." She turned to meet Quinn's eyes. "I don't think he's looked at me in years. I'm just there, you know? And I haven't looked at him, either, not really. And then at the station the other night, I wanted to make love in the office—"

"All those *windows*?" Quinn felt scandalized and intrigued. Making love in front of a window sounded like something Nick would do.

"—and he wouldn't even consider it. He didn't even say, 'Let's try the bathroom instead,' he said, 'After the kids are in bed.' How bad is that?"

Quinn said, "Well—"

"He couldn't keep his hands off me once and now he wants to wait?" Darla's voice rose as her face crumpled. *"He doesn't even see me anymore."*

"Okay, okay." Quinn leaned over and patted Darla's arm. "Okay, we can fix this. We just have to get his attention. I mean, *you* just have to get his attention."

"How?" Darla practically snarled the word. "I almost raped him in the office, and he said no. What more—"

"Maybe you were too subtle." Quinn thought fast. "You have to shock him. Like meeting him at the door wrapped in Saran Wrap or something." She felt a stab of envy for Darla, who was in a relationship with a guy who could appreciate Saran Wrap. Bill would have passed out from the vulgarity of it, and Nick would have taken the Saran Wrap and used it on some other woman.

"Saran Wrap," Darla said.

"Or a really sexy nightgown," Quinn said. "Or black lace underwear—"

"I have a transparent plastic raincoat," Darla said, her voice calm again. "Max's mother gave it to me because it would go with everything."

"That could be good," Quinn said.

"The boys come home late on Friday," Darla said. "Max'll be home alone tonight at five-thirty."

"Tonight?" Quinn was a little taken aback with how fast Darla was moving—thing must really be bad—but she nodded anyway. "Good idea."

"I like this," Darla said. "Great sex in the living room in broad daylight."

"I'm jealous," Quinn said, partly for encouragement and partly in truth.

"This is a plan." Darla nodded, back to her old positive self. "And it's just a little plan, it won't change anything important, just make things the way they used to be." She beamed at Quinn. "This is a very smart idea. Thank you."

Quinn looked down at Katie uneasily. "Don't mention it."

Darla put the car in gear. "Let's go get you an apartment fast. I have to be home by five."

"Look, don't get yourself too invested in this," Quinn said. "A little change, fine, but be practical. Don't expect miracles or revolutions."

"Like you and Nick?" Darla said.

Quinn closed her eyes and thought about Nick. All that zing. "Okay, you're right. We deserve miracles and revolutions. We'll both go for it."

"Damn right," Darla said. "This is going to be great."

"Damn right," Quinn said, and thought, *Oh, boy.*

five

MEGGY HAD found one apartment in Tibbett—"None of the others allowed pets, dear"—and that one was not attractive. "You can't live here," Darla had whispered, staring in horror at the water-stained walls, and Quinn was saying, "I can if it means I keep my dog," when the landlord bent to pat Katie.

A minute later they were out on the street, braced against the gusts of March wind. "I said housebroken only," the man said before he slammed the door on them.

"She is housebroken," Quinn said, thinking evil thoughts about the landlord who clearly did not understand dogs, but Darla looked approvingly at Katie for the first time.

"She knew that was a lousy place to live," she said. "Good dog."

"Well, how's this for an alternative?" Quinn said, glaring at both of them. "Now I have to live with my parents."

"There must be something else," Darla said. "If you're sure you're not going back to Bill."

"I don't like him," Quinn said. "Okay? Can we get that clear? He stole my dog. He's out."

"Right." Darla nodded. "Okay, forget him, I'll never mention him again. How about buying? If you can swing a down payment, mortgage payments could be cheaper than renting."

"Buy a house?" Quinn thought of the Tara-like subdivisions that ringed Tibbett. Buying a house was serious stuff. "What would I do with a whole house?"

"Not all houses are huge," Darla said patiently. "Find a little two-bedroom deal. Your mother works for a realtor, for heaven's sake. Let's go ask."

"Buy a house." Quinn got into the passenger seat again and

let Katie scramble her way into the backseat as she thought about it. A house. Her own house. Independence. Maturity. Privacy. The same flare of excitement that had caught her when she decided to keep Katie and kiss Nick came back. "You know, I could do that. Buy a house. Just me." Her own house. With a fenced-in backyard for Katie. And a couch in the living room for Nick. "I could do that. Maybe. I like it."

"Why do you have that look in your eye?" Darla said. "We're talking about real estate, not sex."

"They're both exciting," Quinn told her. "I'll talk to Mom tonight and see what I can afford, and we can go look tomorrow. Are you busy tomorrow?"

"Only in the morning at the shop." Darla smiled. "And tonight. I'm going to be very busy tonight."

WHEN MAX CAME home at five-thirty that night, Darla met him at the door, naked under her transparent raincoat.

"Hey, babe," he said and kissed her cheek as he pushed past her into their sunken living room. "We've only got—"

"Hey, yourself," she said. "Jeez, you really *aren't* seeing me anymore."

He turned around as she opened the coat. *"What—"*

"I have plans for you." She dropped the coat just as the door opened behind her.

"I brought—" she heard Nick say, and she went cold all over, not hard to do since she was naked and there was a considerable March breeze hitting her backside. Bending over to pick up the coat was not an option, and it was transparent anyway. Before she could think of anything else, she heard Nick say, "Or not," and the door closed again.

"What are you *doing?*" Max looked amazed and horrified, and neither was the emotion she'd been going for. "The *boys* will be in here in a minute."

"I—" She was stuck. "The hell with it." She walked past him, too embarrassed to pick up her coat. Too embarrassed to do anything really but walk into the bedroom and lock the door and sit on the bed with her arms wrapped around her and think about killing herself.

"Darla," Max said on the other side of the door.

"Go away," she said, and then she heard somebody knock on the front door, heard Max open it, heard her sons' voices, one of whom said, "Why couldn't we just walk in?"

"Oh, God," she said, and let herself fall backward. After ten minutes of self-flagellation, she put on her T-shirt and jeans and concentrated on figuring out who she was madder at, Max or Nick. The fact that neither of them had done anything wrong, that she was the one who'd been stupid, didn't make it any easier to forgive them.

An hour later, she was calm enough to go out to her kitchen to make hot dogs for the four of them camped around the TV where they watched the videotape of the last football game, re-running the parts where Mark had made his touchdown.

"The tape just came in this afternoon," Max told her on one of his trips to get food. "Bill called from school. I didn't have a chance to tell you—"

"Not a problem," Darla said, handing him a bowl of popcorn. "Take this out there, will you? Thank you."

Max retreated without another word.

Nick came out half an hour later for a beer.

"Sorry about that," Darla said, wishing Max had been an only child.

"About what?" Nick said. "You got any chips?"

"Sure." Darla reached up into the cupboard, glad to turn her back to hide her burning face. She handed the bag to him across the kitchen island and said, "Thanks."

"For what?" Nick said.

Darla took a deep breath. "For pretending nothing happened so I don't feel bad. It doesn't work, but I appreciate it."

"Well, in that case, it was my pleasure," Nick said. "You have a nice ass."

"Hey," Darla said, her face flaming hotter, but she grinned in spite of herself.

"Not that I'll ever see it again," Nick said and wandered back out to the living room.

Okay, she'd forgive Nick. But Max—

Once they were all fed, she fixed herself a plate and locked herself in the bedroom again.

Few things she'd tried in her life had ever gone so wrong. And Max hadn't helped. He'd just looked horrified that she was naked. Even for a second he could have looked happy—

Of course knowing Nick was right behind him might have had something to do with that, but it was still a great gesture, damn it. Naked right there in the living room, too. She thought wistfully of how exciting that could have been, naked in the living room in broad daylight. They could have—

She saw Max's face again, appalled.

Rats. She bit into her hot dog and thought evil thoughts about Max as she chewed.

AT ELEVEN THAT night, Max stumbled into their pitch-dark bedroom, crawled into bed beside her and whispered, "Now, about that naked bit at the door—"

"Touch me and you're a dead man," Darla said in a voice like lead.

"Good night," Max said and rolled away from her.

WHAT QUINN COULD afford, her mother told her Saturday morning, was nothing she should live in. "Seventy-five thousand, tops," Meggy told her. "And there's not much out there for that. Maybe you'd better stay with us until you patch things up with Bill."

"Give me the list," Quinn said, and picked Darla up at noon, determined to find a place of her own. She'd been thinking about it all night, a cozy little place where she could have people over without worrying about the neighbors hearing through the walls. Up until now, she hadn't done anything worth overhearing, but if she had a house of her own, she might. There was reason enough to buy a house right there.

"So did the plastic raincoat drive Max mad with lust?" she asked Darla as she pulled out into the street.

"No." Darla's voice was flat again, and when Quinn risked a glance, her face was tense.

"You want to talk about it?"

"I met him at the door, naked. Nick was with him. It sort of wrecked the moment."

"Oh." Quinn slumped back in her seat. "Well, you could have sent Nick over to me."

"He hasn't said anything to you yet?" Darla said, perking up a little in shared outrage. "What a jackass."

Quinn glanced at her. "Does that mean you're okay with the Nick thing now?"

"No." Darla settled deeper into her seat and folded her arms. "But if that's what you want, I'm with you."

"Thanks." Quinn's voice sounded as flat as Darla's to her own ears. This depression stuff was catching. "Any ideas?"

"Not yet," Darla said. "I'm still recovering from last night. But I'm not giving up."

"Good," Quinn said. "Let's go buy a house and then we'll think of Plan B for you and Plan A for me."

But after they'd spent the afternoon looking at her options, Quinn had to admit her mother had a point. "They're ugly. Even after I fixed them up, they'd still be ugly, poky little houses. I wanted something cozy and cute and these are all—"

"Really, really ugly," Darla said. "That's why they're cheap. There are two more in this neighborhood—"

"No," Quinn said. "They all look alike. I hate them."

"—and then one on the other side of town that's eighty-five, but your mom wrote a note that it's been on the market for a while so they might come down."

"The other side of town." Quinn sighed and started the car. "Twenty minutes from school and anything else, plus how good can it be if it's been on the market that long?"

Fifteen minutes later, Darla said, "We don't have to actually go in."

The house was tall and skinny, about one room wide, sided in peeling gray asbestos shingles and trimmed in dark gray rotting wood. It had a little side porch, but most of the porch rail had fallen off in pieces. Several of the storm windows were broken, the spouting swung drunkenly from the roof, and the tiny front yard was decorated with two twisted trees, one of which was dead. On one side was another house in even worse condition, on the other a weed-choked empty lot. As a finishing touch, the FOR SALE sign had fallen over.

"We have the key, we might as well go in," Quinn said. "Look at it this way. If it's anything on the inside, I should be able to get a really good deal."

"Quick, before it falls down," Darla said, but she shut up when they got inside.

The downstairs was three rooms in a row, the side porch letting them into the middle room first. Its hardwood floors gleamed in the light from two tall windows framed in wide peeling white woodwork. An archway led into the front of the house, a living room with a bricked-up fireplace framed in book-cases, their leaded glass doors missing most of the panes. Two more tall windows looked out on the deserted street and the dead tree.

"Lots of light," Darla said. "Of course, the trees would give you nightmares."

Quinn turned around, imagining comfortable furniture, none of it stripped pine. A big couch, definitely. "I think I like it."

The other door from the center room led to the kitchen at the back of the house, an ugly little room with gray cupboards and counters, but more light from another tall window and a door with a dog flap to a big yard that was, miracle of miracles, fenced in.

"Maybe a little paint." Darla looked doubtfully at the cabinets. "You know somebody really depressed lived here."

Quinn pulled the retaining board out of the dog door, and Katie sniffed it as if it were the door to hell and then climbed through. After a cautious circuit of the yard—a mass of weeds spotted with barren earth—she stretched out in a run, doing a dog version of *Born Free*. "I really, really like it."

"Because of the backyard?"

"It's big," Quinn said. "If the upstairs isn't awful, I'm buying it."

The upstairs wasn't awful. Two small bedrooms and one big one with another bricked-up fireplace, a bathroom with a claw-foot tub that had once been white, and lots and lots of wonderful light.

"Somebody kicked this door in once," Darla said, stooping to see the woodwork.

"Darla, I can fix all that." Quinn turned to survey the upstairs from the landing and felt the same warm feeling in her solar plexus that she'd felt looking at Katie in the car the first day, much the same warmth she'd felt when Nick had almost kissed her. "I am going to buy this house." She smiled, suddenly euphoric. "You know, three days ago my life was as gray as that kitchen downstairs, and today it's full of infinite possibilities. Just think what tomorrow might be!"

"Yeah," Darla said, looking around. "Just think."

BY SUNDAY NIGHT, Meggy had not only leaned on Bucky to negotiate a sale for seventy thousand, she'd gotten the seller to rent the house to Quinn before the closing. "You can move in Friday," she told Quinn. The look she gave Katie, sitting patiently if nervously on the kitchen tile, said, *And not a minute too soon.*

"Thank you." Quinn hugged her mother. "I'm truly grateful. I know you think I should go back to Bill—"

"Well, now he can move in with you," her mother said. "It's a good house. I had it inspected this morning. Lots of work, but a good foundation. Bill can work on it."

The hell he will, Quinn thought, but she kept her mouth shut.

"You'll need seven thousand for the down payment," Meggy went on.

"Got it," Quinn said. "I have over eleven in savings. I'll even have some left over for furniture." *A new bed. And Nick can help me move.*

"New furniture." Her mother walked to the archway and gazed around the living room, lit only by TV. "It's been years since I did that." Her eyes fell on the couch, currently occupied by her husband who was oblivious to her. "Maybe I'll get a new couch and give you this one."

Nick had blamed the couch, Quinn remembered. *It's this couch.* "I'd love to have the couch," she said. "You can keep Dad, though."

"Mmm," her mother said, and turned to survey the rest of the room. "This place could use some changes."

"Little changes," Quinn said, suddenly nervous.

Her mother's eyes went back to the couch. "Certainly."

Joe looked up and caught them watching him. "We got any beer?"

Quinn turned back to the kitchen to get him one. "Little changes, Mom. Just little ones."

ON MONDAY, QUINN was still sure that buying the house had been a brilliant decision, but her optimism flagged a little as the day wore on and school did not go well.

It began with first period when several athletes scowled at her through attendance and the rest of the students seemed subdued. The word was out that she'd dumped the coach. They'd get over it, but it was still disconcerting since she was used to being liked.

Then the BP stopped her in the hall on her way to the teachers' lounge on her break and said, "I can't believe you're doing this over a dog. Don't you realize what you're doing to Bill? To the school? We have a *levy*, Quinn." She'd stared him down and he'd gone off in a snit, but if anything went wrong with that tenth WBL trophy or the levy, Quinn knew there would be hell to pay and she'd be footing the bill.

Then at lunch, she had to deal with Edie and the faculty.

"Your mom said you left Bill," Edie said, her bright blue eyes watching Quinn across the scarred plastic wood-grained table in the teachers' lounge. "She's a little upset."

"Yep." Quinn popped the top on her Diet Coke, ignoring the avid interest of the rest of lunch group, especially the two women sitting next to them. Marjorie Cantor, the biggest mouth in school, was probably torn between sucking up to Quinn for inside info and cutting her dead for leaving that nice Coach

Hilliard. Tidy little Petra Howard just looked confused. Petra, always vague, had decided the previous month that her students were plotting against her—given Petra's abysmal teaching skills this wasn't complete paranoia—and now she spent as much time as she could in the lounge, hiding out, distracting herself with the lives of others.

"That's a nice sweater, Quinn," Petra said now. "Such a pretty color."

"Thank you," Quinn said, before turning back to Edie. "Mom's always a little upset with change."

"She's afraid you're throwing away security." Edie's lips pursed a little. "Your mother is a great one for security."

"Really a very pretty sweater," Petra said.

"I can make myself secure," Quinn said.

"Hey, I'm on your side," Edie said. "It's your mom who's upset."

"Where did you get that pretty sweater?" Petra said, and Marjorie rolled her eyes. Eavesdropping on sweaters was not going to get Marjorie where she wanted to go, which was deep into the details of the biggest breakup at Tibbett High since the last coach had left his wife for a cafeteria worker.

Quinn smiled sweetly at Petra to annoy Marjorie and said, "It's vintage. I found it in a shop in Columbus the last time I visited my sister."

"I think you're making her reevaluate her own life," Edie said.

"Why would I do that?" Quinn asked, genuinely mystified. "I don't see that what I'm doing has any bearing on her."

"Does it come in other colors?" Petra asked. "I can't wear lavender. I'm too pale." Petra looked like the undead, but it wasn't the fault of her clothing.

"I'm sure it came in other colors in nineteen sixty," Quinn said, trying not to sound exasperated. "It's vintage. There aren't any more." It had also been five bucks, but Quinn saw no point in making Marjorie's day by broadcasting how cheap she was.

"Probably no bearing at all," Edie said, soothingly. "So now that you've got some free time, you can come do the tech for the play. Sets and costumes. The stipend's a thousand dollars, which isn't bad, and if you don't do it, I'll end up with a parent again. Remember *The Sound of Music*?"

Quinn winced. She'd never seen shoddier Alps in her life. "It's every night of the week for ten weeks. That's not even minimum wage."

"Maybe a nice blue," Petra said. "Is it wool?"

"Please don't tell me that's a no." Edie tried to look crushed, but it wasn't in her personality. Fluffy little blondes do not crush.

"I'm starting a whole new life," Quinn said. "I'm going to be selfish." From the corner of her eye, she saw Marjorie lean forward.

"Aren't you afraid the moths will get it?" Petra went on, and Marjorie said, "Petra, for heaven's sake, drop it."

"Well, I'm all for the selfish part," Edie said. "I just wish you'd make an exception for me."

"This is equal-opportunity selfish," Quinn said. "No."

"It's *Into the Woods*," Edie said. "Fairy tales. Trees and towers. Think how much fun."

"No," Quinn said, trying not to design trees and towers in her mind.

"Mothballs," Petra said. "But then they smell so."

"Imagine how bad it could be if you don't do it," Edie said. "You'd really be saving the play if you took it."

"So you dumped the coach, did you?" Marjorie said, evidently goaded past resistance.

"Gotta go," Quinn said and escaped.

Then Bill dropped by the art room—"just to see how you're doing"—and stayed. "You must be getting pretty sick of living with your parents," he'd joked and she'd said, "No," feeling no temptation to tell him about the house, to tell him about anything that might start a conversation. "I'm really busy, Bill," she'd said, and he'd still hung around, while the kids watched, fascinated by the soap opera unrolling before their eyes, some of them actively hostile toward her because she was dissing their coach.

"He's a good guy," Corey Mossert told her when Bill had finally given up and gone, and she said, "Corey, do I mess with your personal life? Then stay out of mine."

When Jason Barnes saw her last period, he just shook his head, but Thea, who was aiding and therefore not distracted by artwork, was harder to put off. "What did he do?" she asked, and Quinn said, "He wasn't the right one. And I didn't want to settle, that wasn't good for either of us."

"What do you mean, you didn't want to settle?" Thea leaned on the desk, checking out supplies as students trailed up to the desk sporadically. "He's the coach, for cripe's sake. He's like the king of the school."

"There's life after school," Quinn told her. "And I don't want to wake up someday wishing I'd gone after what I wanted instead of settling for what I have. Which in this case is what other people want for me, not what I want." She hesitated a little, knowing Thea had parents behind her pushing her into places she wasn't sure she wanted to go. No point in unsettling Thea three months before graduation. "Look, he's just not the right guy."

"Right," Thea said. "How do you know he's not the right guy?"

"He took my dog to the pound."

Thea's eyes widened. "He's not the right guy. So how do you know the right guy?"

Quinn thought of Nick. "Beats me. I know somebody who

makes me want to throw up every time I look at him, but that might be flu."

"No, I know that feeling," Thea said. "So are you going to start dating this new guy?"

"He doesn't seem to be interested," Quinn said. "I may have to make a move anyway, though." The thought of that was terrifying, but the alternative wasn't any better. "Otherwise, I'm just going to sit around getting older waiting for him to figure it out."

"That's no good," Thea said, and when Jason came to the desk a couple minutes later to check out an X-Acto knife, Thea handed it to him and said, "So, you want to go to a movie tonight?"

Jason jerked his hand back and Quinn thought, *Oh, hell.* "No," he said.

"Okay," Thea said and walked into the storeroom behind the desk and shut the door.

"You handled that *beautifully*," Quinn said, torn between smacking Jason and feeling sorry for him.

"Well, she took me by surprise." Jason scowled at the storeroom door. "What was that all about, anyway?"

"I think she wanted to go to the movies with you," Quinn said. "That's just a wild guess, of course."

"What are you on my case for?" Jason said. "What else was I supposed to say?"

"Nothing," Quinn said. "Except maybe you could have said no a little slower."

"She surprised me." Jason shook his head. "Women."

When he'd gone back to his desk, Quinn went into the narrow storeroom where Thea was stocking paint.

"You okay?"

"Yep." Thea handed her the empty paint carton. "I'll get started on the ink."

"Thea—"

"It's all right." Thea picked up the carton of ink from the

floor. "I just thought I'd give it a shot, like you said. It's not like I have anything to lose."

Quinn ached at the determined matter-of-factness in Thea's voice. "Thea, he was just surprised, that's all. Maybe when—"

"McKenzie," Thea said. "He's known me since kindergarten. Do not say, 'Maybe when he gets to know you.' He knows me." She ripped open the ink carton with a lot more ferocity than the cardboard needed. Plastic ink bottles bounced on the concrete floor but didn't break. "Shit." She stooped down and then stopped, looking up at Quinn. "Look. My mom wants me to be valedictorian, my father wants me to get a lot of scholarships for college, and my social life is pretty much studying and aiding for you. It's all about grades and school. And I look at Jason and I see a real life, I mean, a guy who does things. Who's *been there*, you know?"

Since Quinn was pretty sure the only places Jason had been were athletic fields and the backseats of cars with cheerleaders, she didn't know, but then Thea had been even fewer places. "Sort of." *Like Nick*, she thought. *Different from me*.

Thea went on. "And then you said, 'Don't settle,' and I thought—" She shrugged. "It was stupid."

"It wasn't stupid." Quinn bent to help her pick the ink bottles up. "Men don't like surprises. I feel the same way about one of them, and he doesn't want anything to do with me, either."

"Men are stupid," Thea said, and began to shelve the ink.

"Pretty much," Quinn said, and went back outside to her classroom to glare at Jason until he said, *"What?"* and she had to admit he hadn't done anything wrong. Poor Thea.

Her sisterhood with Thea increased tenfold when she went to the station after school to get her books and give Nick back his jacket, her heart pounding like a trip-hammer.

She knocked on the back door as she went in, calling, "Hello? Nick?"

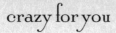

"Over here."

He was tightening the lug nuts on the wheel of an Escort, and she stopped for a guilty moment to enjoy the muscles in his arms, mostly his forearms but also the biceps under his shirt. Nick wasn't muscle-bound, he was too lanky for that, but working in the garage had made him solid and strong, and his arms were great. The rest of him was probably great, too. *You're hopeless*, she told herself, but it was still good to watch. No law against watching. As long as she remembered not to ask him to the movies, she was safe.

Nick stopped and straightened to look over his shoulder at her, and he looked gorgeous. She'd never thought that before, he'd always been just Nick, and everybody knew Max was the good-looking Ziegler brother, but now she saw Nick differently, saw how hot those dark eyes looked and how unruly his thick dark hair was, as if he'd just rolled out of bed. Nick looked like he'd just finished making love, she realized, or maybe was about to start. There was an idea.

Mostly, though, he looked wary, and she knew if she tried to talk about that night on the couch, he'd duck, but she had to say something, so she stuck with her excuse for the visit. "I brought your jacket back," she said, draping it over the work table. "You left it Thursday night." *That night you stared at me*.

Nick nodded. "Thanks."

Okay. "And I came to see if you had any problem picking up the books. I know there were a lot of them."

"There weren't any." He went over to the wall to hang up the wrench. He had great shoulders. Why hadn't she noticed his shoulders before? Where had her mind been, Pluto? He wiped his hand on a rag as he turned back to her. "You and Darla packed them up Friday, right?"

"Right."

Nick shook his head. "They were all back on the shelves.

Alphabetical order. No boxes. Just like you'd never been there."

Quinn leaned against the workbench, her knees suddenly not as strong as they had been.

Bill had unpacked all those books. She thought of him coming home, seeing the boxes, carefully reshelving them by the authors' last names, taking the boxes to the trash, putting things back the way he wanted. She was willing to bet he hadn't even been angry. He'd just put them back where he thought they belonged.

"Have you talked to him?" Nick asked. "Because he doesn't seem to be getting the idea."

"I left him a note," Quinn said, and Nick snorted. "No, a very clear note. And then he called me at Mom's and I told him again. And he said, 'There's no silverware,' and I said, 'It was Grandma's, you'll have to buy more,' and he said, 'But then we'll have two sets.'"

Nick met her eyes on that one. "That's not good."

"And I told him at school on Friday. And I packed up all the books. And I told him again today at school."

Nick dropped the rag back on the bench. "Well, you're going to have to be a lot clearer."

"How?" Quinn said. "How much clearer can I be than 'I've left and I'm not coming back'?"

"Did you tell him why?"

"No." Quinn looked at her feet. "It's hard to explain."

"Well," Nick said reasonably. "What did he do?" He leaned against the wall, his arms crossed, flaunting those great forearms. "It's easier to understand being dumped if somebody tells you why."

Quinn shrugged. "I just realized there wasn't anything there." *And after that there was something between you and me.*

He was nodding at her. "Right, I've been there. The thrill was gone, and it wasn't coming back."

"There never was any thrill." Quinn shoved herself off the

workbench, irrationally angry that Nick had had thrills that had worn off. "You know me. I'm not the thrill type."

Nick unfolded his arms and turned back to pick up the rag again.

"It wasn't just the no thrill." Quinn watched him crouch down on the concrete to polish the Escort's wheel cover. "He kidnapped Katie, and I realized I didn't want to live with a guy who would do something like that because he thought he knew best when he didn't know me at all." The last words came out in a rush. "I may not be the kind of woman who has thrills, but I wasn't going to live with that. And then it felt so good to move out, I knew it was the right thing."

She stepped closer, trying to make him understand because it was so important that he be on her side, not on Bill's, not two guys sticking together, but him and her together. "But I can't tell him that. 'Sorry, Bill, I just realized that you were not only dull, you were clueless about what I need. See you.' That would be cruel." She tried to picture Bill if she said that. "And then he'd say, 'I'll learn what you need,' and I'd have to say, 'Not in a million years,' and then I'd just be being a bitch."

Nick wouldn't look up at her. She should have known better. He hated getting involved. "So I'm sticking with 'We've grown apart,'" she finished. "That doesn't mention that we were never really together." She shrugged then, trying to lighten the silence. "Sorry about the books. I'll figure something out." Nick still wasn't saying anything, so she turned for the back door. "I really appreciate you trying to help."

Still nothing.

She let the door bang behind her, feeling miserable and furious at the same time. A logical woman would have analyzed her feelings and reconciled her thoughts. Quinn just wanted all men dead.

WHEN THE BACK door slammed, Nick stopped polishing the wheel that didn't need polishing and leaned his forehead against the side of the car.

So she thought she wasn't the thrill type. But he'd seen the flicker in her eyes when he'd leaned close to her that night, heard the soft intake of her breath, felt the heat as her blood had flushed close to her skin, and the need to have that all back, to touch her and make her breathe harder, make her blood pound harder, to take that mouth, move his hand down her throat, over her breast—*I could make you the thrill type,* he thought and then tried to push the thought back into whatever dark hole in his mind it had crawled out of.

Hell. He sat down on the cold concrete floor and wished the last half-hour had never happened. In fact, if he was going to erase history, he could do without the last five days entirely.

Quinn was a permanent part of his life—hell, he couldn't sleep with her, he loved her—and *sex* and *permanent* were two words he didn't want anywhere near each other, not in his life, not ever. He had a good life going—lots of freedom and variety, no responsibility, everything easy—and he was not going to screw it up just because he was hot for his best friend.

Forget it, he told himself, and turned back to the other problem, the safer problem, which was Bill.

Bill was a great guy, not deep but honest, hardworking, kind—God, he sounded boring, what had Quinn seen in him?— so why was he acting like she couldn't leave him?

Nick leaned back against the wheel cover and tried to put himself in Bill's place, something he wasn't very good at since he usually didn't care what other people did. Okay, he was Bill. He'd been living with Quinn—his mind swerved a little there, trying to go into the corner where the underwear memory lived—and she moved out. This shouldn't be hard; women had been getting fed up with Nick and dumping him for years, and it had never bothered him much.

But suppose it was Quinn. Suppose he'd been used to coming home every night and finding Quinn on the couch reading, or laughing on the phone with Darla, or showering—*don't think about that*—and then one day he'd come home and there was a note.

The showering part was distracting him, lot of soap in that particular image, but he tried to imagine a note that said, *Dear Nick, I'm gone,* and it bothered him a lot more than he'd expected. No more Quinn in his life, no more laughter and bright cool copper hair, no more arguments or "Guess what?"s or surprises like ratty little dogs with persecution complexes.

And if he'd been Bill, no more rolling into bed at night and feeling all that softness against him, no more running his hands down her body, no more taking that lush, hot mouth, feeling her hair slide like silk against his skin, feeling himself slide hard deep inside her—

"Okay," he said out loud and stood up.

Quinn had problems. Bill wasn't going to give her up easily. Nick could understand that, he wouldn't have, either, but Bill was going to have to because Quinn wanted out.

"Then we'll have two sets," Bill had said. And he'd smiled when she'd told him she was moving out.

So it might be a good idea to keep an eye on Quinn. Nothing intense, just a brotherly eye, because all Bill needed was to get used to the idea of Quinn being gone, and things would be fine.

Nick shoved all thoughts of Bill and Quinn and showers and beds out of his mind and turned back to the Escort.

And wondered what color underwear she'd had on under that sweater.

six

BILL HAD sent Quinn two dozen red roses when she got home the next Tuesday night. He called so she could thank him, and she said, "Bill, it's over. Don't send any more flowers," before she hung up on him and dialed Darla.

"Red roses," she said when she'd explained. "Isn't that just like him? The most generic gift in America."

"He's trying to be nice," Darla said.

"No, he isn't," Quinn said. "He's trying to ignore reality."

"He probably thinks if he ignores it, it'll go away," Darla said. "Men don't like change." She sounded grim as she said it.

"Well, it's not going to go away," Quinn said. "I have an appointment tomorrow morning at the bank to get a loan application for my house, and that'll be the end of it. Even Bill is going to have to accept I'm gone after that."

"I wouldn't count on it," Darla said, but the next day Quinn walked into bronze and marble lobby of the First National Bank of Tibbett on her planning period, feeling as though she was declaring her independence.

Across the lobby, Barbara—elegant in a powder-pink Chanel-style suit, pale stockings, pink heels, and new hair streaked light brown in a loose French twist—conversed with great adult seriousness with a chubby guy in a gray suit. Quinn tugged a little at her peacoat, uneasily conscious of her own jeans and canvas flats. She'd put on her good navy blouse to do business, even though that meant by the end of the school day she'd have destroyed it with clay and paint, but it didn't seem enough now. She should have dressed better to go that deeply into debt.

Barbara saw her and waved, and Quinn went over and said, "My mother called about a loan appointment," which made her feel stupid in addition to guilty. She was thirty-five and her mother was calling about her loans?

Barbara nodded. "You're buying the old house out on Apple Street, right?" She didn't seem particularly pleased about it.

"Well, you know, it's time I stopped renting," Quinn said, wondering why it was time. The idea of owning her own place, of being free and adult and independent, had been heady, but being in the bank was reminding her that "owning a house" actually meant "owing a lot of money." She smiled at Barbara, trying to calm her own nerves. "You like owning your house, don't you?"

"No," Barbara said.

"Oh." Oh, hell.

"I'll get the paperwork." Barbara pointed behind her. "Take a seat at the second desk."

Quinn nodded and went to sit on the edge of the massive green leather chair beside the massive mahogany desk. She felt like an obedient twelve-year-old and had to resist the urge to slump down and kick the legs of the chair. Why was buying a house making her regress?

When Barbara sat down with a sheaf of forms, Quinn said, "Why don't you like your house? Because maybe this isn't something I should do."

Barbara put the papers down and said, "Owning a home is an excellent investment that will appreciate over time. Rent is an expense, but a mortgage payment is an investment in equity. And your interest is tax-deductible, so it's a very sound financial move."

Quinn looked at her doubtfully. Bank Barbie. "Then why do you hate it?"

Barbara shifted in her chair. "A house really needs a man," she said finally. "Things go wrong, and then you have to hire people to help, and so many times they're not competent, and it becomes difficult because you don't know. Men know, the competent ones. So there really should be a man."

So much for Barbara, the feminist woman of finance.

Barbara smiled at Quinn. "But that won't be a problem for you, since you have Coach Hilliard. He looks very competent."

"I don't have him anymore," Quinn said. "I returned him. The house is just for me."

Barbara's face relaxed into sympathy, Bank Barbie disappearing. "I'm so sorry, Quinn, that must be awful. I just hate it when they let you down like that."

Quinn wanted to say *like what?* but that would result in talking men with Barbara, and all she really wanted was the loan. Sort of.

"You think you can count on them," Barbara went on, "and then something comes up and they don't come through for you, and you think, 'Why did I bother? I can be helpless without you easier than I can with you,' and they just don't get it."

I don't get it, either, Quinn thought, but she nodded.

"But then you're good friends with Darla Ziegler, aren't you?" Barbara smiled with her whole face this time. "Her husband is *very* competent."

"Yes, he is—" Quinn began, and then she thought, *Oh, no*.

"I heard he even does the plumbing at their house." Barbara's face took on a faraway look. "The kind of man you can count on. She's so lucky." She pulled herself back. "So I'm sure you can call him. He'll know everything."

"Barbara, if you hate owning a house that much, sell it," Quinn said. *And stop vamping married plumbers and electricians.* And possibly mechanics.

"I can't," Barbara said. "It was my parents'. And it's a wonderful investment."

"Maybe you could take night courses in plumbing," Quinn said.

Barbara drew back, plastic again. "I take night courses in investing. Now you'll need to fill out these forms and attach the proper documentation . . ."

Quinn listened with only part of her mind, the rest of it trying to decide if Barbara's interest in Max warranted saying something to Darla. Probably not, since there wasn't anything to go on, it wasn't as if she was dropping by the station or anything.

Life had been so much simpler a week ago. Her teaching, her apartment, her friendship with Nick—she felt lost for a minute, missing him since he was avoiding her like commitment—but of course, a week ago there had also been Bill and no Katie.

Barbara was pointing at a form with one perfectly shaped shell pink fingernail. ". . . Fill in this information and sign right here. Do you have any questions?"

Any questions. If she signed right there, she'd be sixty-three thousand dollars in debt and much of her savings would be gone.

But she'd also be free. An adult woman who owned her own house. And couch.

"No questions," Quinn said. "I'm sure I'm doing the right thing."

On her way back to school, she stopped at the only furniture store in Tibbett and bought a massive queen-size golden oak fourposter bed to celebrate. After her old twin beds at home and the double she'd shared with Bill, it looked like a golden oak football field, and twelve hundred dollars was a lot of money to impulse, but it felt so right she didn't even hesitate.

She had some plans for that bed.

AFTER SCHOOL THAT afternoon, Bill sat on the edge of one of the weight benches while Bobby finished lifting and tried to deal with the thought he'd been fighting all day: Quinn was buying a house.

He'd run into her—well, he'd been waiting for her by the art-room door—when she'd come back from wherever she'd gone on her planning period, and he'd said jovially—just like they were still together because they were, really, this was just a temporary thing—"Where have you been, young lady?" And she'd looked at him without smiling and said, "The bank. I'm buying a house."

A house. It made him ill to think of it. And then he'd found out it was that old derelict house on Apple Street of all places. An old house in an old neighborhood too far from school for their kids to walk. What was she thinking?

"You don't look happy, Big Guy." The BP came over to stand beside him in hunter green designer sweats. Bill closed his eyes and thought, *Go away, Bobby, before I step on you.* That's what Quinn always said, "He's such a bug you want to step on him." Once she'd said, "Don't you just want to slap him when he calls you Big Guy?" and he'd said, "No, of course not, he's smaller than I am." Besides, poor old Bobby didn't have much of a life. Bill had a sudden realization of what his own life would be like without Quinn—like Bobby's—but he shoved it away immediately. Not a possibility.

Bobby sat down beside him, a coordinating towel around his neck, his eyes at Bill's shoulder level. "Still woman trouble, huh?" he said, and Bill thought about catching him across the nose with his elbow. Just a thought; he'd never do it. "Can't live with 'em, can't live without 'em."

What was that supposed to mean, anyway? He'd had no trouble living with Quinn. And he sure wasn't going to live without her.

"But you can't let it affect the team," Bobby went on. "You got to be up for the guys, you know?"

Bill looked down at him. "Are you telling me there's something wrong with my coaching?"

"Whoa!" Bobby stood up. "Hey, no, you're the best, we all know that." He looked thoughtful. "Although we did lose tonight. Not that I'm complaining."

"What a twit," Quinn used to say. She was right.

"But, attitude is everything, right, Big Guy? And let's face it, your attitude isn't what it used to be." Bobby settled in on the padded scarlet bench, a weightlifting man of the world. "Now, I don't want to put any more pressure on you, but the levy—"

"I know about the levy," Bill said. "The team will do fine. Everybody loses sometime."

"It's not just the levy," Bobby said, the bluster gone from his voice. "It's my job."

He sounded so vulnerable, Bill actually paid attention. "What about your job?"

"I'm only principal for the rest of this year," Bobby said. "They just gave it to me because I was the assistant principal and they didn't want to do a candidate search till spring. Hell, they don't even have to do a search, Dennis Rule from over in Celina wants it bad, and he's been a head principal for ten years there. Experience." Bobby said the word as if it were something obscene.

"Well," Bill said mildly, "you're doing a good job—"

"It's not enough." Bobby's voice was intense. "But if I pass the levy, they'll have to give it to me. And then we'll have the stadium and the fieldhouse started next year, and more championships—" His eyes stared into space, seeing a glowing future. Then he came back to earth. "But only with the championship this spring and the levy. I need you on this, Big Guy. So what can I do for you? You name it, you got it."

"You can't do anything," Bill said, thinking of Quinn in a

house without him. If she stayed with her parents, she'd have to come back to him, but if she bought a house—

"You'd be surprised what I can do," Bobby said.

"Okay." Bill stood up. "Stop Quinn from buying a house in the wrong part of town. That would cheer me up."

"She's buying a house?" Bobby frowned.

"Never mind." Bill began his final check of the weight room. No point in spending the rest of the night with Bobby. "What I meant was, there's nothing else you can do."

"Oh, I don't know." Bobby got that intense look on his face that meant he was thinking. "Is she going through the First National?"

"What?"

"For her loan. Is she using the First?"

Bill stopped. "I don't know. That's where we bank."

Bobby nodded, satisfied. "Then that's where she'll go. Not a problem."

"What the hell are you talking about?"

Bobby folded his arms, cocky as hell. "Carl Brookner is a vice president there."

Big deal. The president of the Boosters was a bank vice president. "So?"

"So I just mention that maybe Quinn isn't the best loan risk since she's been acting so strangely, like moving out on you, and he'll review the loan and refuse it."

He wanted to say, No, that's not fair, don't do it. But he didn't. Anything that kept Quinn from moving into that house was good for her in the long run. He couldn't stand the thought of her staying there permanently, it wouldn't be safe, it would be a lousy place for their kids, it wasn't a place they'd bought together, she couldn't stay there, she couldn't, it would be bad for her.

"What do you say?" Bobby said.

"Do it," Bill said.

"HEY, I HEARD you went to the movies," Darla said, when Lois came into the break room that afternoon.

Lois shrugged. "I like Tom Cruise. Matthew was paying. It's no big deal."

"Pretty big deal, dating your ex-husband," Darla said, and watched Lois shrug. "Not to mention, making him pay. Literally."

"Not ex-husband exactly," Lois said. "I haven't signed the papers yet."

"Good," Darla said. "I never sign papers. They only get you into trouble."

Lois's lips tightened. "It's Bank Sluts that get you into trouble."

"Right." Darla considered telling Lois that no Bank Slut ever broke up a strong marriage and decided not to. Let Lois blame Barbara if that was what it took to get her marriage back.

"She's probably on the prowl for somebody else now," Lois went on, her face darkening.

"What's her hair look like?" Darla said, remembering Debbie's theory.

Lois snorted. "How would I know? Like she'd come here to get it done."

Quinn breezed in then, glowing with excitement over her new house. "It's so darling, Lois," she said, dropping into one of the avocado armchairs. "And I just filled out the loan papers this morning, so it really is happening."

"I've been by this house," Lois said. "Darling it's not."

She left the room, and Quinn said, "What's wrong with her?"

"She's dating her husband," Darla said. "You think she'd be happy about that, but she's still fixated on Barbara."

"Dating her husband?" Quinn frowned. "Why would she be happy about that?"

"You know, something different." Darla let her mind slide away from the something different she'd tried to put in her own marriage.

"What's different? Matthew was a loss even before Barbara got him. I can see why Lois is depressed at the thought of dating him again."

"He's her husband," Darla said with no enthusiasm.

"Right," Quinn said, obviously filling in the blanks. "So what are you going to do about Max?"

"Something," Darla said. "I'll think of something. Just not now. Give me some gossip. Did you get the loan through Barbara? Tell me what her hair looks like."

"How'd you know about her hair?" Quinn said. "She's changed the color. It's pretty, sort of streaked brown, but it's a shock. She's always been blonde, but it's definitely light brownish now."

Darla felt a twinge. Something not right there. If Barbara was going after Nick, she should have been deepening it to dark brown like Lisa's. "Light brown?"

Quinn nodded. "It's up in a twist like yours, only not so tight. Sort of like a Gibson Girl. She looks really, really good."

Like yours.

"Darla?"

"Like mine?"

"Looser than yours. Fluffier, sort of." Quinn gestured with her hands. "Like yours but not. With tendrils of hair around her face. You know."

Except she had those wisps at the side that make it look so sexy,

Debbie had said. *Poor old Bea just looked like she had a bagel on her head, but Barbara looked great.*

Darla touched her own tight French twist, the same tight knot she'd worn since high school.

Boring.

Max.

"Are you okay?" Quinn said.

"I'm fine," Darla said. "Just fine."

"No, you're not," Quinn said. "Talk."

"I'm going to." Darla picked up her purse. "To Max."

MAX WAS BENT over a Sunbird when she came in, and Darla noticed with complete dispassion that he still had a great butt. That was one thing you had to give the Ziegler boys: they kept their bodies.

And she'd gotten the good-looking one, too. Nick had been the wild one, the one whose face had been thin with too many bones in it so he'd looked older than he was in high school. Max had been the handsome one, the nice one with the cheerful face. His mother had said, "Well, you got the good one, he'll never give you any trouble." People had been a little nervous around Nick, but everybody loved Max.

Still did, evidently.

He raised his head and started when he saw her. "Hey," he said. "I didn't hear you come in. What's up?"

"Why didn't you tell me Barbara was after you instead of Nick?" Her voice was clear, but her words seemed very far away to her, as if somebody else was saying them.

He put the hood on the Sunbird down, testing it more carefully than he had to in order to make sure it had caught. "No reason to."

"A known homewrecker is chasing my husband and you didn't see any reason to tell me?" Really, it was amazing how calm her voice was.

Max didn't seem impressed. "Since I'm the husband, and I have no plans to cheat, no. I didn't see any reason." He folded his arms across his workshirt and leaned against the car, which for placid Max was attack position. Every fight they'd ever had, he'd stood just like that.

"You let me think it was Nick," Darla said.

"It didn't hurt anybody."

"It made me look like a fool."

Max shook his head, clearly disgusted. "No, it didn't. The whole town knows I'd never cheat on you."

It struck Darla with sudden clarity that he never would. He'd fallen in love with her at eighteen, he'd married her, he had two sons with her, he'd built a house with her, and now he had every intention of dying with her, and he'd never do anything to upset that.

"You have everything you've ever wanted, don't you?" she said, appalled, and she was even more appalled to realize that she couldn't think of anything else she wanted, either. Their lives were over. They were on the downhill slide. "That's why you were so mad about the raincoat thing the other night. It screwed up your routine."

"I was surprised, not mad," Max said, looking mad. "And I don't want Barbara."

"I almost wish you did," she said and he scowled at her.

"Well, that's a jackass thing to say."

Darla felt her anger like a hot flash. "Don't call me a jackass—"

"I didn't call you a jackass." Max folded his arms tighter. "I said what you said was a jackass thing to say, but if you keep on like this, I may—"

"Hey, guys," Nick said, coming in from the back lot. Then he got a good look at both of them and said, "Oh, hell," and backed out the door again.

"Fine," Darla said. "But I would appreciate it if next time you did not lie to me."

"I did not lie," Max said.

"You didn't tell me the truth," Darla said.

"That's not necessarily lying." Max unfolded his arms and walked over to the sink, where he began to wash his hands. "I'm not attracted to her. At all. And even if I was, I wouldn't cheat on you. I have a family."

"Well, that's real big of you, Max," Darla said. "The family and I appreciate it."

"Also I love you," Max went on. "Although right now I have to wonder why."

"I love you, too," Darla said. "And I'm doing a little wondering myself." She walked over to the door and opened it. "Get in here before you freeze," she yelled to Nick who was shooting a basket and knocking icicles off the hoop. "The fight's over."

But it wasn't, she knew. It wouldn't be over until she figured what the hell they'd been fighting over.

She had a real good idea it wasn't Barbara.

QUINN STARTED HER move on Friday after school by loading a nervous Katie, her grandmother's silver, and nine garbage bags of clothes into her car and driving to her new house. Edie and Meggy met her there and began to polish floors, moving on to windows while Quinn wiped down shelves, hung up her clothes, and put the silver away.

"This place really is beautiful, Quinn," Edie said when they were done. "Lots of lovely quiet."

"It's a risk," her mother said. "I don't know what people are going to think, you living alone out here. And your next-door neighbor is Patsy Brady, for heaven's sake, and you know *her* reputation."

Edie rolled her eyes, and Quinn said, "Mom, stop it. I don't care what other people think. I can't live my life for other people, I have to live it for myself."

"Oh, well, sure, that *sounds* good—" Meggy began.

"It is good." Quinn stood in the middle of her house, feeling invincible. "I'm happier than I've ever been. The risks I'm taking like keeping Katie and buying this house"—*and wanting Nick*— "are making me feel alive." She looked around at the now-gleaming floors, at the tall windows with all the light streaming through. "How can you look at this and not think it's wonderful? Can't you be glad for me?"

"I am glad for you," Meggy said. "It's just, all these changes—" She picked up her purse and sighed. "Never mind, I'm probably just jealous."

"You want a new house?" Quinn said, confused, but Meggy shook her head and went out the door.

"It's lovely, Quinn," Edie said. "Have us all over for dinner when the furniture is in."

"Right now that's the pie safe, the washstand, Mom's red couch and armchair, and our old twin beds," Quinn said. "Although I did order this gorgeous bed for me, too. I deserve it."

"Yes, you do." Edie kissed her on the cheek as Meggy honked the horn outside. "Have a good life here, Quinn."

"I'll do my best," Quinn said, and then left to pick up Darla at the Upper Cut so they could clear out the housewares department at Target together, leaving Katie to explore her new house and yard with her usual suspicion and dread.

"This is fun," Darla said two hours later, folding the last of Quinn's new mint green towels into the old-fashioned wall cupboard built into Quinn's bathroom. "Maybe I'll hit the savings account and buy everything new." She shoved aside a pile of Quinn's nightgowns to make room for towels and said, "What's this?"

She pulled out a wad of white chiffon and shook it free and Quinn made a face. "It's a nightgown Bill got me. Isn't it awful? It made me feel like a virgin sacrifice. And then when I put it on, he could see right through it so he hated it."

"Right through it?" Darla held it up in front of her and looked at Quinn through the filmy cloth. "Oh. And he hated it?"

"Bill isn't into sexy," Quinn said.

"Max is," Darla said. "Or at least he used to be."

"Then it's yours." Quinn waved her hand. "Use it with my blessing."

"There's a thought." Darla wadded the gown up again and jammed it into her bag where Katie sniffed it and then sighed because it wasn't food. Darla moved to the sink and opened the wall cupboard to stack soap and toothpaste into the cabinet. "You bought two toothbrushes?"

Quinn looked at the ceiling. "I bought a bed, too. You never know when you're going to have somebody sleep over."

Darla shook her head. "If you're talking about Nick, that'll be never. He's allergic to sleepovers. Lisa got so frustrated she showed up on Christmas Eve and told him she was staying so they could wake up on Christmas morning together."

Since Lisa was history, there was no reason for Quinn to feel jealous, and there was especially no reason for her to feel jealous since she had no relationship with Nick at all, but she did. Really, she was hopeless. "At least Lisa went after what she wanted."

Darla snorted. "Yeah, but she didn't get it. When they came to dinner, she was fuming. She said when she woke up, Nick was out in the living room asleep in his armchair. And then she was expecting a ring and got a CD set." Darla closed the cabinet door and stuffed the now-empty Target bag in the trash. "And that was it for Lisa."

"Was Nick upset when she left?" Quinn hated how needy she sounded.

"He was relieved." Darla's voice was sympathetic. "He always is. Round about the one-year mark, he gets itchy."

"With me, it was at the half-hour mark," Quinn said.

"Well, he'll have to go longer tonight," Darla said. "He has a lot of furniture to unload." She checked her watch. "They should be at your mom's right about now. Let's go."

Quinn thought about seeing Nick again and felt like throwing up. "Oh good."

BILL WATCHED QUINN and Darla drive away and scowled at the empty house. It was ugly, dirty and gray and skinny and derelict and isolated, and he hated that she was going to live there—especially live there with that damn dog, especially live there without him.

He got out and walked around the place, shaking his head at the patchy ground, full of weeds and stones, and when he let himself in the backyard through the alley gate, it was worse. Then the dog burst through a flap in the back door, barking at him hysterically, trying to get him in trouble, and he retreated to the gate before anybody could catch him there and jump to the wrong conclusion. He was just there to protect Quinn, to find out how bad the place was, and it was so bad, he knew he had to get her out of there somehow.

"What're you doing?" a woman called, and he jerked around to see a blowzy-looking brunette leaning over the fence.

"Meter reader," he called cheerfully, keeping his face averted as he waved and went through the gate. The dog followed him through, still barking.

If the dog wasn't around, Quinn wouldn't need a house.

He slammed the gate so the dog was outside in the alley— maybe it would get hit, it was dumb enough—and then he got in the car and headed for a pay phone. He'd call the pound and tell them a vicious dog was loose. Quinn couldn't blame him if the dog got out, that was the dog's fault. And the pound would call him since he'd paid for the license. "Put it down," he could say. "I think it's dangerous." That was the God's honest truth, too. It was dangerous.

As he drove away, he could see the dog in the rearview mirror, sniffing garbage cans, not even trying to run away.

Dumb mutt. It deserved to die.

THEY ALL UNLOADED the furniture from Meggy's and carried it into the house under the appreciative eyes of Patsy Brady, who called out, "Hello, Gorgeous," from her front porch as Max carried in an armchair.

"You get all the hot women," Nick said, and Max said, "I'm going upstairs to put that bed together. You go talk to her."

"Nah," Nick said. "I know when I'm outclassed. Once they see you, I'm history."

"This thing is huge," Max said half an hour later, tightening the last bolt. "She have some plans we don't know about?"

"I have no idea," Nick said, but it was hard to look at the bed, glowing like the floors even in the growing twilight, and not think of Quinn on it, in it, under him. *Knock it off*, he told himself, and then he thought about her some more.

"We have a problem," Darla said behind him, making him jump in guilt. "We seem to have lost that damn dog."

"She's nowhere in the house or the next-door yards," Quinn said behind her, her voice a little shaky. "I don't get it. The gate is still closed and there are no holes under the fence. I checked the alley anyway, and she's not there. The next-door neighbor said there was some meter reader here. Maybe he let her out."

"Is this a sort of skinny black ratty dog?" Max said, looking out the front bedroom window. "Because there's one of those in the street, and there's an Animal Control truck headed its way."

Quinn was down the stairs faster than Nick had ever seen her move, and he followed her through the dining room and out the front door just as Katie sniffed her way into the front yard.

Animal Control slowed to a crawl.

"I'll go call them off," Quinn told Nick. "You get Katie."

Katie danced around the yard, looking for trouble, watching him bright-eyed. He took a step toward her and she crouched down, her bony butt in the air, ready to play.

"I'm not chasing you, mutt," he said to her, and she cocked her head at him, clearly ready to make a break for it if he came closer.

"Cute. You run in the street, you're hamburger," he said, knowing as long as he talked to her, she'd listen. "So why don't we just end this now?"

He took a step toward her, and she danced away, never taking her eyes off his face.

Okay, fine. Part of him wanted to just let her run away—she was the one who was causing all the trouble, breaking Quinn and Bill up, screwing with his life—but Quinn had asked him to, and he didn't want Katie getting hurt, even if she was a rat on stilts, and besides, there was Animal Control.

So what did he have that this dog wanted?

There was probably a Burger King bag someplace in the truck. "How do you feel about really old fries?" he called to the dog, and she danced closer again, two steps forward, one back.

He opened the passenger door to the truck and leaned in, feeling under the seat for possible trash, and Katie leaped in, scrambling across his back to sit in the driver's seat.

Nick got in and slammed the door, trapping her inside with him. "Gotcha."

Katie put her paws on the driver's side window and looked out anxiously, probably wondering why nothing was moving. She looked over her shoulder at Nick and whined.

"We are not going for a ride," he said, and she barked at him.

Actually, it wasn't a bad idea. As long as she thought she'd always get a ride if she got in the truck, she'd be a piece of cake to catch, so if he took her around the block, he'd be solving a lot of future problems for Quinn.

Also he could stall going back in that light-filled house full of Quinn and beds for another fifteen minutes. He slid across the seat, picking Katie up to trade places, and backed the truck out of the driveway, waving to Quinn as he went.

Katie immediately climbed in his lap to press her nose against his window.

"There's another one on your side," he told her, but she was light and she didn't squirm, and after the first minute, she sighed and sat down and leaned against him without trembling as he drove, watching out the window with her chin on his shoulder as the world went past.

She was a good little dog, Nick realized. She still looked like hell, of course, but she was a nice little dog. He scratched her behind the ear, and Katie leaned against his hand a little, the same way Quinn had that night.

Quinn had been so tempting there in the dark, so yielding.

And she was so off-limits he didn't even know why he was thinking about her again.

He finished his circuit and pulled in the driveway, and Quinn came over to the truck, crossing her arms over that fuzzy purple sweater to keep herself warm. She looked great. He opened the door and handed Katie out to her, saying, "She likes to ride, so that's an easy way to catch her."

"Thank you," Quinn began, smiling up at him with that lush mouth, all huge eyes and warm curves, and he cut her off with, "Don't mention it, glad to help. Well, you're all moved in, so I gotta go." He slammed the door and waved as he backed out of the drive, and she watched him go with her mouth open.

It wasn't until he was all the way back to the station that he realized he'd left Max behind.

BILL WAITED DOWN the street until Darla and Max left. Then he parked in Quinn's driveway and knocked on the ugly black front door—a door that had too much glass in it to be safe, another reason he really had to get her out of there. When Quinn opened it, she looked so beautiful that he just stared at her for a minute. She said, "Bill?" and he smiled and said, "I have a car full of your books. Where should I put them?"

She hesitated for a minute, and then she stepped out on the porch with him. "We can stack them in the dining room for now."

She helped him carry the books in, which was great because it meant she was with him, but not great because it meant he'd get done twice as fast, that he wouldn't have enough time to talk to her, to make sure she was all right, to make her talk to him again the way she used to. He needed to see her more often was the problem, so on one of his trips in, while she was at the car, he opened the shutter on the far window so he could see in if he ever had to. Just to make sure she was all right. It was the window that was behind the fence on the side with the vacant lot, so nobody would see him and stop him on checking on her.

The damn dog growled at him, and he fought back the urge

to kick it. It was supposed to be gone by now, run over or in the pound, not here. But kicking it would be stupid. She might catch him doing it, and that was all he needed to make Quinn suspicious that he was the one who'd let the dog out.

When he came back in two trips later, she'd closed the shutter again—had she realized what he was doing?—so when she left for the last box, he reached over and snapped one of the lower slats off its staple so it wouldn't go up any more. It wasn't much of a change, he wasn't even sure he could see through it, but it was something.

Anything so he could see her, see what she was doing, be with her until she came to her senses again.

"That's it," she said as she came in with the last box. She was a little breathless and her cheeks were red from the cold and she was so beautiful, he took a step toward her and reached for her.

She shook her head and stepped back as the dog growled again. "No," she said. "I'm really sorry, but no. I'm happy, and I'm not coming back. This is my house now. I'm staying."

And there was nothing he could do but nod and smile and wish her good luck even though he felt like hell, like shouting at her, like grabbing her, like making her listen.

Thank God Bobby had stopped her loan and she'd be out of there soon. And once she was out of there, she'd have to get rid of the dog, and things would be back to normal again. If it hadn't been for Bobby stopping that loan, he didn't know what he would have done.

DARLA HAD DROPPED Max off at the station, and he called a little later to say that moving Quinn had put them behind, and that he and Nick were both working late to catch up. Darla felt one tiny twinge—*are you with Barbara?*—and then stifled it, knowing Max wouldn't lie to her. "No problem," she said in her best Understanding Wife voice. "I'll keep dinner hot for you."

"Don't bother," he said.

Don't bother? "Well, I'll be here whenever you get home," she chirped, determined to make this work.

"Good," Max said, sounding a little confused. "That's where I figured you'd be."

She'd fed the boys, argued with them about their homework, and was packing them off to bed when Max finally came home, covered in grease and exhausted. By the time he got out of the shower, the boys were asleep, so he plopped himself down alone in the dark living room to watch the news in the TV's weird blue light, turning down her offer of a late dinner.

"I appreciate it," he said. "But I'm beat."

"No problem," she said brightly and went off to lock herself in the bathroom.

She took her hair down in the bright light from the round bulbs that surrounded their huge mirror, and she brushed it until all the kinks from the pins that had held it fast in her French twist were gone and it flowed silky, way past her shoulders.

Max loved it down. She used to trim it to get rid of the split ends, just half an inch, and he'd say, "You cut your hair."

"Just a little," she'd say and let it fall over him, tickle his skin, and he'd pull her close—

How long had it been since he'd done that?

She clamped down on critical thoughts. It didn't matter. Tonight, they'd be what they'd used to be.

She flipped her hair back over her shoulders. She was getting a little long in the tooth for hair this length. If she'd been her client, she'd have said, "Cut it, go for something snappier, more sophisticated." Long hair like this only worked on waiflike women, anyway. It was for little girls, perennial Alices.

And for women with husbands like Max.

She ignored her sensible long flannel nightgown hanging on the back of the door—she had at least a dozen, all gifts from her mother every Christmas—stripped off her clothes, and slid the white chiffon gown over her head. It felt like cream sliding over her skin, cool and smooth and liquid; it rippled around her like a waterfall. She flounced it a little to straighten it, and then watched it settle around her curves. You could see through it, her nipples were dark circles and down below—

If Max looked horrified at this, she was divorcing him and Barbara could have him.

She swished around the bathroom a little, not taking her eyes off the mirror, watching the chiffon settle and slide as her hair floated about her shoulders, turning herself on with how good she looked, how lovely the chiffon felt, how nuts Max was going to go when he saw her.

She heard him come into the adjoining bedroom and unlocked the bathroom door, waiting for him to walk through the door to get ready for bed. Maybe they wouldn't even make it to the bedroom. Maybe he'd just boost her up on the counter. They'd done it that way in the station bathroom once and that had been at the station, not in their own house—surely he couldn't say no in his own house. He sure hadn't said no in the station. She shivered a little remembering it.

They'd done it other places, too. Like in her bedroom while her mother slept next door; Debbie had been at a slumber party and Darla had whispered, "I want a party, too," and Max had climbed a tree and almost killed himself getting in her window. And in the backseat of Max's old clunker, a hundred times it seemed like, although it couldn't have been more than a couple dozen, really. Even in the front seat of the station truck once. They'd taken it to the drive-in because the seat was higher, they could see better, and then they'd only seen the first half of the first movie. *Hours,* she thought. *We touched each other for hours.* It had been the first time she'd come, the first time she thought, *I get it,* the first time she'd realized why girls were dumb enough to get pregnant because you'd take chances for that kind of glory.

She could really see her nipples now, poking against the chiffon, and she wanted him so much she was breathless with it.

Which was when she realized he wasn't coming in the bathroom.

She opened the door into a pitch-dark bedroom. "Max?" she said and walked cautiously to the bed in the light from the bathroom, trying not to trip over anything that might be in her path. "Max?"

She turned on the bedside light. He was stretched out on top of the duvet, his handsome face slack in complete unconsciousness.

"Max?" She crawled on the bed and shook him a little. "Honey?"

He took a deep breath in stages, almost sighs, and she realized from seventeen years of sleeping with him that he was out cold. Even if she managed to wake him up, he'd just blink at her; he'd still be asleep, really.

This was what she got for waiting until bedtime.

Of course, when she didn't wait for bedtime, he was horrified. Just like that damn Bill.

She was so mad, she punched him in the shoulder, and he frowned, but he didn't wake up.

She let herself fall back onto the bed beside with a scream of frustration, but that didn't wake him up, either.

Nothing was going to wake him up. Not even the trump for the second coming.

Just thinking about coming made her furious all over again, so she punched him one more time, then crawled under the covers to put herself to sleep.

SATURDAY MORNING, DARLA got out of bed, and Max peered at her blearily as she headed for the bathroom.

"What are you wearing?" he said, still half asleep, sounding vaguely interested.

"Nothing you'll ever see again," she said and slammed the bathroom door.

seven

WHEN CARL Brookner called Quinn from the bank later that Saturday morning, she was sitting at her island counter on one of her new white counter stools eating her breakfast pancakes in her house—*her* house—while her dog sat at her feet hoping patiently for leftovers, rolling in the whole experience and loving it. This was all hers, all this sunshine and comfort and freedom and polished wood, a place to make new plans and begin new adventures. Like Nick. She was going to have to get a lot more aggressive about Nick—

Then the phone rang and when she answered, Carl Brookner said, "Ms. McKenzie? There's a problem with your loan. I'm afraid we're going to need twenty percent down instead of ten."

Quinn stood stunned for a moment. "That's another seven thousand dollars. Why—"

"Right," Brookner said. "We're holding your check for the first seven thousand until the closing on April fifteenth, of course, so you can bring the rest by then. You know how it is, with you being a single woman and all. We just need a little more up front."

But I don't have it. Quinn hung up, feeling scared and guilty. This was what messing with banks did to you: made you feel inadequate and poor. She looked around her sunny kitchen. And vulnerable. Last week this time she hadn't known she wanted this house. Now she was terrified she'd lose it.

She picked up the phone and dialed Darla, ready to dump her troubles, but Darla got to hers first.

"You can have your nightgown back," she said as soon as she heard Quinn's voice.

"You're kidding."

"He was so tired he passed right out." Darla sounded defeated. "He never even saw it."

"That's my fault." Quinn patted her lap and Katie jumped into it, politely not eating off Quinn's breakfast plate although she stared at it with an intensity that made her quiver. "The move. Maybe—"

"No," Darla said. "It wasn't the move, it's our marriage. Nothing is going to work. I'm doomed."

"No, you're not." Quinn broke off a piece of pancake and fed it to Katie, who sighed with gratitude and relief before she took it. "We just have to time this better. Send the kids to sleep someplace else so you can start earlier in the evening when he's not so tired."

"And to think I used to fight this guy off me," Darla said. "Now I have to fit his biorhythms."

"Yeah, well, his brother isn't exactly a ball of fire, either," Quinn said.

"Maybe it's genetic."

"No, it's the routine," Quinn said. "They're both used to the way things have always been, and they're holding on to that. We just have to shake them up a little so they notice things are different. Blast them out of their routines."

"Blast," Darla said.

"Yeah." Quinn nodded. "I've been thinking about this, and I think we're both going to have to get a lot more aggressive." Katie nudged her arm with her nose, and she fed her more pancake.

"Aggressive." Darla took a deep breath.

"The other times were just practice runs," Quinn said. "This next one will work."

"Maybe." Darla's voice was doubtful. "Enough of this. Tell me something cheerful. How's life as a homeowner?"

"My loan just went bad," Quinn said.

"What?" Darla sounded outraged, which felt good.

Quinn explained, ending with, "I have some money left in my savings, but I'm still about five thousand short."

"I'll give it to you," Darla said. "We've got money in the college funds—"

"No. But I could use another kind of help."

"Anything."

Quinn swallowed. "I can probably get three thousand on the cash advance on my Visa."

"Oh, God, the interest," Darla said.

"I'm not in a position to be picky. But I'm still two thousand short. And tech director for the play pays a thousand."

"Go for it."

"Yeah, except it's sets and costumes and I don't know a damn thing about sewing and hair."

"I'll do it," Darla said.

"I'll pay you back later," Quinn said. "When I'm solvent again, I'll give you half the pay."

"No, you won't," Darla said. "Think of it as a housewarming present. In fact, think of it as a down payment on my rent because if Max doesn't respond pretty soon, I'm moving in with you. At least you pay attention to me."

When Darla had hung up, Quinn tipped Katie off her lap and called Edie. "Is that tech offer still open?"

"Yes," Edie said immediately. "We start Monday, six o'clock. It's yours, and I'm so relieved. I thought a parent was going to have to do it again this year."

"If you can think of anything else," Quinn said, "I need two thousand dollars by April fifteenth."

"You won't have this money by then," Edie said. "You'll get half by the fifteenth, minus withholding, and the rest at the end of May. How about the lights contract? That's another seven fifty."

"I don't know anything about stage lighting," Quinn said.

"Neither do I, and I've been doing it," Edie said. "Take the contract."

"Right," Quinn said. "I'll take it." She hung up and did some fast figuring. If both contracts paid half on the fifteenth, and she used her Visa, and she didn't eat for the next month . . .

She'd still be short.

"I should never have blown that two twenty-nine on that extra toothbrush," she told Katie, who looked worried. "No more throwing away money on long shots."

Katie sighed and lay down at Quinn's feet, her head on her paws.

"My sentiments exactly," Quinn said.

BILL TRIED TO talk to Quinn the next week at school, for her own good. "This house is a bad idea," he told her. "It's falling down, and you can't fix it. Why don't we—"

"Bill, there is no we," Quinn said. "And the house is fine. If anything needs fixed, there's Nick or my dad or Max. Or me. I can learn to fix things. I'm staying in the house. Now go away, I have to teach."

"Nick." He shook his head. "Even Max. That's a bad idea. People will talk."

"Bill," she said, closing her eyes, shutting him out. "Go away."

It was frustrating because she was so hard to get hold of since she was now putting all her energy into some damn play Edie was doing and roping Jason and Corey into it, too, by promising students extra credit if they worked on it; but the good thing was, that gave him a reason to stop by after school the next day. "Play practice doesn't start until six," she told him when he tried to discuss the boys' involvement with her. "If it gets in the way of ball practice, they can quit the play." When he stopped by again the next day, she said, "Bill, we have nothing to talk about ever again. Go away, *please*," so he was forced to do something to bring her back. Patience was all well and good, but it was time for some offensive action, and he knew what he had to do: get rid of that damn dog and that damn house.

The next day, he signed out on his planning period and went to the house. It was such a horrible place, there had to be something wrong with it, something dangerous, something he could use to get her out of there. He was just going to walk around a little; but knowing that slut of a woman next door was probably watching, he parked on a side street and let himself quietly into the backyard through the alley gate again.

Once there, walking around the yard wasn't enough. He really needed to see inside, to see all the horrors that were waiting for her there, all the possibilities for convincing her to leave. He tried the door, but it was locked; even jiggling the handle and leaning on it didn't budge it, although it did bring that damn dog to bark at him, pulling back a lip to snarl, too. Damn thing was dangerous, it would bite Quinn, he was right to have tried to have it put down. He looked next door to see if that woman was watching and went to the other side of the house. Only a vacant lot on that side. Safer.

He tried the side door, but it was locked, and then the basement windows—it would be a squeeze, but he could come out through a door, after all—and they were all locked, but while he was leaning on one, it cracked and broke so that he could reach through and open it, and after that, sliding through into the basement was fairly easy.

When he went up the basement stairs, the dog went crazy, snarling but backing up as he climbed. He looked around the kitchen—pretty, cozy, freshly painted blue and white with Quinn's *Night Kitchen* print on the wall next to her red colander just like it had been in their apartment—and tried to ignore the damn yapping, but finally he'd had enough and he opened the back door and kicked it yelping out into the yard. Even if the nosy bitch next door looked out, she'd just see the dumb dog. He was safe.

He went into the dining room and found himself in a lot of warm sunlight, some from the tall windows on his right—his window; he looked at the broken shutter with affection—some from the matching windows in the living room at the front of the house, through an archway. But the place was dingy and cold, old plaster with cracks and woodwork with peeling paint, and the sunlight wasn't enough to make it better.

Unfortunately, plaster cracks and ugly paint weren't enough to get Quinn out. He'd have to find something much worse.

He moved into the living room and stood in the middle, turning slowly. There was an old red chair by the front windows with an octagon table beside it. Beside the chair was a brown basket made of wide strips of wood. Bill sat down and opened it. Yarn and stuff, Quinn's crochet.

She'd be making a blanket for their baby. When she came back to their apartment, they'd sit and watch TV, and she'd crochet for the baby.

The yarn felt soft and weightless in his hand, a sort of denimy blue color; Quinn knew they were going to have a boy. Like Jason Barnes. They'd call him Bill Junior, but Quinn should have part of his name, too, and Quinn could be either a boy or a girl, so William Quinn Hilliard it would be. A great name. He let his hand close on the yarn and it became a fist. A really great name.

He let the yarn drop and stood up.

There were bookcases around the fireplace full of Quinn's art books—he tensed a little, thinking, *Those books belong in our apartment*—and he let his hand slide over the smooth surface of shelves and the mantel, touch the face of an absurd gold clock there, linger on the spines of her books, drift over the polished top of the octagon table. If he touched these things, they'd be his, too.

On the other side of the room, the old red couch from her mother's took up too much space. The damn thing was huge, six feet long, almost a bed. The thought made him clench his fists again, but there was no reason. If she really wanted that couch, they could have it at their apartment. With a nice tan slipcover. Late at night, he and Quinn could stretch out on that couch and watch the news, the weather, the scores, flip between the late night shows and laugh. And then he could turn the TV off with the remote and reach for her—

His breath came quicker and he tried to turn his thoughts. This wasn't about sex, they'd never been about sex, they were about better things, family and school. He looked back at the chair—it was safer to think about—and saw the yarn again. He bent down and picked up a ball of the yarn, a small one, one she'd never miss, and shoved it in his jacket pocket. He'd keep it as a reminder that she'd be back with him crocheting for Bill Junior soon.

He caught sight of the clock on the mantel and straightened. He was running out of time.

He went to the front door and then remembered the back way was better, he was parked in back. But as he turned, he saw a key on the bookcase closest to the door. He tried it in the front door and it worked.

Of course she'd keep a key close to the front door. The doors had glass windows, so she had to have a key lock on both sides, but she'd keep a key near for convenience, in case of fire. That just made sense.

He weighed the key in his hand.

If he had his own key, he could come in any time, look around, make the plans they needed for their future.

Except Quinn would miss it if it weren't there.

And he had to get back to school, he'd taken too long to get in, he was running out of time.

He went out to the car, holding the gate open just long enough for the dumb dog to rush out yapping. Then he closed the gate, trapping the dog outside again, and drove off. On the way back to school, he dropped the key off at Ronnie Headapohl's hardware store and asked for a duplicate. When he got back to school, he used the pay phone in the hall to report that a dangerous dog was running loose on Apple Street and had bitten him. Yes, it had broken the skin, it should be put down. He gave his name as Harvey Roberts and made up an address to make the complaint official, and then he hung up feeling as though he'd made huge strides even though he hadn't found anything wrong with the house.

Two hours later, he signed out of school on his lunch break, picked up the key, and went to Quinn's again. The dog was nowhere around and the new key worked perfectly. He put the original back on the shelf and went back to school relieved. There he found a message from Betty at Animal Control that his dog had been picked up and had reportedly bitten somebody.

"We've been having trouble with it," he told her when he called back after school. "I hate to say this, but just put it to sleep. It's going to be easier on all of us that way. I'll come in and pay the fee tomorrow."

He hadn't lied, he thought as he hung up. Once things were back the way they belonged, life really would be easy for everybody again.

"SO IS LOIS still dating Matthew?" Quinn asked Darla over pizza after school.

"Yeah, but she doesn't seems too happy about it," Darla said.

"It's like without Barbara to bitch about, she doesn't have a life. She keeps needling me about her, like I'm going to bond with her and do a Bank Slut duet."

"It must be tempting," Quinn said.

"Not really." Darla put her pizza slice back in the box half-eaten. "Max wouldn't cheat. Hell, he doesn't even have the energy to do me, let alone Barbara."

"I was thinking about that," Quinn said. "It occurred to me that a nightgown that appealed to Bill was probably not something that would appeal to Max, anyway. Like maybe you should go for something really in-your-face."

"How about I grab him by the throat and say, 'Fuck me or die'?" Darla said.

"I was thinking more about black lace," Quinn said. "You know, something incredibly tacky. The kind of thing guys like and we laugh at."

"I don't know—"

"Look, you've learned a lot," Quinn said. "Don't ask him in front of windows or other people, and don't wait until he's too tired. I'd say you're almost there. Don't give up now."

"You really think so?" Darla shook her head.

Quinn leaned forward and closed the pizza box. "I know so. Come on, let's hit the mall right away. I can't stay long, Katie's home alone, but I can sacrifice another hour to save your marriage."

"Can I?" Darla said.

"Hey," Quinn said. "No defeatism. Let's go buy you something that'll drive your husband crazy."

"He already has one of those," Darla said. "Me."

IN THE FIVE days since Nick had helped Quinn move he'd managed to push her to the back of his mind where she lurked and made him uneasy. That was the trouble with change, he told himself. It never made you feel calm. The best he could do was ignore the fact that she existed, always difficult but then impossible when Bill stopped by the station after practice.

"Talk to you for a minute, Nick?" Bill called out, and Nick straightened from over Pete Cantor's Jeep and said, "Sure. What's up?"

"It's about Quinn," Bill said, and Nick thought, *Oh, hell, I never touched her.*

"I know you've been helping her," Bill said, "and I appreciate it, but I don't think that this move is good for her."

Nick let go of his guilt gratefully and regrouped. "What?"

"That house," Bill said, looking like a wise but regretful Viking. "It's a bad idea. She's there all alone, and the place is going to fall down around her ears any minute."

"Meggy says it's sound." Nick turned back to work. "I really wouldn't worry."

"What does Meggy know?" Bill shook his head. "We really have to get her out of there."

Nick stopped. "Bill, she likes it there. I think she's staying."

"If you hadn't helped her move—" Bill began, and his voice sounded tight, almost angry.

"Of course I helped her move." Nick frowned at him. "We all did."

"Well, stop," Bill said. "It's bad for her. And people are going to start talking. People who don't know you two are like brother and sister. You want to ruin her reputation?"

Nick tried to think of something to say, but all he could come up with was "What the hell are you talking about?"

"You helping her move. People are going to start thinking she's just one of your . . ." Bill's voice trailed off as he searched for a word.

"One of my what?" Nick said dangerously.

"Girlfriends," Bill said. "You know, the kind of girl you date."

Nick controlled his temper. "Bill, I don't give a damn what people think, and if Quinn does, she'll tell me to butt out. I haven't seen her since we moved her in, and I'm not planning on going over there any time soon, so if that's what you're worried about, you can forget it."

Bill's face cleared. "Thanks, Nick. I knew you'd understand."

Then you know more than I do, Nick thought, but he watched Bill leave without saying it. He'd had enough conversation with Bill Hilliard for one afternoon. In fact, considering the conversation, that was probably enough for a lifetime.

Ten minutes later, when somebody pounded on the back door, he thought, *Oh, Christ, not again*, but when he opened it, Quinn was standing there, her face pale in the cold, and in spite of all his rationalizations and promises to Bill, he was so glad to see her he almost reached for her.

"What's up?" he said, deliberately keeping things light and distant—reaching would be bad—and she pushed past him into the garage. She had on a blue down parka that made her look huge, jeans, and black rubber boots with buckles. She looked like a clown, and he should have been grateful, but his first thought was to wonder what she was wearing under all of it. Then he saw her face and he stopped thinking obscene thoughts.

"Katie's in the pound," she said, her voice on the edge of panic. "I called to report her missing, and they said they had her but I couldn't have her back because I wasn't the licensee and that she'd bitten somebody and they're going to *destroy her*—"

"Wait a minute, wait a minute," Nick said, wanting to put his arm around her and knowing better. "Start over. How did she get in the pound?"

"I don't know," Quinn said. "The gate was shut, but she got out anyway, and now they're going to *kill her*."

The fear on her face made him sick. "Tonight?"

She shook her head. "I'm not sure. I went over there, but they said the licensee has to come in, and Bill had told them to go ahead because if she'd bitten somebody she was dangerous. They won't give her back to me because the license is in Bill's name, and he won't answer the phone when I call, so he might already be out there signing to have her killed because he *hates* her—"

"Who'd she bite?" Nick said, trying to make some sense of it. Katie wasn't a biter.

"I don't know. They said somebody called in and said he'd been bitten by a dog that was running loose, and when they went to check, they found Katie." Quinn swallowed in a pathetic attempt to get calm. "And now they have her—"

"Oh, hell," Nick said. "Let's go talk to them." He picked up his jacket, knowing he was making a huge mistake and glad anyway because he was going to be with her again.

"They said no," Quinn said, her voice quavering. "I went there already and they said no. I couldn't even see her."

"Well, we'll talk at them until they say yes," Nick told her, not having any idea of what he was going to do. It sounded good though, and Quinn tried to smile.

"Thank you," she said. "I know I'm a hassle but I really need you on this."

"You're not a hassle," he lied. "Come on, let's rescue a dog."

THE TRUCK TOOK the miles to the pound without any problem, and Nick had plenty of time to think about Quinn next to him. It was a real turn-on being alone with her in the dusk, but then he'd known it would be a turn-on being alone with Quinn any-where, which was why he'd taken so much care *not* to be alone with her. Of course, the thoughts he'd been having lately weren't helping, filled as they were with bright underwear that was filled with Quinn until he stripped it off her and bounced her on that huge bed—

Stop it, he told himself. The woman's dog was in danger, for Christ's sake. She was upset. What kind of a creep would think about doing her at a time like this?

His kind of creep.

Beside him, Quinn scrubbed at the window with her sleeve, and he tried to see her the old way, the way she'd used to be before she'd come to occupy his thoughts permanently. *This is Quinn*, he kept telling himself, but as a warning it was losing power. It was Quinn he wanted.

"There's the drive-in, it's right after that," Quinn said, and he felt her soft, urgent voice in his solar plexus. *This is Quinn*, he told himself again, and his solar plexus said, *Sure is. Go for it.*

"The turn is right up here—there it is!"

Quinn grabbed his arm and he tried not to think about her so close as he pulled in and parked in front of the shelter. The place was deserted, not a car in sight, and he had a bad feeling that there wasn't going to be anyone to talk to. He glanced at the clock on the dash. Six-fifteen. Not good. "You stay here."

"No," Quinn said, and when he knocked on the door, he could feel her close behind him and it took everything he had to resist the urge to lean back into her. "Hello?" he called and pounded on the door this time.

"They've gone, they're closed," Quinn said in his ear, and he flinched at the warmth of her breath.

He tried the door but it was shut tight. "It's no go," he said, and she said, "Break it down. They have my dog."

He turned to her and said, "Quinn, I am not going to break a door down, especially a door to government property. Get a grip," but she looked up at him, her hazel eyes huge in the dusk, and he had to do something soon or he was going to grab her.

"My dog's in there," Quinn said, and he said, "Oh, hell," and turned and walked around to the back of the shelter where the pens were. At least a dozen dogs came out to see what they were doing, barking their heads off, and the last one in the last pen was Katie.

"Oh, no." Quinn ran to the pen and fell to her knees. "Oh, baby, I'm so sorry. I'm so sorry."

The little rat did look pathetic, shivering in the cold, its wiry little body pressed desperately against the mesh in a futile attempt to get to Quinn.

"Okay," Nick said, "we'll get here first thing in the morning and—"

"They'll kill her," Quinn said.

"So we'll get here really early—"

"No," Quinn said. "I'm not leaving her."

"Quinn, be reasonable—" Nick began, but she jerked her head up and said, "That's what *Bill* would say. This is not about being *reasonable*. This is about loyalty and love and trust and betrayal, and *I am not leaving this dog. They're going to kill her*."

"Oh, right," Nick said. "You're going to sit here and freeze to death."

"There's a blanket in your truck," Quinn said. "Leave me that."

"I'm not leaving you," Nick said, outraged. "What kind of guy do you think I am?"

"Well, I'm not leaving Katie," Quinn said. "So whatever kind of guy you are, that makes two of us."

"Oh, hell." Nick looked down at Quinn, immovable and irresistible, and at Katie, shuddering against the wire.

Against his will, he began to plan. The fence was only about six feet and it was smooth at the top. Getting over it was unfortunately doable. Illegal as hell, but doable.

"It's okay," Quinn said. "Just give me the blanket and go home. I know there's nothing you can do."

And to think that she had once been the *quiet* part of his life. "Okay," Nick said. "I'm going for the truck. You get away from the fence."

"I told you, I'm not leaving her," Quinn said, and he said, "Neither am I, but if we're going to get her out, I'm going to have to back the truck up here."

Quinn's mouth fell open. "You're going to get her out?"

"It's either that or stay here and freeze my ass off with you," Nick said. "I like you, but there's a limit to what I'll put up with to be with you." *Not much of a limit, though.*

Quinn stood slowly. "You are the most wonderful man in the universe," she said, looking into his eyes with so much hero worship that he felt hot even in the cold. "I'll never criticize you again, ever, I swear."

"Good," Nick said. "That's almost worth going to jail for. Now get your butt out of the way while I go get the truck."

It wasn't hard getting over the fence once he'd backed the truck up. The difficult part was convincing Katie to come to him since she ran back inside as soon as he landed on the concrete beside her. Quinn called her and coaxed her until she edged her way out again, slinking submissively along the pavement, and when he reached out and grabbed her, she peed on him as he scooped her up.

"I'm really sorry about that," Quinn said as he handed the dog over to where she stood in the back of the truck. She took the dog into her arms and said, "Oh, *Katie*," and cuddled the dog to her, and he was struck by the irony of the dog getting caressed and kissed while he stood shivering in the pound in a pee-stained jacket.

"You're going to owe me big for this," he told her and grabbed the top of the fence to climb back.

"Anything you want," she told him, and he thought of several things even before he began the climb back over.

He'd just landed back in the truck when the police cruiser came around the corner of the shelter.

DARLA STARED IN her bathroom mirror, appalled. Forget that the thing she had on was called a merry widow, not the best omen under the circumstances. Forget that it was black lace and scratchy, forget that it was so tight her breasts stood out like they were propped on a shelf, forget that the bikini that had come with it was so brief there wasn't enough bikini wax in the world.

Concentrate on the fact that she looked like a rogue dominatrix.

She put her hands on her hips, which didn't help, and confronted her own personality. *Confronted* was a good word, she thought. Confrontational, abrasive, domineering...

If Max didn't have a submissive side, she was toast.

Or maybe not.

She let her hands drop and tried to look less angry. It was the anger that was doing it, she decided. The anger that she was having to try this hard to seduce her husband, to wear this stupid lace thing that Quinn assured her was sexy—"He'll have a heart attack," Quinn had told her. "Can I borrow it if I ever get Nick?"—to plan what *he'd* used to plan, coax, and seduce her for.

He'd been so good at seducing, too. "Nothing below the waist," she'd tell him, really meaning to be a good girl this time, if her mother ever found out she'd be in so much trouble, "I mean it, Max," and he'd say, "Sure," and kiss her, and his hands would be so hot, and she'd feel herself going soft all over, and pretty soon they'd both be breathing into each other's mouths, letting their hands travel, and he'd say, "It would feel so good," and she'd be dying for it—

"Max!" Darla said, and opened the bathroom door to go into the bedroom. "Could you come in here for a minute?"

No, that wasn't the plan, she tried to remember what the plan was, but all she really wanted to remember was the way his hands had felt—

"What?" Max said.

He stood in the bedroom doorway, a *Sports Illustrated* in his hand, and it took him about half a second to switch from mildly annoyed to astounded.

"Sweet Christ," he said.

"Nope," Darla said. "This is pagan. We're going to hell. Let's make the most of it."

She walked up to him and he dropped the magazine to put his hands on her automatically, sliding them around her waist, which was cinched tighter than usual, smaller, so that his hands on her waist made her feel sexy, and she arched her hips into his as she kissed him.

He kissed her back immediately, hard, just like the old days, spontaneous and urgent, and she wanted him so much—

Then he broke the kiss and said, "What is this?"

She froze, literally cold all over with rejection. "What?"

"Is this about Barbara?" He dropped his hands from her waist.

"Because we've been married a hell of a long time and you've never pulled this stuff before."

Darla felt her breath come faster, and it wasn't from lust. "I don't believe this."

"I told you, you don't have to worry about Barbara." Max's voice was tight with anger. "I told you, but you don't trust me. *Our marriage is fine.*"

"The hell it is," Darla said, and stomped back into the bathroom to slam and lock the door. She peeled the merry widow off and left it on the floor while she yanked on her long flannel nightgown. Obviously her mother knew her better than she did. *"You've never pulled this stuff before,"* Max had said. Just not a sexy woman. Can't even seduce her own husband.

"Darla?" Max said through the bathroom door.

"Go to hell!" Darla said, and sat down on the floor and cried because she was so damn mad.

She was pretty sure it was because she was so damn mad.

NICK TOOK OFF his pee-soaked jacket and flannel shirt and tossed them in the back of the truck before he climbed in the cab beside Quinn.

"He really isn't going to arrest you, is he?" she asked, and Nick sighed and said, "He already did."

He started the truck. "The only reason I'm not in jail and Katie's not back in the pound is that it would take too much trouble to do the paperwork on me and get the shelter people out here." Tibbett's police force wasn't known for its aggressiveness in its best moments, and Gary Farmer had never been one of its even mediocre moments. "We're just damn lucky it was Gary and not Frank Atchity."

"I'll tell them it was my fault," Quinn said.

"We'll tell them your dog got stolen, and it has a medical condition," Nick said. "A urinary problem that needed attention."

"I'm really sorry about your jacket," she said. "Aren't you cold in just your T-shirt?"

He looked over at her, cuddling her dog in the growing twilight, her eyes huge and grateful and her body undoubtedly round under that down coat. "No," he said, and told himself that he was not going in her house when they got there, that he was just going to pull up out in front with the motor running.

"I'm truly grateful," Quinn said, and he considered not stopping at all, just slowing down enough so she could jump out with the dog.

But when he got to her house, a U-Haul was parked out front and all the lights were on inside.

"You know anything about this?" he asked, and when she said, "No," he turned off the motor and followed her inside to find out what else cataclysmic was going wrong in her life.

WHEN SHE WALKED in the door, the first thing Quinn saw was a lot of furniture from her past. Her mother's dining-room table was in the dining room with its full complement of chairs and her living room had three familiar end tables and an extra armchair.

"Quinn?" her mother said, and Quinn turned to find her standing in the doorway of the kitchen. "We just brought you a few things." Meggy looked flushed and harried, but she was smiling, a real smile, full of excitement, a smile Quinn couldn't remember seeing before.

"Mom?"

"We knew you needed furniture, and we had the U-Haul, so we just brought all the extra stuff over," Meggy said.

"We?" Quinn heard Nick close the front door behind her. Her mother's smile faded a little as she saw him. "We who? Why did you have a U-Haul? What extra stuff?"

"Edie," Meggy said and went back into the kitchen, and Quinn looked at Nick, who shrugged.

"If you don't need me anymore—" he began and she said, "I need you." He looked doubtful, so she said, "The least I can do is give you a thank-you beer. Come on," and when she went out to the kitchen, still carrying Katie as if she might disappear, he sighed and followed her.

Edie was putting Meggy's mixing bowls in the cupboard.

"You bought new bowls?" Quinn finally put Katie down and got a beer from the fridge.

Meggy said, "No, Edie's were nicer."

Quinn handed Nick the beer. "What does that have to do with you?"

"I'm moving in with your mother," Edie said. "She decided that if you could change your life, so could she." She looked over at Meggy with fond approval.

Meggy added, "Edie and I spend so much time together that we though it'd be easier just to live together."

Quinn looked from her mother's beaming face to Edie's and said, "Live together."

"Yes," Meggy said proudly. "It's all because of you. You said you didn't care what people thought, that you had to live your life for yourself, and all I could think of was how much I wanted to do that, too, to go for it all." Meggy smiled at Edie, happier than Quinn could remember seeing her in years. "And then we talked and decided it would just be so *convenient*. And Edie moved in tonight, and I'm so happy. I've wanted this for *years*."

"Years." Quinn looked over at Nick, who avoided her eyes. "And how does Daddy feel about this?"

"We haven't told him yet," Meggy said. "He's bowling."

"That'll teach him," Nick said, and Quinn glared at him to shut him up.

"So you and Edie have moved in together without telling Daddy," Quinn said, trying to regroup.

"He's probably not even going to notice unless I stand in front of the TV," Edie pointed out.

"I'm only doing what you said to, dear," Meggy said. "Going for it all. You were right."

"This wasn't what I had in mind," Quinn said.

"Well, we have to go." Edie picked up her purse, brisk and matter-of-fact as ever. "Your father will be home any minute and he's going to need an explanation."

"That I'd like to hear," Nick said, and Meggy ignored him to kiss Quinn good-bye.

"I just want to be happy, Quinn," Meggy said, and then they were gone.

Quinn leaned against the counter and said brightly to Nick, "So. This is new."

Nick nodded. "Interesting night you're having."

She met his eyes. "They're not moving in together so they can go to garage sales, are they?"

"Nope."

Quinn swallowed. "Did you see the way they looked at each other? For years, she said. How could I have missed this? How could I have been so blind?"

"Well, they haven't exactly been advertising. And who thinks about their parents' sex lives, anyway?" He looked slightly revolted as he said it. "I don't want to think about it now."

"I'm not ready for this." Quinn said. "This is my *mother*. She doesn't do things out of the blue. She just stands there in the middle of everything and stays the same." Katie got up and headed for the dog door, and Quinn went to watch her, still talking. "I can depend on her to be boring. I don't like this at all. It *changes* things."

"I know how you feel," Nick said, and took his beer into the living room.

eight

QUINN NEVER took her eyes off Katie for the five minutes she was out in the cold, but she thought about Meggy the whole time. *Years*, she'd said. *I've wanted this for years.* And now she was going after what she wanted, so happy, glowing at Edie. Okay, so it was selfish for her to just dump on Joe like that, selfish to turn everybody's life upside down, but still . . . she was so happy.

Well, good for her, Quinn decided. Whoever had come up with the idea that women were supposed to sacrifice for others was probably a guy anyway. Good for Meggy for going for it. Katie came back in, and Quinn shut the dog door so she couldn't get out again and then began to plan. Nick was in the living room and so was the couch. And he'd just rescued her dog without her even asking. She should show her gratitude for that.

Whether he wanted it or not.

When she went into the living room, Katie tiptoeing cautiously behind her, Nick was standing by the stereo with a CD in his hand looking as hot and heroic as ever, but when he heard her, he dropped it back on the stack with the others and stepped away, looking guilty.

"Music?" she said, and he said, "No."

It sounded as if he was saying no to more than music. Of course, she was in her fat coat and clunky boots, and she'd just gotten him arrested, so he probably wasn't in the mood to neck. But she was. She'd wanted him right there on the pavement when he'd told her he was going to rescue Katie. And she and Darla had made a pact to be more aggressive. Darla was wearing black lace, for heaven's sake. And then there was her mother and Edie. The least she could do was make an effort.

Nick shoved his hands in his pocket and ignored her, looking hot and nervous, and she thought, *He's up to something or he'd have left by now.* That was encouraging.

"I should go," Nick said. "I have to work tomorrow." But he didn't move.

Quinn took off her coat and threw it on the chair behind her. "So my mother's going for it all." She wandered over to the stereo, trying to look casual as her pulse pounded, and picked up the CD he'd dropped: Fleetwood Mac's *Greatest Hits*. He must have dug that one out of the stack. What the hell. She punched the button and slid the disk in the tray. "Well, good for Mom. I mean, we only get one shot at life. Shouldn't we make the most of it?"

The first bars of "Rhiannon" filled the room. Not one of Quinn's favorites. She turned it down to background level so they could talk. Or so she could. Nick wasn't helping much. "I mean, shouldn't we make it as exciting as possible? Since we're only here once?"

Nick was looking at her funny, probably because she was talking like a beer commercial. Quinn drifted past him—not easy to do in rubber boots—and sat down on her mother's red couch. They'd been on the couch when things had heated up before. She wasn't proud; maybe it would work again. She unbuckled her boots and felt him sit down next to her, and her pulse went into overdrive. So far, so good. She kicked off the boots and wiggled her toes. "Listen, I'm really grateful for everything you've done for me tonight." She stole a look at him under her lashes.

He looked grim, staring at her, his arm stretched along the back of the couch.

She leaned against the back of the couch and then rolled her head closer to his hand. "You stuck with me through everything. You really are my hero."

"You know you're driving me crazy, right?" he said.

"Well, I was hoping." Quinn tried to keep her voice from shaking. "I've been thinking about this a lot."

Nick's face was like stone. "This is a bad idea. You're my sister-in-law."

"Ex-sister-in-law. Twenty years ago. Darla says the statute of limitations is up."

Nick closed his eyes. "Darla knows about this."

"Well, of course, Darla knows about this."

"This is not what I want," Nick said. "You're my friend. My best friend. I need to keep you that way."

Quinn would have kicked him out for being a wimp if he hadn't just rescued her dog and she hadn't wanted him so much. "So why are you here on this couch then?"

"You're right, it's the couch," he said, refusing to look at her. "Classical conditioning. It's not me, it's the couch. Let's go in the kitchen."

But he didn't move.

"I like this couch," she said, and he finally looked at her, his eyes dark and hot on hers, and her throat went dry.

"So do I," he said.

She swallowed and leaned forward a little so that her cheek brushed against his hand. "You know, we can't just keep pretending this isn't here, this thing between us."

"This is dumb," he said. "This is such a dumb thing to do."

"No, it isn't—" she began, and then he slipped his fingers into her hair, his hand real on her, not a fantasy, and she stopped, a little breathless, wanting him, afraid of him, not sure what to do next.

He said, "This is dumb, but I've been thinking about this since the last time we were on this damn couch, so just this once." He slid his hand to the back of her head to bring her face closer to his. "Maybe this'll be really lousy and we'll never have to do it again." He sounded a little out of control, and she held her breath as he leaned closer—amazing to have him that close, to feel how warm he was, how dark he was—and then he brushed her lips so softly he almost wasn't there, making her heart clutch, tantalizing her until she wanted to grab him, climb into him, and make him kiss her harder. She caught his T-shirt in her fist, pulling him closer, and his mouth moved deliberately on hers then, tempting her, making the heat flare in her, and she leaned closer as he pulled away.

"Damn, not lousy," he whispered and she said, *"More,"* and he closed his eyes and kissed her again, harder this time, his hand tight on the back of her head as her heart pounded and she clenched her hands in his shirt and pressed against him to make the kiss last longer, forever. He pulled back, and she leaned forward, her mouth close to his until she was almost in his lap, trying to find him again, to draw him back, to learn his kiss and everything else she could get from him.

"Bad idea," he said like a warning, his voice husky, and she said, "Kiss me *hard*," and wrapped her arms around his neck, and he pulled her tight against him, tipping her back against the couch so she lay trapped in his arms as she stretched against the lovely hard length of him. His hands slid down her back, rough hands that made her hot and nervous at the same time. This was Nick, and that seemed exciting and dangerous but safe because it was Nick and he was kissing her, long lovely minutes of kissing her—time evaporated while he kissed her—heating her, scaring her, thrilling her because he wanted her so much and he was so rough. She moved closer, and he shuddered and pulled her hips to his and licked into her mouth. She touched his tongue with hers, and he rolled her down onto the couch cushions, twisting so she was under him, pressing her down with all his hot weight, pushing his thigh between hers and making what had been undefined heat suddenly fuse and flare so that she dug her fingernails into his back.

His body was harder under her hands than she was used to, leaner than Bill, more graceful, less gentle, and she tried to find her place with him, find his rhythm as he kissed her and moved against her, but it was confusing because there was so much heat and because he was Nick, insistent and hot on top of her, taking her mouth the way nobody had ever taken her body, but still *Nick*, and that kept getting in her way at the same time it made her breathe faster. Nick's heart was pounding, too, she could feel the beat of it, but then he eased his hand up her side—the flannel of her shirt so worn that she could feel how hot his hand was through it—and she forgot his heart and tensed because it was Nick touching her, and then he slid his hand under her breast and then over her breast and cradled it, stroking through the flannel, and she shuddered because the heat and the pressure felt so good and his mouth was so lush on hers. He tightened his hand on her and then stopped, frozen for a instant, the darkness evaporating from his eyes while she pressed against him and he pulled away.

"What?" she said, rising to meet him, holding on to him, and then she heard it, too. Somebody was ringing the doorbell, holding his finger on it so it was one long trill.

Nick's eyes focused on her. "Christ," he said and rolled away to stand up, all in one motion, pulling Quinn into a sprawl on the couch because she was holding on to his shirt.

"Nick?" she said as he pried her fingers from the flannel, and then he was on his way to the door, shaking his head, and she heard him open the door and say, "Oh. Hi, Joe," and she put her head against the back of the couch and exhaled her frustration through her teeth.

Her father came into the living room carrying the portable

TV from his bedroom and a garbage bag that looked to be full of clothes.

"Hi, Dad," Quinn said, trying to look unheated.

"Your mother threw me out," he said, sounding equally astounded and outraged. "I asked her for a beer, and she just threw me out."

"I don't think it was the beer," Quinn said. "Was Edie with her?"

"I thought it was menopause." Joe put the TV on the end table near the archway and looked for an outlet. "I mean, she came in and said Edie was going to stay for awhile, and I said, 'Whatever,' and she started yapping that I never listen to her, and I asked her if this was menopause, and she sort of screamed that was two years ago, and threw me out." He looked at Nick. "Can they get that twice?"

Nick looked at Quinn and closed his eyes. "No. Well, I have to go."

"Oh, no, you don't." Quinn stood up and glared at him. "You stay right there." She turned to her father and said, "There are twin beds in the second bedroom upstairs. Pick one. I have to talk to Nick."

"The game's on," Joe said.

"The game's always on," Quinn said. "And here's the bad news: I don't have cable."

"Ah, hell," Joe said and went upstairs with his garbage bag.

Quinn turned back to Nick. "What do you do, pay people to interrupt us?"

"Don't start." Nick shook his head at her, looking appalled. "One kiss, right, Jesus, and you say *harder*. No. This was a mistake."

"Okay, you're kidding me, right?" Quinn held on to her temper because screaming wasn't going to help even if it would have felt good. "You're going to do this to me *again*?"

"I think it's your hair." He looked up at the ceiling, anywhere but at her. "I must be nuts. Fucking nuts."

"My hair." Quinn felt herself flush again. "My hair. You grope me on my couch and then tell me no because of my hair." She picked up a couch pillow and clutched it to her middle, wrapping her arms around it so she wouldn't hit him. "You're right. You are nuts."

"You look just like you did at sixteen," Nick said. "Except older."

Quinn hadn't realized she was gritting her teeth until she exhaled and her breath rushed out like a hiss.

"I didn't mean it like that." Nick closed his eyes and let his head fall back. "I'm having a bad day."

"You're having a bad day?" She felt her temper rise, a flood of heat that made her head ache. "The bank turns down my loan, my dog gets kidnapped, my mother comes out of the closet, my father moves in with me"—her voice rose to a shriek—"and my ex-brother-in-law refuses to sleep with me, but *you're* having the bad day? *I don't think so!*" She flung the couch pillow at him, aiming for his crotch, and he just stood there while it bounced off him.

"The bank turned down your loan?" he said.

"Forget the loan." She took a deep breath so she could stop shrieking.

Nick took a step back. "Hey, this isn't just my problem. You said 'ex-brother-in-law.' You knew this wasn't going to work, or you wouldn't think of me like that. Not while I was—" He broke off. "I don't want to talk about it."

"This is not about me," Quinn said. "I was ready to take off my clothes and do anything you asked."

Nick closed his eyes again. "Don't do this to me."

Quinn wanted him dead. "I'm not doing anything to you. I'm

not the problem here, you are. Why did you kiss me if you weren't going to follow through?"

"I was going to follow through," Nick said. "I *wanted* to follow through, believe me. But you—" He spread his hands and bounced them once in the air, as if trying to force the words he needed. "I can't do it. I've been thinking about doing it, God knows lately it's all I've been thinking about doing, but then I look at you, and you're Quinn, not some fantasy, and I love you but not this way, and I can't, so we're not going to. Ever. This didn't happen, and it's not going to happen again."

He pushed past her to pick up his coat, and she said, "You know, you can't keep rewinding and erasing reality whenever you want to. It happened. You kissed me."

He shrugged on his coat, refusing to look at her. "I don't want to talk about it."

"You *groped* me."

"I *really* don't want to talk about that." He pulled his keys out of his coat pocket and pointed them at her. "We don't do this again. No more big eyes at me on the couch."

"Oh, it's *my* fault."

"Yes." Nick turned and went through the dining-room arch to the front door, and Quinn followed him, wanting to throw herself in front of him and drag him back to the couch, but also wanting to kick him hard. "It's your fault," he said. "Ever since you picked up that damn dog, you've been different. I never did stuff like this before, I never even thought about this before until you changed." He stopped to yank open the door. "Not for a long time, anyway."

Quinn glared at him. "What's *that* supposed to mean? A long time ago you had thoughts? I can't believe you're going to just leave me like this."

"Good night," Nick said and slammed the door behind him.

"The hell it was," she yelled at him through the window in

the door. When he didn't yell anything back and just kept walking to his truck, she looked down at Katie who'd come to see what the commotion was about. "My hair," she said to the dog. "He turned me down because of my hair."

Katie cocked her head, a little nervous and clearly doubtful.

"I know, I'm not buying it, either," Quinn said, but when Nick's truck pulled away, she went to stare at herself in the hall mirror. So she still wore her hair the same as in high school. Big deal. Dumb excuse.

In the living room, Fleetwood Mac sang, "Go Your Own Way."

"What are you, the fucking sound track?" Quinn said, and stomped in to punch off the stereo. So much for Nick's taste in music.

"Quinn?" Joe called down from upstairs. "Do you have an extra toothbrush?"

"In the cabinet," she snarled up at him and then went out to the kitchen and dialed Zoë's number.

When her sister answered, Quinn said, "I think Mom's gay."

"What?"

"Our mother is a lesbian. Just a guess, but she and Edie have not been swapping recipes, they've been swapping tongues."

"I'll be damned." In the background, Quinn could hear the rumble of Ben's voice, and then Zoë's voice, slightly muffled as she turned away to say, "No, nothing's wrong." When her voice came back clear, she sounded bemused. "How's Dad?"

"I don't think he's caught on yet," Quinn said. "He has, however, moved in with me."

"Oh, God, Quinn, I'm sorry." Ben's voice rumbled again, and Zoë said, "I told you, there's nothing wrong. Your mother-in-law's a dyke, that's all. Go away."

Quinn heard Ben's laugh over the phone, and then Zoë saying, "I'm not kidding, but I'll never get the details if you don't let me talk." Then Zoë's voice came back clear. "You know, you have to hand it to Mom, she's not real focused, but she does tend to get what she wants."

"Yes, and wouldn't it have been an excellent idea for her to bring us up the same way?" Quinn started to pace, stretching the phone cord.

"You sound a little annoyed," Zoë said. "I'm still not sure how I feel about this except that it's a little weird to find out Mom has a sex life besides Dad, but then I imagine it was a little weird for her, too, after all these years. So when did she finally figure this out?"

"You don't get it." Quinn sat down on one of the counter stools, and Katie curled up at her feet, convinced Quinn wasn't going to do anything rash for awhile. "She says she's wanted this for years."

"What?"

"Yeah," Quinn said, feeling vindicated by Zoë's outrage. "Yeah, all that time she was shoving us down the straight and narrow and fetching and carrying for Dad, she had Aunt Edie on the side."

"Do you know how many times she told me sex wasn't necessary and I should stop chasing boys?" Zoë's voice went edgy with betrayal. "And all this time I thought she was practicing what she preached, poor boring Mom."

"Probably as many times as she told me I was smart for not having sex," Quinn said. "I told her losing my virginity had been awful, and all she said was, 'Well, that's sex for you.' She told me it was boring and you told me it was overrated, and between the two of you I've been settling because I thought that was all there was, and now I'm mad."

"Shut up," she heard Zoë say, and then she said, "Not you, my husband, the comic. He says she was probably hoping we'd chase girls. I told you sex was overrated?"

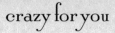

"Several times. I couldn't figure out why you kept going back for more, and I finally decided it was to drive Mom crazy."

"It probably was," Zoë said. "I didn't really get the hang of it until I was almost thirty." Ben said something in the background, and she said, "No, not you, but you're good, too. Will you go away so I can have this conversation?"

"It was bad with Nick?" Quinn felt guilty for asking but she had to know.

"Not bad, just not that good," Zoë said. "I was nineteen, what did I know? And God knows, *Mom* was no help."

"Well, didn't he know? I always had these huge fantasies about what great sex you were having on the couch."

"Nick was nineteen, too," Zoë said. "Most of what he knew, he'd figured out with me. The Quick and the Clueless, that was us. And all that time, *Mom*—"

"So great," Quinn said. "So just great. You end up divorced, and I end up with one boring guy after another, and Mom gets a lifelong relationship with Dad *and* with Edie. I'm *annoyed* with her."

"Imagine how Dad feels."

"Right now, he's chalking it up to menopause."

"Oh, hell. Do you want me to come home?"

"And do what? Show Dad the closet Mom just peeked out of? He'd only look for a cable hookup."

"You don't sound so good."

"I'm having a rough night." *Your ex-husband just said no to me again.* "People are thwarting me."

"Fuck 'em if they can't take a joke," Zoë said. "Go get whatever you want, Q. I did, finally, with Ben, and evidently Mom has, too. So can you."

"I'll remember that," Quinn said. "Now tell everybody else to give it to me."

———

QUINN WALKED INTO the Upper Cut the next morning on her planning period looking for Darla. Debbie waved hello across four stations and three women wrapped in scarlet plastic aprons.

"Hey, honey," she called, looking weirdly like the late Princess Diana under her new blonde haircut. "Heard about your new house."

Two of the women turned to see who had a new house while the third went on describing her argument with somebody. "And then *she* said—"

"Darla here?" Quinn asked as she made her way back to Darla's station.

"Any minute." Debbie sprayed the confection of champagne blonde hair she'd just raised to new heights in front of her. "How's that, Corrie?"

Corrie Gerber's wizened little face peered out from under a pile of frozen curls, looking like a mouse caught under a Baked Alaska. "Perfect, Debbie, just like always."

"We try to please." Debbie whipped the plastic apron off Corrie, brushing little bits of hair from her shoulders. "There you go, honey. You be careful on the way out. The floor gets slippery here."

Corrie eased herself out of the chair and stood, not even five foot tall, checking the top of her head in the mirror. Over her shoulder, she caught sight of Quinn, who'd been trying hard not to stare at her, and said, "Heard about you. Went and dumped the coach and now you're living in that old house out on Apple. What's wrong with you, girl?"

"I'm a feminist," Quinn said. "We get irrational urges."

Darla blew in behind her, in such a tense hurry she was almost on top of Quinn before she said, "Whoa, what are you doing here? Hey, Corrie, looking good. Is my eleven-thirty here, Deb?"

"No," Debbie said. "But then it's Nella, so no big surprise. What's with you? You're wound today."

"Work me in," Quinn said to Darla. "I want a haircut."

"Sure, what the hell. You could use a trim." Darla waved her toward the chair, brittle as hell, and Quinn said, "You okay?"

"Later," Darla said. "Trim, coming right up."

"No," Quinn said. "A cut. Cut it all off."

All three of them turned to her.

"Honey, no, not that beautiful *hair*," Debbie said.

"You turning into one of them lesbos?" Corrie said.

"Are you sure about this?" Darla asked.

"Yes," Quinn said to all of them. "Lop it off." She sat in Darla's chair and skinned her hair back from her face. She looked like hell but she looked different.

"Well, not like that." Darla smacked Quinn's hand until she let go, and then fluffed her hair a little around her temples.

"Shave it off," Quinn said.

"Something I should know about here?" Darla said.

Quinn looked in the mirror at Debbie and Corrie, listening avidly. "Later."

Darla turned to them. "Anything else we can do for you, ladies?"

"Just lost her mind," Corrie said and went tottering off to pay for her hair.

"I'll just clean up my station," Debbie said. "Won't be in your way at all."

"Yes, you will," Darla said. "Give us ten minutes. Go get a Coke."

Debbie got the same look on her face she used to get when Darla wouldn't let her play with the big girls, and Quinn would have bet she was going to whine, "That's not fair," just as she had a thousand times while they were growing up. Instead, she sniffed and flounced off to the break room.

Darla pulled open her drawer and got out her scissors case. "Now give or I don't cut."

"Nick kissed me last night. A lot," Quinn said and saw Darla smile behind her in the mirror, relaxing a little for the first time since she'd hit the shop.

"Excellent. Now explain the cut."

"Then my father came in, and he used it as an excuse to just stop." She clenched her teeth just thinking about it. "He just *stopped*." Quinn met Darla's eyes in the mirror. "I said, 'Listen, I've changed,' and he said, 'You look the same,' and when he was gone I looked in the mirror and I do. I wore my hair like this in high school. It was a little longer but just like this, parted in the middle. I want to be new and this will be one way to show *everybody* that I've changed, and I'm not going back. Cut it off."

"Come on back," Darla said. "I'll hose you down and then we'll do it."

"Wait a minute," Quinn said. "I forgot to ask. Did the earth move last night?"

Darla's face was like stone in the mirror.

"Oh, just hell," Quinn said. "What is *wrong* with them?"

"What's wrong with us?" Darla said.

Their eyes met again in the mirror, and Quinn said, "Cut my hair. Cut it all off. Make it as different as possible. Make it so different I can't ever go back to where I was before."

Darla nodded. "You got it."

"Not yet," Quinn said. "But I'm going to."

nine

WHEN NICK hit the bank at ten, the place was almost empty, so Barbara's voice echoed a little.

"Nick!" she said, smiling like a bank president. "It's too early for the deposit."

"Max'll bring the deposit in later," he said and watched her face light up. Jesus, Max had troubles. No wonder he'd been so cranky all morning. "I need some help here."

"Of course." Barbara switched off the light in her face and became Bank Barbie again. "What can I help you with?"

Nick cast a quick look around the bank but nobody seemed to be listening. He leaned forward, and Barbara leaned, too, evidently caught by his aura of conspiracy. "Quinn's bank loan got turned down."

She straightened. "It couldn't have."

"Shhhh," he said, and she leaned forward again.

"It couldn't have," she whispered. "Her credit is good. Who told you that?"

"Quinn," Nick said. "Could you look—"

"Wait here," Barbara said and marched off.

His approval rating of Barbara shot up. Of course, what she was doing was entirely unethical, but it was in a good cause, Quinn's cause. Not that he was involved with Quinn.

Nick leaned against the counter and solidified his noninvolvement while he waited. Quinn could be responsible for herself, but the refused loan thing seemed fishy, the kind of thing a friend would look into for another friend, and therefore not real involvement at all. He wasn't anywhere near her, no touching no thinking about her underwear—he thought about how soft the flannel of her shirt had been last night, how much softer she must have been under it, how she'd turned under him and tilted her hips and how he'd almost lost his mind—he was definitely not going near her again until this heat streak he was going through had passed.

Barbara came back, bright red spots high on her cheeks from what turned out to be outrage. "They changed her loan status," she said. "They didn't turn her down, they just asked for a twenty percent down payment. And she doesn't have it."

"Why'd they change it?"

Barbara leaned closer, her lips pressed together. "I shouldn't tell you this, but they shouldn't have done it, either. Her boss wrote a letter that said she was acting crazy, 'unstable,' he said."

"Bill," Nick said.

"No, her boss Robert Gloam," Barbara said. "I saw the letter."

"Yeah, but Bill put him up to it." Nick's last vestige of sympathy for Bill vanished. "How much is the down payment?"

"Fourteen," Barbara said. "But she'd already put down seven."

"I'd like to transfer some funds," Nick said.

"To Quinn's loan?" Barbara shook her head regretfully. "I can't do it. It's in her name and—"

"You want them to win?" Nick said.

Barbara bit her lip.

"She doesn't deserve this," Nick said.

Barbara thought for ten long seconds, and then she nodded. "You're right, she doesn't. Where do you want it transferred from?"

"I have some CDs in the safe deposit," Nick said. "Nobody needs to know about this, okay?"

"This is really nice of you." Barbara smiled at him approvingly, a bank teller's smile, remote and uninvolved.

It was a relief after Quinn.

"You're supposed to take care of your friends," Nick said, and Barbara stopped.

"Yes, you are." She looked at him with real warmth for the first time. "You certainly are."

"Right," Nick said uneasily.

Barbara beamed at him.

DARLA SECTIONED QUINN'S damp hair and thought about Quinn and Nick and change and Max. One thing about Quinn going short: people would finally see those great cheekbones. And maybe Nick would finally see Quinn, which would be a good thing. Maybe.

She looked over Quinn's head to her own neat French twist. Much neater than Barbara's version of it, which was softer, sexier.

Hell.

"Since high school," Quinn had said. Well, that's how long she'd been growing hers, since senior year when she'd caught Max looking at some junior cheerleader and all he'd said was, "I like long hair." Instead of saying, "I don't, and you look at her again, you're dead," she'd stopped cutting hers.

"Darla?" Quinn said, and Darla said, "This is a good idea."

She cut Quinn's hair in a layered cap, parting it on the side to deemphasize the roundness of Quinn's face, amazing herself with how much Quinn changed with each snip of the scissors. She looked older when Darla ran a comb through her hair for the last time, but she looked better, too. Sharper. Faster. Sexier. So much for long hair having sex appeal. "What do you think?"

Quinn nodded, her face a little bleak but determined. "It's a shock, but I like it. Once the shock's over, I'm probably going to love it." She shook her head back and forth. "I used to be able to feel my hair swing when I did that."

"Those days are over," Darla said. "Want a blow-dry?" But

then Nella came in, half an hour late, and said, "I'm not late, am I?" and Quinn stood up, dumping swathes of coppery hair as she did.

"Not at all, Nell," Darla lied. "Sit down. Be right with you." She followed Quinn out to the counter and said, "That one was on me. Call me later." When Quinn was gone, she went back to the break room to find Debbie.

"My twelve o'clock here?" Debbie said, her voice a little frosty.

"No. Can you cut my hair later?"

Debbie's jaw dropped. "Your hair?"

"Yeah," Darla said. "I want it short. Pixie short."

"Oh, my God." Debbie's frost thawed at the news. "Max is going to kill you sure as look at you."

"It's my head, not Max's," Darla said, and went back out to do Nella before Debbie could point out that Max was the one who had to look at it.

That was his problem.

QUINN SAT IN the car outside the station, trying to get used to her new haircut. She stared into the mirror on the back of her visor, twisting her head from one side to the other, but all she could think was *short*.

Well, the hell with it. She had a good cut, Darla didn't do bad ones, so she'd be fine. She flipped the visor up, took a deep breath, and went in to talk to Nick.

He was deep in conversation with Max, both of them frowning, and she had the distinct impression that they weren't talking about cars. She let the back door slam behind her, and they both turned and lost their frowns in surprise, but Nick got his back again in a hurry.

"What did you do to your *hair*?" he said. "Are you *nuts*?"

"No," she said. "And you can stop saying that. I'm grown-up. I'm thirty-five."

"That would explain the maturity you showed last night," Nick said.

"Last night?" Max said.

"Your brother made a move on me last night and then told me I wasn't the type to pet," Quinn told him.

"I don't want to know this," Max said, and retreated into the office, slamming the door behind him.

"Nice," Nick said.

"Listen, the last time you pulled this on me, I was polite," Quinn said. "But you just used up all my polite. What the hell are you doing to me?"

Nick tensed even more, glaring at her. "I don't know. I just know I'm not going to do it again."

"Well, why not?" Quinn walked closer so she could smack him or jump him, depending on how the conversation turned out. "I'm all for it, or I will be after I get finished wanting you dead."

"You're important to me," he said, and her anger evaporated. She swallowed. "Oh."

"I don't want you to be just another . . ." He searched for the word.

"Bimbo?" Her anger began to condense again.

"I don't get involved," he told her. "I don't do responsibility. I like my life the way it is, and I like you in it, but you stay a friend because that way I can keep you around forever." He didn't look happy about his plan, but his jaw was set. "Having sex with you would be wrong, it's not the way we are. So I'm not going to do it."

"Then why did you kiss me?" she said.

"I was stupid," he said, and she felt deflated.

Really, what could she do? Force him to make love to her?
She wasn't even sure she was ready for that. She'd done about
all she could. At least she'd confronted him. The sensible, safe
rationalizations piled up and buried her resolve.

"Okay, fine." She backed up a step.

He looked miserable. "I don't want to hurt you. I never
wanted to hurt you. I'm really sorry, Quinn."

"Not a problem," Quinn said. "I'm not the sensitive type.
Sturdy. Competent. Dependable."

"Quinn—"

"No need to get involved at all," she said brightly, backing
toward the door. "I'm completely responsible for myself. So
we're fine."

"Don't do this."

"So I'll be seeing you." She bumped into the door and felt for
the handle. "Best of luck in the future."

"Quinn—"

She met his eyes and playing fair lost its appeal. "You are not
going to forget me," she said, her chin up. "I don't give a damn
what your plans are, you still want me. Just don't expect me to
sit around waiting until you get your commitment problem
worked out because I'm getting a brand-new life with this haircut, and it's going to include a brand-new sex life, too. Sorry
you won't be joining me."

She swung open the door and stomped outside, flinging herself into her car and starting the motor immediately in case he
followed her out, which of course he didn't.

"Nice job," she told herself. Now she had to get a sex life
since she'd threatened him with it. And she had no hair. And
her father was living with her and using Nick's toothbrush.
"The hell with it," she said and went back to school.

———

MAX POKED HIS head out of the office. "She gone?"

"Yes." Nick stared into Eli Strauss's Honda. "Permanently gone."

Max nodded, still safe in the office. "Is that good?"

"That's perfect," Nick said savagely.

"Well, good." Max shook his head. "Why'd she cut her hair like that?"

"I have no idea," Nick lied.

"I hate short hair on women," Max said. "Makes 'em look tough."

"Yep," Nick said, planning on killing Max if he didn't shut the fuck up and leave him alone.

"So you made a move on Quinn, huh?"

Nick swung around and glared at his little brother.

"I'll just be here in the office," Max said and went back in.

Nick worked for another hour on the Honda without paying much attention to what he was doing. Mostly, he was fuming at Quinn. What an overreaction, big deal, a couple of kisses—his mind slid away from the mind-blowing heaviness of her breast in his hand—and she was acting like they'd—his mind ricocheted off what she was acting like they'd done, the things he hadn't gotten to do, the way that soft flannel would have parted under his hands, the way Quinn would have rolled hot in his arms—he put his hands on the edge of the Honda and thought, *I am such a hypocrite, and she was not overreacting.*

Suppose they hadn't stopped, suppose he'd pulled that shirt off her, those jeans, suppose they'd had sex—

He'd never be able to leave her. Life without Quinn wasn't possible. She was one of the people he loved, like Max and Darla and the boys. She stayed.

But life with Quinn in his bed on a permanent basis wasn't possible, either. He liked living alone. And if he slept with

Quinn, she'd want to move in or want him to move in with her, and he'd never be alone again, and she'd definitely want to talk about the relationship. Nightmare time. He had the perfect life, the perfect apartment, he'd done the right thing. He wasn't the type to take care of people, he didn't want responsibilities, he wanted to do what he wanted when he wanted, free to sleep with anybody and wake up alone—

He straightened at that thought. He hadn't slept with anybody since Lisa. That was before Christmas. He'd been alone and Quinn was alone, and they'd just lost their heads. As soon as they both dated somebody else, *slept with* somebody else, the problem would be solved.

Except he didn't want anybody else, and if she really made good on that dumb threat to have sex with another guy—

The back door slammed again, and he turned so fast he bruised his shoulder on the hood of the Honda, but it wasn't Quinn, it was Darla, and her hair was gone. It was short, like Quinn's, only shorter.

"Jesus," he said. "What did you guys do, join a cult? Max is going to throw a fit."

"Screw Max," she said, and he put his head back under the hood of the Honda because life outside of auto mechanics was just too damn emotional.

"WHAT DID YOU *do to your hair?*" Max said.

"I cut it off." Darla closed the office door behind her. "I wanted something different so—"

"Well, I don't." Max folded his arms across his chest and glared at her. "I can't believe this. What the hell's the matter with you?"

"There's nothing wrong with me," Darla said, holding on to her temper with every cell in her body. "I just think we're stagnating. We're the same—"

"I want us the same," Max said, still seething. "I worked my butt off to get us here—"

"Hey, I worked, too," Darla said.

"—and now we've got life just the way we want it—"

"The way *you* want it."

"—and you want to *change things?*" Max was so mad he looked away from her. "Just for the sake of change, you want to screw up a perfect life."

"It's not perfect for me," Darla said, and then Max did look at her. "It's been the same old thing for years, Max, we need to keep growing or we'll just—"

"You mean I'm not perfect for you," Max said.

"No." Darla shook her head, her heart beating faster. "No, you're the perfect man for me, you always have been, I love you—"

"Then why this?" Max said. "Why all that stupid sex stuff?"

Darla went cold. "I wanted some excitement. Evidently you don't."

"We're exciting enough," Max said.

"No," Darla said through her teeth. "We're not."

Max stared her down, as mulish as only Max could be. "You mean I'm not exciting enough."

"Yes," Darla said.

Max nodded, too mad to talk.

"I want something different for us," Darla said.

"Well, I don't." Max uncrossed his arms and turned away. "So I guess you're going to have to find something different on your own."

"Guess so," Darla said, and stomped out of the office. On her way she passed Nick bent over the Honda and said, "And you're a jackass, too," and then she went out and slammed the door.

———

"WHAT'S WITH THE haircut?" Thea asked Quinn later that afternoon, and Quinn said, "Sometimes you have to do radical things to make people really see you and realize you're not who they thought you were." When Thea turned thoughtful, Quinn added, "Which does not mean you should cut your hair."

"I know," Thea said. "I like my hair long. But you're right about people not seeing you. I mean, the whole school probably thinks you're just the coach's girlfriend and the art teacher who fixes things. They don't see you're a real person at all."

"Thank you," Quinn said. "That's enormously cheering."

"Well, now they will," Thea said. "You dumped the coach and cut your hair. They're going to have to look at you differently now."

"We can only hope," Quinn said.

"I think that was *very* smart of you," Thea said. "The getting people to look at you differently part, anyway. I gotta admit I really liked your hair long."

Thea was up to something, and Quinn didn't feel any more reassured when Jason came up to sign out an X-Acto knife fifteen minutes later, and Thea said sweetly, "I owe you an apology."

Jason gave her the same nervous look he'd been giving her ever since the movie fiasco.

"You know, for when I asked you to the movies." Thea radiated earnestness. "I was really using you, trying to make my life different."

"Oh," Jason said, clearly not following at all.

"I just wanted something more exciting than studying all the time. And I figured if I went out with you, there'd be parties, drinking, sex in the backseat, that kind of stuff."

"What?" Jason said.

"It wasn't fair." Thea smiled her apology. "I mean, imagine

if you'd asked me out to use me for sex. That would make you a real creep, and here I was doing it to you. So I'm really sorry."

"Wait a minute," Jason said.

"It won't happen again," Thea said soothingly and went into the storeroom.

"She's yanking my chain, isn't she?" Jason said to Quinn.

"I'm sure she's truly sorry," Quinn said.

"She shouldn't say that stuff about looking for sex," Jason said. "She'll have every creep in the school on her butt."

Quinn tried to look as innocent as Thea. "Why do you care?"

"Look, she's a nice kid." Jason sounded exasperated. "She's not my type, but she's a good person. Tell her to knock off that sex talk or she's going to get in trouble."

"I'll pass that along," Quinn said, and when Jason finally went back to his table, she went into the storeroom. "That was an incredibly evil thing to do," she told Thea.

"Paybacks are a bitch," Thea said. "Besides, it's not going to keep him awake nights, thinking about what he missed. He's not interested."

"He seems concerned," Quinn said. "And he's right, you probably shouldn't spread that bit about the sex around."

"Like I would." Thea grinned. "But he did look at me differently for a minute, didn't he?"

"Yes," Quinn said. "He was appalled."

"Beats bored," Thea said. "And I didn't have to cut my hair, either."

The last bell rang fifteen minutes later, and Quinn grabbed her coat and ran, trying to avoid Bill and the BP, only to run into Edie instead. They hadn't had much chance to talk at lunch with Marjorie loudly expressing her opinion that people knew who to blame for the team's three losses, and Petra darkly muttering about the evil that lived in students' hearts, especially the pervert boy students, and where had Quinn gotten that lovely blouse?

"Sometimes I think everybody in this school is crazy," Edie said as they went out the back door.

Quinn nodded. "The BP is driving me there. Every damn day he's on me for something else. It's like being nibbled to death by ducks. Ducks in letter sweaters."

"He doesn't have a life," Edie said soothingly. "You do. Your hair looks great, by the way."

"I don't have a life that I've noticed," Quinn said. "Pretty much the same old thing as far as I can see. Except for you and Mom."

"Quinn—" Edie began, and Quinn said, "No, it's okay. As long as you're both happy, I'm happy for you. And I'm sure I'll grow to like living with Daddy. He seems fairly simple in his needs."

"I'm so sorry," Edie said.

"Don't be," Quinn said. "Everything's going to be fine."

But at five-thirty that night, in the middle of making brats and sauerkraut for her father before heading off for play practice, Quinn heard the doorbell and opened the door to find Darla with a suitcase, a pixie cut that took about ten years off her age, and a strained expression on her face that put the years right back on.

"Love the hair," Quinn said as she stepped back to let her in.

"I'm moving in for a little while," Darla said. "If that's all right."

"Uh, sure." Quinn searched for something tactful to say and finally settled for directness. "What happened?"

"He didn't like my hair." Darla put the suitcase down where Katie could sniff it. "He said, 'What the hell's the matter with you?' and I said, 'I want something different,' and he said, 'Well, I don't,' so I left for awhile. That's different."

The old Darla would have said it with a glint in her eye, but this one just stood there, looking as tense as Lois. Maybe this was the kind of tension you got when you separated from a husband. Not that Quinn would ever know.

Darla wasn't saying anything else, so Quinn said, "Yes, it is different," to encourage her. Nothing. "Well, come on upstairs and we'll move one of the twin beds into the office."

"Why?" Darla picked up her suitcase again, making Katie skip back a step.

"Dad moved in last night. I'm assuming you don't want to share a bedroom."

"Your mom and dad have a fight?"

"No. She's in love with Edie. We haven't mentioned this to Dad yet."

Darla blinked at her. "Right. And you and Nick?"

"I'm annoyed and he's in denial."

"Well, at least we're all out of our ruts," Darla said and headed for the stairs.

LOOKING BACK LATER on the next two weeks, Quinn wondered how any of them survived.

Darla stubbornly refused to go home and Max just as stubbornly refused to admit there was anything wrong. "She's being unreasonable," he told Quinn. "She knows I'd never cheat." "This isn't about Barbara, Max," Quinn said, and then Max got that mule look on his face and refused to talk any more.

"It's hopeless," Darla told her later. "But at least I'm not living the same damn life I was before. I've stopped thinking about screaming all the time. You don't mind if I stay here, do you?"

"No," Quinn said. "It's kind of fun. And it's not like I have a life, anyway. I'm turning into my mother after all; she had Edie and I have you. Not in the same way, of course."

"You never know," Darla said. "We live together for ten or twenty years, we may see the light."

Not that Edie and Meggy's life was perfect.

"Edie's so quiet," Meggy told Quinn when she dropped Edie off at play practice. She checked to make sure that Edie was across the stage out of earshot, and then she said, "She keeps going in the bedroom and closing the door, and when I go in there, she's *reading*."

"She's an English teacher," Quinn said. "They do that."

"She's just used to being alone too much," Meggy said. "Poor Edie."

Quinn thought about her own house, full of ESPN now that Joe had the cable hooked up, and Darla's boys who came to dinner every night, and Darla's mother who stopped by every night, too, to see if Darla had come to her senses yet and gone back to Max who was a good provider. "Yeah, poor Edie."

Later that night, Edie cornered her and said, "Your mother is driving me crazy. She keeps bringing me things, asking me what I want for dinner, telling me to put down my book and come watch TV with her."

"I'm sure it just takes a little getting used to," Quinn said. "It's only been a couple of weeks. She spent almost forty years with Daddy and you've always lived alone. There's bound to be some adjustments." She thought of Joe, settling into life on Apple Street because he thought it was going to be temporary, sure he'd be moving home to his big TV before the World Series started.

"I loved living alone," Edie said.

"Well, then, why did you move in?" Quinn said, feeling exasperated and then feeling guilty for feeling exasperated.

"Because she was so excited about it." Edie looked rueful. "She kept saying how we could finally be together and how could I say, 'I like living alone'? That would have been terrible."

Quinn thought about her mother's face, beaming at them all that night in the kitchen. "You're right. I couldn't have said no to her, either."

"I'll get used to it," Edie said. "Heck, I'm spending so much time on this play, I won't be around much anyway."

Bill, on the other hand, was around all the time, dropping by Quinn's room to discuss Jason's participation, even though she'd told him over and over she wasn't interested in talking to him. "I'm just worried he may be overextended," Bill said, inviting her to worry with him.

"That's Jason's business," Quinn said, and turned her back on him to teach.

The BP wasn't nearly as tactful as Bill. "You're ruining the team," he told her when he called her in the last Wednesday in March, the fifth summons he'd given her that month. "Jason Barnes's discipline has gone to hell, and Corey Mossert's getting to be just as bad. You tell them they're off that crew, or I will."

"Then you will," Quinn said. "They're eighteen, Robert. They're capable of making their own decisions about extracurricular activities."

"Baseball is not an extracurricular activity." Bobby's eyes were lit from within by religious fervor.

"Right," Quinn said and escaped to the outer office. "Is he getting loonier or is it just me?" she asked Greta.

"It's just you," Greta said, without looking up from her typing. "He's always been a bedbug."

And if that wasn't enough, somebody kept reporting her to the housing authorities and she had to put up with one inspection after another—water, foundation, pest control, gas leak, fence, on and on—until she was so worn down by the hassle that she almost wished she'd never bought the house.

"Somebody is out to get you," Darla said.

"The thought occurred to me," Quinn told her. "I asked Bill

to stop calling the city on me, and he said he wasn't. What do you do when they stonewall you like that?"

"I moved out," Darla said. "But you've already done that so you're stuck. Which reminds me, the mail came. You have another notice from the city."

Bill wasn't the only one stonewalling her: Nick dropped off the face of the earth. They'd talked every day for years, and now, suddenly, he just wasn't there. Quinn was mad, then hurt, and finally just lonely, missing the huge part of her life he'd occupied. This was what he'd meant by risking their friendship, and she tried to regret the night on the couch and then gave up. She'd wanted exciting and he'd given it to her; how could she regret that when she wanted more? She fought the urge to confront him and decided to wait him out. Tibbett wasn't that big, he couldn't ignore her forever. Sooner or later he'd have to come back or at least acknowledge in some way that she existed.

She hoped.

THE SAME TWO weeks weren't any better for Nick.

He'd talked his way out of jail by paying the fines for trespassing and for Katie. The pound was really not interested in pressing charges since the phantom caller never showed up to pursue the dog bite report, so Katie was put on probation after Quinn promised never to let the dog out of her sight outside the house again and took out a license in her own name this time.

But if the Katie problem was solved, the Quinn problem wasn't. No matter how virtuous he tried to feel about walking away from the couch, he couldn't help thinking about what would have happened if he hadn't. His libido was showing Technicolor movies with SurroundSound of What Might Have Been, and the knowledge that Quinn was exasperated but willing did not make his life easier. *Just once*, his id would whisper.

*Just once, to get it over with, so you can stop thinking about it.
She'll be like all the rest then. Do it just once.*

This was such a bad idea that when Max came into work two
weeks after Darla moved out and said, "I'm going to Bo's tonight, want to come?" he didn't say, "I don't want to get involved with a married guy trolling for women at a bar," he said,
"Yeah." Anything was better than another night thinking about
Quinn.

Unfortunately, Joe was standing beside him when he said it.

"Great idea," Joe said. "I'll come, too. In my own car, though,
in case I get lucky."

"Lucky?" Nick said and felt ill.

"Well, it's probably going to take Meggy another couple of
weeks to start missing me," Joe said. "No point in just sitting
around waiting. Right, Max?"

"Right," Max said with no enthusiasm whatsoever.

The night went downhill from there.

There wasn't anything wrong with Bo's Bar & Grill. Nick
had spent plenty of good times there: the beer was cold, the
pizza was hot, the jukebox wasn't too obnoxious, and they only
did karaoke on Wednesday nights so it was easy to avoid. The
place wasn't attractive—lots of scarred Formica tables and
stainless-steel chairs that probably looked like hell in the daylight—but nobody went to Bo's for the decor. They went for
the booze, the TV, and the company. Tonight, Nick could have
done without the company.

"So this is where you meet women," Max said as he sat down,
trying to sound like a man of the world and sounding instead
like a high school freshman trying to sound like a man of the
world.

Joe leaned on the bar and surveyed the place. "Great pickings.
Way to go, Nick."

"We're not staying long," Nick said and ordered a beer.

The way he figured it, Joe would get bored and begin watching the game that was always on the TV over the bar. And women would start hitting on Max pretty soon—there was that face, after all—and he'd get spooked and want to go home. Then they could all go to Max's since Joe would go anywhere there was cable, and he could get out of this nightmare.

"Hey, Nick," Lisa said from behind him, and he froze.

"Hi, Lisa." He turned around to be polite. "How you doing?"

"Lonely," she said, smiling at him, young and beautiful and nothing he wanted at all.

"Sit right here, little lady," Joe said, moving down a stool to make room between them, and Nick shot him a dirty look while Lisa boosted herself up on the stool. "I'm Joe." He leaned toward her smiling even wider than she was smiling at Nick. "Can I get you a beer?"

"Uh, sure," Lisa said, looking at Nick, but he felt Max lean into him and turned to see what Max was trying to get away from.

"You're new here, aren't you?" a neat little blonde was saying to Max.

"Uh, Max," Max said, holding out his hand for the blonde to shake.

"Tina," she said, taking his hand and holding on to it. "Very pleased to meet you."

"Uh, um, how about a beer?" Max bumbled, gesturing with the bottle he held in his left hand, since Tina had taken permanent possession of his right. "What do you say?"

Tina dropped his hand as if it were slime and said, "You *creep,*" and stomped off.

"What did I do?" Max said, panic making his voice higher than usual. "I thought you were supposed to offer them booze."

Across the room, Tina whispered to her friends and they all glared at Max.

Nick looked down at the beer bottle clutched in Max's left hand. "Well, this is just a guess, but it might have been the wedding ring."

"Oh, hell." Max put the bottle down and tugged at his ring, but it wouldn't budge.

"What's up?" Joe called across Lisa and then he saw Max pulling at his ring. "Good idea." He slipped his off and put it in his pocket while Lisa watched. "My wife left me," he told her sorrowfully. "After thirty-nine faithful years, she threw me out."

"That's *terrible*," Lisa said. "Thirty-nine faithful years." She shot a look at Nick under her lashes. "Now that's commitment."

Nick turned back to Max, who was still yanking on his ring. "You know, that's probably a sign you shouldn't be here."

"You sound like Quinn," Max said, still grumbling. "Signs. Hey," he called to the bartender, "You got any butter?"

"Max, give it up and get her back," Nick said. "You don't want anybody here, you want Darla."

"She left me," Max said, that mule look back on his face. "It's been two weeks, and all she'll say is she wants something new." He looked around Bo's as if it were Sodom. "Well, this is new. Damn it."

"I think she probably meant something new with her." Nick looked at him in disgust. "I can't believe you're fucking up your marriage like this."

Max glared at him. "Is this your business?"

"Great." Nick went back to his beer. "Fine. Go for it. Knock yourself out."

They sat in silence for a couple of minutes, and then Max said, "I don't notice you hitting on anybody."

"I'm resting," Nick snarled.

"You going to call Quinn?"

"No."

"And you think I'm stupid. Quinn wants you, you dumbass."

"Well, I don't want her," Nick said, thinking about hitting on Lisa to get Max off his back and dropping the thought immediately.

"Yeah, right." Max sounded normal again, now that he was arguing. "You've wanted her forever."

"Aren't you supposed to be picking up women?" Nick said, and before his sentence was finished, a woman sat down beside Max and said, "Hello, Max Ziegler, what are you doing in a place like this?"

Max jammed his left hand in his pocket and turned. "Oh, hell. Hi, Marty."

Nick squinted past him. Marty Jacobsen, one of Darla's regulars. Good. Served Max right. He hadn't wanted Quinn forever. Just for the past twenty years.

"Darla know you're out tonight?" Marty said, leaning into him a little.

"Nope," Max said, leaning back a little. Nick nudged him upright, and he said, "Just out with Nick and Joe." He pulled his left hand out and looked at his watch, flashing his wedding ring under her nose.

"I heard she left you." Marty leaned a little closer. "Must be pretty dumb to leave a great guy like you."

"She's just staying at Quinn's for awhile," Max said nervously.

"Heard about that, too." Marty nodded, sympathetic. "Must be terrible for you, finding out like that."

"Finding out what?"

"First Quinn's mom and Mrs. Buchman and then Quinn and Darla."

Nick laughed as he realized what Marty was getting at, and she straightened, glaring past Max at him. "Not that I think it's wrong or anything. I mean, Darla's still going to do my hair."

"What are you talking about?" Max said, mystified.

"I just thought, if you wanted, you know, *reassured*, that I could help." Marty batted her eyes at him. "I'd love to help."

"Marty, they're not lovers," Nick said. "They're just working on the play."

"Lovers?" Max said.

"You men are so blind," Marty said. "Quinn left the coach, didn't she? Like the best guy in town?" She shook her head. "And then they cut their hair like that. It's obvious."

"Lovers?" Max said to Nick, his brows drawing together, as the thought took hold and he got angrier.

"Not lovers," Nick said. "Jesus, Max, get a grip."

"Yeah, but people *think*—"

"So how about a beer, Max?" Marty said. "I sure am thirsty."

"Sure," Max said, signaling the bartender and putting a bill down on the counter. "Lady'd like a beer." He nodded to Marty. "Well, gotta be going. Nice seeing you."

He slid off the barstool to Nick's relief and Marty's disappointment, and said, "Joe?"

Nick turned to see Joe leaning against the bar talking to Lisa and two of her friends, a redhead and a brunette.

"Now what you got there," Joe was saying, "is probably a bad washer if your sink is really old."

"It's really old," Lisa said, beaming up at him.

"Well, I could come over and fix it tomorrow."

"All right." Lisa slid her eyes to Nick to see if he was listening. "You and I have a date tomorrow."

"I don't believe this," Max said under his breath.

"We're leaving, Joe," Nick said. "You have a good night."

"I plan to," Joe said, toasting him with his beer.

Lisa ignored Nick completely.

"We're going to have to do that again real soon," Nick said as he followed Max out to his car.

"Shut the fuck up," Max said.

ten

BILL'S TWO weeks were hell, too.

First of all, Quinn had cut her hair and he hated it. *Hated it*. It gave him a headache to look at it. She'd looked so sweet before, like a mother, like his girl, and now she was different, farther away from him, and he *hated it*.

Of course, it would grow back. She was just going through a phase, and when they were back together, he'd say, "Please don't cut your hair again," and she'd be sweet like always, and it would grow back.

He couldn't wait.

In the meantime, the BP was getting out of control. "We'll start a rumor she's screwing around with Jason Barnes," he told Bill, almost cackling he was so happy. "That'll get Jason off that damn play and make her come back to you to save her job. Pretty good, huh?"

Bill looked at him as if he were demented. "Quinn wouldn't get involved with a student."

"We don't know that." Bobby shook his head. "She's been acting strange and that kid is always with her. I wouldn't be surprised—"

Bill glared at him and he broke off. Quinn was not involved with anybody else, especially not a student, especially not Jason Barnes who was practically a son to him, Quinn was not with anyone else, nobody but him.

"It'll work," Bobby said, and Bill shook his head but let him go. He had a plan of his own.

He'd realized finally that Quinn was going to be stubborn about owning a house after she'd withstood all the city inspections he'd sicced on her in the past two weeks, so he'd decided he'd just find a good house for them to share. He really didn't know why he hadn't thought of it before, it was so obvious, so he'd call Bucky at the real estate office and when he found the perfect house, he'd show it to her, and she'd realize his was the better choice, and they'd move in together, and her hair would grow back, and he could concentrate on the team again. Not that four losses were anything to worry about.

"I'll take care of Quinn," Bobby said, "you just concentrate on winning," and Bill ignored him because he'd had another idea.

People thought Jason and Quinn were together because they were working on the play. Well, *he* could work on the play. He could see Quinn every night if he helped with the tech. With that and the house—

Things would be back the way they should be in no time.

On Monday. the BP called Quinn to his office on her planning period.

"What is it this time, Greta?" Quinn asked.

"You're ruining his life." Greta kept typing, but she did manage to shoot Quinn a sympathetic glance. "At least life as he knows it. Go on in, he's waiting."

Bobby's glare as she came in was even more self-righteous than usual.

"We have a problem," Bobby said.

"Don't we always?" Quinn didn't try to keep the exasperation from her voice.

"As I've told you, Jason Barnes has been coming late to weightlifting and leaving early." Bobby's lips tightened and almost disappeared. "His involvement in this play is hurting his athletics. It has to stop."

"And as I've told you, nobody's forcing Jason to work on the play," Quinn said. "I really don't see what I have to do with this."

"People have remarked on your relationship with this boy," Bobby said. "I don't want to have to call his parents."

Quinn went cold; this wasn't the BP being a twit, this was the BP being dangerous. "What people and what relationship and why would you call his parents?"

"People have seen the two of you together," Bobby went on. "There's a suggestion of intimacy."

"He's one of my students," Quinn said. "He's a great kid, but he's a kid, that's all."

"You've been talking and laughing." Bobby glowered at her. "He follows you around, and you encourage him and he's not concentrating on the team. I've seen the way you—"

"I get it." Quinn folded her arms and glared down at him. "You're the 'people,' and you're mad because you want Jason off the play and me back cooking dinner for Bill." She wanted to kill the little tick where he sat; who was he to try this garbage on her?

"Others will notice," Bobby said. "They probably—"

"Yeah, after you point it out so that even giving the kid homework will look like a come-on." Quinn shook her head at him. "You're not going to blackmail me with my reputation, Robert. I can't believe you and Bill would stoop this low. You should be ashamed."

"I've got nothing to be ashamed of," Bobby blustered. "Nobody could ever accuse me of being too close to a student—"

That was for damn sure, they all thought he was a dweeb.

"—so the very fact that you're vulnerable should tell you something." He paused, smug, and she wanted to smack him because he was right. "You know better than this; teachers have to be above suspicion. You tell Jason he can't work on that play anymore. Send him back to Bill where he belongs."

"I'll tell Jason you and Bill are concerned about his weight-lifting," Quinn said. "Anything else, you're going to have to do. But I promise you this"—she leaned forward, intense because she was so furious—"you start any rumors about Jason and me, and I will file a grievance against you that will make Carl Brookner think you're scum."

He went white then, his brows drawing together in fury, and she felt better. It was the smug part that made her nuts.

"As long as you don't say anything to anybody," Quinn pointed out mildly, "you're not vulnerable. And if you don't say anything, there won't be a problem because the only person around here with a slimy enough mind to even think I'd fool around with a student is you."

"You be careful," Bobby said. "You just be careful. People notice. People talk. They already think you're crazy because you broke into the pound to get a dog."

Quinn shook her head and left, pausing on her way out of the outer office to say to Greta, "You know, I think he's losing it."

"I'm sure of it," Greta said. "Oh, and you had a message from the bank. Something about your loan."

"Oh, hell," Quinn said, but when she called, Barbara said, "I just wanted you to know your loan is through. You can come in any time and sign the papers."

Quinn's mind went blank. "My loan? What loan? I thought I needed more down payment."

"It's through," Barbara said brightly. "Come in any time."

That wasn't like Bank Barbie, ducking a financial question. "I'll come on my planning period," Quinn said. "We'll have a nice long talk."

Barbara looked a little nervous in her neat gray gabardine suit when Quinn got to the bank. "I'm going to lunch in five minutes," she told Quinn sliding papers across the desk to her. "If you'll just sign—"

Quinn nodded. "Good. I'll come with you."

"Well . . ." Barbara looked flustered.

"I want to know what happened," Quinn said.

Barbara blushed. "I promised him I wouldn't tell."

"Him? Him who?"

Barbara looked over her shoulder and then whispered, "Nick."

"Nick?"

"Shhhh."

"We are definitely going to lunch," Quinn said grimly.

Half an hour later at the Anchor Inn over French silk pie, Quinn was still grappling with the enormity of it. Nick wouldn't speak to her, but he'd pony up half the down payment for her house. Exactly what train of thought had taken him there, she wasn't sure, but she knew she was both grateful and furious— grateful that he cared that much and furious that he'd done it. Bill had gone behind her back to screw up the loan, that she was pretty sure of, and now Nick had gone back there, too, to rescue her, treating her as if she were a child.

"I can't believe this," she told Barbara.

"I think it's wonderful," Barbara said. "He's taking care of you. You're so lucky."

"I'd rather take care of myself," Quinn said. "I'd rather he treated me as if I were capable of taking care of myself."

"Why?" Barbara looked at her so blankly that Quinn said, "I don't get you. You have a real career at the bank, and you make good money. Why are you so fixated on getting a man to support you?"

Barbara drew back, two spots of color flaming in her cheeks. "I don't need a man to support me. I'd never depend on a man for money."

"Oh." Quinn blinked at her. "Then why do you keep dating married men?"

"I *don't*," Barbara said, and the distress on her face was real. "I truly don't. I never date them until they're separated. It's just so hard to find somebody to take care of you, you know? When you find a good repairman, you know you're lucky."

Quinn thought back to the string of men who'd tromped through her house on all those inspections. She'd looked at every one of them and thought, *Are you taking me for a ride on this? Because I don't have a clue what you're talking about.* "Okay, I'm with you there, but they end up living with you, Barbara."

"Only three of them," Barbara pointed out.

"You're only twenty-eight," Quinn said. "Three married men by the time you're twenty-eight is statistically significant."

"I don't date them while they're married," Barbara insisted. "I'd never date a married man. It's just that when I find somebody who's really good and can fix things, I have a lot for him to do."

"So he comes over a lot." Quinn nodded for her to go on.

"And then sometimes they ask me out," Barbara said. "But I always tell them that even though I'm really, really grateful for how hard they've worked, and that I think they're wonderful, because they are, I couldn't possibly go out with a married man. Because I couldn't."

"And then they leave their wives," Quinn said, light dawning. She could just imagine Matthew, after umpteen years with Lois bitching at him, having a young, beautiful blonde telling him he was wonderful.

"And then for awhile it's wonderful," Barbara said, almost to herself. "And I feel so safe, and I know who I am because I'm with this wonderful man who knows everything." She came back to earth and said, "But it always turns out he doesn't. It's so disappointing because they always say they do, you know? But they don't, and you can't trust them after all."

"I think you're supposed to love them for themselves," Quinn said.

"Well, I do," Barbara said. "Until they fail me."

Quinn went back to the essentials. "Why would you want somebody who would dump his wife?"

Barbara looked dumbfounded. "People get divorced all the time. Nick's divorced, and you're with him."

"No, I'm not," Quinn said. "He's not even talking to me."

"Then why did he pay your loan?" Barbara said. "He must think he's with you."

"I don't know what he thinks," Quinn said. "I'm not even sure what I think. My world is going through a weird phase."

"Darla Ziegler is living with you, isn't she?" Barbara said.

Quinn frowned at her. "*No*. She's just staying temporarily to work on the school play." That sounded so lame she could see why Barbara wouldn't buy it, so she ditched the excuses and went for the truth. "She hasn't left Max. They're still married."

"If I had somebody like Max, I wouldn't move out and leave him alone," Barbara said. "I heard he was at Bo's last night. That's terrible."

Bo's. Oh, hell. "They are not getting divorced, Barbara," Quinn said. "Forget it."

Barbara flushed, and Quinn felt sorry for her. "You'll find somebody wonderful who knows a lot who's not married," Quinn told her. "It's bound to happen."

Later, driving back to school, she realized that had been pretty patronizing. It wasn't as if she were doing any better than Barbara, really. Barbara was at least getting her house worked on. Quinn couldn't even get the guy she wanted to pay attention to her (although he'd pay her down payment, the dumbass), and she couldn't get the guy she didn't want to leave her alone. *Fix your own life before you start on Barbara's*, she thought.

She started with Jason. "Mr. Gloam is upset that you're doing both the play and baseball."

"I'm not the one screwing the team up," Jason said.

"He seems to think that would be me," Quinn told him. "He also implied that our relationship might be, uh, more than teacher and student."

"He's whacked," Jason said.

Quinn moved back as Thea came out of the storeroom with more paper. "I think so, too, but he can make life hell for me, so I'd appreciate it if you'd stand at least twenty feet from me at all times."

"You're kidding." Jason looked disgusted.

"What's wrong?" Thea said, and Jason said, "Gloam thinks I've got the hots for McKenzie."

"He's just trying to blackmail me into kicking Jason off the crew," Quinn told her. "He doesn't really believe it."

"You're not going to kick me off, are you?" Jason said, and Quinn shook her head. "Good," he said. "This place is crazy." He looked at Thea as he said it, and then went back to his seat, only to get up a few minutes later and say to her, "Listen, Thea, if Gloam shows up at practice, I'm sticking to you. Maybe he'll think I'm after you instead of McKenzie and get off her back."

"Are you that good an actor?" Thea said coolly, and Jason shook his head and said, "This place is *definitely* crazy."

"Not just this place," Quinn said and thought about Nick. He'd paid off her loan. He should be thanked for that. Her pulse kicked up a little at the thought. Exciting wasn't turning out to be as easy as she'd thought it would be, but it was definitely worth pursuing. After ignoring her for two weeks, Nick should definitely be thanked.

Whether he wanted to be or not.

———

DARLA WAS JUST finishing up Joan Darling's blow-dry when Max came into the Upper Cut.

"There's your husband," Joan said.

"Is that who that is?" Darla said. *Shut up, Joan*.

"You been gone so long you probably forgot," Joan said.

"There you go," Darla said, shutting off the dryer before the back of Joan's head was completely done. Let her walk around like that for awhile.

"You and that Quinn aren't fooling anybody," Joan said as she got up. "We all heard the rumors, and Corrie Gerber said that Quinn admitted it right here in this chair."

"Admitted what?" Darla said, but then Max was there, saying, "I need to talk to you," and she walked to the break room with him following her while Joan watched them, avid for news to spread.

Max closed the door behind them. "How long are you going to pull this crap?"

"Which crap?" Darla said. "Living with Quinn instead of you? Until you give me a good reason to come home."

"Well, I've got one for you," Max said. "There's a rumor going around that you and Quinn are sleeping together."

Darla laughed. She couldn't help it, he looked so indignant. "So are you afraid we are, or disappointed we aren't?"

"It's not funny." Max glared at her. "You're making me a laughingstock."

"I don't see how," Darla said. "You should be getting a lot of sympathy. I bet those cookies are just piling up over there."

Max's face got red. "You really think I'd cheat on you? You really do?"

"No," Darla said. "But I really think you still don't get it." He looked so unhappy she wanted to put her arms around him,

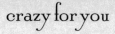

but that would just get her back where she'd been. "We need a change, Max. We need to really look at each other again, take risks again, remember what it was like to really live again. If I come home, it'll be like it always was, and I can't stand that." She stopped, knowing from the look on his face that he wasn't getting it, that he was getting angrier instead. "Forget it." She turned back to the door. "Just forget it."

"Look, just tell me what you want and you can have it," he said, his voice tired with exasperation.

"If I tell you, it doesn't mean anything," Darla said. "It isn't anything specific. I just need you to realize that we're turning to stone and we're not even in our forties yet. I tried to do something different, and you wouldn't pay attention. Now you try something. Surprise me. Prove to me we're still alive."

"I have no idea what the hell you're talking about," he said.

"Well, that's why I'm sleeping with Quinn instead of you," Darla said.

LATE THAT AFTERNOON, Nick bent over Marcy Benbow's Jeep and thought about Quinn. And sex. He wasn't comfortable with the two ideas in the same sentence, but he couldn't get them out of his mind. So maybe he could talk her into doing it once, so they could get it out of their systems and go back to where they'd been before. One shot, that's all he wanted. One chance to rip that underwear off her and roll her over and then back to the good old days like before. One fast forbidden fuck, and then—

Out front, a car door slammed and Barbara Niedemeyer walked toward the station door. She'd driven in her mom's Camry this time, which made sense since they'd fixed everything on her own car. Nick ducked under the hood of the Jeep, planning on being too busy to talk. Ever since he'd paid the rest of Quinn's deposit, Barbara had been beaming at him equally with

Max. She was a nice woman, but not one he wanted anything to do with. Especially since his mind was full of Quinn and—

"Nick," she said, and he jumped because she'd drifted right up next to him. Damn woman moved like a cat. "I have to talk to you."

"Sure thing," he said and straightened.

"Quinn knows about the loan." Barbara looked guilty and delighted at the same time. "She asked where the money came from, and I had to tell her. I couldn't help it."

"It's okay," he said, and thought, *Hell*.

"She was a little upset," Barbara said, and Nick winced. "But she was okay by the time we were done with lunch."

"Good," he said. "Well, thanks." He nodded his good-bye and bent back under the hood hoping she'd leave, but just then Max came out of the office.

"Bringing your mom's car in this time?" he called to Barbara jovially.

"I'm worried," she said as she went over to him and handed him the keys. "She's not getting any younger, and I want to make sure her car is safe."

"Not a problem," Max said. He filled out the work order, chatting as he wrote, and Nick stopped working on Marcy's car when he realized that Max was taking his time, not trying to get rid of her.

No, he thought. *Oh, hell, Max, don't do this*.

"So how you getting home?" Max said when he'd put the key and work order in the office.

"It's not that far," Barbara said. "It's nice out today. I can walk."

"I'll take you home," Max said.

"We got a lot of work here," Nick said loudly from behind the Jeep.

"Dinner break," Max said. "You hungry, Barbara?"

Oh, shit.

"I did have a light lunch," Barbara said, her voice full of delight.

"How about the Anchor Inn?" Max said. "You've been giving us a lot of work. Only fair for me to buy you dinner."

"Could I see you for *just a minute*?" Nick said.

"I'll wait in the car," Barbara said, and smiled at them both before she went out.

"Don't start with me," Max said to Nick.

Nick glared at him from behind the Jeep. "You are a fucking moron. Darla's going to rip you in half, and that's if you're lucky, because otherwise, she's going to leave your ass cold, and then where will you be?"

"Right where I am now," Max said mulishly. "She doesn't take care of what she's got, she's gonna lose it."

"Maybe that's the reason you lost yours, you butthead." Nick slammed the hood of the Jeep down. "When was the last time you took Darla to the Anchor Inn?"

"She left me because she wasn't getting bad lobster?" Max shook his head. "That's crap."

"Well, what was she getting?" Nick leaned against the Jeep, a lot more upset than he wanted to be. "If I had a wife like Darla who met me naked at the door, I wouldn't be dating Bank Barbie. But you, no, you sit down and watch football tapes with me while she locks herself in the bedroom. What the hell was that all about, anyway?"

Max turned away. "I got to go now."

"She probably cut her damn hair so you'd pay some attention to her," Nick called after him. "Then you go to Bo's. You're fucking up here, you dumbass."

Max turned at the door. "So why did Quinn cut hers, smart guy? I don't see you doing real good, either."

"Quinn is a friend," Nick said.

"You are a jackass," Max said and went out to meet Barbara.

IT WAS ALL Quinn could do to keep her mind on the play tech that night. She was definitely going over to Nick's after practice to thank him. Even if she hadn't decided he was her ticket to excitement, she'd have had to go thank him. That was reasonable.

Maybe she'd go braless.

On the other side of the stage, something fell over with a crash, and she shoved Nick out of her mind and crossed to check out the new disaster. Jason and Corey were setting up the cardboard tube trees the Art Ones had painted, and she got there in time to see Corey pick up a tree trunk and hear him say, "That Thea. She's something. How'd I come to miss her?"

"You're still missing her." Jason centered the dented trunk on the wheeled platform they'd be rolling it around on and began to bolt it down. "Forget her."

"You going there?" Corey said.

"Nope. Not my type."

Jason, you jerk. He was Nick all over again.

"Everything okay here?" Quinn asked.

"Just fine." Jason shoved his hand into the trunk to push the dent out.

"Okay," Quinn said and retreated to test the trees they'd already bolted. She was still within earshot when Corey looked back at Thea, bending over to hand one of the techies some duct tape at the edge of the stage, and said, "She's my type. Look at that butt."

"No," Jason said, still tightening. "Not your type."

Corey looked at him exasperated. "If she's not yours, she can be mine."

"She's nobody's." Jason stood up. "Check out the second stepsister. She's in our chem class. You missed her, too."

"Which one?"

"The one with the big—"

"Got it." Corey took another look at Thea.

"No," Jason said. "Go ask the chem for help with your labs. You need it."

Corey shrugged and said, "Whatever," and went over to the chem.

She looked amazed and delighted to see him.

"You want to tell me what that was all about?" Quinn said, coming out from behind the tree.

"Nope." Jason picked up the tech plan to take it to Thea.

"She's allowed to go out, you know," Quinn said.

"Not with Corey," Jason said, and they both jumped when Bill said, "Quinn?" from behind them.

"Hey, Coach," Jason said, and immediately crossed the stage to Thea.

Subtle, Quinn thought, and turned to face Bill.

"I thought maybe I could help," he told her. "You know, an extra pair of hands."

"No," Quinn said, putting as much finality into the word as she could.

"Quinn, we need to be together." Bill smiled at her, the same old smile that always said *I know best*, and Quinn felt her temper spurt.

"I can't make this any clearer," she said. "I don't care if you start rumors about Jason and me—"

"*I didn't,*" Bill said, outraged.

"—I don't care what you do, we are not together and we're not going to be."

"I didn't start that rumor," Bill said. "I swear—"

"I believe you," Quinn said. "That was the BP, I'll give you that. But no more of this. Leave me alone. Go."

He started to say something and then shrugged. "Maybe later," he said, and she gritted her teeth as he trailed off the stage, making her feel guilty and then angry because she felt guilty. It wasn't her fault. She was allowed to leave a man she didn't want.

And seduce one she did.

At nine that night, after the last kid was gone and she'd checked the stage door to make sure it was locked, Quinn took off her bra and drove to Nick's apartment, feeling cold and queasy from nerves and lack of underwear, still not quite sure what she was going to say to him—she'd rehearsed a hundred different conversations but none of them had seemed anything but desperate—and hoping the lack of support under her sweater might make a lot of conversation unnecessary anyway.

She climbed the stairs at the back of the station to his door, and when he opened it and looked startled to see her, she just said, "I heard about the bank loan," and pushed her way past him, praying he'd give up and jump her fast so she could get past the nervous part.

"That was no big deal," Nick said, but when she turned to face him, he'd shut the door and was looking fairly tense.

"It was Bill," she said. "He went behind my back to screw it up."

"That's what I figured."

"And then you went behind my back to fix it," she said. "Pretty patriarchal of you, wasn't it?"

"What?" He looked a little confused. "You're mad?"

"Not really." Quinn wandered over to the bookcase so she wouldn't have to look at him because he looked so good, tall and relaxed, his shirt open at the neck. He was barefoot, too, and that seemed amazingly sexy.

What were they talking about? The loan. "I'd just like to know what's going on in my own finances," she said, trying to keep her voice even. "Instead of having the two of you duke it out behind my back."

"It was more sneaking around behind your back," Nick said. "Which isn't that hard to do since I haven't seen you much."

Her heart lurched a little at that; he sounded annoyed. Maybe he'd missed her. "The play's taking up our time," Quinn said. "It's going to be wonderful. Edie—"

"Want a drink?"

Quinn nodded.

He wasn't throwing her out. He was plying her with liquor. These were good signs. While he went to get the Chivas, she flipped through his CDs, her hands shaking a little, looking for something vaguely seductive, something that wasn't "Bolero." When she found Fleetwood Mac's *Greatest Hits*, she slipped that in the player. It had worked at her place. If only she had her mother's couch here—

"Rhiannon" started, and Quinn flinched and hit the "up" button until she got to "Hold Me." There was a great song. Catchy title. She turned to see Nick stopped in the doorway to the kitchen, a drink in each hand, a funny expression on his face.

"What?" she said, walking toward him to get her drink.

"Interesting choice in music," he said. "So, you mad or not?"

He watched her seriously, meeting her eyes, and she felt her breath go because he looked so good, lean and dark and dangerous. She was almost afraid to make love with him, he was so different from anybody she'd ever slept with, but she was more afraid not to. She'd been missing out long enough.

"I'm not mad," she said. "I'm grateful. I love the house. Thank you. I'm going to pay you back, of course, but thank you."

"You're welcome."

His eyes were still on hers, and the more he looked at her, the warmer she felt. But he was looking at her a lot, and that made her uneasy, too. She sipped her Chivas, trying to think of a nice topic of conversation. The weather had been good lately. Maybe—

"So why are you here?"

Quinn choked on her Chivas and then swallowed, wiping her mouth on the back of her hand. "To say thank you." His eyes were intent on her, watching her, predatory, not like he'd ever looked at her before. Even the time he'd kissed her, he'd been more reluctant than anything else. Something had changed. He wasn't reluctant any more.

So maybe this wasn't a good time. She could be reckless another day when he didn't look so much like a serial killer. "Well, now that I've said thanks—"

She handed the Chivas back to him and he put it on the bookshelf, still watching her, half amused now because she was flustered.

"—I'll just be going." She looked up at him again, at his lovely hot eyes on hers over his glass, smug. She waited until he was drinking and then said, "Actually, I came to sleep with you."

Nick choked on his Chivas.

Good. "But of course, you're not interested—"

"Once." Nick put his glass down a lot faster than she'd ever seen him move before.

She felt the ground tilt under her. "What?"

"Just once, to get it out of the way." Nick sounded completely reasonable, as if he were telling her to get teeth checked twice a year. "That way we can both stop thinking about it."

Once, to get it out of the way.

So much for the great affair that would make her exciting. She opened her mouth and closed it again, trying to think of a witty and urbane way to tell him to go stuff himself and his little one-night stand, too. "So you've been thinking about it, have you?"

"Hell, yes." He leaned against the bookcase so sure of himself she wanted to smack him. "So have you."

"Once, to get it out of the way, huh?" Quinn's voice shook a little with rage. Over her dead body. No, over *his*, the bastard. "That's your plan?" She glared at him. "Who the *fuck* do you think you are?"

"I think I'm the fuck you want," Nick said, and when she swung on him, he ducked under her arm and caught her to him, taking her mouth with his so completely that she stopped swinging to enjoy the heat and shudder he kissed into her, so relieved to finally have his arms around her.

Then she pulled away and said, "I'm furious with you," and he said, "You'll still say yes," and pulled her back and kissed her again, sliding his hand under her sweater, moving his hands hard over her breasts and making her moan while she grappled with sanity.

The problem was the pleasure, she decided as she tried to get her mind out of the gutter. He was acting like a twit instead of Nick, all superior and macho, but he had beautiful hands, and he was finally really kissing her, kissing her stupid for that matter, his hands so hot on her that she shuddered and twisted, and when he slipped his tongue in her mouth she gave up and leaned into him.

"The bedroom is this way," he said when they came up for air.

She said, "We're still going to have that fight," and he said, "Later," and she thought, *Right. Later.*

eleven

NICK PULLED her onto the bed and rolled her under him, and the weight of him was so erotic that she wrapped herself around him and arched up into him. She could make him pay for that "I'm the fuck you want" crack later; right now she just needed him. He yanked her sweater up over her head and then kissed her hard on the lips, licked her throat, found her breast and drove her crazy, pushing her toward a hot darkness, a place she'd never been before because she'd never been with anybody like Nick before, the dangerous kind of guy, the kind of guy who'd say, "I'm the fuck you want," which turned her on and made her want to kill him all at once, the kind of guy who made a woman mindless—

Almost.

There was a part of her that wasn't cooperating, that was still a little mind-whacked that she was with Nick, that wouldn't give up hanging on to reason, that wouldn't give up *thinking*. His mouth would move on her breast, and she'd go under, loving it, squirming under him as the dark closed in, and then she'd remember, *wait a minute, this is Nick*, and she'd feel herself break through the surface *do I really want to do this? the hassle could be enormous*, and then he'd suck harder, or bite her shoulder, or yank her zipper down—*oh, god, that feels good*—and she'd go under, mindless until logic would pop her to the surface again, *are we sure about this? is this something I'll regret?* After half an hour, she felt like a fishing float. What did they call them? Bobbers, that was it. She felt like a—

Nick slid his hand into her underpants and she went under again, only to bob up again in a minute when he shifted to yank her jeans down.

Okay, I'm pretty sure this is what I want, it's why I came over here, but Zoë is going to kill me—

Actually Zoë wasn't her problem, it was this concentration thing: lust or logic, lust or logic. If she didn't get her mind around one or the other soon, she was going to go crazy from carnal whiplash.

She really wanted the logic, she decided as Nick tugged her jeans down past her knees, the part of her that could step back and say coolly, "Well, he's a little rough, but he seems to know his way around a vulva," the part that wouldn't go into the dark beckoning void she started to slide toward if she wasn't thinking. It wasn't as if she hadn't had sex before, it wasn't as if she hadn't had orgasms before, plenty of them, lovely little vanilla orgasms, and now there was Nick and he seemed to be dealing in dark chocolate and she just wasn't sure she was the dark chocolate *type* and if not—

Nick licked her stomach and went lower, and she let her head roll back and dumped logic for a minute. Then she shoved his head away so she could kick her feet free of her jeans without braining him, and he stripped off his shirt and pants, and they were naked. He was gorgeous, lovely and lean and loosely muscled, reaching for her—

"Well, this is different for us," she told him brightly, trying to be urbane and cope with the situation as he rolled against her.

Oh, hell, we're naked.

"Different, fine," he said, his voice husky and his eyes unfocused, and he pulled her close on top of him—all that hair on his chest where Bill had been smooth—and slid his hand down her stomach so that her mind flipped and flopped—*lovely hands, really*—slid his hand between her thighs so that she lost a good five minutes just moving against him—*yes, there*—his fingers slipping inside her—*don't stop*—he rolled on top of her, the stroke and the pressure of his hand dragging her under again—

This is Nick, logic said. *Isn't this interesting? Note the differences from the other times—*

She felt him lean across her, his weight squashing the air out her lungs—*not very erotic*—and then realized he was going for a condom in the bed table drawer—*there, see, a gentleman—*

And then he spread her legs with his hips, his hand slipping between them, making her crazy, mindless again, his fingers finally parting her—*wait a minute*—and then he was inside her, and she arched under him because it was so good being filled like that, solid, hard, and full, arched to take all of him she could, digging her nails into his shoulders because he felt so amazingly good.

He said something, choked it out, and she couldn't hear through the haze of heat, but the sound of his voice was enough to get her mind back.

Am I doing this right?

He thrust harder inside her and she fell into him again and then climbed back out—*let's not lose our heads here*—then he moved again and she went back to heat and shudder and rhythm—his rhythm—*I think I'm off a beat, if he'd slow down, I could catch up, it's sort of a rumba*—She'd never had second thoughts like this before in bed, but she'd never been this terrified and bedazzled, either. A woman could lose control doing this. Imagine the problems that could lead to.

Nick moved higher up her body and rocked into her, and she lost herself again, only to reel herself back because she should be doing something productive, surely he was used to more, all those agile twentysomethings he'd dated, *and I could stand to lose a few pounds, too, well, ten, not a few*—

He slid out of her, and she clutched at him, but he kissed her hard, then moved down to take her breast just as hard, then moved lower to bite her stomach and lick into her—*so wet,* she thought, *why would he want*—and then his tongue found her and she writhed under the shock, his hands held her hips in place and she couldn't bring her mind back any more, he was too much, and she moved into the tension he was building, crying out mindlessly as the dark loomed in front of her. She was going to fall if he didn't stop—*don't stop*—and then he did, and she reeled herself back, grateful and disappointed until he slid up her body again and plunged into her hard. He rocked into her, saying *yes* in her ear, not gloating at all—*Oh, God, Quinn*, he said—and made her clutch inside, made her twist against him, and she caught herself once more—*what are you doing? you're out of control*—before he ripped her back down to his darkness, his hand rough on her face, his eyes black from being tight inside her. He said, *"Come on!"* through clenched teeth, and she looked into his eyes and he was *Nick*, and that was all she needed to break under him, shocked and startled, fast and sharp and hard.

Then he collapsed against her, and she clutched him as she tried to remember how to breathe. He slid off her body, letting his hand slip across her stomach where he'd been, down between her legs so she moaned, up to her breast so she rolled to feel the pressure. Then he leaned over and kissed her breast—she curled into him—and then her mouth—he tasted hot and strange and delicious—and then she let her mind come back permanently while he rolled over on his back beside her.

"My God," Quinn said.

Oh. HELL. NICK thought.

It was hard to feel depressed after good sex, but he was managing it. It had been a great idea, sleep with her once, kill the magic, go to work the next morning a new man, free of all those stupid fantasies once he knew that she was just like all the other women, lovely, fun, worthwhile, but still one of a series, women who'd slept with Nick Ziegler.

Except she was still a mystery, and he wanted her again.

Get out of this bed, he told himself, but his hand went to her anyway, she was so hot and round, and he raised himself up on his elbow, so tired it took all his energy just to look.

She didn't look like Quinn, not with short tousled hair, not naked and flushed with sex, not curled next to him mindless and sated. She looked exotic and erotic, she radiated heat, she was the kind of woman every man wanted to fuck, and he wanted her again. He studied her body, trying to make her ordinary, gauged the slope of her breast, noted the faint appendix scar on the swell of her stomach, measured the thickness of her hips, not a perfect body, not unless you wanted to sink into those hips, not unless you wanted a woman who was lush with flesh, hot and strong and giving. He slid his hand down her stomach so he could watch her arch and moan like any woman—*Make her real*, he thought, *make her like anyone else*—but she blushed and curled toward him instead, covering her breasts with her arm, using her thigh to push away his hand, modest after everything they'd done, and he wasn't tired any more.

"Nope," he said and pulled her arm away. He bent to take her breast in his mouth, felt her nipple harden on his tongue, the heat from her body on his hand, and she was so soft as she shuddered under his touch that he tightened his hand on her to feel her flesh mound between his fingers. He slid his hand down her back, bumping over vertebrae as he sucked and made her sigh, curved down to the round fullness of her butt, pulled her close to touch her everywhere, all his fantasies made flesh, wanting her under him and open again, wanting her soft and round and wet and moaning. He kissed her hard, stroked down her

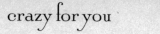

stomach, slipped his hand between her legs, and looked at her and looked at her and looked at her, taking her all over again with his eyes.

"You're staring," she whispered, and grabbed at his hand, trying to pretend she wasn't dizzy and only looking dizzier because she was pretending. Confused by the heat, she was gloriously vulnerable and absolutely his.

"I get to stare," he said. "It's my bed. I get you any way I want." He thought about rolling her over, pushing against her firm butt, cupping her full breasts from behind; about pulling her down to straddle him on the end of the bed, impaling her while he took her breasts with his mouth; about going down on her, licking into her, tasting how hot and wet and sweet she was, driving her mindless—

She leaned up suddenly and kissed him, surprising him as she slipped her tongue into his mouth, and then she pushed him down onto his back and pinned him to the bed, all soft flesh and searching hands, biting his lip, moving against him. When he laughed and looked up at her, suddenly she looked like Quinn again, only Quinn transformed, her eyes dilated with lust, her mouth bruised and red because he'd taken it so hard so many times, Quinn looking debauched, like she'd been thoroughly had, done, laid, screwed, bit, sucked, and fucked—

"Jesus, you're beautiful," he said and took her mouth, her body hot under his hands, his hands tight on her flesh, full of her flesh, *this is mine*, wanting to make her part of him, take her, claim her, absorb her, invade her, *keep her*—

He stopped, his breath rasping, appalled at the way he wanted her and wanting her anyway. Keep her?

Get out.

He closed his eyes so he wouldn't see what he was giving up and rolled his hips to tip her off and then rolled the other way to sit on the edge of the bed. "I'm starving," he said, reaching for his pants, trying to keep his voice from shaking. "How about a pizza?"

Quinn struggled to sit up, ungainly in her surprise, still coming back from the heat. It took everything he had not to jump her again.

"Pizza?" she said, disbelieving, and he tossed her sweater to her so he wouldn't have to look at how amazing she was naked.

"We burned up a lot of fuel," he said, making his voice chipper. "Any preferences?"

"Preferences." She sat there naked with the sweater in her lap, and he turned away from her so he wouldn't have any more stupid thoughts.

"Pepperoni, mushroom—"

"I'm not hungry," she said flatly.

"Well, I am." He escaped into the living room, shoving all naked memories of her away, and tried to figure out how the hell he was going to get her out of his apartment. Maybe he could send her out for pizza and then move. That would be right up there with the rest of his bright ideas lately.

But when she came out fully dressed five minutes later, she picked up her coat without prompting.

"I'm going to go now," she said, "but I have to tell you, your finish needs work. Really lousy, Ziegler."

He was torn between feeling insulted and feeling relieved. "Hey, you came."

"I was being polite," she snapped, and stomped out the door.

"You were not," he yelled after her. He'd felt her give under him, felt her arch and shudder and go soft till there wasn't anything left in her, and he'd had to work damn hard to get her there, too. He tried to feel aggrieved, but all he could feel was how great it had been to work that hard on Quinn's body.

Quinn's body.

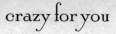

"The hell with it," he said, and went to shower and change his sheets, determined to get her completely out of his apartment forever.

BILL SAT IN his car across the street from the service station and watched Quinn drive away. She'd been with Nick over an hour and he felt jealous, knowing they'd sat up there talking and laughing the way he'd seen them together a thousand times. Nick wasn't anything to worry about, he was just Nick, but the time he had with Quinn, inside with Quinn, Bill envied that. He'd sat outside the school while she'd finished practice, laughing and talking with the kids inside—he was sure she was laughing and talking—and then he'd followed her to Nick's and pictured them laughing and talking inside. It was so unfair that the closest he could get to her was outside in a car, waiting and watching, that was so unfair, he *hated it, hated it*—

He took a deep breath and rubbed his head which had started to ache again. Then he put the car in gear. He'd drive by her house to make sure she got home all right, home to her dad and Darla, home where she'd laugh and talk more, without him, but that was all right, because they'd be together soon.

He'd see to it.

WHEN ZOË ANSWERED the phone, Quinn took a deep breath, and said, "Why did you and Nick break up? You never wanted to talk about it, but I need to know."

"Because I left him," Zoë said. "Is he all right? Why do you keep asking about him?"

"He's fine." Quinn searched for a reason besides *I just slept with him and he got strange at the end. Is that normal?* "He just broke up with Lisa. That's like his twentieth girlfriend since you."

"Is he upset about it?" Zoë said.

Quinn thought back to Nick rolling hot on top of her. "Not so's you'd notice. I just wondered."

"It was a long time ago," Zoë said. "I told you, I think I married him to piss Mom off and get out of Tibbett. And he was fun until we ended up in Dayton, and he worked all the time and then just sort of vegged when he came home."

"Vegged?"

"You know, read, played ball with the guys, that stuff."

"He still does that," Quinn said. "He and Max have a hoop out back of the garage."

"Well, see." Zoë's voice sounded eminently reasonable. "I was pretty much there for sex, and I got bored. What is this about?"

"He only wanted you for sex?" Quinn hated saying it. For one thing, she didn't want to be reminded that he'd *had* sex with Zoë.

"No, that's the only thing I wanted him for. I don't know what he wanted me for. A wife, I guess." Her voice grew thoughtful. "Although he was never very possessive. It was more like I was just along for the ride. After three months, I made him take me home to see you and Mom, and I was so happy to be back in Tibbett that I knew something was wrong. When we went back to Dayton, I left. Couldn't take it anymore."

"Are you sorry?" Quinn asked, wanting absolution, wanting Zoë to say, *Take him, he's yours*.

"No. Is he?"

Quinn thought back to the few times he'd mentioned Zoë. He'd said her name without inflection, like anybody else's name, nothing special. "I don't think so. He doesn't seem like he's hiding anything."

Zoë's laugh snorted over the line. "Then he isn't. Nick couldn't hide anything if he tried. What you see with Nick is what you get."

Quinn had a sudden sharp image of Nick lean and naked beside her. "Okay."

"He was fun, just no zazz." Zoë didn't sound broken-hearted, and then her voice faded as she turned away from the phone to say, "Yes, you have zazz. That's why you've got me."

Quinn heard the rumble of Ben's voice and then Zoë laughed, and she felt a twinge of envy. It must be wonderful to live with a man you loved and who loved you, the way Ben and Zoë lived. "How did you know Ben was the one?" she asked suddenly. "How were you so sure? You just met him at work, how did you know?"

"I didn't really meet him at work," Zoë said. "I mean, I told you and Mom that, but actually, he picked me up in a fountain."

"What?"

"There was this fountain outside our building." Zoë sounded embarrassed. "And I went out there one day, really depressed because I was almost thirty, and I was never going to have kids, and I wanted them, and because I was wearing a suit and being normal instead of, well, you know—"

"Instead of being Zoë," Quinn said, knowing exactly.

"And I took off my shoes and pantyhose and went wading in the fountain because that's what I would have done before I got to be a suit, and I didn't even know Ben was there until he said, 'You have great legs.' He was sitting on the other side of the fountain with his pants rolled up and his feet in the water, looking at me through those horn-rim glasses, and I thought he was trying to pick me up, so I shut him down. And he said, no, it was just a scientific observation because he was happily married and the father of a fine son named Harold—"

"You're kidding me," Quinn said.

"—and I told him only a sadist would name a kid Harold, that my daughter was Jeannie and she was the star of her ballet class—"

"This is *great*," Quinn said.

"I know," Zoë said. "I felt like me again. And then we told each other about how great our spouses were, and somewhere in there I realized he was lying in his teeth, and I told him I was actually a Russian spy with a license to kill, and he said, 'I've always wanted to have sex in the afternoon with a Russian spy with a license to kill,' and I said what a shame it was that he was married to such a wonderful woman or we certainly *could* have had sex, and he said 'She left me,' so we spent five days in a suite at the Great Southern and then eloped to Kentucky."

"What?"

"Yeah," Zoë said. "That's why I told you we met at work and we'd known each other a long time. Dumb, huh?"

"It's wonderful," Quinn said. "No wonder you don't miss Nick."

"Hey, Nick was a good guy," Zoë said. "Just not the right guy. Why are you asking about him so much anyway?"

"I've just been thinking about the way we used to be," Quinn said truthfully. "Who we all were back then. Who we are now."

"Yeah, well, I bet Nick's the same now as he was then. Guys don't change. Nick was always sports, cars, and sex."

That sounded like Nick.

"Not that that was bad; I just got so tired of Fleetwood Mac I was ready to scream—"

Quinn went cold. "What?"

"Fleetwood Mac. He liked to fuck to Fleetwood Mac, and I will bet you a nickel he still does. Ask Lisa. I bet she's heard 'The Chain' so many times she can come to it without him."

"I'll kill him," Quinn said.

"What?"

Well, there she was. One of a series brought to you by Nick Ziegler. Music by Fleetwood Mac. The bastard.

"Quinn?"

He'd even pulled it out of her CD stack that night after Meggy and Edie had left. Making his move, changing his mind. She'd put it on. He'd kissed her because of Fleetwood Mac and stopped kissing her because of her hair. Then she'd cut her hair and—"I'm going to kill him."

"You slept with him." Zoë's voice was flat.

"Yep." The more Quinn thought about it, the more her blood boiled.

"Well."

"Well, what?" Quinn said, ready to fight with anybody.

"Well, nothing. Except that you slept with my ex-husband, and you're my sister, and we sound like one of Jerry Springer's greatest hits."

"I thought you didn't care who he slept with."

"I don't." Zoë sounded a little surprised. "I care who you sleep with, though."

"Well, you can stop caring because I'm never sleeping with anybody ever again." Quinn thought of Nick naked and hot on top of her, and shoved the thought aside. "Never."

"It was that bad?"

"No." Quinn tried not to think about it. "I just can't believe he used Fleetwood Mac on me, too. He kissed me halfway through 'Hold Me' and had me naked by 'You Make Lovin' Fun.'"

"I don't think we ever made it to 'You Make Lovin' Fun,'" Zoë said. "That was at the end of the album. He didn't last that long. I'm not kidding about 'The Chain.' If I hadn't made it by then, I wasn't going to because he was done."

"He's changed," Quinn told her. "'Hold Me' was on its second play by the time I came. I don't believe this."

"I don't remember 'Hold Me' at all," Zoë said. "The *Rumours* album, right?"

"They've made a few others since you were eighteen," Quinn said. "This was the *Greatest Hits*."

"And I imagine he's been making a few with it, too," Zoë said. "He was always good at taking girls to bed. The rat bastard."

"He still is," Quinn said. "I'm so mad I could spit."

"I can't believe he seduced my little sister," Zoë said. "He was always sex-crazed, but I thought he'd have *matured*—"

"I seduced him," Quinn said.

"What?"

"I went over to his place so he'd take me to bed." Quinn felt stupid saying it. "I wanted to know what it would be like. So I went over and propositioned him."

"Oh." Zoë regrouped. "So why are you mad at him? I mean, I'm mad at him because you're mad at him, but now I don't know why you're mad at him. Was it bad?"

"I thought I was different." Quinn felt like a fool while she was saying it.

"You probably were until you went to bed with him," Zoë said. "You have to be the only woman he was ever close to that he'd never seen naked. Besides his mother and Darla."

"Thank you," Quinn said. "That makes me feel so much better."

"In fact, he was probably closer to you than anybody he'd ever seen naked. He was never very good at combining emotion and sex. Don't expect a lot of phone calls discussing the relationship."

"I can't believe I was so dumb," Quinn said.

"Tell me again why you did this," Zoë said. "Because for the life of me, I can't figure it out."

Because he's darling. Because he's sexy. Because I trust him. "Because I wanted to be like you, I think. Exciting instead of just . . . there."

Zoë didn't say anything for so long, Quinn thought they might have lost the connection. "Zoë?"

"I'm thinking. What happened all of a sudden? You never wanted to be me before. You left Bill, you slept with Nick. What's with you?"

"I don't know. I just wanted . . . different."

"Well, you got it. You want me to come home for a while?"

"No." Quinn sighed. "What can you do? I'll get this figured out."

"Well, I can castrate Nick with a dull spoon. I told him once I'd do it if he ever touched you, so he's probably expecting me."

Quinn sat up straighter. "What do you mean, you told him once?"

"I caught him looking at you. You were just a baby and he had that look in his eye. I couldn't believe it."

"How old a baby?"

"We were married. We'd just come home and—"

"Sixteen," Quinn said. "Nineteen years ago. He waits nineteen years, and then he plays Fleetwood Mac."

"You may be taking this too hard," Zoë said. "It's just sex, not death. Unless you're hooked."

"I'm not hooked," Quinn said, fairly sure she was telling the truth. "I just thought the sex would be exciting, and I wanted some exciting sex before I died."

"Wasn't it?"

"I don't know," Quinn said. "I was trying to figure out what the hell was going on most of the time and then all of a sudden I was coming. It seemed so unlike me to be doing that with Nick."

Zoë's laugh cackled through the line. "Sounds great. Not."

"Toward the end it was," Quinn said, trying not to sound wistful. "Shortly after 'No Questions Asked' it approached excellence. Then he got hungry for pizza, and the whole thing went to hell."

"You sure you don't want me to come home?"

"Positive," Quinn said. "I can handle this. I have dull spoons of my own."

"Let me know," Zoë said.

"Oh, yeah," Quinn said. "I'll keep you posted."

"SO HOW WAS your hot date with Barbara?" Nick asked Max when he came into work the next morning.

Max snarled at him and went into the office.

"You're number four, you know," Nick called after him, needing to spread his own misery. "Pretty soon Barbara's going to have get one of those number things like they have at Baskin-Robbins. Now serving."

He heard Max slamming drawers and felt about as pleased as he could for how pissed off he was.

"You guys can form a club," Nick went on, talking at the top of his lungs. "The Promise Breakers. You can stand up at the beginning and say, 'I'm Max and I'm a—'"

"You got a reason for busting my chops on this?" Max said, standing in the door to the office.

"Yeah." Nick folded his arms and leaned against the work-bench. "I do. I like Darla."

"I don't," Max said.

"The hell you don't," Nick said. "If you didn't care, you wouldn't be this damn mad. And you wouldn't have pulled that jackass stunt last night."

"I didn't sleep with her," Max said. "I took her home right after the Mud Pie. She's the most boring woman I've ever met."

"That's because you've been living with Darla for all these years," Nick said. "She sets a high standard."

"Fuck off," Max said and went back into the office, and that was the last voice Nick heard until Quinn walked into the garage three hours later.

"FLEETWOOD MAC," QUINN said and watched with satisfaction as Nick raised his head up from the Honda he was working on so fast he smacked himself on the edge of the hood.

"What?" He rubbed his head and looked at her across the car. "Don't sneak up on me like that. Where'd you come from? Why aren't you at school?"

"I signed out," Quinn said. "I'm on my lunch break. Don't change the subject. You did me to Fleetwood Mac."

Nick looked over his shoulder and then came around the car to take her arm. "Could we talk about this over here, please?"

When they were in the back of the garage, Quinn said, "I thought I was different."

"You are different," Nick said. "What are we talking about? Different from what?"

"Different from all the other women you've—" Quinn struggled to find a word that wasn't gross or bland.

"You are different from all the other women I've." Nick sounded grim. "Which is one of the reasons I didn't for so long."

"Well, it's so good to finally be one of the club," Quinn said.

"What the hell are you talking about?" Nick frowned at her. "You knew I wasn't a virgin. Why are you so bent?"

Quinn swallowed, trying to keep her voice firm. "You did Zoë to Fleetwood Mac, too."

"Hell, I do everybody to Fleetwood Mac," Nick said, and then he winced and said, "Let me put that another way." Then the other shoe dropped. "You told Zoë?"

"Dumb me, I thought I was different, not just one of a series," Quinn said. "I can't believe this."

"I can't, either." Nick scowled at her. "You're mad because I like to do it to the Mac? Swell. Pick another group. I'm flexible. You're the one who put it on the stereo." He sounded sarcastic, not apologetic. "I can't believe you told Zoë."

The last thing she needed was sarcasm.

"You're very flexible," Quinn said. "Zoë mentioned that when we talked. You also seem to have developed staying powers."

He scowled at her. "I was eighteen when I was with her, cut me a break."

"Aside from that," Quinn went on with savage cheerfulness, "according to our comparisons, you haven't changed much."

Nick closed his eyes. "I don't want anything to do with this."

"Well, you should have thought of that before you turned on the stereo, you jerk." Quinn glared at him. "I can't believe I was just like the others."

"You weren't just like the others," Nick said. "You're still not. None of them ever creeped me out like you're doing."

"Wait a minute—"

"Also, you're the one who turned on the stereo, not me, babe." Nick folded his arms. "You were the one who cut your hair and came up with no bra and put 'Hold Me' on."

"Oh, this is my fault." Quinn fought back the urge to pick up a wrench and deck him with it, mostly because he was right. If she'd stayed out of that apartment—

"And then you had to call Zoë," Nick said. "She's probably sharpening her scissors now." He leaned against the car and crossed his arms. "You know, it's just dawned on me. This isn't about me at all."

"The hell it isn't," Quinn said, indignation making her voice rise.

"This is about you wanting to be Zoë." He looked at her grimly. "That night on the couch, you said you wanted to be like Zoë. The only reason you slept with me is because Zoë did."

"That's not true," Quinn said, pretty sure it wasn't. "I really wanted you. And you really wanted me, too, damn it." When he just shook his head as if he was disgusted at her, she said, "Fine. I just wanted you to know that that was it. Never again."

"Fine," Nick said, and Quinn felt the word like a stab.

"Glad to see you're taking it so well," she said. "I really changed your life, didn't I?"

"You were fun," Nick said. "A lot of hard work, but fun. But I don't need this kind of hassle, and I sure don't need to be your ticket to Zoë."

He half-turned to go back to the car, and Quinn kicked him hard. *"Hey!"* he said, nursing his shin as he turned back to her.

"That's just until I can find a dull spoon," she said, and stomped out.

NICK WATCHED HER go and tried to feel good about it as he rubbed his shin. She had a kick like a mule. There was a good thing: he wouldn't be getting kicked again. Another benefit: he wouldn't wake up alone and remember that he'd fucked his best friend. And he wouldn't remember how much he'd enjoyed it, either, taking her like that, making her want him, making her come when she'd been fighting it, watching her move because of what he was doing to her—

No, it was a *damn* good thing Quinn had called it off because that meant he didn't have to. His lucky day.

"What was that about?" Max said from behind him.

"Not much." Nick straightened and limped back to the car.

"I don't think I've ever seen her that mad." Max sounded pleased.

"And you never will again," Nick said.

"Am I missing something good?"

"No," Nick said, and Max gave up and turned to go back to the office.

"Oh, hell," he said, and Nick looked up to see Barbara heading for the door.

"Go," he said, and Max escaped out the back door.

"Is Max here?" Barbara said thirty seconds later, poking her head around the door.

"He had to go out for a minute." Nick leaned against the car and really looked at Barbara as a possible woman for the first time. Medium height, slender, a little vague but not dumb. Clean and neat and pretty. A man could do worse, especially if by doing it he could save his brother and escape from two homicidal sisters. He wanted to say, "How do you feel about Fleetwood Mac?" but instead he put the hood on the Honda down and said, "I was just going to break for dinner. You busy?"

"Me?" Barbara blinked at him.

"Would you like to have dinner with me?" Nick said, gently because she was so taken aback. "I'll even spring for the Anchor Inn instead of a Big Mac."

"Oh." Barbara stood there, stuck as always.

"I fixed your heater." Maybe if she was grateful.

"What?"

"The one that stuck? I fixed it, not Max. Come have dinner to thank me." He smiled at her, the smile that usually made women smile back.

"You fixed my heater?"

"Right," Nick said, regretting ever starting the conversation.

"That was really nice, what you did for Quinn."

"What?" Nick said, startled. "Oh, the loan thing."

"Really nice." Barbara smiled. "Taking care of her like that. I'd love to have dinner."

"Terrific," Nick said, and wondered why if everything was going his way, he felt so lousy.

BILL STOOD ON the porch of the Apple Street house after school—he was never going to call it Quinn's and she wasn't going to be there much longer anyway—waiting for Quinn to answer the bell. He was happier than he'd been since she'd moved out, happier really than before she'd moved out, because his life was finally completely on track and he was really paying attention. Spring was in the air, they had a whole future to plan, everything was going to be—

The door swung open and Quinn stood there in a paint-stained chambray shirt, a two-inch paintbrush in her hand. She looked flushed and beautiful, and just for a moment she took his breath away and he wanted to touch her so much—

"Bill?"

"You look great," he said.

The damn dog came snuffling up and growled at him. "Quiet, Katie," Quinn said. She wasn't smiling at him at all. Well, that would change.

"Get your coat." He grinned at her, encouraging her to smile, too. "I have something to show you."

"Bill—" She stopped, looking at him as if she was angry. "I'm not in the mood for this. I've had a really bad day."

"It'll only take a minute." His grin widened. "This will turn your day around."

"I doubt it." She took a step back and began to close the door. "I have to go."

"Wait a minute." He put his hand against the door to hold it open. "You don't understand. I found us a house."

"You what?"

"I found us a house." This was going to be great. "It's in the development behind the school, walking distance from both the high school and the elementary. The kids'll have to ride the bus to junior high, but that's okay."

Quinn looked stunned. "What kids?"

"*Our* kids." He almost laughed, she looked so surprised. He'd just swept her right off her feet. "It's a great house. Four bedrooms, big backyard, huge basement—"

"Bill, we're not having any kids."

"—and wait'll you see the family room, the kids—"

"Bill!"

He stopped, jerked out of his plans by her scowl.

"We're not having any kids," she said. "And I'm not buying a house with you. I bought this one yesterday. You can buy that one, but I already bought this one. So we're not buying one together. We're not doing anything together." She stopped, and he could hear the blood pound in his ears. "I'm sorry, but I've told you over and over. We're not getting back together."

"How could you buy this house?" he said.

"Bill, I told you I was going to—"

"How did you get the loan?" he asked before he could stop himself, and she grew still.

"I had to put more money down," she said finally. "Was that your idea?"

There was something pressing on his chest, making it hard to breathe and hard to see, too, for some reason. "Quinn, you shouldn't be here alone," he began and then his mind went blank because he couldn't explain that it was for her own good, that he hadn't really done it, that she shouldn't hate him—

The damn dog nosed its way past her leg and began to bark at him.

"You screwed up my loan," she said over the dog's yapping. "You keep calling the city on me, you had Bobby threaten me with Jason, and you stole my dog *three times*—"

"No," he said, trying to make her listen.

"—Stay out of my life."

Quinn slammed the door and left him alone on her porch, trying to breathe in enough air so he could say the words that would bring her back, but his lungs just couldn't suck enough in.

It'll be all right, he told himself as his mind slid around the panic. It would be okay. So the new house was out, well, that was all right, maybe this house wouldn't be that bad. Really, it wasn't that bad. It was small, he didn't know how many bedrooms, but maybe they could build on. Yeah, that was it. They could build on.

He walked off the porch and around the side of the house to the gate to the backyard, walking carefully because he felt a little dizzy. The backyard wasn't huge, but it was big enough for the kids until they got to junior high age and then they'd be at the school most of the time anyway. Lots of room to run drills at the school. A small backyard here would mean less to mow. That was good. They could put an addition on, an extra bath and bedroom above, a family room below, and still have enough room for a deck. Not a problem. He should have been more flexible from the beginning. It was his fault. He should have listened to her. He felt much calmer. This house was fine.

He turned to go back toward the gate and saw movement in the kitchen. He moved closer to the side window and squinted through the lace curtain. It was hard to see because the light wasn't on inside, but he could make out Quinn at the sink, working her hands back and forth on something, probably the brush, probably cleaning the brush. He stood and watched for awhile as she bent over the sink, the curve of her bottom so familiar he felt as if he could reach out and pat her, just like he used to, except he never had, he realized. He wasn't a patter, Quinn hadn't seemed like a woman who wanted patted, but now he wanted to. He felt closer to her now than he had when he'd been with her, maybe because she didn't know he was there so she couldn't shut him out, couldn't make her eyes go blank the way she always did now when he tried to talk to her. He couldn't understand it; he was giving her so much time. When was she going to stop this and let him back in?

It started to rain, and when he looked up, Patsy Brady had come out to take in her crummy lawn furniture and was looking at him with interest. This is *ridiculous*, he told himself and ignored her to head back to the car. Anyone would think he'd lost Quinn. Things were going to be fine. He'd be patient and understanding and things would be fine. It wasn't as if he *couldn't* get in to her. He could get in any time.

He trudged back to the car, reminding himself to call Bucky and tell him the house hunt was off and thinking about packing his stuff for the move to Quinn's house. He probably wouldn't need all of it since she'd acquired some extra furniture, but a lot of that was hand-me-downs and junk that she might not want after he brought her their pine furniture from the apartment. They'd have to talk it over when he got ready to move.

Just thinking about talking things over with Quinn again made him feel better. He imagined their conversations all the way home.

"HEARD THE BANK Slut's dating your husband," Lois said in the break room of the Upper Cut the next day.

Darla's heart leaped to her throat, but she forced herself to lean back against the couch and say, "Did you now?" as if it didn't matter. *Max.*

"Took her to dinner Monday night," Lois said with smug satisfaction. "The Anchor Inn. She had lobster."

"Anybody who has lobster at the Anchor Inn deserves what she gets." Darla concentrated on keeping her breathing even. "So how's Matthew?"

Lois's satisfaction faded. "He's moved back in," she said, her chin in the air. "I'm taking him back."

"Good for you," Darla said. *You deserve each other.*

"We'll see," Lois said. "We'll just see how he acts." She didn't seem particularly pleased.

Quinn breezed in and pushed past her to sit in the armchair across from Darla. "Hey, Lois," she said. "What's new?"

"Matthew moved back in, and Max took Barbara to dinner," Darla said calmly, meeting Quinn's startled eyes without a flicker.

"Interesting," Quinn said, and shut up until Lois gave up and left. Then she said, "Max did what?"

"Lois said he took her to dinner Monday night." Darla swallowed. "Lobster at the Anchor Inn."

Quinn looked miserable. "He's trying to make you mad."

"It's working." Darla leaned forward to rearrange the magazines on the coffee table so she wouldn't see the sympathy in Quinn's eyes. "I thought he didn't like change."

"You want to go back to him?" Quinn asked.

"I can't." Darla dropped the magazines and slumped back. "What's changed? If I go back, things are going to be the same, and that's the reason I left." She felt misery rise like nausea in her throat. "If I go back, and Max doesn't have a clue why I left, he'll just think I've been a bitch and he'll never trust me again. If he doesn't see—"

"What if he never sees?" Quinn said. "Are you just going to wait forever?"

"Look who's talking," Darla snapped. "You're not doing anything, either."

"Well, actually, I did." Quinn looked miserable. "I slept with Nick last night."

"Oh. Damn." Darla regrouped. "So how was it?"

"It was strange," Quinn said. "Good strange until the end and then just strange. He's definitely not interested in a replay. It's over." She slumped a little. "Not that it ever really started."

"Oh, just hell," Darla said.

"Pretty much," Quinn said.

twelve

BILL DECIDED he really needed to see the interior of Quinn's house to plan the addition they needed. Which meant he had to go inside again. It was unavoidable. He had to.

The dog barked as he came in, so he picked up a bottle of window cleaner Quinn had left out—that was like her, careless—and sprayed it in the dog's eyes. The mutt shrieked and went under a chair, and Bill laughed and measured the kitchen, planning the addition, making notes in his pocket organizer. When he was done there, he went upstairs to make notes for the second-story part of the addition, his heart now pounding for some reason.

It was dimmer upstairs. The narrow hall had only one window and it looked out on the blank brick wall of the house next door. Five doors off the hall. Too many. Too crowded.

The first one at the head of the stairs was Quinn's bedroom.

He stopped in the doorway because it was so hers that it hit him like a fist to the chest. Then he stepped in and took possession. Quinn wouldn't care, she'd be glad.

She'd left a mess as usual, drawers shut crooked, closet door half open, the bed unmade—that was his Quinn—but it was still the bedroom he remembered from their apartment before she'd moved out, her grandfather's washstand and the pie safe she used as linen cupboard and—

He slid his eyes away from the bed. The bed was new. He had their old bed. He'd bring it here when he moved in and then things would be the same again. There was a heavy lamp beside the bed and that was new, too, with a glass shade, and he hated it because it wasn't theirs. They'd get rid of it when he moved in.

Her bunny slippers were kicked off near the fireplace—she had a fireplace in the bedroom, now that was wonderful—and the slippers looked so funny and so Quinn, tumbled over each other, almost as if they were doing it—

His eyes slid away from the bunny slippers and back to the bed.

It was rumpled, the thick blue blanket and the blue and yellow quilt rolled back together, the bottom sheet still curved with the print of Quinn's body. He walked over—no reason to feel breathless, everything was fine—and let his hand rest where she'd been. It was cold, she'd been gone for hours, and he lay down where she'd been just for a minute, and put his throbbing head on her yellow pillow—bright like Quinn—and smelled her warmth and her laughter—was it her shampoo really? she didn't wear perfume; no, it was Quinn—and almost wept because he wanted her back so much.

Not that she was gone. She wasn't. They were just in a readjustment phase. Things would be fine.

He lay there for awhile, thinking of how fine things would be, of how they'd build a fire in the fireplace and then hold each other here, right here, and she'd be under him again and—

His mind went dull as he thought about having her again, thought about how she'd lay quiet in his arms, about how he'd have her soon, here, in this bed, he'd take her back here—his breath came faster and he squeezed his eyes shut until he couldn't see anything anymore.

Then he got up and slowed his breathing, made himself calm, taking one last look around their bedroom, not wanting to leave, or if he had to leave, wanting to take her with him. Something that was like her.

He slipped the pillowcase off her pillow and held it to his face, breathing her in.

Her pillow lay white and naked on the bed. That wasn't right.

He went to the bottom shelf of the pie safe and got a new yellow pillowcase. He put the clean one on, and then folded the used one, that one that had Quinn on it, under his coat.

And then he went back to school, carefully locking the door behind him so nobody could get in to hurt her.

The BP met him at the weight-room door.

"Bill," he said. "You got to pull yourself together."

"I'm fine," he said, thinking about swatting Bobby like a gnat.

"It's still that woman, isn't it? I don't see why you don't just forget her," Bobby shook his head. "She's not worth it. Why don't you—"

"She's worth it," Bill said through clenched teeth. "We're going to be together, so just butt out, Bobby."

The BP winced at the "Bobby," and Bill realized he'd slipped, he should have called him "Robert," but really that was what he deserved for doubting Quinn.

"We lose three more games," Bobby said, "we don't even go to regionals."

"It's not going to happen," Bill said and pushed past him.

"Where do you go on your planning period, anyway?" Bobby called after him, and Bill ignored him.

They'd be in the regionals. They'd even win the tournament. Once he got Quinn back, everything would be fine. He'd see that it was fine.

He'd make her see tonight.

QUINN WAS ALONE in the art storeroom getting brushes for the techies that evening, still fuming over Nick and how stupid she'd been—it wasn't as if he hadn't had a track record of non-involvement, for heaven's sake—when Bill came in and stood by the door, blocking her from the rest of the art room. When she turned and saw him filling the doorway, her heart clutched for a minute because he was so big and she was so alone. The kids were all down on the stage, nobody there to hear her yell if she needed help...

But that was dumb. This was Bill, after all.

"You scared me," she said, wanting to walk forward so he'd step back and let her out of the closet but afraid to, afraid he might not step back.

"I just wanted to talk," he said, smiling at her.

She hated that smile. "Bill, we have nothing to talk about and I'm late." She did walk forward then, and he didn't move, so she stopped. "You're in my way."

"I can't be in your way," he said. "We belong together. Your way is my way."

"*No,*" she said, and he said, "If you'd just listen, we'd be okay again."

"There isn't any 'we.'" Quinn heard her voice shake a little. "There never was, Bill. We never connected at all."

"Of course, we did," he said. "We're getting married as soon as—"

"*No!*" she said, and his face changed, twisted for a minute before it smoothed and he said, "It's okay, we can live in the Apple Street house."

She put out her hand to one of the shelves to steady herself, dizzy with how angry she was, that he wouldn't listen, that he wouldn't see how much she'd changed, and scared, too, although that was ridiculous, this was Bill. "We are not getting married," she said as calmly as possible. "I don't love you. I never did. It was a mistake and it's over and you're never moving into the house on Apple Street. Now let me out."

His jaw clenched, and he said, "You're not listening." She moved forward then, determined not to let him stop her, saying,

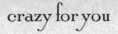

"Let me out!" but he slammed the door shut in her face and trapped her inside.

"Bill?" Quinn said and pounded on the door. "Let me out! This is ridiculous. I've told you—"

"Just *listen*," he said from outside. "I've made plans. I know you think there's not enough room, but we can put an addition on."

He went on to her growing horror, explaining how they'd build on the house, where they'd put the doors and windows, where their kids would sleep, and Quinn felt paralyzed, trapped not only in a cold storeroom but in the cold world of Bill's denial while he talked on and on in his calm teacher's voice, sounding as sane as anybody.

He broke off in the middle of explaining the deck they'd build out in back, and Quinn pressed closer to the door to find out why.

"Have you seen McKenzie?" she heard Jason ask. "We need her down on the stage, and Mrs. Buchman said to try here."

"Jason," Quinn called before Bill could say anything, "I'm in here." She rattled the storeroom doorknob, but it wouldn't budge. Bill must be holding it. "Let me out, Bill," she said. "I have to go work on the play."

"We're talking," she heard Bill say to Jason. "She'll be down later."

"*No!*" Quinn heard the panic in her voice and forced herself to be calm. Catching Jason in the middle of this wasn't a good idea. "Jason, go get Mrs. Buchman, please. And Mrs. Ziegler." She was pretty sure Bill wasn't violent, just detached from reality and that only in reference to her, so if Edie and Darla came in, he'd see the absurdity of the whole thing and open the door.

She hoped.

"Coach, we really need her now," Jason said. "I think you'd better let her out."

"She'll be down as soon as we're finished talking," Bill said kindly. "You go on now."

"Well, I can't," Jason said. "We're out of red paint and the extra's in the storeroom."

It wasn't a bad lie since Bill didn't know the play stuff was kept in the stage storeroom, but he wasn't buying it. "She'll bring it down when she comes."

"I need to go now, Bill," Quinn said. "You're holding up our practice. Let me out."

"We really need her, Coach." Jason's voice was close now, as close as Bill's, and Quinn imagined them standing there side by side at the door, Jason almost as big as Bill, Jason at eighteen practically a man, strong from weightlifting, ready to face Bill down.

No, she thought, and opened her mouth to tell Jason it was all right, but then the doorknob turned, and Jason opened the door, gently shoving Bill out of the way with his elbow as he did so.

"You're late," he said to her, his voice deliberately cheery. "You're in trouble now."

She slipped out past him, ignoring Bill standing desolate behind him, trying not to shake as she headed for the door, Jason close behind her, shielding her.

"Wait," Bill said, and she turned, reaching out to hold on to Jason's arm as she did. "You forgot your paint," Bill said, and she shook her head.

"I'll send somebody else for it," she said and escaped into the hall, still holding on to Jason.

"You okay?" he said when they'd turned the corner into the main hall, when she felt safe enough to let go of him.

"Yeah," she said.

"That was weird."

"Very," she said and swallowed.

Jason put his arm around her. "Don't walk around here alone anymore. You keep Corey or me with you. That was really bad."

Hearing him say it made it worse, having a student know, but Quinn shut her eyes and nodded, knowing he was right.

Jason squeezed her shoulder. "It'll be okay," he told her, and then he looked past her and dropped his arm.

She turned and saw Bobby glaring at them. What the hell was he still doing here this late? Stalking her?

That wasn't funny, she realized. Not funny at all.

"Ms. McKenzie, I'd like to see you in my office," he said, his voice icy.

"Not now, Robert," she said, her fear morphing into anger as she looked at his silly, stupid face. "But you might want to go check on your baseball coach. He just trapped me in my storeroom." Bobby stiffened a little, suddenly wary, and she added, "There's something really wrong with him, Robert. Really, really wrong. You're going to have to talk to him. Keep him away from me."

"Don't be ridiculous," Bobby said, but he took off down the hall.

BILL SAT IN the empty art room, tense with frustration. Jason had meant well, but he'd ruined everything. She'd been listening to him, quiet in there, he'd been explaining it so well, if he'd just had a chance to finish—

"Bill?" Bobby said from the doorway. "Are you all right? What happened?"

"She won't let me take care of her," Bill said. "She's just all caught up in this play and she's so busy—"

"Look." Bobby came in and sat down next to him. "I think you should stay away from her—"

"If she'd just stay still enough to listen," Bill said.

"Yeah, well, I could break her leg," Bobby said sarcastically.

"But even then she'd just get crutches and walk off. She's done with you."

"You don't understand," Bill said. "We belong together."

"Right," Bobby said. "After baseball season. You'll have the whole summer to get her back."

Bill frowned at him. "That's too long. I can't wait that long."

"Look, Bill, don't make me get nasty," Bobby said. "I could screw things up for you, I'm the principal, you know, but I won't because I don't want you worried about anything but the team."

Bill stood up, sick of the team. "There are more important things than baseball, Robert," he said, and walked out of the room, fairly sure that Bobby couldn't think of one.

That was really sad.

"HE WAS CRAZED." Quinn told Joe and Darla at home later that night. "I couldn't believe it. He thinks he's moving in and we're having kids."

"I'll talk to him," Joe said, and Quinn looked at her father in surprise. "I'll tell him to leave you alone."

"It won't do any good," Quinn said. "*I* told him that, and he didn't believe me." She smiled at her dad. "But thanks, anyway. I told Bobby to take care of him. Maybe—"

"It's not enough," Joe said and Darla said, "He's right, Quinn. If Bill's trapping you in storerooms, he's gone over the edge. We've got to do something."

"What?" Quinn said. "Call the police and say Bill Hilliard, the Hero of Tibbett, locked me in my storeroom and wouldn't let me out? It sounds like a kid's prank. I mean, who would you believe, Bill or the woman who stole her dog from the pound?"

"Let me say something to Frank Atchity," Joe said. "We play

poker. Let me just give him a heads-up on this. And from now on, you don't go anywhere alone."

"For the rest of my life?"

"He's right," Darla said. "No place alone. And you tell the BP that if he doesn't call Bill off, you're going to the police. That should do something."

As it happened, the first person Quinn saw when she got to school the next morning was the BP, vibrating by her classroom door.

"Jason *quit*," Bobby told her as she unlocked it. "He quit the team cold this morning, just like he didn't owe Bill anything."

Oh, hell, Jason, Quinn thought, and then she flipped on the light and went into the room. "Look, I'm sorry but I'm not surprised. He watched Bill wig out last night. I'm not kidding, Robert, there's something really wrong there. You either keep Bill away from me or I'm going to the police for a restraining order. And you can just imagine what kind of rumors that will start. Good-bye levy."

Bobby turned purple. "This is all your fault. All he wants is you, although God knows why. You're the most ungrateful—"

"Bobby, will you *forget it?*" Quinn turned on him. "What do I have to do to—"

"Just until June," Bobby said. "That's all I ask. Just go back to him until we get the trophy and I'll help you move out afterward myself."

"You're as crazy as he is," Quinn said. "*No.* And you keep him *away* from me. Or else."

"This is your fault," Bobby said and walked off, and Quinn thought, *That's what everyone else is going to think, too.* Bill had been perfectly normal until she'd left. Well, as normal as any coach in America.

Her homeroom kids started to file in, still half asleep and

sullen as always, and Quinn shoved all thoughts of Bill away so she could get attendance taken. There was at least one part of her life that was under control: she could still count kids. But all the way through the roll call, Bill lurked in the back of her mind, refusing to go away.

She really was going to have to do something. She just didn't know what.

JASON HAD QUIT. Bill tried to understand it, how Jason could leave him after four years. Four years of football and baseball, and then Jason just stood there at morning weightlifting, his eyes blank, and said, "Sorry, Coach. I'm just not interested anymore."

"Jason," Bill had said, but Jason had just shaken his hand and left the weight room.

Bill looked at Corey Mossert and said, "Talk him out of it."

Corey shook his head, too. "Something happened yesterday after school. He didn't tell me what, but he's real sure this is what he wants. He's gone, Coach. Let it drop."

Bill felt cold. That thing in Quinn's room. When he was trying to talk to her, Jason had butted in and ruined it. What had Quinn said? What had she told Jason that had made him want to quit?

He had to do something. He had to do *something*. His headaches were getting worse. Nothing was going right. Nothing was going right.

So he went back inside Quinn's house on his planning period—he had to, he'd forgotten to measure the upstairs the previous time so he had to—and inside, he felt better. It was almost like being inside Quinn. No, no, he didn't mean that, he meant with Quinn.

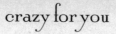

He couldn't wait to move in.

The dog went under a chair as soon as it saw him, snarling at him but staying away. On his way up the stairs, he noticed how flimsy the railing was. Just bolted to the wall. It could come loose any time. If he lived here, he'd make sure there was a better railing. She really needed him there.

He slowed as he neared the top of the stairs. Maybe that was it. Maybe if she realized how much she needed him—

He went back downstairs to the back porch and found Quinn's toolbox. With the screwdriver he loosened the bolts on the stair rail, and then went through the house, loosening other screws, to doorknobs and outlet plates, loosening the wires behind the plates, too. He thought of other things he could do. He could loosen the gas lines so there'd be just a little leak, nothing big. The steps to the front porch were awful. He could weaken one so it would go later, so everything wouldn't be bad at once. He could loosen a porch rail. He could do lots of things. She'd need him again.

When he went upstairs an hour later, he was brisk, sure he'd be moving in soon. The second door up there was another bedroom, set under the eaves, with a twin bed, probably Quinn's or Zoë's from when they were kids, and he smiled, cheered because it'd be such a great room for their boys. The two rooms at the back of the house were an office with the other bed and a bathroom. The bathroom was just too small, they'd be extending that out, and maybe putting another one behind it, enlarging the office to a master bedroom with the master bath right off it, behind the old bath, that was the way it would go. Just right.

Bill made notes of the measurements and then pocketed his measuring tape and organizer. He had everything he needed, everything would be easy now, once Quinn realized how much she needed him. Once she called him back.

And she'd be so surprised when he showed her the plans after he moved in. "Silly," he'd say. "You knew we'd need more room. You should have known I'd plan it."

On the way down the hall, he opened the fifth door out of curiosity.

Quinn's closet.

He could see the sleeves of her dresses. The green print one she'd worn the first time they went out, the blue checked one she'd worn with a jacket for fall open house, the red plaid flannel one she'd worn to the last basketball game they'd gone to—he clutched a little there, they'd been so happy—the black one she wore to teach in when the kids weren't doing something messy, and the brown patchwork print one and the denim one and—

He closed his eyes because his chest hurt. He couldn't be having a heart attack, he was too young and healthy. Indigestion maybe. He should lie down.

Once in Quinn's bed, the quilt pulled over him, he felt better. For a moment he was almost angry with her, she was being so stubborn, she deserved what he'd done to her house, if she'd just listen to him, she could be here with him, under this quilt, she wouldn't *listen*, if he could just *make her listen*—

He thought about making her listen, about what he'd have to do to make her listen, what she deserved for not listening, so angry, he was so angry because she wouldn't *listen*—

He breathed harder, the room went away, and he thought about Quinn, about making her listen, about making her take him back, she'd have to take him back now, this had gone on long enough, it was enough, enough, enough—

When he was calm again, he told himself the old story, that things would be fine, that she'd listen now—*it's been two months*—just a little more time, and things would be fine, and she'd listen—

No, she won't.

He felt himself clench again, like a giant fist, and rolled out of the bed. He was fine, she'd listen, things would be okay.

He went around the room, opening the closet door—this one was her shirts and skirts, jeans folded on the shelf above—opening the pie safe—sheets and pillowcases, T-shirts—opening the washstand drawers—

Quinn's underwear. *My secret life*, she'd called it. Absurd colors, screaming pinks and metallic golds and acid greens and—

He plunged his hands into the drawer, into the lace and the satin and the silk—"I have to dress like a dockworker to teach art," she'd said once, "but I can be all dressed up underneath"— all the stuff he didn't really like, not really, all those weird, bright colors, that wasn't how he wanted Quinn, bright and hot; his Quinn was clean, white, plain, good—he clenched his fists around the vile stuff—*his*, she should know she was his.

He threw the underwear back in the drawer as if it were unclean, contaminated, it contaminated her, he wanted to rip it up, shred it, burn it so it never touched her again, and he gathered it up in handfuls to do that, and that's when he saw the white at the bottom of the drawer.

They weren't plain white cotton, they were lacy and brief, bikini pants—not the kind that really covered her up, but they were white, like a bride's, and he picked them up, holding his breath. Some guys called them panties but that always seemed dirty to Bill, so he just called them underpants, a nice clean name, these were mostly lace with just a strip of white satin down the crotch—*crotch*, not a word he wanted to use with Quinn, harsh—satin down the crotch, the part that went between her legs, the part—

He shuddered a little, and shoved the drawer shut, still clutching the panties.

Underpants.

They were white lace. She could wear them when they got married.

She had to listen. He had to make her listen. He'd been patient long enough. You waited for awhile to give women time, but then you had to be firm.

He'd be firm and she'd understand. She'd be grateful, she'd want this over, too. She'd come back to him, wearing these panties, open her arms to him, open herself to him in the dark—

It would be fine.

He held the panties and tried to slow his breathing, and he was looking at them, just looking at them, when Bobby said, "So this is where you go on your planning period."

Bill jerked his head up, and Bobby leaned in the doorway, smiling.

"This is really pathetic, Hilliard," he said.

"How did you—"

"I followed you." Bobby shrugged. "You're losing it, Hilliard. More important, you're losing games. Can't have that." His voice was insolent and his face was smug.

Bill swallowed. "Get out of here."

Bobby shook his head. "It's too late for that. Go ahead, put those things in your pocket if that's what you need, but we have to get out of here. I really wouldn't want to explain this to anybody."

"You don't understand," Bill said. "This isn't—"

"I understand plenty," Bobby said. "Now shut up and get out of here before you get caught. Jesus, you're a fool."

"You can't talk to me like that," Bill blustered, but he felt cold. His world had been wrong before, but not this wrong.

"I can talk to you any way I want." Bobby's smile was ugly. "After this?" He nodded toward the panties, still clutched in Bill's hand. "I'm the Big Guy now, and you do what I say." He jerked his head toward the stairs and then walked toward the door, acting like he was sure Bill would follow him.

And dizzy with confusion, his headache back again in full force, Bill did.

"WHAT THE HELL is she *doing*?" Max said, slamming down the office phone.

Nick raised his head from the Subaru he was working on and squinted out the window. "Who?"

"Not out there. Darla." Max sounded exasperated. "She just left a message on our machine that the boys should come to dinner again. Not me, just the boys."

"She probably thought you'd be eating at the Anchor Inn."

"Fuck you," Max said. "This is stupid. We're married. She should be home."

"Yep."

"It looks weird. People are talking, damn it."

Nick kept his head under the hood. "Maybe if we were nice to them, they'd let us watch."

"You can make jokes," Max said. "You're not missing anything."

The hell I'm not.

"It's been over a *month*," Max seethed. "I didn't go this long in high school."

"Oh," Nick said. "That's why you're so grumpy."

"Wouldn't you be?"

Nick thought about telling him it didn't matter how long it had been, it was the idea it was never going to happen again that was making him nuts, but he didn't. Some things he just wasn't interested in discussing with Max even if he couldn't help thinking about them himself.

He had to fight the urge every day to drop by Quinn's house to see if she needed anything. Like him inside her. Of course with Darla and Joe there, he was out of luck, and Quinn wasn't stopping by his place any more, so short of jumping her on the street, he was pretty much screwed. Or in this case, not. Which was good. She was just a friend, and anyway, his attention span was not that long. He should have been past this by now. He was not the kind of guy who obsessed over women.

He wanted her naked under him again.

No, he didn't.

"I've been over to the Upper Cut," Max said, lost in his own problems. "She says no. I can't figure out what to do. I go to Bo's and she laughs. I date Barbara to make her jealous, and she tells me to avoid the lobster next time."

"I told you that was a dumb move," Nick said.

Max ignored him. "I tell her to tell me what she wants, I tell her she can have it, whatever it is. She says if she has to tell me, it doesn't mean anything."

"I hate that one," Nick said, his sympathy veering back to Max.

"She wants change," Max said. "I like our life. Why should I change?"

"To get your life back?"

"She's my wife," Max said stubbornly. "She belongs to me. I'll just wait. She'll come to her senses."

Before you've lost yours? Nick wanted to say, but it was fairly clear that Max's mind had already gone seriously astray, and Nick wasn't in any position to criticize since he wasn't doing any better. After all, he was still fixated on a woman he was never going to see naked again, never hold, touch, stroke, squeeze, bury himself inside—

Not that he wanted to. Much.

"Go over there and kidnap your wife," Nick said. "The hell with waiting."

Max snarled at him and went back in the office, and Nick stared at the Subaru and tried to get a calm rational grip on the way he felt about Quinn without actually thinking about the way he felt.

Okay, everything was under control. He'd lost her before for two weeks after the night on her couch, and that had made him edgy but only because he liked having her around, liked hearing her voice, her laugh, seeing her face, watching her hair swing— *Quinn, her hair cropped, twisting under him, beautiful cheekbones, the shape of her skull under his hands as he pushed into her*—really liked her as a friend for companionship and conversation. Like reading the articles in *Playboy*, which were damn good.

And now it had been almost a week since he'd seen her— *naked, round and wet*—and he wanted her back.

To talk to.

He couldn't believe how much he missed her. As a friend. She'd been his best friend, and now she wasn't in his life anymore—*See*, he wanted to tell her, *this it why it was such a bad idea for us to have sex, I knew this would happen, I told you so*— and he missed her. Talking to her.

He hadn't really appreciated how important conversation with a woman was until he'd spent time with one who didn't have any. Barbara was a perfectly nice woman aside from her addiction to married blue-collar workers, but if he never had to spend another five minutes with her again, it would be too soon.

Quinn had always had plenty to say. They'd talked about books and movies and people and her teaching and his abysmal dating habits, but it wasn't until his week dating Barbara that Nick realized that it was Quinn's conversation he missed most. They were friends. They should be talking.

And that was why he wanted her back. He nodded. That was good. Reasonable. Sensible.

He loved Quinn like a sister, so of course he wanted to be

with her. It wasn't her body he loved—*lush and tight and slippery under him*, never mind that sister thing, bad analogy, forget that, don't go there—no, it was her mind he loved, who she was, Quinn, the person, not Quinn the body.

Perfectly reasonable.

But the problem was that—entirely separate from the love thing, the two things were totally different, not even in the same universe, completely apart—he craved her body shuddering hot under his.

That made sense, Nick told himself. That was fairly simple. It was like separation of church and state, integral to the continued freedom of both. Love over here, sex over there. No mixing.

Of course, it was easier if there were two women involved instead of one. In fact, he realized now, one of the things that had made his life so easy up until now was that he'd loved Quinn and slept with other women. So since it was easier to find women to sleep with than to love, he'd just keep loving Quinn— he didn't think he could stop anyway—and find somebody else to fuck.

The memory of her body came back to him—hot and yielding under his hands, the way he'd learned her, felt her, sensed her, known her, made her shudder and made her come—and that made him hard all over again.

He had to have her again, or he wasn't going to get anything done.

Nick leaned on the Subaru, almost defeated. Okay, there was no need to panic. He could still do this. He just had to remember to keep the two things separate. Love the mind, fuck the body. That way when he stopped fucking the body, he could still love her mind.

Clearly logical. Maybe he could talk her into buying it.

But first he had to convince her to let him near her without kicking him.

The phone rang while he was trying to think of a way, and when he answered, Joe said, "Nick? Could you come over here when you're done tonight?"

"Here?" Nick said. "You mean Quinn's?" He couldn't possibly be this lucky.

"Yeah," Joe said. "Quinn just fell down the stairs and messed up her ankle. The stair rail came loose."

"Oh, hell." Nick's libido evaporated with his concern. "Is she all right? You need me to take her to the hospital?"

"Darla's taking her." Joe's voice sounded grim. "I think somebody loosened that rail. It's supposed to have three screws in each bracket and there was only one in each. I put it back up, but it's loose now. And when I got home last night, I smelled gas, somebody'd messed with the valve in the basement, and when I went down there, I found a broken window. Anybody could have gotten in here. I think this place is booby-trapped."

"Who—" Nick started to say and then stopped. "Not Bill?"

"I don't want to believe it, but yeah, after that thing in the storeroom, that's my guess, too."

"What thing in the storeroom?" Nick said, and as Joe told him, his concern for Quinn morphed into rage, much easier to deal with than love and fear. "Christ," he said. "You should have called me and we could have both gone to see him."

"Quinn said no," Joe said. "You know how she likes things calm. I think she thought if she was patient and didn't cause a fuss, he'd just give up, but after this, we got to do something. I got a call in to Frank Atchity, and I'm going through the house now, but I want somebody double-checking me on this. If you—"

"I'll come over now," Nick said. "So will Max. It's Saturday, we can close an hour early."

"Thanks," Joe said.

"My pleasure," Nick said.

thirteen

NICK BROUGHT deadbolts, and they put them on all the entry doors and the door to the basement. Then they began to check everything, starting in the basement. Two hours later, they only had the downstairs done.

Bill had been thorough.

It seemed as if everything with a screw or a nail in it had been loosened. Wires had been frayed, pipes unscrewed slightly, a leg on the couch weakened, cans poised to fall out of cupboards. "It must have taken him hours," Max said finally, and Joe shook his head, years as an electrician and general handyman behind him. "Always takes longer to fix than it does to screw up. You don't have to be careful when you're screwing up." Nick stayed silent, testing everything he found twice, feeling more and more outraged with every sabotage they found.

They were just heading for the stairs to do the second floor when the phone rang, and Nick picked it up.

"Hello," he said, and Zoë said, "Who is this?"

"Oh, good," Nick said, her voice coming back to him over twenty years. "You I needed right now."

"Nick?"

"Yep."

"So I hear you're fucking my sister."

"Every chance I get," he said. "She's not here. I'll tell her to call you."

"Wait a minute, if she's not there, what are you doing there?"

When he'd told her, she was silent for a minute, and then she said, "Shit. Move in with her."

"What?"

"Move in with her. She loves you, you love her, and that nutcase needs to know that. Stop screwing around and move in."

"It's not that easy," Nick said.

"Oh, grow up," Zoë said. "You've loved her forever. Stop being a baby."

"Gee, I've missed you," Nick said. "I'll have Quinn call you."

"Do that. But in the meantime, you stay there and watch out for her. I mean it, Nick," she added, annoying him as much as ever. "Don't screw up." Then she hung up.

"Who was that?" Joe asked as he came down the stairs.

"Zoë," Nick said, hanging up the phone.

"You do have an interesting life," Joe said and got a screwdriver from the drawer. "What'd she say?"

"She wants me to move in with Quinn," Nick said.

Joe smiled. "That's my Zoë. Hell of a kid." He started back up the stairs, but stopped as the front door opened and Quinn hobbled in, Darla's arm around her, holding crutches. Quinn's ankle was taped, and there was a big Band-Aid on her elbow, but the part that made Nick sick was the bruise on her forehead.

"You look like hell," Max said, and Joe glared at him.

"I'm okay," she said to all of them. "It looks a lot worse than it is." She put her crutches under her arms. "I won't even need these by the end of the week. It's just to keep my weight off the ankle. It's just a sprain—"

"A bad sprain," Darla said grimly, closing the front door behind them.

"—and I'll be completely back to normal in a couple of weeks." Quinn took a deep breath and smiled, and Nick thought, *I'll kill him. He ever gets near her again—*

"But I'm going to bed now." Quinn headed for the stairs, clumsy on her crutches. "I'm tired as hell."

Nick moved to pick her up but Joe got there first. "Let me carry you," he said, and scooped her up in his arms.

"You'll break your back," Quinn protested, dropping her crutches. "I can walk."

"Nope." Joe carried her up the stairs while Nick followed behind in case he dropped over from a heart attack.

Joe dumped Quinn in the middle of her big oak bed and leaned against the wall for a minute. "Used to do that when you were little," he wheezed. "You've put on some weight."

Quinn grinned up at him. "I love you, Daddy," she said, and when Joe grinned back, Nick was struck for the first time by how alike they were. Meggy and Zoë were the scatty ones who got all the attention while Quinn and Joe went with the flow, just sort of solid and there, nobody really noticing them. Except that Quinn was everywhere he went now, a permanent part of his thoughts, every day. But then she always had been. He just hadn't been tormented by her before, the way he had for the past few weeks.

Or terrified for her, the way he was now.

"I love you, too," Joe said gruffly when he'd caught his breath. He kissed her on the top of the head. "Stay there for a while until I get my breath back. I got to get more exercise." He shook his head and left, and Nick, unable to think of anything else, went over to the bed and pulled the pillow she wasn't leaning on out from under her quilt.

"Sit up," he said, and when she did, he stuffed it behind her. "You got any more pillows?"

"Why?" Quinn frowned at him. "This is plenty. Thank you."

"For your foot. Your foot should be up." He opened the pie safe behind him and found a blanket. "This'll work." He rolled it into a thick tube and then lifted her bandaged foot gently, stuffing the blanket under it. "It won't swell so much if it's up. You got a cold pack? I can go—"

"This isn't like you," Quinn said. "Relax, I'm fine."

"Right." Nick backed up a step. "Anything else? Diet Coke? Food?"

"I'm fine," Quinn said, and he backed up another step. "I really am, Nick. This is sweet of you, but I'm great. Darla and Dad are going to drive me crazy waiting on me hand and foot. You don't have to do this."

"Right," Nick said again, and looked at the shadows under her eyes and the bruise on her forehead. "I'm scared for you," he blurted. "I never thought he'd hurt you."

Quinn shook her head. "I don't think he meant to. He probably didn't think it through that far. He's in trouble."

"Screw him." His voice was sharper than he'd meant it to be, and Quinn looked concerned.

"Listen, it's okay." Quinn's voice was the same as always, practical and sure. "I've got Darla and Dad here, and a ton of people at school, and Darla and Edie at play practice. I'm safe."

"You really think Darla's going to be able to protect you from Bill?" Nick said incredulously. "I think—"

"Hey, who would you rather meet in a dark alley?" Quinn grinned, and Nick had to admit it wouldn't be Darla. She had a real mean streak when she was riled.

"Just be careful," he said, and she sighed and said, "*I will*, okay?"

"Okay," he said and turned to go, stopping only when she said, "Nick?"

He looked back at her, leaning toward him a little, her copper hair mussed from the pillow, her eyes huge and beautiful.

"Thank you," she said. "Really. You're a good friend."

He swallowed as the word *friend* knifed through him. "You need anything, you call."

"I will," she said, and there wasn't anything else he could do but leave her and go out into the hall.

Friend. Well, that's what he wanted. Everything back the way it was.

Max came out of the bathroom. "Sonofabitch frayed the cord on her blow-dryer. He could have electrocuted her."

Nick felt cold. "We check everything in this house three times. Every damn thing."

When Nick left two hours later, he saw Patsy Brady watching out her front window, and on a hunch, he went up and knocked on her front door.

"My lucky day," she said when she opened it.

"Not really," Nick said. "Have you seen anybody hanging around the house next door?"

Patsy lounged in the doorway, her terrycloth robe pulled carelessly shut. "Next door. The teacher's place."

"That's it."

Patsy shook her head. "Just the big guy."

Nick stiffened. "Big guy?"

"Yeah." Patsy shifted and so did her robe. "Big blond guy hanging around her backyard. Let her dog out once."

"You recognize him?"

"Nope." Patsy shifted again, her robe now close to qualifying her for indecent exposure. "You want to come in?"

"No," Nick said. "Did he look like Coach Hilliard?"

"Nah," Patsy said. "I've seen him down on the field. This guy is big but the coach is huge."

"Sometimes guys look smaller up close," Nick said.

"No shit," Patsy said.

Nick said, "Okay, let's try this another way." He picked up a yellowed ad circular from Patsy's porch and got his pen out of his workshirt pocket to write Frank Atchity's number on it. "If you see this big blond guy again, will you call this number?"

"This yours?" Patsy said, one eyebrow raised.

"The sheriff's," Nick said. "Please."

"The sheriff? No way." Patsy drew back and Nick said, "Wait a minute then," and scratched out the first number and wrote two others down.

"Call me then," he said, handing it to her. "The first one's my work number and the second one's my apartment. Call as soon as you see him."

Patsy frowned at him but she took the paper. "What's going on?"

"Somebody booby-trapped her house." Nick jerked his head toward Quinn's. "She fell down the stairs and screwed up her ankle."

"Shit." Patsy looked at the number again. "Yeah, I'll call you. That sucks. I thought he just had the hots for her, you know? Looking in the window. Big deal."

"He's dangerous," Nick said.

"So are you." Patsy looked him up and down. "But I guess you're hers, right?"

"Right," Nick said, just to keep things simple.

"Lucky her."

"Not really," Nick said. "I'm a pain in the ass. Look, thanks for helping. We appreciate it."

Patsy pulled her robe closed. "Hey, we girls gotta stick together around here what with the way men are." She shook her head. "Sonofabitch."

"Right," Nick said.

He walked off the porch feeling vindicated that he'd been right and even more afraid for Quinn than before, trying to figure out how to protect her. She'd be all right at home as long as Darla and Joe were there, but she wasn't home all the time, there was school and that damn play—

And under it all, he wanted her. Needed her, which was worse, but there it was.

An hour later, he was home, still trying to figure out how to get back next to her—maybe send her flowers for a start?—when Joe called him.

"We talked to Frank Atchity," he said. "Tried to get him to come out and get fingerprints. He's not real interested."

"Why the fuck not?" Nick said. The Tibbett police force wasn't exactly *NYPD Blue*, but Frank had always been competent before.

"We've got no proof." Joe sounded disgusted, too. "It's an old house, the city has already been here a dozen times for violations, so the gas leak and the broken window just sounded like business as usual to him. And Bill is God around here, all that charity shit he does and the work with the kids. Frank just didn't want to hear it. He said he'd come out and look tomorrow, but he didn't sound too interested."

"Fuck," Nick said again. "I'll talk to him."

"No," Joe said. "Let me handle it. I'm her father. I play poker with him. I'll make him do something when he comes out tomorrow."

Nick fumed until Edie called at eight that evening. "Hey, Nick," she said. "Quinn and Darla are doing the tech for the play, but we're running out of time and could use some help on lights and sound. I was wondering—"

"Joe called you," Nick said, knowing he couldn't get that lucky twice in the same day.

"Yes," Edie said. "He's worried about her. So am I."

"Me, too," Nick said. "I'll be there. So will Max. She'll never leave my sight."

"Just like Bill," Edie said.

"Nothing like Bill," Nick said.

Monday morning, he called the florist and had them send a dozen red roses to Quinn at school. It wasn't much, but it was a start.

ON MONDAY, QUINN was on stage leaning on her crutches and talking to Thea about the backdrop when she saw Nick come in the back door with Max, and she stopped in midsentence, a little breathless just because he was there. She tried to tell herself he was a pizza-loving, red-rose-sending loser but every cell in her body strained to get to him anyway.

"Who are they?" Thea asked.

"Mrs. Ziegler's husband and brother-in-law." Quinn put her eyes back on the backdrop cartoon where they belonged.

"The cute one's the husband and the hot one's the brother-in-law, right?" Thea said.

"Good guess."

"So who's the brother-in-law to you?" Thea said.

"Absolutely nobody. Okay, if we thin the dye as we go toward the top—"

"And I thought I was obvious about Jason," Thea said. "That is not nobody. Even if you didn't know who he was, he wouldn't be nobody."

"Trust me," Quinn said. "He doesn't even exist."

"What did he do?"

"Thea," Quinn said sternly.

"Just asking." Thea looked past Quinn's shoulder. "Hi."

"Hi," Nick said, and Quinn shivered a little, he was so close.

"I told you on Saturday, I'm fine," she said without turning around. "You don't need to be here."

"I was asked," he said, still close behind her. "Edie sent for me."

She swung around on that, trying not to enjoy having him near her again. "She did not."

"Your light booth," Nick said, looking down at her with those dark, dark eyes. "She wanted an electrician."

"You are not an electrician."

"Sure I am." He smiled at her and scrambled her thoughts. "Joe taught me."

She turned her back on him. "Edie's down in the front. With Darla. Walk to the edge of the stage, you'll see her."

"Okay," Nick said.

When he was gone, Thea said, "He must have done something really lousy."

"Worse than that," Quinn said.

"So bad he doesn't deserve another shot?"

Quinn looked up to see Thea watching Nick with sympathy. Probably relating to her own problems with Jason. "I gave him three shots. He blew all three."

"Oh." Thea's sympathy returned to Quinn. "One of those." She looked back at Nick. "He's really hot, though. Is he the one you were talking about? The one who made you want to throw up? Did he send the roses? How'd you get him?"

"I don't have him," Quinn said. "And I don't want him."

"You have him," Thea said. "I got a contact high from standing next to you when he looked at you."

"Beautifully put," Quinn said. "Now, about the dyes—"

After Thea had gone to work on the backdrop, Quinn sat on the edge of the table and tried to be practical about her life again. Clearly, being exciting had just screwed things up for everybody, including her, especially her love life. Nick was great as a friend, a disaster as a lover. She needed somebody dependable, somebody who would stick around and wake up with her, somebody she could count on—

Oh, hell, that wasn't what she needed, that was Bill. At least, it was Bill before the storeroom and the sabotage.

Across the stage, she heard Nick laugh, and her eyes stole to the edge of the stage, to where he was grinning down at Edie,

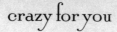

who looked up at him gratefully. Nick, broad-shouldered and slim-hipped—*Nick who did you to Fleetwood Mac*, her practical side pointed out—Nick who'd moved hard between her thighs and bruised her mouth—*Nick who dumped you for a pizza*, practicality reminded her—Nick who'd made her come so hard she was blind and breathless—*Oh, hell, take him back*, practicality said. *Orgasms like that don't grow on trees.*

And then she'd end up alone again. She felt her throat tighten and knew that orgasms weren't enough, she needed the stuff Zoë had with Ben, the attention and the security and the outright demonstrations of love, the stuff she'd been doing without all these years. And Nick couldn't give it to her. She'd looked at him too many times the way she was looking at him now, aching to have him hold her while he turned his back on her.

So he was just a friend. A distant friend.

She turned her back on him and concentrated on her work.

WHEN QUINN GOT to practice on Tuesday, Nick was there again.

"Okay," he told her when he met her at the prop table. "The light booth is now safe once more, or as safe as it's going to get. This place is old."

"Thank you very much for your help," she said. "You can go now."

"So we're doing the spots now," he went on, staring up at the light strips. "I need to know where you want them and what color gels you need."

She blinked at him. "We have crew guys who can—"

"They can." Nick transferred his attention back to her and made her breath come faster. "But only if somebody shows them how. The lighting is a full-time deal and you've been putting it off and your dress rehearsal's in three weeks. Edie gave me a stage lighting book, and I read it last night. I know how to do this. So I'm going to help."

Quinn swallowed. "This is nice of you."

"Not really," Nick said. "I like it."

"Oh."

"You've got some good kids here, and Edie is working her butt off. It's a good project. You deserve the support."

She watched him to see if he was snowing her, but he was looking up above at the spots again, frowning at the rigging.

"That catwalk does not look safe," he said. "Don't send kids up there."

"Well, then you're not going up there, either."

"I'll be careful. I have a lot to live for." He dropped his eyes to hers. "I have to have you again before I die."

Her knees gave way and she sat down hard on the stool.

"Your ankle okay?" Nick said, instantly concerned, and she said, "Fine. Everything's fine here."

"Listen, I screwed up." He came closer as he talked, making his voice low. "I'll probably do it again, and I know you're hurt, and this isn't the time. But I want you back."

She stuck out her chin so it wouldn't quiver. "You never had me."

"The hell I didn't," he said, and the heat in his voice made her dizzy. "I had you to talk to and laugh with, and I had you naked and coming, and you remember all of it."

"Oh, sort of," Quinn said faintly. "I remember the pizza, definitely."

"You remember the good times and you remember the sex," Nick said. "You remember coming your brains out even while you fought it, which for the life of me, I still don't get. The next time we do it, you cooperate."

Quinn got her voice back. "Fleetwood Mac was playing, right?"

"Damn good music," Nick said. "Be as bitchy as you want, I don't care. But when you're tired of making me pay, we're going to laugh again, and then we're going to be naked."

Quinn tried to think of something snappy to say besides *Thank God*, but his eyes were on the lights again.

"This place was built with chewing gum and string," he said, disgusted, and started for the catwalk. "Find your lighting plan, will you?" he called back. "I'm not a mind reader."

"Thank God," Quinn said.

BILL SAT IN the dark parking lot and watched the students leave one by one. He'd been there every night since Quinn had said no, trying to catch her alone so they could sit in the car and talk, but she always came out with Darla, and sometimes with Jason and Thea, too, and Nick and Max and Edie were there, she was never alone, and that's how he needed her. Alone. So he could talk to her. So he could make her *listen*.

He was considering ways to get rid of Darla when the passenger door opened and Bobby got in.

"You know, Hilliard," he said, in the snide tone he'd taken to using since that day in Quinn's bedroom, "stalking is against the law."

"I'm not stalking," Bill said. "Get out of my car."

"You've been here every night," Bobby said. "Not good. Somebody sees this, they could get the wrong idea." He snickered. "Or the right one."

"Get out," Bill said.

"I don't want to see you in this parking lot again," Bobby said, as if what he said mattered. "I want you at home fixing your coaching."

"There's nothing wrong—"

"You lost twice this week already," Bobby said. "One more, we don't even go to regionals."

"There's nothing—"

"I'll tell Quinn."

Bill thought about hitting him, thought about shoving that snide grin down his throat, thought about grabbing Quinn when she came out—what could Darla do, after all?—thought about—

Bobby opened the door. "Go home. Now." He slammed the door shut and stepped back and then just stood there, waiting.

Across the parking lot, Quinn came out with Darla, laughing at something she'd said, swinging on her crutches toward the car. They got in Darla's car, and Bill heard the engine start and saw the taillights come on, cherry red in the dark.

When they left, so did he. There was nothing else there, nothing to stay for, only Bobby, sneering after him in the dark.

ON WEDNESDAY, QUINN sat on the edge of the prop table, double-checking her schedule and trying to forget her day. Things were getting worse, not better, and she couldn't think of a way to fix them. In fact, she was so tense lately, she was actually making them worse. At lunch, Petra had been nasty, shooting ugly looks Edie's way and sniffing about the poor coach and perverts, and Quinn had said, "Petra, forget it," and then Marjorie had come in and slammed the paper down in front of Quinn and said, "This is *your* fault."

Since the headline was about the new sewers in Tibbett, Quinn looked at her calmly and said, "Excuse me?"

"This," Marjorie snapped, and flipped to the sports page. The headline read TOURNAMENT WOES FOR TOOTHLESS TIGERS, and Marjorie's finger shook as she stabbed at it. "You've ruined everything."

"Fuck off, Marjorie," Quinn said. "You want the tournament that bad, you sleep with Bill."

Marjorie sucked her breath in so hard she choked.

"I enjoyed that," Edie said mildly, and Marjorie stomped out again, probably to report her to the BP.

"Pervert," Petra said to no one in particular.

"Petra, the baseball team plans to kill you after the last game," Quinn said. "I'd leave now if you want to live to June." When Petra had scurried out, Quinn had said, "Well, I think we've pretty much hit bottom here," and Edie had said, "Don't count on it."

Looking across the stage now, Quinn crossed her fingers. Maybe—

"Can I talk to you a minute?" Max said.

Quinn jumped and then said, "Sure. How's the sound?"

"The sound I can fix on my own," Max said. "Darla I need help with."

Quinn looked at him warily. "I don't think—"

"How's the sound?" Nick said, from behind her.

"Fine," Max said. "Go away."

"I can't tell you what to do about Darla," Quinn said. "You're the one she wants, so you're going to have to figure out what she needs."

"That's not what we heard." Nick came around the table and sat down close beside her, and she tried hard not to be glad. "Max and I would be pissed about the two of you, but we're kind of hoping you'll let us watch."

Max glared at him. "Would you go away?"

You really should move, Quinn told herself, but that would be petty. And not nearly as much fun as staying where she was. Quinn turned to Max. "She just wants it to feel new again."

Max looked exasperated. "We've been married seventeen years. You want to tell me how to make that new?"

"No," Quinn said. "I don't want anything to do with it."

"You could give him some hints." Nick's voice was low next to her, close, almost in her ear. "Max isn't being boneheaded about this for a change, he just doesn't get it. And neither do I."

Quinn thought, *No kidding*, but she said, "Okay, she wants to feel special, like she's not just your wife."

"Okay," Max said. "I send her flowers."

"Not if you ever want to see her again."

Max looked at Nick who said, "That makes no sense to me, either."

"Women," Quinn explained, as if she were talking to kindergarten kids, "like to feel the man they're with actually sees them as different and special. Every guy on the planet sends flowers; it's generic. If you're going to send flowers, they have to be really special, something that shows you know her." She glared at Nick. "Red roses are not special. Neither is playing the same music for every woman you ... date." Nick rolled his eyes, and she ignored him to turn back to Max. "Darla doesn't feel as if you see her anymore. It's more than being taken for granted, she feels like she's disappearing. And she tried to get you to notice, but you wouldn't."

"I told you so on that one," Nick said to Max.

"So she moved out so you'd have to look at her," Quinn finished. "And now you have to prove to her that you really see her and hear her, that she's not just wallpaper in your life."

"That's the dumbest thing I've ever heard," Max said.

"What's she wearing?" Quinn said.

Max looked around. "She's not here."

"She's doing final fittings in the hall, but you saw her earlier. What's she wearing?"

"I never in my life noticed what she was wearing," Max said. "I'm a guy. Cut me a break."

"I came home on leave once," Nick said, "and all I heard the whole damn night was 'Darla's red sweater.' You couldn't get over it."

"That's because I wanted to get into it," Max said, but he looked thoughtful. "I wonder if she's still got that."

"If it was nineteen eighty-one," Quinn said, "my guess would be no. Forget the red sweater. Where did you have the best times when you were courting, and please don't feel you have to share the details."

"I wouldn't mind," Nick said.

"There was one night in her bedroom with her mom next door," Max said. "For some reason that drove me crazy."

"You're kidding," Quinn and Nick said together.

"Her mom?" Nick added, looking ill.

"No, you know, the thought of us getting caught," Max said. "I really felt like I was getting away with something."

"Knowing her mother, you were," Nick said, but he still looked revolted.

"Well, her mom still lives in the same house," Quinn said doubtfully. "I suppose you could try it there again. If you could convince Darla to go see her mom again on a day that wasn't a major holiday."

"I don't want to see her mother," Max said. "This isn't helping."

Nick snapped his fingers. "The drive-in. You came back from the drive-in one time when I was home and you acted like you'd seen God."

"Oh, yeah." Max grinned to himself. "That was the first time—"

"What?" Nick said.

"Never mind." Max stopped grinning. "You really think if I take her to the drive-in—"

"It's been closed for years," Nick reminded him.

"—that would do it?"

"No," Quinn said. "But that's the kind of thing she's thinking about. The way you used to see God in her at night, and now all you're seeing is the evening news. She wants to know you've changed, that you're ready to take chances with her again, that you see her."

"Oh, great," Max said.

"Told you so," Nick said. "You should have sent us all out for pizza that night she was naked."

"I don't know why you're being so damn cocky," Max said to him. "You're not doing any better than I am." He looked at them both with disgust and went back to the sound system.

"Good point." Nick smiled at Quinn, and her pulse kicked up. "You want to give me a few hints, too?"

She looked away from him. "No."

"Sorry about the roses," Nick said. "Let me start again. I want you back. You want to go to the drive-in?"

Yes. "No."

"Well, what do you want?"

Honesty, Quinn decided, would end this conversation faster than anything. She looked him in the eye. "Commitment."

Nick winced. "You want commitment after doing it once?"

"No," Quinn said. "I want commitment after a lifetime of loving each other. But"—she held up her hand as he started to protest—"I'll settle for you staying the night. The whole night."

"I'm hell to sleep with," Nick said. "I kick the covers off. You wouldn't like it."

"I'll adapt. Just promise me you'll stay."

He looked at her skeptically. "That's it?"

"That's a start."

"Okay." His eyes shifted away from hers. "I'll stay."

"You lie," Quinn said.

"Of course I lie." Nick sounded exasperated. "You're living with Darla and your dad. You really think I'm going to wake up with them? Go downstairs and say hi over orange juice?"

Across the stage, the BP climbed the stage steps and began to talk to Edie, whose face twisted as he leaned toward her. "Oh, hell," Quinn said and stood up, and Nick looked past her and said, "I'm with you. Let's go."

Nice, Quinn thought as she headed off to save Edie. Not good enough, but nice.

fourteen

BOBBY SHEERED off when he saw them coming, and Edie said his main complaint had been that they weren't slamming the door to the parking lot hard enough—"It's been left open three nights so far," he'd blustered—but that didn't seem enough to upset Edie the way he had. She was still pale on Thursday night when Jason interrupted Quinn's concentration by asking, "Why is she talking to Brian?", exasperation making his voice sharp.

Quinn looked away from Edie and saw Thea on the other side of the stage, laughing with the boy cast as Cinderella's Prince. "She's just being friendly."

"He's the biggest hound in school." Jason narrowed his eyes in accusation at Quinn. "And you had to make things worse by casting him as a prince. Way to go, McKenzie."

"I didn't cast him," Quinn said, and then to pour salt on the wound, she said, "Maybe he's asking her to prom."

"Prom is not for weeks yet. He is not asking her to prom."

"You never know," Quinn said. "Leave her alone. She'll find somebody to go with."

"Thea shouldn't be with somebody," Jason said. "I can't believe this."

"I can't believe you." Quinn smacked the script down on the table to get his attention "If you're this jealous, why aren't you dating her?"

Jason shrugged. "She's smart. She'll want to talk Shakespeare or something."

"Well, you're smart, too." Quinn shook her head. "I don't get this. Just ask her out, for heaven's sake."

"I did," Jason said, hell in his voice.

Quinn sat down so she could concentrate. "What happened?"

He shrugged again, painfully nonchalant. "I told her we should go out so people wouldn't think I was hot for you. She said people didn't think that and thanks anyway." He looked at her, suddenly concerned. "Hey, don't worry, nobody thinks that. I just thought it would be a good way to, well, you know, ask her."

"No," Quinn said. "That was a lousy way. Go tell her you want to go out with her for you, because you want to be with her."

"I can't do that." Jason's expression looked vaguely familiar, and then she realized where she'd seen it before: on Max and Nick. It was that mule I-don't-want-to-hear-this look.

Quinn stood up carefully, her voice brisk again. "Then you'll never date her. No big deal."

"Says who?" Jason said, outrage in his voice.

Quinn leaned against the table. "Jason, for crying out loud, just go over there and ask her out and be honest. She likes you. She wants to go out with you. She just doesn't want you doing her any favors."

Jason looked back at Thea, who was laughing at something Brian had said. "If she likes me, why is she messing with him?"

"Because you're ignoring her and she'd like to have children someday. And that is my final word on this subject." Quinn picked up the prop box. "Here, take this over to her and tell her I said the two of you should run inventory."

"That's lame."

"So are you. Go."

Quinn took her crutches and went to lean against the wall, where she could see them better. Jason carried the prop box across the stage, looking grumpy and vulnerable, and for the first time she wasn't worried about Thea. If Thea was lousy to him because he'd been such a dope—

"So what do you do when you're not getting dates for techies?" Nick said as he dropped a coil of wire on the prop table.

"I think about my own lousy love life," Quinn said, refusing to look at him. "Which has gotten so much better since I don't have any. A huge improvement."

He came to stand in front of her, making her see him, and he looked dark and hot and dangerous, and she realized she was enjoying it all, him chasing her for a change. He smiled at her, confident as ever. "Okay, I'll say this again, I screwed up."

Quinn stuck her chin out. "You certainly did."

"Well," Nick said, "Jason screwed up, and you're hoping Thea's going to take him back anyway."

"Jason didn't pancake on Thea three times."

"I did not pancake the third time." Nick came closer, blocking her off from the rest of the stage, and her pulse kicked up as she edged back until she was flat against the wall. "I may have made a small musical error and blown my dismount, but pancake, no. As I keep reminding you, you came."

"I faked it," Quinn lied.

"You did not," Nick said. "You were like wet Kleenex afterward."

"Thank you," Quinn said. "That's very romantic. You can go now."

"You liked it," he said, and she refused to meet his eyes.

"Some."

"A lot." He leaned over her, his hand on the wall above her head, and she could feel herself flush, just because he was that close. "We should try it again. Why should Jason and Thea have all the fun? Want to talk Shakespeare with me?"

Quinn put as much scorn in her voice as she could. "You don't know Shakespeare."

" 'Love is not love which alters when it alteration finds,' " he said. "And I didn't even alter. Except I'm smarter. No Fleetwood Mac, which is a crime because they did some good stuff."

Quinn tried to glare at him without meeting his eyes. "Where'd you read the sonnets? They putting them on cereal boxes now?"

"College," Nick said. "GI bill, remember? Business major, English minor. Good for seducing women. 'The grave's a fine and private place/But none, I think, do there embrace.' Be a shame if we never tried again and died not knowing."

"I can live with that."

He leaned closer, his cheek almost touching hers, and whispered in her ear, " 'License my roving hands, and let them go/Before, behind, between, above, below.' " His breath was warm on her skin. "Let me touch you again. Come back to me, Quinn. I'll drive you out of your mind, I swear."

She felt her breath go. "Who was that one? I got Marvell, but not—"

"Donne. My favorite." He looked down into her eyes, so close. " 'Thy firmness makes my circle just/And makes me end where I begun.' Come home with me tonight."

His mouth was so close to hers she thought about taking it, right there on the stage, everybody watching, but she'd been here before. "No," she said, so dizzy she wasn't even sure what she was saying. "Don't stand so close. People are going to notice."

"Screw people," he said, but she shoved past him to cross the stage to Edie, feeling rattled.

"You okay?" Edie asked. "You look feverish."

"I'm trying to remember why I'm saying no to Nick." Quinn shook her head. "I had a good reason."

"Fleetwood Mac," Edie said.

"I like Fleetwood Mac," Quinn said, and then she got a good look at Edie's face, pale and drawn, and forgot about her own problems. "What's wrong? Are you sick?"

"It's nothing," Edie said. "Really."

"It's the BP," Quinn said, and watched Edie's smile evaporate. "What did he do?"

Edie closed her eyes. "He's had parent complaints."

Quinn frowned. "About the play? That can't be. We—"

"About my morals." Edie looked ghastly as she said it.

"Your morals?" Quinn felt her temper rise as she thought about Bobby's smug little face. The treacherous rat. "That's not parents, that the fucking BP. Don't worry, I will fix this. Tomorrow morning, I'll make him sorry he ever lived."

"Is he in there?" Quinn said the next morning before school, and Greta nodded. She looked tired, and Quinn would have stopped to find out what was wrong, but she had a principal to maim first.

She slammed into Bobby's office and said, "Robert, you have gone too far."

"Greta, where's my coffee?" he said, and from outside, Greta said, "On the corner of my desk."

"Well, bring it in here, damn it." The BP's voice was full of exasperation.

You are such a moron. "Robert, you have to stop harassing Edie."

Greta brought the coffee cup in and set it in front of him. "Was that so hard?" Bobby said to her, and she ignored him with studied completeness as she left. "That woman's got to go," he told Quinn and sipped the coffee. He made a face. "It's cold, too. It's always cold."

"Robert, are you listening to me?"

He shoved the cup away. "She has to go," he said, and Quinn stopped.

"Greta?"

"No," he said, "although I've put her on notice, too. I mean Edie. We can't have her type here."

Quinn swallowed so she wouldn't start screaming at him. "Her type has been teaching here for thirty years," she told him as evenly as she could. "She was Teacher of the Year three years ago. Her students adore her. Parents ask for her—"

"That was before," Bobby said. "They're not asking for her now." His voice was smug.

"What did you do?" Quinn said, already knowing.

"When they call, I have to tell them the truth," he said. "I think our teachers should have the highest morals—"

"Why did they call?" Quinn leaned over the desk, aching to smack his stupid little face. "You started it, didn't you? You told a couple of people she was morally unacceptable, and they started talking, and then—"

"Quinn, she's a lesbian," Bobby said. "An open lesbian. She's influencing children. Look at Thea Holmes."

Quinn straightened in confusion. "What's wrong with Thea Holmes?"

"All that black clothing," Bobby said. "She wears those heavy shoes."

"This is a joke, right?" Quinn said. "Not even you can be that much of a moron. Thea wears Doc Martens. They all do. And just to usher you in to the twentieth century before it's over, you cannot tell a lesbian by her feet." She shook her head at him, hating him suddenly, amazed by how much she loathed him. "I don't believe this."

"She could be dangerous to our children," Bobby said stubbornly.

"How?" Quinn was so enraged her voice broke.

Bobby's mouth got smaller and tighter and he glared up at her. "Just being around her is an influence."

"Oh, absolutely." Quinn held on to the desk because she was shaking so hard. "That lesbian stuff is highly contagious. Why, yesterday I was having a Coke with Edie, and I was suddenly overcome by the urge to go down on Darla."

"There's no need to be offensive," Bobby said, drawing back.

"You're right, you're offensive enough for both of us." Quinn loomed over him, making him meet her eyes, so intense she almost lifted the desk. "Listen to me, you little worm. You give Edie any more trouble, you *cause* Edie any more trouble, and I will hunt you down and make you wish you'd never been born."

"Is that a threat?" Bobby said.

"Hell, yes, it's a threat," Quinn said. "The best thing I could do for this school is get rid of you completely, and don't think I can't do it. You cause any more trouble for me and mine, and I'm going to stop working around you and go through you. You leave her alone."

She swung around and saw Marjorie Cantor standing in the doorway, quivering with delight. Marjorie was probably going to throw out a hip getting to the teachers' lounge with this one. "Anything there you missed, Marge?" Quinn said. "Instant replay?"

"Well, really," Marjorie said. "I just wanted to give Robert the textbook inventory." She drew herself up until she looked like a dingy pouter pigeon, all ruffled dignity and outraged innocence, but the gleam was there in her eye.

"Wonderful," Quinn said and turned back to Bobby, who was glaring at her with what looked like terrified rage. "You stick to counting textbooks and leave teaching to the pros like Edie. We put up with you because you don't get in our way much; but you start screwing with the quality of education around here by running off our best teacher, and we'll take steps."

She shoved past Marjorie and into the outer office where Greta was shaking her head over her keyboard.

"How can you stand him?" Quinn asked and Greta said, "Who says I can?" and kept on typing.

———

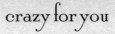

THE BP LAY low for the rest of the day, but even so by nine that night, Quinn was exhausted from both moral outrage and plain hard work. Plus her ankle ached from her first day off crutches. She sat on the edge of the prop table on the gloomy stage and tried not to let pain and tiredness drag her into depression. Most of the kids had left; Edie had gone home still pale and unhappy; even Darla had gone back to Apple Street early with Max since the sound and the costumes were done, leaving the car for Quinn to drive home on her own. "Don't go into the parking lot alone," she'd said to Quinn, "make Nick walk you out," but Quinn hadn't seen Nick since he'd come in, and now he'd probably gone, too. He hadn't even said good-bye. It wasn't like him to give up that easily.

It wasn't like him to leave her alone.

Of course, Bill hadn't come near her for a week, so that threat was probably over. Her dad had made Frank Atchity talk to him; maybe that had brought him to his senses—

"I'm going, McKenzie," Thea said from beside her. "I'm the last one. You need anything before I go?"

"Nope." Quinn tried to sound nonchalant. "How are you doing?"

"Jason's taking me home," Thea said, and then she grinned. "I can't believe it. He came over last night when I was talking to Brian and said, 'Go away,' and Brian sort of got huffy and left, and then he said, 'I want to be with you.' I wasn't exactly sure what it meant, but it sounded good."

"He's trying," Quinn said. "Cut him a break. Guys are inept."

"I am," Thea said. "And he's not that inept."

Quinn raised an eyebrow. "Oh?"

"He took me home last night," Thea said. "Good kisser."

Quinn laughed, delighted that something in her life was finally going right. "Good for you."

"Hey, Thea!" Jason called from the door. "I'm getting old out here."

"You'll get old whether I'm there or not," Thea called back.

"Yeah, but it'll be more fun if you're here," he said, and Thea flushed.

"See you," she said to Quinn, not taking her eyes off Jason, and then she went to him.

Jason grinned and waved at Quinn and then let his arm fall around Thea's shoulders. She glowed up at him, and Quinn ached inside for them. *Horrible things are ahead of you*, she wanted to tell them, but she didn't. Maybe there weren't horrible things, if you paid attention to what you wanted, if you were honest with yourself and didn't settle.

The door clanked behind them, and she almost called, "Slam it or it won't lock," but they were gone before she could. She could get it later. She had all the time in the world, alone.

" 'Had we but world enough, and time,' " Marvell had written, " 'This coyness, lady, were no crime.' " Nick reciting poetry to her, who'd have thought it? And today the florist had shown up again, this time with gold and copper Gerbera daisies. *They look like you*, Nick had written on the card—really written it, in his handwriting, not the florist's, he'd gone to the shop—and she'd put the vase in the middle of the dining-room table and the huge flowers had glowed there, bright and ridiculous. It was impossible not to smile when she saw them, impossible not to feel warm.

"Where'd you get those?" Darla asked when she got home, and Quinn had said, "Nick," and felt stupidly proud of him, trying to hide it because Max still wasn't getting it.

Then she saw the huge purple orchid pinned to Darla's T-shirt and winced. It had scarlet and gray ribbons trailing from it, truly the ugliest corsage she'd ever seen. "Max?"

"Yeah," Darla said, and grinned. "Isn't it great?"

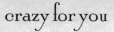

No, it's ugly. "I didn't know you were an orchid fan."

"I'm not." Darla's grin widened. "Homecoming, nineteen eighty-one."

Quinn started to laugh. "He got you an orchid for *Homecoming?*"

"Yeah." Darla unpinned the corsage carefully. "It was our second date, and everybody else had these huge yellow and white mums, and I got this ugly orchid. And I said, 'Thank you,' because it was Max and I would have worn stinkweed for him, and he said, 'I knew it had to be different because you're not like the other girls.' I damn near died on the spot."

Quinn stopped laughing. "Where'd he ever find—"

"He didn't. He had it made special." Darla's voice shook a little. "I called the florist. They had to send out for the orchid. The girl on the phone apologized for the colors, she said Max insisted it had to look just like this."

Quinn felt her throat get tight. "He's trying. He's listening."

"I know." Darla sat down at the table. "I was really hoping for something big, you know." She looked down at the orchid. "But this is good. I mean, this is great. It's so sweet. It's so Max."

"You're going back to him," Quinn said.

"I have to." Darla leaned back, her grin fading completely. "The boys have been pretty understanding about this, considering, but they need a mother at home. And Max needs a wife. That's me." She met Quinn's eyes. "He really tried. And he did pretty good. That's enough."

"I should be happier about this," Quinn said. "I really want you back with Max. I guess I was hoping he'd sweep you off your feet."

"I'll go home Saturday morning," Darla said. "We'll have most of the tech in place then. Max can wait another two days. You'll have Joe here to keep you safe—"

"You can go home tonight," Quinn said.

"No." Darla had looked at the orchid again. "I guess I'm still hoping he does that sweeping thing you talked about. Selfish, huh?"

"At least you'll always have orchids," Quinn had said.

And she'd have daisies.

She thought about it again now, as she stood on the dimly lit stage. So Nick wasn't good with commitment and he wasn't moving in and he wasn't ever going to sweep her off to the Great Southern for five days and elope with her to Kentucky. But he'd always love her, even if he'd never say it, she knew he'd always love her, no matter what. And she loved being with him and making love with him—she was pretty sure they'd get it right the next time—so it was time to stop being romantic and hoping for anything else. If Darla could be happy with orchids, she'd make do with daisies.

Quinn straightened her shoulders and went to the light box. The stage dimmed as she flipped the lights off one by one until only the last big ceiling light shone high above, making the catwalk look like black net far above her. Tomorrow, she'd take him back, she decided as she stood in the shadows at the side of the stage. It wouldn't take much to get him at this point; if she smiled at him, he'd probably take her on the prop table. That was pretty flattering, come to think of it, to have somebody like Nick just waiting for her.

So maybe she'd wait to tell him until everybody had left, like now, except by then she'd be this tired, too. Still, there was something melancholy and romantic and sexy about a theater in the dark, even a high school theater with gym mats and fake bushes piled around the edges. Maybe if she smiled at him to-morrow night, he could take her on the wrestling mats at the back of the stage, a sort of pseudo-rape fantasy because she'd be too tired to contribute. He could do all the work. Screw equality.

She rubbed her hands up and down her arms and wished he

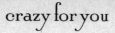

were there and they were talking the way they used to, that they were making love, and then she told herself that it wouldn't make any difference if he were, she couldn't make love here. If the BP was getting his knickers in a twist about Jason throwing longing glances her way—not to mention Meggy and Edie in the privacy of their own home—imagine what he'd do if he caught Nick throwing body parts her way.

She bent to pick up her bag, and it felt good to bend over, to stretch a little. She straightened and turned to press her back against the cool tiles of the stage wall, rolling her shoulders to ease the muscles in her back and shoulders, muscles that still ached from her week on crutches. It felt so good that she dropped the bag and kept stretching, pushing her arms up the wall over her head, flexing her calves, making her whole body feel the stretch and the cool, cool tile. She let her arms slide down the wall until her crossed wrists rested on top of her head, and closed her eyes and imagined how Nick would be the next night, strong beside her, under her, on top of her, doing things that threw her off balance and made her hot and then made her come. Just Nick, the pure pleasure of sliding against him, listening to his low laughter against her neck and the deep sigh of his breath as he moved inside her—

"What are you doing?" Nick said.

She almost let her arms drop when his voice came out of the darkness, but he didn't sound amused, he sounded distracted, and as she gathered her scrambled thoughts, she realized that she must look pretty interesting with her arms above her head like that.

"I'm stretching," she said. "Where are you?"

She heard his feet hit the floor—he must have been on the catwalk ladder—and then heard him walk toward her across the hardwood floor, finally coming into the pool of light cast by the last overhead lamp. The light made the planes of his face sharper, made his hair gleam black, and he looked tall and lanky and strong in his paint-stained T-shirt and jeans, the hottest thing she'd ever seen.

"You shouldn't be here alone," he said. "You know that. It's dangerous," and she said, "I'm not alone. You're here."

"That's even worse." He came closer to stand in front of her, not smiling.

Come and touch me, she thought.

And he came closer.

"Thank you for the daisies," she told him, meeting his eyes. "They're perfect. I don't know how to thank you."

Nick's voice was husky in the dark. "Oh, yes, you do." He took another step closer, until he was almost against her, his eyes black, casting her in the darkness of his shadow.

"I have no idea what you mean." Quinn met his eyes and didn't look away, lifting her chin when the staring match moved past comfortable and made her heart pound. Then he smiled, and she shivered a little and smiled, too, a slow curve of an invitation, daring him while her heart thudded.

"Well, you could let me do this." He put his hand on her crossed wrists and rested against them, just firmly enough so she couldn't move them. It had been so long since he'd touched her that she let her eyes go closed just from the sheer pleasure of the heat of his hand on her wrists. "And this." He took his free hand and hooked a finger inside the opening of her chambray workshirt to pop the first button.

"Hey." Quinn leaned forward to pull her arms down, and his hand closed hard on her wrists.

"And this." His free hand was on her breast, his thumb tracing a circle over the cotton of her shirt while he smiled into her eyes, his breath coming faster. She shivered, and he let his thumb slip into the vee of her shirt, into the warm hollow between her

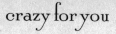

breasts, popping another button, making her breasts tense and lift against him.

Quinn felt her breath go. "Just for a couple of daisies? I don't think so." *Keep going*.

He popped another button. "Think again."

He leaned to kiss the hollow of her neck, and she sucked in a sharp breath as his lips tickled her throat. Then he kissed her again, lower this time, as he popped the rest of her buttons, one after another, slowly, echoing the buttons with kisses above, until her shirt fell open as he licked into the warm place between her breasts. He pulled her shirt open further, his hand sliding against the satin of her bra, baring her to his eyes—"Hot pink plaid, huh?" he said—and looked at her with such satisfaction and possession that she went dizzy with anticipation. Then, after what seemed like hours, he bent to trace the swell of her breast with his tongue, and she began to shudder and soften inside.

She could see the curve of his bicep against the edge of his T-shirt sleeve as he pinned her hands to the wall, the strong line of his neck, feel his hand on her wrists, the other pressed hot against her ribs as he moved his tongue across her skin. She ached to feel him under her hands, to pull his T-shirt up and pull him to her, to feel the fur of his chest tickle against her breasts and the muscles in his back flex under her fingers. "Let me go," she whispered. "Let me go so I can touch you."

He lifted his head to stare into her eyes—*don't stop*—and shook his head, smiling at her and sending heat into her bones. "Not a chance," he said, and kissed her on the mouth, taking her voice and her breath as he licked into her, making her squirm against him as he pressed her against the cool wall. His hand curved around her breast, his thumb stroked across her and then hooked around the edge of her bra, and she felt the satin slide across her nipple as he pulled the cup down, felt her whole body stiffen against him. Then his hair tickled softly on her throat as he bent to her, and she shuddered at the damp heat of his mouth on her, shuddered harder when he began to suck, shuddered harder still when he didn't stop.

"Let me go," she said, and tried to pull her hands from his grip so she could touch him as she rolled her hips toward him, but he tightened his hold, crushing her wrists together, stretching her arms higher, his lips moving against the swell of her breast, moving to bare the other, to tease her again with his mouth. His free hand moved to her zipper, easing it down, and she said, "No," but she pressed against his hand because it felt so good and she wanted to feel him everywhere. His hand slid around her waist, into the back of her jeans, into the stretchy silkiness of her underwear, around her curves there and under to hold her tight against him, shoving fabric down until she felt the denim and rayon crumple around her thighs. He pressed her back into the cold, smooth tile with his hips, pulsing against her while he smiled against her mouth. Then she felt his fingers slide into her, the hot slick inside of her, and she moaned softly because he felt so good.

"Louder," he said in her ear as he stroked her. "Scream," and she shook her head but breathed faster, sighing with his hand.

Somewhere something moved, muffled, and she tensed. Nick stopped, too, still looking into her eyes but distracted, as if he were listening for something. It was so quiet, all she could hear was Nick's breathing.

He was breathing pretty hard.

"We better stop," Quinn whispered, but there were no more sounds, she wasn't even sure she'd really heard the first one, she wasn't really sure she cared, so she pressed against his hand, and when he moved his fingers inside her again, she let her eyes go closed.

"I don't think so," Nick whispered against her ear. "I think we do this now. Right up against this wall."

She shivered. It was dumb to do this here, she should be saying no, telling him they could do this at home, at his place, even in the truck, but it felt so good right now, and she thought about what it would be like to not think about it once, to just be, to take into herself the darkness he'd tried to give her the last time, the darkness her mind had kept pulling her out of, the darkness she could feel moving into her now.

"It's been so long," he said, his voice low. "So long since I've been inside you, watched you come, made you come."

He slid his fingers higher, stroked her faster, made her breath go and her throat dry. "Nick—"

"So we do it now."

His voice hummed in her blood. "Nick—"

"I'm going to take you hard against this wall," he whispered into her ear as his fingers moved into her. "Harder than you've ever been had before. So hard you're going to feel me with every move you make for a week. You're going to remember you were mine every time you breathe."

She shuddered under the tickle of his breath, under the pressure of his hand, but mostly under what he'd said—*you're mine*—and the dark washed over her in slow waves, syncopated with his hand. His fingers slid inside her, and she thought, *Go into it*, and gave herself up. The heat and the prickle in her blood spread low and thick, and she moved with it, against Nick's hand but with his rhythm, and she thought about his hand to make things darker, Nick's fingers, long and strong and square-tipped, alien inside her, invading her, moving into her slick folds and then out to her hard little center. *There*, she thought, and when his fingers slid wetly there, she said, "*There,*" out loud, and moved to help him, shivering at the stroke.

"There," she said again, just to say it, and when he bent his head to her breast, she said, "Oh, *there*," and stretched to meet him.

Everything in her that was practical said, *You know you heard something*, and she ignored it and went into her body and what Nick was doing to her, into his fingers inside her, his hand holding her helpless, his body pressing hers—the heat was everywhere—into his mouth sucking her hard, his fingers faster there, his hand bruising her wrists—*I'm going to take you hard*—into the heat of him, the roughness of him, the darkness of him, the difference and the danger of him, into—

"*Into me*," she whispered, and all sanity died as his fingers left her, left her so empty she cried out *Oh* and rocked forward, her hips following his heat, pressing against his fingers as they moved down his own zipper, pressing until his hand was on her again, not just his hand, and she felt him thick between her thighs. She breathed, "*Yes*," into his mouth as he kissed her, felt his body slide down hers until his hand moved between her legs and guided him hard into her.

She shuddered at the shock of him, then deliberately opened herself to the dull thudding of her blood as he moved inside her, pinning her against the wall with each thrust of his hips. *Into me*, she told herself and thought of him smooth and thick sliding inside her, splitting her softness open, hard inside her, all the way inside her, into the hot and the slick and the pink of her, taking him, all of him. It was breathtaking, astounding, going into herself like this, thinking about herself like this; she'd had men inside her before but *she'd* never been there, never known herself thick with heat and succulent the way she loved herself now, could love herself now because she trusted him so completely that she didn't have to think of anything else. For the first time, she was more real inside than out, all blood and flesh and nerve and mindless, endless pleasure filled with Nick.

He lifted her hips with his, pushing her up on her toes with each breath he took, thrusting her off balance each time, trapping her against the cold, smooth wall. The tingle in her blood turned to crackle, a dark itch under her skin that made her writhe, and she almost pulled her mind away but didn't, not this time. *Into me*, she thought again, and willed herself to take in the darkness, to feel herself swell and clench, and when she opened her eyes and found him staring at her, she took him in, swallowed him with her eyes and made him hers.

"Quinn," he whispered and let go of her wrists to cradle her face and kiss her, and she clutched him and gave herself up. He whispered her name over and over as he moved inside her, looked in her eyes as he took her, and when she dug her fingernails into his shoulders, he slid his hands to her hips to move against her harder, faster, shuddering, never taking his eyes from her, his fingers digging into her flesh, all of it part of the dark surging through her body, everywhere, swelling into her fingertips, her breasts, her thighs, her lips, everywhere she opened to it.

"Oh, *God*, Quinn," Nick said, intent on her eyes. He kissed her hard, and the dark deepened and tightened. She writhed against him as it burned and spread and throbbed, and she shuddered with it, making small breathless cries as Nick thrust into her—Nick hot in her, mindless in her, thick and hard in her—her blood screaming, tight, everything inside her tight, tighter—tighter—and then she cried out "Nick" and came, staring into his eyes, crying again with each break and shudder, each spasm flinging her into the next, hard, hard again, hard again, hard again, over and over and over, until she clung to him, defenseless and open and ecstatic, safe in his arms, not caring about anything except how dark and beautiful and shattering it was inside her.

Then she collapsed and he held her tightly because her knees had gone and there was nothing left of her except ache and quiver and satisfaction. He felt so good against her—his worn T-shirt soft under her cheek, his chest hard under the shirt, his hands digging into her back—and then he bent to kiss her, his mouth soft on hers, and she sighed from the sheer rightness of it.

A few minutes later, he whispered, "Imagine what we could do in a bed."

"I don't want to imagine," she said, and her voice came out thick and low. "I want to know."

His arms tightened around her. "Your place or mine?"

"Yours." Quinn moved her face against his shirt, still clinging to him, her knees like rubber. "Max took Darla back to my place a hour ago, and I want to scream again."

When Nick was gone to get the truck—"Let me warm it up and bring it to the door," he'd said, laughing, shrugging on his flannel shirt. "The last thing I want is you going cold on me or the damn thing stalling"—she stood alone on the stage, hugging herself because they'd done it right, she'd done it right, and anything seemed possible. Darla would go back to Max, the play would be a hit, Bill would find somebody else, and she and Nick could drive each other into hot, wet darkness forever.

She picked up her bag and went out to meet him in the dark parking lot, her heart tripping, letting the door slam shut behind her and yanking on it to make sure it was locked. If the BP found it unlocked, there'd be hell to—

"We need to talk," Bill said behind her.

fifteen

NICK SAT in the truck and tried to tell himself that things were just fine, that the separation of church and state was still intact, but it wasn't working. His democracy had turned to theocracy, and he didn't care. Somewhere in the middle of fucking Quinn against a wall, he'd stopped thinking incoherent thoughts that could be summarized as *this is phenomenal sex*, and realized that Quinn was murmuring *oh, yes, there,* breathing his name, taking him without question, giving without reservation, staring into his eyes, being Quinn the body he craved and Quinn the woman he loved, one and the same, and everything fused, and he fell and made love to her instead.

Oh, hell, he thought now from habit, but he was too elated to be depressed. Holding her and loving her and needing her and having her all at once had been a mind-bending experience, one he intended to repeat every chance he got. Forever. Assuming he could pull that off.

"Don't fuck this up," he told himself now. "Do not fuck this up."

Of course, she was going to be skeptical. *You pancaked on me three times*, she'd said, so she'd need some reassurance when she got in the truck that they weren't going out for pizza.

Okay, she'd get in the truck and he'd tell her he loved her.

No, he wouldn't. Jesus, this would be the worst time, right after sex, she'd never believe him, especially given the stuff he'd pulled before. They could never have pizza again. Why hadn't he said, "Let's go out for broccoli"?

Okay, he couldn't tell her tonight, so maybe tomorrow. He could take her home tomorrow after the play stuff was done and not jump her until he'd told her.

No, that wouldn't work, either, she'd think it was just a ploy to get her into bed. So he could tell her and then not sleep with her tomorrow night.

Fat chance.

This wasn't going to work. Besides, he didn't want to tell her anyway, how could you just say something like that? No wonder guys sent flowers. More daisies. He could write it on a card.

No, he couldn't.

Okay, so he was going to have to get used to the idea before he started actually talking about it. Oh, hell, he was never going to talk about it. Maybe she'd just know. Maybe if he stayed the night, she'd figure it out.

But then he'd have to actually stay the night.

He flinched a little at the thought, and then he thought of holding her close and safe—holding Quinn close and safe, loving her, feeling her warmth all night, waking up next to her, not having to wait to hold her again—and he stopped flinching and told himself it would be okay. He could get up really early. It would be fine.

He started the truck and thought, *Well, what am I going to say to her when she gets in?* and turned the truck off to think again.

SHE LOOKED PALE, Bill thought. Pale with bright spots on her cheeks, sick, she needed him to take care of her. "Come home," he said, and she shook her head and laughed, but there was something wrong with her laugh.

"You scared me." She tried to laugh again.

Wrong. Wrong. His head started to pound.

She pulled away. "Bill, you cannot even believe how tired I am. I can't talk right now."

"Come home," he said and tried to take her hand, but she jerked it away, too, like there was something wrong with him, there wasn't anything wrong with him, and she said, "Bill, I'm tired."

She tried to move around him and he blocked her, just took one step, not touching her, just to stop her. "Come home," he said. "We can talk."

"I don't want to talk, Bill." Her voice was flat again, not pretending any more, he'd known that laugh was fake, and now she was just saying she didn't want to, like she didn't owe him, like it wasn't her fault—

"I want to talk," he said, and crowded her closer, liking the way she stepped back—now she was paying attention—so that he moved closer and closer again until she was up against the building, nowhere to go.

Now she'd talk to him, damn it.

"Stop it." She put her hands out to wave him away. "Just stop it. This is stupid."

She shoved at him a little, and it made him mad, she was shoving him away, but it made him want her, too, her hands on him, and that was wrong, this wasn't about sex, and then she said, "Bill," and tried to move around him and he caught at her wrists to hold her there.

She shut up then, she knew he was serious, she was going to listen this time.

"Just tell me what I did so wrong so I can fix it and you can come back." He heard his voice, and it sounded thick, like there was a lump in his throat, the way people sounded when they were going to cry, and that wasn't his voice at all.

"You didn't do anything wrong." She tried to twist her hands away and he held her tighter, felt the fragile bones in her wrists crunch together, saw her take a sharp breath, frown at the pain, and thought, *Now you'll listen,* thought about shoving her against the wall, shoving himself against her, just to feel her again, just to—

"Let go, Bill." Her face was wrong, she was frowning at him, she was all wrong. "It just wasn't right. It's nobody's fault." Her voice shook a little, and that made him tighten his hands again. She looked afraid, she was really paying attention now, he could talk to her now. "Let go of me," she said, and he watched her try to be calm, that was his Quinn, nothing she couldn't handle, nothing she couldn't make all right. Except this. He was the one in control now.

She squirmed under his hands again and he felt hot, felt like pushing at her, pushing against her, all her softness was supposed to be his, it was his—

"This is ridiculous, Bill," she said sharply. "You're hurting me."

That's the only way you listen, he wanted to say, but he couldn't waste the time, he had to make her see—"What wasn't right?" he said. "You owe me that, what was so goddamn wrong you had to leave? You just tell me that."

"Bill, I don't like this." She tried to make her voice firm, he could tell she was trying, but she quavered anyway, and he thought, *Good. Good* for somebody else to feel some pain instead of always him, *good* for her to know who was in charge. "Let me go," she said, and he felt the heat flare again because he wasn't going to. She was just out of luck because he wasn't going to.

"I don't *like* letting you go." Bill had to push the words out, his throat was too tight, she had to understand, he'd *make* her understand just how *wrong* she'd been to leave him in that *tomb* of an apartment. He shoved her into the brick again, bouncing her with his words to make her listen. "I don't *like* coming home and finding you not there." And watching her through windows,

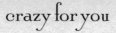

always shut out, that was her fault. He pulled her up and shoved her into the brick harder. "I don't *like* never seeing you. I don't *like* the way you won't look at me, the way you treat me like I'm not even *there*, so I guess we've *both* got some things we don't like."

"I'm going home." Quinn tried to jerk her wrists free, but there was no way, not anymore, he'd had enough, so he pulled her close and then shoved her really hard against the building to make her listen, and her head smacked against the wall, and she cried out and blinked back tears, pain, he knew about pain, and he was glad.

He pressed her wrists into the bricks, one hard on each side of her head so she couldn't turn away, putting his face close to hers so she'd have to look at him, have to see him. "I did everything right, I was everything you needed, and you left me because of that damn dog. You were happy with me," he said, and her voice choked as she said, "Bill—"

"You *were*," he said, "you *were*, you *were*, you *were*—" He shoved her wrists into the brick on each *were*, glad she winced when he did it, breathing heavier each time she did, glad she was paying attention, feeling really good, feeling really really *good*, but when he pulled back to shove her into the wall again, she wrenched herself away, throwing herself sideways, trying to get away. He said, *"No,"* and grabbed at her shirt, but she wouldn't stop, he felt it give suddenly, and then she was running from him, limping and stumbling, her shirt was in his hand and her bare back was pale in the dark night as she ran, and all he had was her shirt, that was *wrong*. He yelled, "Goddamn it," and threw the shirt away to run after her, to get her back, she couldn't get away again, she was not going to get away again.

He caught her in three strides, grabbing at her bare arm, feeling her warm flesh under his fingers as he yanked her back and yelled, *"Stop running from me."* He swung her around—she was naked, almost naked, one of those loud bras, awful pink, she was so round, he reached for her, wanting to dig his fingers into her—and she screamed, *"No!"* and kicked out and caught him on the knee. The pain shot to his groin, the knee gave way, he buckled to the pavement, losing his grip on her as he went down, grabbing out again even as she stumbled back and ran again. He tripped to his feet and went after her, just as a truck came around the corner, and his mind screamed *No* just like she had because the truck slowed down.

QUINN SHRIEKED. *"NICK,"* his name tearing at her throat, and the truck slid to a stop close to her. She lunged for the door just as Nick opened it from the inside and Bill grabbed her from behind again, yanking at her arm, and she wanted to scream and scream, grappling for the door, for Nick's hand, anything to be with him and safe and away from the madness behind her.

"Christ!" Nick lunged across the seat as Quinn grabbed for him. *"Let go of her!"*

He caught the hand she flung at him and hauled her into the cab, dragging Bill behind her into the doorway. Her shoulders ached as they pulled her between them, and she clutched Nick with all the strength she had left, digging her fingers into his hand, leaning toward him, trying to become part of him again so Bill couldn't drag her back.

"Don't let me go," she said to Nick between gasps, and he said, "Don't worry."

His face looked dark as he leaned across her, pinning her to the seat with his shoulder, keeping her safe with his weight. He glared down at Bill. *"Bill, let go of her now."* He started to shove past her to get out of the truck and Quinn held on to him.

"No," she said. *"No, you don't leave me, no."*

"We need to talk," Bill said, still holding on. "Just talk. This is between us, Nick. Nothing to do with you." His voice was thick with tension and rage, and Quinn wanted to throw up; she'd never heard Bill like that before. Breaking into her house could have been just malicious, but this, this was madness. Then he said, "Give her back to me," and Quinn panicked.

"Don't let me go," she said to Nick, not knowing what he could do, holding on to him for dear life. "Don't leave me, don't let me go."

Nick took a deep breath, and then set the emergency brake with his free hand. He eased himself around her, pushing her with his hip so that she slid over toward the driver's door, almost lying on the seat because Bill was still holding on to her wrist, trying to pull her out. Nick leaned against her arm, blocking her from Bill's sight—he felt so good and solid, like an anchor, like her last hope—and began to pry Bill's fingers from her arm. He said with calm ferocity, *"You're hurting her, Bill,"* and that was when Bill finally let go.

Quinn felt so relieved she almost wept, crossing her arms in front of her, hugging herself to ease the aches in her shoulders and wrists, feeling naked and exposed in just her bra. Her shirt was back someplace on the pavement along with everything she'd ever known about herself and the world. Things like this didn't happen to her. People didn't hurt her. She didn't get this scared. She was the one in control, she could fix anything, she—

"Don't get between us, Nick." Bill stood close, making his body a block so Nick couldn't close the door. "I know you're a good friend, but this is serious. Don't make me come in there after her."

His voice was so calm that Quinn thought, *He really is insane. He's gone completely round the bend.* He could do anything and think it was right. Even hurt her. Even drag her off just because he thought she belonged to him.

"Here's the situation, Bill," Nick said in the same calm voice

Bill was using. She could feel him shaking, hear the strain behind his voice as he fought his temper to stay in control. "You can undoubtedly kick my ass in about thirty seconds, but you can't do it and grab Quinn, too, and that means she'll have thirty seconds to lock herself inside this truck and dial nine-one-one on the cell phone while we're beating the crap out of each other. Then you can explain to Frank Atchity why she's so upset and I'm bleeding, and he's already got some pretty good suspicions about you. Or you can let me take her home, and we can decide what the fuck is going on tomorrow. Your call."

Bill looked like a maddened bull, but then he looked past Nick's shoulder into Quinn's eyes. She drew a shuddering breath, and his face changed. "Don't cry," he said to her. "I just need to talk."

"Later," she said to appease him. "Much later." *I hate you. I never want to see you again. Ever. I hope you die.*

"I'm going to take her home now," Nick said. "Step back so we can close the door."

Bill stood there for a minute, the longest minute of Quinn's life, and then he stepped back, and Nick pulled the door shut and locked it. "Jesus, that was bad," he said, and turned to put his arms around her.

She leaned into his arms, pressing against him, trying to feel warm and safe, and when she said, "I'm okay," he said, "No, you're not. Somebody you used to care about just hurt you."

His arms tightened around her and she clutched his shirt and sobbed once—she hadn't meant to at all, it just came out—and he held her close until she felt her breathing slow again. "Take me home," she said into his shirt. "Get me out of here."

Nick kissed her forehead. He let go of her to take off his flannel shirt and drape it around her, and then he climbed over her to get back to the driver's seat. Quinn took one last long shuddering breath and turned to get her seat belt. Through the window she saw Bill across the lot, standing there, her shirt in his hand, watching them. "Get me *out of here*," she said, and Nick looked past her and said, "Jesus," and floored it getting her away from him.

NICK TOOK HER home—trying not to shake, trying to be the practical, calm, soothing one when all he wanted to do was kill Bill—and they walked in the dining room to find Max and Darla sitting in strained silence.

"What happened to you?" Darla said when she saw Quinn's face. "Nick, what did you—"

"It wasn't Nick," Quinn said. "It was Bill. He grabbed me. He's out control, completely out of control."

"The police," Darla said, and Nick said, "Damn straight."

Quinn collapsed into a chair. "I hate this. I hate this. Why couldn't he just give up and let me go?" She put her head down on the table, and Darla went to stand beside her and stroke her hair.

Nick felt like hell.

"It's not your fault," Darla told her. "He's crazy."

"We're calling the police *now*," Nick said, needing to do something, and Quinn raised her head and said, "Not now."

Nick said, *"Quinn!"* and Darla said, "Just give her a minute. She's not going to talk to anybody like this."

"Oh, yeah?" Max stood up, as tense as Nick. "Suppose that loon comes here after her. Nick calls the police."

"He's not going to come here," Quinn said tiredly, and Nick wanted to hold her, to tell her it would be all right, that he'd be there, that—"My dad's here. Darla's here—"

"Not anymore, she's not," Max said. "This is it." He turned

to Darla and said, "I know you want to wait until Saturday, but it's time for you to come home. You are not staying here with that asshole on the loose."

Darla shook her head, incredulous with him. "I can't leave Quinn. Bill—"

"She can come home with us," Max said at the same time Nick said, "I'll stay with Quinn."

"Or Nick can stay with her," Max said, picking up the thread smoothly. "But you don't stay here. It's dangerous."

"If it's dangerous, then I'm definitely not leaving her." Darla's voice was stubborn but uncertain. "Nick won't stay, you know how he is—"

"Hey," Nick said, feeling outraged and guilty all at once. Of course he'd stay. Okay, so generally he wasn't much for sleepovers, but this was different. He'd stay. At least until Bill was in jail with a good long sentence.

"—and I can't leave her alone," Darla finished.

"It's okay—" Quinn began, and then Max said, "The hell with this, you're *going*," and picked Darla up over his shoulder.

Nick winced, and Darla said, *"Wait a minute,"* and squirmed to wriggle down.

"Probably not a good idea," Nick told Max under his breath, but he opened the door anyway, and Max carried her out.

Darla said, "I said, *wait a minute,*" as they hit the porch, but Nick said, "Don't hurry back," and shut the door behind them. He leaned against the door and locked it, throwing the deadbolt.

Quinn stood, tense and strained. "That's my best friend. I object."

Nick came toward her. "No, you don't. You're as glad as I am they're back together. Come on—"

"Back together may be premature," Quinn said. "She didn't seemed charmed by that. Just like I wasn't charmed by Bill."

Nick stopped, appalled at the comparison. "That's different. This is her husband."

"I'm not sure." Quinn limped into the living room and sank onto the couch. "I'm not sure about anything anymore." She rubbed her ankle. "Bill was never like this before, grabby, physical. He's changed. Maybe Max has, too."

"I sure as hell hope so." Nick came to stand in front of her. "That's why Darla left him. I thought change was what you guys wanted."

"Not like that," Quinn said. "I don't understand Bill at all."

She looked tired and confused and hurt, and Nick felt like hell again. "I do. I think he's a jerk and we're calling the police right now, but I understand him. He thinks you belong to him."

"Listen, I have told him—"

"You told me, too, and I didn't go away." He sat next to her on the couch, taking her hand, trying to make her understand so she wouldn't look so lost. "For the past two weeks, I've waited, and I've watched you, and I knew you'd come back to me because you belong to me. Every guy thinks that about the woman he loves."

Quinn jerked her head up at "loves," and he ignored it to go on.

"It's the reason I trapped you against that wall after you blew me off for those weeks. I took you back." He felt a wave of heat even as he said it. He wanted her again, wanted to take her like that again, feel her give herself up like that again, and then Quinn closed her eyes, and he felt like hell. "Sorry."

"I'm not." She opened her eyes again and looked at him fully. "I was just overwhelmed by how sexy that was. Politically incorrect as hell, but really, really sexy."

He wanted to bend her back right there on the couch, and he felt guilty for wanting to, she'd been manhandled enough for one night. But he still wanted to. "Look, I know it's not right, but that's the way it is. I watch you walk across the stage, and I look at your butt and I think, *That's mine*. I watch you stretch up to take a paint can from Thea and your shirt gapes open and I think, *That's mine*. I listen to your voice and your laugh and I watch your eyes and your mouth and I think, *That's mine*. Even when you were saying no, you were mine. It doesn't go away. You can't talk me out of that. Every move you make belongs to me. I know it's wrong, and I don't care."

"Oh," Quinn said.

"And the problem is, Bill doesn't even know it's wrong. He just knows you're his and you're not with him."

Quinn swallowed. "He's never going to see the truth, is he?"

"Yes," Nick said. "He's going to see it, but it's going to take more than talk. I don't know what it's going to take, but I know it's going to be more than you saying, 'Bill, it's over.' You could say it to me and I'd never believe it. You're mine. Just like Darla belongs to Max." He spared a thought for Max, who'd just kidnapped his wife. "I hope."

"I can't cope with this right now." Quinn collapsed against the back of the couch. "I know that's weak, I'll handle this tomorrow, but no more tonight."

"You need ice on that ankle before we call the cops?" Nick said, and she shook her head.

"No." Quinn shook her head. "No police. I can't face them tonight. Tomorrow, I'll do it, I swear. But not tonight."

Nick started to protest and then saw how exhausted she looked. He was staying with her, and Bill wasn't going any place. "First thing in the morning, then, you promise."

"Tomorrow," she said, nodding.

"Okay." He held out his hand. "Come on, gimpy. Let's go to bed."

"Oh, you really are staying?" Quinn took his hand, and he looked down to see her wrists scraped raw. From far away he heard her say, "Dad's upstairs, you know. You don't—"

"What happened to your wrists?"

Quinn looked at her hands. "Oh. Bill scraped them against the bricks."

"That's it," Nick said. "He goes to jail forever. The sonofa-bitch—"

"It's not that bad—"

"Fuck him. He goes to jail." Nick gritted his teeth, and then shut up when he saw how upset she was. "Tomorrow. Where's your first-aid stuff?"

"Kitchen," Quinn said. "I don't think he realized—"

"Screw what he realized," Nick said. "He goes to jail."

DARLA STOLE A look at Max as the truck bumped down the road. She didn't think he was mad, but he wasn't saying anything and she didn't know what to say, so she couldn't start a conversation. She'd already tried, "Quinn needs me," and gotten back, "Nick's there," so now she sat silent wondering how she'd gotten into this mess.

She'd wanted excitement. Well, she'd gotten that. And now she'd gotten an orchid and been kidnapped by her own husband. That was interesting, even if they were going back to the same old life at home—

It was right about then that she noticed they weren't on their way home.

"Max, where are we going?"

He turned instead of answering, and she realized they were out on the edge of town, and then he hung a sharp right and skidded into the first lane of the old drive-in.

"This has been padlocked for years," she said. *"Max, look out!"*

He kept driving toward the padlocked chain, and she flinched when they hit it, breaking it and a headlight at the same time.

Maybe he was mad.

He drove straight for the back of the lot, and she thought for a moment that they were going to go through the back fence the way they'd gone through the chain, but he swerved at the last minute, making the truck fishtail in a half circle, and brought them to a stop in the last row of the theater.

"Haven't done that in twenty years," he said, his voice deep with satisfaction.

"More like fifteen," Darla said.

The lot stretched out for an acre, ghostly posts marking row after row of parking spaces, the speakers long gone, some broken spiral cords still bouncing in the wind. The screen ahead was smaller than she remembered it, but the old concession stand was about right, a cinder-block rectangle with the best barbecue and the worst restrooms in Tibbett. They'd come here a lot, both of them just babies, seventeen, amazed by life and by each other and especially by sex.

Maybe that's why Max had brought her out here, sex in the front seat again. Well, it was a nice idea, she thought tiredly, but they could just go home to bed. That's where she'd be for the rest of her life anyway, home. Why put it off?

Max cut the engine and turned to her, leaning back against the seat. "We had some good times here." He smiled at her, acting a little nervous, which was the way he'd been back then, come to think of it. "Remember?"

"Yes," Darla said. "Pretty exciting."

"Yeah." Max nodded, clearly at a loss for what to say next, and she felt awful for him. He'd gotten her an orchid, for heaven's sake. That was enough.

"It's okay, Max," Darla said. "I know we can't get that back. And it's pretty sweet of you to bring me out here to remember."

"No problem." He shrugged.

His voice was offhand, but the way he sat wasn't, his hand tense on the steering wheel, so clearly unsure that her heart melted. He was so much dearer now than when he'd made her shiver here all those years ago. You got some good trade-offs when the excitement went, she realized. He might have been more exciting in high school, but she'd never trade the man he was now for the boy he'd been then, sweet as that boy had been.

"So." He turned to look at her and then evidently lost his courage. "What's new?"

"Aside from Bill mugging Quinn?" she said. "Not much. And you?"

He shrugged again. "Oh, I've made some changes."

"Right." Darla sighed, feeling sorry for both of them. "It's okay, Max. I give up. I'll come home."

"You don't have to give up," he protested. "I've taken some risks. Hell, I took Barbara to dinner. That was a change."

"Yeah, I loved that one," Darla said flatly.

"And the play." Max sounded as if he was digging for stuff. Probably was, poor schmuck. "I really am into that play. That's a big change." He nodded in the dark. "And I'm cooking dinner, did I tell you that?" He nodded some more. "Buying stuff and cooking it. I'm not bad, too."

"I'm not surprised." Darla felt her throat catch. He was trying so hard. "You've always been good at everything. It's okay, I'm coming home, you don't have to—"

"And I"—he looked around a little wildly—"and I bought this drive-in." Darla jerked back. "You what?"

Max nodded, now a lot surer. "I bought this drive-in." He looked at her and nodded again. "Bought it this afternoon. The station's doing good, no point in risking that, but I thought, 'Well, a new generation ought to have what we had,' so I bought it. Took a chance, what the hell."

Darla's mouth fell open. He'd bought a drive-in. In a million years, she'd never have seen this one coming. Just like she hadn't seen the orchid coming, but this—

This was huge. Sweeping. "Max," she said, her voice breathless.

He swallowed. " 'Course I'm going to need help with it. Can't start a business by myself." He turned to her, looking as vulnerable as a seventeen-year-old. "I thought we could do it together. Like the old days when you ran the register at the station." He tried to look offhand, but she could see the tension in his eyes. "You in?"

"Of course I'm in," she said, surprised to find tears choking her voice. "I can't believe—"

He leaned over and kissed her then, solid and so Max, and he felt so good she grabbed onto him, kissing him back, holding on to him for dear life.

"Don't leave me again," he said into her hair. "Don't ever leave me again."

"I can't," she said. "I can't leave you alone, you're too unpredictable. God knows what you'd buy next." She kissed him again, hard, so glad she could, so glad she was with him again. "Oh, I missed you. I'm so happy. I can't believe it, I'm so happy."

He laughed, and she could hear the relief there, and with the relief all the tension left him, and he was Max again. "Have I ever told you how sexy you look in a T-shirt?" he said, and she shivered as she felt his hands move down her back.

"No." She shook her head, swallowing tears. This was no time to cry. "You never did."

"You're even sexier out of it," he said and slid his hands under her shirt.

She moved closer to him and breathed him in, closing her eyes as she felt his hands move against her skin. "I missed you so much."

"Thank God," he said and stripped the T-shirt up over her head.

"Max, we're in public." She shivered in the cool air, crossing her arms over her bra.

"No, we own this place, it's not public." He was looking at her in the twilight, his eyes roaming hot on her, really looking at her, and she stopped covering herself. "I know you're hard to get," he went on and flipped open her bra catch, one-handed, just like the old days. "I know you don't put out." He pulled her bra off her shoulders and slid his hand to her breast and she closed her eyes. "So we can just pet until you say stop." He bent his head and kissed her breast. "I swear I'll stop when you say stop." He leaned over her, so close he was almost on top of her, his hand sliding her zipper down, his body hot against hers.

"Don't stop," she said, as he bent to her again. "Do it all." She started on his buttons by feel since his head was in her way. "Just don't tell the kids at school. I want them to think I'm still a good girl."

"Best I know," Max said breathlessly, and she pulled his shirt open and climbed into his lap.

OUTSIDE QUINN'S HOUSE, Bill watched through his shutter. Quinn and Nick were in the living room where he couldn't see—he should have broken a shutter in there, too, should have thought ahead, he could do that tomorrow—but they might come back through when Nick went home, so he stood and watched an empty room. Then they did come in, heading for the kitchen, and he slipped into the backyard to look through the lace curtains of that window. Nick was opening a cupboard.

Quinn had her wrists under running water, and he winced, realizing he'd hurt her more than he'd thought. If she'd just listened, he wouldn't have hurt her. Bill scowled at the dog as it stood on its hind legs to see what Quinn was doing. The damn dog had started it all.

Nick took a box down from the cupboard and dropped it on the counter. He picked up a blue-checked towel and when Quinn held out her wrists to him, he patted them dry, carefully, and Bill felt his throat catch. It should have been him, not Nick who got to comfort her, not Nick the old friend who couldn't hold her later. Friends were fine, he was glad she had Nick, but it would have been better if Nick hadn't been there tonight. If he hadn't, Quinn would have gone home with him, he would have been the one drying her wrists.

Nick opened the box and took out a roll of gauze and began to wrap it around her wrists, bending his head close to hers to see what he was doing. Too close. If anyone saw them it would look funny, that close, even if it was good old Nick. Nick wrapped her other wrist, taping the gauze in place carefully, and then Quinn said something to him, and he laughed, way too close to her.

Bill frowned. She should be careful. Nick could get the wrong idea.

Nick picked up the gauze again and wrapped it once around her wrist—that made no sense, she was bandaged—and then around her other wrist, wrapping them together, winding the gauze loosely as he laughed into her eyes. Quinn lifted her arms, and Nick bent under them, straightening so her wrists were locked behind his neck and her body fell against his.

The extra gauze unrolled from her wrists to the floor. Bill concentrated on the ribbon of cotton snaking its way down Nick's back, tried to ignore the way Quinn laughed up at Nick, the way she pushed herself against him, the way Nick's hands went to her

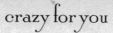

hips—there was a rushing noise in his head—and then Nick kissed her, hard, not a friend's kiss, a lover's kiss, they were lovers, Nick was kissing her hard, his hands were on her butt, in the back of her jeans, her hands gripped the collar of Nick's T-shirt—that was worse, the air left Bill's lungs—twisting the material as if she wanted to rip it off, and then Nick pulled Quinn toward the stairs, still kissing her, kissing his Quinn, Nick had no right, that damn dog dancing around them—

It wasn't until they disappeared, until they'd been gone minutes, maybe hours, Bill couldn't tell, that he realized all the screaming he'd been doing had been silent, that it was all inside his head.

QUINN WATCHED NICK peel off his T-shirt. He had such a lovely body and she was going to have it. Again. Only this time, she could touch him. Nick all over her, inside her, to wipe away all the bad memories. She thought about Bill and went cold for a moment before she pushed the thought away. Nick was here. She was safe. "Hurry up," she said.

"Shhhh." Nick looked back at the closed door. "Do not wake up Joe. I'd just as soon he didn't come in and pull up a chair."

He stripped off his jeans and he was beautiful. She whispered, "I'm crazy about your body. Get it over here."

"Pushy." He slid under the sheets to hold her, hard against her softness, and she rolled until she was on top of him.

"You're mine," she told him.

"Works for me." He ran his hands up her sides until she caught at his wrists and pulled them over his head.

"You are going to feel me for a week," she whispered, moving against him.

"Honey, I already feel you every minute of the day." He lifted his face to kiss her, taking her mouth, licking into her and making her shudder again. "I've been thinking about you for so damn long it's a miracle I get anything done. Every time you turn your back on me, I want to bend you over something, and every time you don't, I want to take you against a wall, and if you're not around I close my eyes and imagine you're naked and I'm inside you." He kissed her again, making her blood heat with his words and his mouth and his long, lovely body shifting under her.

Quinn was breathless. "This domination thing doesn't seem to work when I do it," she grumbled, trying to be cool, but he was hard under her hips and she tensed against him just to feel him thrust back.

"Oh, I don't know." Nick kissed her neck, evidently unconcerned that she held his hands. "We get some leather and handcuffs in here, you could do some damage."

Quinn let go of him. "I can do some damage without leather," she whispered and began to kiss her way down his chest.

"Oh, Christ," she heard Nick say as she ran her tongue across his stomach. "You're right. I'm yours."

Damn right, she thought, and took him.

NICK WOKE UP the next morning at eight, as usual, with the covers kicked off, as usual, and with Quinn's head against his arm, not as usual. He felt a spurt of panic, and then she stirred in her sleep, and her hair slid silky against his skin, and he remembered the stage the night before and Bill and felt a rush of relief that she was safe with him. She moved again, and he thought, *This is good*, and rolled against her back to feel how warm she was all over.

He was sliding his hand up to her breast when Darla knocked and came in without stopping, saying, "Max is waiting, I just came back for my—"

Nick froze. Eight a.m. was not his best time for fast thinking even when he wasn't naked in a strange bed.

"Nice ass," Darla said. "Not that I'll ever see it again."

"Thank you," Nick said, and she left, shutting the door behind her.

"What was that?" Quinn said sleepily.

"You owe me for that," he told her, rolling her over. "Come here."

"For what?" Quinn said, but she came anyway.

QUINN SAT AT the breakfast table an hour later and tried to make sense of her life. Talk about the good, the bad, and the ugly. She was going to have to go to the police, Bill was out of control, and that made her feel like hell. He'd been perfectly sane until he'd gotten involved with her, and he probably would be again once he forgot her. Maybe if she waited—

She thought of him shoving her against the brick the night before. There was compassion and there was stupidity. She was going to the police.

Nick came in, dressed in his workshirt and jeans, his hair still damp from his shower, and she remembered the good part. "You are gorgeous," she said, and he said, "Nope, that's Max," and kissed her, reminding her that she was in love on a sunny Saturday morning.

"No, that's you," she said. "Definitely you."

"Well, glad you think so." He leaned back against the sink with such tense nonchalance that she knew something was wrong. "Because you're going to be waking up with this face from now on. I'm moving in."

Quinn sat back. He looked uncertain as he said it, defiant and sort of miserable. "Why?"

He rolled his eyes. "Because you need somebody to take care of you. Hell, what kind of guy would I be—"

"I'm going to the police today," Quinn said. "My dad is here. You don't have to stay."

He stopped, taken aback. "I thought you wanted—"

"I want you to move in," Quinn said. "But only when you want to for you, not for me. I don't need any favors."

"Don't start this." He turned to the fridge and got out the milk. "There is no way you're going to tell me we're not together after last night."

"Of course we're together," Quinn said. "I love you." She waited for a minute to see if he'd say it, too, and then went on. "That doesn't mean you have to live here. You like your space and your privacy. Dad's here to keep Bill out until the police take care of him. You don't have to move in."

He stood there with the milk carton in his hand, frowning at her. "That's not it. I want to take care of you."

Quinn tried not to wince at the echo of Bill. "I know. But you don't have to. You stay at your place where you're happy and I'll live here. And we'll see each other every day just like we always have, only now we'll be having lots of great sex, too." She smiled at him. "I'm pretty sure that's your idea of the perfect life, isn't it?"

"Yeah," he said and drank some milk from the carton.

"Well, then, everything's great," Quinn said, ignoring the carton.

"Yeah," Nick said. "Thanks."

sixteen

NICK STOPPED by the police station on his way to work and filed a complaint, telling them to expect Quinn, but when Frank Atchity called from the station later that morning, he wasn't reassuring.

"We talked to Bill before he left for the game at noon," Frank said. "He seems to think you're exaggerating things."

"She has marks on her wrists from him," Nick said, outraged. "He hurt her."

"The principal was there and he said Bill had told him that, ah, Quinn, well, likes things rough." Frank coughed a little. "Bill agreed."

Nick almost went through the phone he was so mad. "Quinn does not like things rough. That asshole grabbed her in a dark parking lot and terrorized her."

"How do you know she doesn't like it rough?" Frank said.

Nick heard the suspicion in his voice too late. "I just know. She's not that way."

"Because I'm against guys beating up women, but I'm also against getting caught between two guys being played by a woman. And she hasn't been in to press charges, either."

"Oh, hell, Frank—"

"See, the thing is," Frank said. "I'm the sheriff, not just Joe's poker buddy. I need evidence. And I need Quinn in here with a complaint before I can get real aggressive about looking for it."

"She'll be in," Nick said, grimly. "And she is not playing anybody. That guy is out of control."

"So you staying over there to protect her?"

"No," Nick said.

"Real worried, huh?"

"Frank—"

"Get her in here," Frank said. "Or forget about it. One or the other."

Nick slammed down the phone and turned on Max when he came in a few minutes later. "You're late."

"Yup," Max said, obnoxiously cheerful. He started to whistle, and Nick thought about killing him.

"I gather you got your wife back?"

"Oh, yeah," Max said, and then he got a little less cheerful. "Uh, that reminds me."

Nick felt suddenly wary. "What?"

"You want to buy a drive-in with me?" Max asked with studied innocence.

"No," Nick said and headed for the Ford in the last bay.

"Nick," Max said.

Nick stopped and closed his eyes. "Why would I want to buy a drive-in?"

"Because I told Darla last night I'd already bought it, and I called this morning and the damn thing is a hundred and twenty thousand, and I could use a co-signer."

Nick turned to him. "You told her you bought the drive-in?"

"Hey," Max said. "It was the smartest idea I'd had in a long time." He turned thoughtful. "It worked, too. The sex was great."

Nick stared at his brother. He wasn't joking. "You bought an abandoned drive-in so you could have sex with your wife?"

Max shook his head. "This wasn't just sex. I saw God again. A hundred and twenty thou is a small price to pay."

Nick snorted. "Yeah, as long as I'm paying half."

Max scowled at him. "Yes or no?"

"Yes," Nick said. "But only for Darla." He shook his head and then had to laugh. "A drive-in."

"Hey, we might make some money off it," Max said.

"Only if we show *Sorority Sluts in Heat* to minors."

"I'm not proud," Max said and picked up the next work order.

Fifteen minutes later, from under the hood of a Chevy, Max said, "Thanks."

"No sweat," Nick said.

"WAS THAT MAX dropping you off?" Debbie said to Darla when she got to the Upper Cut.

"Yep," Darla said. "I moved back in last night. He bought me a drive-in."

"That dump out on the old highway?" Debbie blinked at her. "Why?"

"To get me back," Darla said. "Isn't that the most romantic thing you've heard of?"

"I'd rather have roses," Debbie said.

BILL SAT IN the weight room, ignoring Bobby and thinking about Quinn. Now that baseball was over, he could see her more, work on the house.

"You dumb *ox*," Bobby said in his face. "You're not even *listening* to me. I lie to a cop for you today, and then you do the most piss poor job of coaching I've even seen in my life. *We're not even going to the regionals*."

"Leave me alone, Bobby." Bill got up. "I have things to do."

"We lost that game on *coaching*," Bobby spat. "You *fucked it up*. This is *your fault*."

"I don't care." Bill flipped off the lights in the weight room and turned for the door. "Hell, it's just baseball."

"Just baseball?" The BP almost lost a lung, he screamed so

loud, and Bill laughed at him. What a twit. Quinn had been so right.

"Funny, huh?" Bobby got up close, in his face. "I'll tell you something funny. I was here last night, checking the stage door because that bitch you're so obsessed with is incompetent." He stopped, fuming. "She *threatened* me and she's *incompetent*."

"She's not incompetent," Bill said. "She's careless sometimes"—*she let Nick touch her*—"but she's not incompetent."

"Oh, yeah?" Bobby rounded on him, sneering. "Well, I came back to check the stage door last night, it was unlocked *because she's incompetent*, and when I came in, I saw *her*. And you know what she was doing?"

"Bobby, I don't care," Bill said. "Get out of my face."

"She was *fucking that mechanic*." Bill flinched, and Bobby's voice went low and evil. "Up against the wall, like a whore. Right there on stage. I watched them. While you waited out in the lot like the *dumb ox* you are, that *slut*—"

Bill backhanded him. It was easy, like swatting a fly, and when Bobby didn't get up, Bill nodded and left.

There was one thing he owed Bobby for, he thought as he packed his clothes into his matched suitcases. If what he said about Quinn was true—which it probably wasn't, Quinn was a good person, she wouldn't do that, she was probably just kissing Nick, which was bad enough, and then Bobby with his dirty mind came in, he was glad he'd hit Bobby—well, it was time he moved in. It had worked before, just moving his stuff into her apartment a little at a time, and she hadn't objected, Quinn wasn't difficult, so he'd just move his clothes in, and then he could move the furniture later.

Really, he didn't know why he hadn't thought of it before.

But when he was on her front porch and he'd unlocked the front door, it still wouldn't open. The key turned in the lock, but the door wouldn't budge. And when he went into the side yard, the broken window was fixed, with a piece of wood nailed across it so even if he broke it again, he'd still have to get through the wood.

It was like she was trying to keep him out. He felt his temper rise and calmed himself. It was just a mistake. She wanted him in there. She'd realize that when he moved in.

If he could get in.

He left his suitcases on the front porch and went to the back door, a little worried about trying it with that damn dog around, the dog would bark and bring the neighbor, the dog would scare Quinn, but while he was standing in the backyard, he heard her shower start—her bathroom window was open, if it wasn't on the second floor he could climb through—and he realized that Quinn at least wouldn't hear him or the dog as long as she was in the shower. And she took long showers. Sometimes he'd stand in the bathroom just to see her come out of the shower, toweling her hair, so beautiful, so round—

He picked up a piece of broken concrete from near the step— the first thing he was going to do once he was moved in was clean up this yard, it was a disgrace—and smashed the window in the back door. Then he reached through and turned the key in the lock—so careless of her to leave the key in the lock with the window right there—and then when the door still wouldn't open, reached in and felt around until he found the deadbolt. She was trying to keep him out. Silly thing. He threw the deadbolt and opened the door.

The dog was there, of course. He walked to the front door with the damn thing yapping behind him, and opened it, turning the key, throwing the deadbolt she'd thought would keep him out, and then he turned and grabbed the mutt before it could scoot away, holding it away from him while it shrieked and peed, and then he took it out on the front porch and threw it as hard as he could into the front yard.

It rolled once and lay still.

Good riddance. He picked up his suitcases from the porch and took them upstairs to his bedroom to unpack.

QUINN'S AFTERNOON WITH the police had been less than productive. She'd filed her complaint, explaining what happened to Frank Atchity, who looked at her without much sympathy but without any antagonism, either. Just the facts, ma'am.

"What I'd like to do is talk to Bill again," Frank had said. "He'll be back from the game this afternoon. I'll give you a call then."

"Can I get a restraining order or something until then?" Quinn said. "I really don't want him near me. He scares the hell out of me." She thought of Bill looming over the night before and shivered in spite of herself. "It's like he's living in a different world. He really thinks we'll get back together, even though I keep telling him no. I mean, I moved out and bought a house. How much more can I do?"

Frank's voice had a little more sympathy this time. "I'll get a judge on the restraining order. You go on home, and if he comes over, don't let him in."

"He has a way in," Quinn said. "We don't know how, we think maybe the basement, but he got in to do all that sabotage. We put on new deadbolts, but—"

"You just relax," Frank said. "We'll get this handled one way or another this afternoon. We're talking about the coach here."

"I know who we're talking about," Quinn said. "He's dangerous."

When she got home, the house was empty. "Daddy?" she'd called, but only Katie came running, anxious as ever, and for once Quinn knew how she felt. She locked all the doors, throwing the deadbolts before she sat down in the living room and told herself not to be ridiculous. She had things to do, Frank Atchity would stop Bill, her dad would come home, everything would be fine.

She'd wandered through the house, double-checking windows, while Katie followed behind her, and she finally realized that as long as the dog was quiet, there wasn't anyone around. She had the perfect Bill alarm in Katie since Katie hated Bill with all the passion in her little dog body. If Katie was quiet, she was safe.

She'd gone upstairs and made the bed and thought about seeing Nick again. *Tonight*, she'd thought. He'd be back tonight. And other nights until he got used to being with her, and then maybe he'd want to move in. Even if he didn't, they were together, and that was pretty damn good. She could even wear Saran Wrap, or that merry widow thing Darla never wanted to see again. She tried to picture herself in black lace. Nah, she was more red and purple satin. She went to the bathroom to search through her nightgowns for something truly outrageous for Nick to rip off her, and then looked at the clock. Four. He got off at five.

Katie's toenails had clipped in the hall outside the bathroom, regular walking, no problem, so she'd stripped off her clothes for a shower. With any luck at all, Nick would get here before Joe, and they could do something loud all by themselves.

The shower felt wonderful, waking up every nerve Nick had played with the night before and the morning after, and she thought hot thoughts as she soaped herself all over. Maybe they'd do it in the shower. That kept her mind occupied until she snapped the water off and shook herself a little. Definitely in the shower. She threw the shower curtain back.

"Hello, Quinn," Bill said.

———

WHEN NICK OPENED his door at three-thirty, Joe was standing there with his portable TV and garbage bag.

"I'm moving in," Joe said, pushing past him.

"The hell you are," Nick said.

Joe dropped his bag and surveyed the apartment. "This is it?"

"It's plenty big enough for one." Nick opened the door. "Thanks for stopping by."

Joe shook his head. "I won't be in your way. I have a date in three hours." He winked at Nick. "Taking Barbara to the Anchor Inn."

"Barbara?"

"Had a job at the bank and we got to talking."

"I bet you did." Joe wasn't budging so Nick shut the door. "Why aren't you at Quinn's?"

Joe snorted. "Right. Like I'm going to bring Barbara back to my daughter's house."

"You're not bringing her back here, either," Nick said. "There's only one bed."

Joe shoved some books and papers off Nick's end table and set the TV down. "So, you'll be at Quinn's." He looked pointedly at Nick's TV. "You got cable?"

"Joe, you're not staying," Nick said, but Joe was already wandering toward the kitchen.

"I've seen coolers larger than that refrigerator," he said when he came back with a beer. "Once you're out of here, I'll get a bigger one."

"I'm not leaving," Nick said.

"I thought you were moving in with Quinn." Joe twisted the cap off and slugged down some beer while Nick thought about killing him.

"She said no," Nick said.

Joe stopped in mid-gulp, choking a little. "What did you do?"

"Nothing." Nick sat down, tired of resisting Joe and thinking about Quinn. "You can stay until seven if you shut up, but you're not spending the night here. Go to Barbara's place."

"You're going to leave Quinn alone with Bill on the loose?" Joe shook his head. "I thought you were better than that."

"Joe, I tried." Nick sat back. "I told her I needed to be there to take care of her, and she said she could take care of herself."

"Independent. I raised both my girls that way." Joe raised the bottle in a toast to himself and drank. Then he wiped his mouth and said, " 'Course, you know that."

Nick narrowed his eyes. "Don't start."

"I raise two women for you to marry, and you won't even let me stay at your place." Joe shook his head. "No gratitude. 'Course, I can see why you'd be a little annoyed about Zoë, she's a handful. But Quinn? Easy as pie to live with. What a sweetie. Can't think why you didn't stay and argue your way back in."

"Joe."

Joe ignored him to look around the room. "Christ, how long were you planning on living here, anyway?"

"Forever," Nick said coldly. "I take it back about staying until seven. You can go—"

"Forever, huh," Joe said. "You got a refrigerator Ford wouldn't put in a camper, your bookshelves are cement blocks and planks, and your TV doesn't even have cable." He met Nick's eyes. "Your forever looks pretty temporary to me."

"That's very deep, Joe," Nick said. "Finish your beer."

Joe chuckled and wandered into the bedroom, probably scoping out the place for future use, and Nick looked at his bookcases and thought, *Maybe I should build some in.*

The thought held no appeal. So he'd still have block and plank bookcases at eighty, so what? They'd still hold up his books.

Except he couldn't imagine himself here at eighty. He never had. Joe was right; somewhere far back in his mind he'd always assumed this was temporary. This was where his mom and dad had lived when they were first married until they could afford a real house, where Max and Darla had lived at first, and he realized now that he'd thought he'd move, too, someday.

"I've seen bigger bathrooms on airplanes," Joe said as he came out of the bedroom.

"Joe—"

"Still with a little fixing up, this could be a real good bachelor pad."

"You're making me sick," Nick said. "This is not a pad and you are not a bachelor."

"Neither are you," Joe said. "You're just too damn dumb to go back and demand to live with your wife. You're going to marry her sooner or later." Joe went back to the kitchen as he spoke and began to open cupboard doors.

"Speaking of living with your wife," Nick said pointedly, "how's Meggy?"

"She's doing real good." Joe pulled out a bag of pretzels and tasted one. "Stale. You should have those airtight cannister things that Quinn has. Even keeps Cheetos crisp." He brought the bag into the living room and sat down.

"Get out, Joe," Nick said without heat.

"You're just going to sit here then." Joe chewed his pretzel. "Best thing that ever happened to you's out on Apple Street, but you're going to sit on your ass here in this dump."

Nick stood up. "Door's over there."

"What did she want that you didn't have?" Joe said. "Why'd she throw you out?"

"She didn't throw me out." Nick walked to the door and opened it. "She said I couldn't move in until I wanted to live there more than I wanted to live here."

Joe looked around. "Doesn't seem like a lot to ask."

"Out," Nick said, and Joe put the pretzels down.

"You're under some stress," he said. "I'll leave." He picked up the TV and then bent to pick up the bag. "Ouch. Hell." He straightened and then looked relieved. "Thought I threw out my back. That'd be a hell of a thing with a big date tonight."

"A tragedy," Nick said. "Be careful on the stairs."

Joe nodded and headed for the door.

"So you going back to Quinn's?" Nick said, trying not to feel guilty.

"Nah, I think I'll go home."

"To Meggy?"

"I figure Edie's about ready to move out," Joe said. "A little Meggy goes a long way if you're not used to her. I'm used to her."

"I don't think it's going to be that easy," Nick said, and Joe shook his head as he stood in the doorway.

"You don't think at all, son," he said. "That's your problem. You just follow your hormones around instead of thinking about what you're doing." Joe leaned against the door frame as he began to wax philosophical, his TV still tucked under his arm. "Now, when you think about it, relationships are like cars."

"They are not," Nick said.

"The good ones are built to take the bumps, they got good shocks, if you know what I mean. Meggy and me"—Joe grinned—"we got good shocks."

"I've got another one for you," Nick said. "Meggy and Edie are sleeping together."

"I know." Joe's grin widened.

"You know?"

"Hell, yes. Been going on for years." Joe shook his head in admiration. "She's an exciting woman, Meggy is. Likes variety."

"I don't want to know this," Nick said.

"Like I said," Joe told him as he started down the stairs. "You don't think enough."

Nick closed the door and looked around. Frayed carpet,

fourth-hand furniture, block and plank shelves—the place looked like he didn't care. Probably because he didn't. It wasn't permanent.

"Fuck," he said. "I like living alone." He sat down in his armchair and spilled Joe's beer. He got a towel from the kitchen—Christ, it was small after Quinn's—and mopped up the beer from the floor—damn nice floor, too, every bit as good as Quinn's—and then sat down to read.

Quinn would be home by now. She'd be napping, or crocheting, or goofing around in the kitchen, playing with Katie, maybe calling Darla. If he'd gone home to her, she'd be talking to him now.

Well, there, see? Talking. How could he read if she was talking?

He looked down at the book he wasn't reading now because he was thinking about Quinn. If he wanted to read, there were six rooms there to find privacy in. And also six rooms to find Quinn in.

Still, how could he give up all of this? He looked around the apartment again and it looked awful, cold and ugly, no light and no couch and no Quinn.

"I'm happy alone," he said out loud, and looked down automatically to see if Katie was tilting her head at him, quivering like the neurotic little rat she was.

Right, no Katie.

Fuck.

He really should be there. Bill might still be out there if Quinn hadn't filed charges. In fact, she probably hadn't filed charges. That would be like her, not wanting to cause a problem she'd have to fix. He'd better go over there and make sure she'd filed charges.

He put the book down and got up to go to Quinn's. *Don't come back until you're coming back for you*, she'd said.

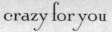

So he'd lie.

He was heading for the door when the phone rang. When he picked it up, Patsy Brady said, "You told me to call you if something was wrong."

Nick went cold. "What?"

"That little dog's out again," Patsy said. "It was walking funny and crying, so I let it in the back gate and it tried to get in the back door, but it couldn't so I went to let it in—"

"Call nine-one-one," Nick said. "I'm leaving now."

"—and that's when I saw the window on the back door was broken," Patsy finished. "That poor little dog ran right through the glass—"

"Fuck!" Nick slammed the phone down and ran for the door.

QUINN'S SCREAM ECHOED in the tiny bathroom, and Bill smiled. "Hey," he said. "It's just me."

She jerked the shower curtain in front of her and said, "Get out. *Get out of here!*"

"Now, just be calm." He smiled again, reassuring her. "Just think about this for a minute."

"Bill—"

"I know you're upset right now, but that's really just stubbornness. You knew we'd get back together sooner or later, and I think it's time. Really, it'll be okay."

Quinn clutched the shower curtain and tried to stop shuddering as he smiled encouragingly at her. *Stay calm and you can fix this.* Okay, he was nuts but he wasn't violent.

Yet.

Her heart leaped and she gritted her teeth. No, she could fix this. It would be better if she wasn't naked in the shower, though. Of course, that had probably been Janet Leigh's last thought when Tony Perkins dropped by.

"Why are you hiding behind that curtain, silly?" Bill said and Quinn forced herself to smile.

"You scared me," she said. "I wasn't expecting you. Uh, could I have a towel, please?"

Bill said, "Oh. Sorry," and handed her the towel from the rack behind him.

"Thank you," she said, and wrapped herself in it, feeling less vulnerable once she was covered. Not a lot, but some. She pushed the shower curtain back and stepped out of the bathtub, her wet hair dripping. "I'll just go get dressed and be right back," and he said, "I'll come with you and we can talk," and followed her down the hall, speeding up when she did.

She tried to close the door to the bedroom in his face, but he stopped it with the flat of his hand, so she retreated to the other side of the bed, knocking over the suitcases he had stacked beside the foot of her bed. They fell lightly, as if they were empty, sliding against each other so that she moved back, staring at them as they came to rest.

"Sorry," he said, "I'll store those in the basement later," and she yanked the top drawer of her washstand out, looking frantically for clothes to stave off whatever he intended to do between now and that "later" he was planning on.

Her underwear was gone. All of it. In its place was his clothing, T-shirts, jockeys, socks.

"Where's my . . . stuff?" she said, trying to sound normal.

"That trashy underwear wasn't you," he said. "You're not like that."

Yes, I am. "Okay," she said, and grabbed one of his T-shirts from the drawer. "Okay, fine."

"We'll have a lot more closet space when we put the new addition on," he said, stepping over the suitcases so he could sit on the bed. "I thought we could go out for dinner tonight and talk about it so we could get started on it as soon as school is out."

She looked at his calm, sure face and tried to decide if he'd get homicidal if she told him the truth. Maybe the best way to handle this would be to not disagree, to just ignore what he was saying. She pulled his T-shirt over her head, hating it that it was his T-shirt but not in a position to be fussy. She kept the towel wrapped around her under it like a bulky sarong even though the T-shirt went to her knees. The more fabric between them the better.

"My dad's living here, you know," she said offhand. "He should be back any time now."

Bill shook his head. "I doubt it. Edie moved back to her apartment, so he's probably at your mom's."

"Edie moved back?" Quinn felt dumbfounded and then alarmed. If her dad wasn't coming back—

"It was all the mothers could talk about at the game," Bill said. "I heard Darla moved back with Max, too. That's when I knew it was time for us."

"Bill, there is no 'us.'" Quinn watched him cautiously to see if he looked annoyed.

"Of course there is." Bill shook his head, patient as always. "You were like this the last time I moved in. I kept suggesting it and you said no, and then I just moved in and things were fine. And it was the same way with the new apartment. Once I moved us, you were happy." He shrugged. "Sometimes you don't know what you want until I show it to you."

Quinn opened her mouth to protest and then shut it again. He was right. Not about what she wanted, but she had given in all the other times. He wasn't crazy to think it would work again.

He was just crazy, period.

"I didn't want it," she said carefully, watching his eyes to see if he'd go rogue on her. "I just didn't want to cause a problem by arguing about it. It was stupid of me, and it's what got us into this mess now, but I didn't want it."

"We're just like we always were," Bill said, almost to himself, and she said, "No. Bill, look at me. I've *changed*."

He grinned at her. "You look just the same as always to me. You used to sleep in my T-shirts sometimes, remember? This is just like always."

"It's not like always. I told you, I've *ch*—"

"People don't change," he said. "They think they do, but they really don't. Down inside, they're the same. Look at Max and Darla. And your dad's probably going to move back with your mom. Just like I'm back with you. People do stuff, but they don't really change."

"Well, *I* did," Quinn said. "And I'm not—"

"No, you didn't," Bill said. "You cut your hair, big deal, it'll grow back. Next September you'll be back teaching art again with long hair, just like always. You're the same." He waved his hand around the room. "You've got the same furniture in this bedroom, the same pictures on the walls. You hung the colander next to that kid picture in the kitchen, the same place it was in both our apartments. You didn't change."

Quinn blinked at him. He was right.

"And I know you think I don't belong here, but you wait." He nodded at her. "It'll be like it always was."

"I'm in love with Nick," she blurted, as much to prove to herself that she'd changed as to him.

"No, you love him," he corrected her gently. "You always have. You just got confused about the kind of love it was because I wasn't with you."

"I'm sleeping with him," Quinn said. "I'm pretty clear on how I love him."

"No," Bill said, his face darkening, and she remembered where she was and how much trouble she might be in. "You just tell him you don't love him that way. It was a mistake. He'll understand. You know Nick, he doesn't like to get involved anyway."

"Okay, you have to listen to me," Quinn said, as quietly as she could. "I think you're right about me not changing"—he smiled at her—"because I think I've always loved Nick."

"No."

"I think I loved him when I talked Zoë into marrying him," she said, keeping her voice as calm as possible. "I think I just didn't believe he was anything I could have. That's why I wanted to be Zoë. So I could have him. Because I've always loved him."

"No," Bill said, standing up.

"And he's always loved me." Quinn backed up a step, still talking in her everything-is-fine voice. "And now we're together the way we should have been from the beginning—"

"No!" Bill said.

"—so you'll have to leave now."

"That's *ridiculous*," he snapped. "I'm unpacked. I'm not leaving, all my clothes are here."

She started to argue, and then somebody banged on the back door and they both froze for an instant. She heard Katie's toenails on the kitchen floor, heard Katie yelping, and Bill said, "Goddamn it, I got rid of that dog. Who the hell—"

"You *what?*" Quinn shoved past him and ran out on the landing as Katie limped up the stairs, shrieking in pain and anger. *"What did you do to her?"* she screamed at Bill and scooped up Katie to cuddle her, to find out what was wrong.

"That dog goes," Bill said in his Master of the Universe voice, and when she turned, he was reaching for her.

"No!" she said, and ran down the stairs, taking the treads two at a time to get Katie to safety.

"Damn it, Quinn," Bill said behind her, and she hit bottom just as she heard the thud of his feet on the top stair. *"Give me that damn mutt,"* he said and she turned in time to see him lose his balance and grab the stair rail. It came out of the wall when he put his weight on it, and he screamed and slammed into the opposite wall as she ran into the dining room, Katie still clutched shivering in her arms.

She heard him land hard at the bottom of the stairs, but by then she was at the front door, fumbling for the key as she heard him curse and try to stand. She cradled Katie in one arm as she got the key in the lock, got it turned, got the door open, and then his hands were on her, yanking at the T-shirt, trying to get to Katie. She fell through the front door as his fingernails raked her back, and she stumbled across the porch and onto the steps, grappling with Katie as she tripped and grabbed the porch rail, which came loose in her hand, a chunk of it coming with her as she fell into the grass. She let Katie go and yelled, "Run, Katie, run!" scrambling to her own feet as she turned back to face Bill, who hit the top step, his face contorted with fury, and broke it in two. He pitched forward and landed hard, lashing out to smash his fist into Katie as Quinn screamed, *"No!"* and fell over him to shield her.

"I'll kill that damn thing," Bill said, and shoved Quinn hard to get past her as he climbed to his feet. She scrambled to her feet in front of him and said, "Stop it, *let her alone*," and he slapped her, knocking her back out of the way.

"I told you," he said to her, his voice calm and sure. *"You're not keeping that dog."* He moved past her and reached for Katie, who cowered back, shaking and yelping, and Quinn grabbed the piece of broken porch rail from the grass and smacked it into the back of his head.

He shook his head once, like a bull, and turned on her. *"Give me that damn thing."*

She backed up a step. "You listen to me," she said, seething. "I hate you. I hate everything about you. I want you off my property and out of—"

He tried to grab the rail and she smacked it into his hand, catching him across the knuckles and making him swear.

"Just get *out*," she said, and he grabbed for her again, and that's when Katie bit the leg of his jeans and yanked, trying to pull him back. He turned and swatted at her, making her yipe again, and Quinn lost it completely and smashed the rail hard into the back of his head.

He staggered and jerked around, and she swung again, connecting solidly with his ear. "Don't you *ever*"—*smash* as he fell back, shaking his head—"come near"—*smash* into his shoulder—"my dog"—*swoosh* a miss as he ducked—"or me"—*smash* into his neck, making him fall to his knees—*"again!"* She raised the rail to hit him the last time, this time between the eyes, the *hell* with fixing things, and then somebody grabbed her from behind and dragged her away, and she struggled to hit him, too, until he took the rail away from her and said breathlessly, "I think you made your point. Knock it off."

"Nick?" she said, and Nick held her tight for an instant before she struggled free and said, *"Katie."*

She swung around to see Katie snarling at a groggy Bill, who had fallen back onto the grass. Beyond them, Frank Atchity's patrol car pulled up.

Frank crossed the lawn at his usual leisurely pace as Quinn dropped the porch rail and tried to look innocent.

"I kinda see your point about the coach," Frank said to her when he was looking down at Bill. He shook his head. "I don't think she likes it this rough, Bill."

Bill let his bloody head fall back, and while Frank recited Miranda, Katie moved in and started to bark.

"I'm moving in," Nick said to Quinn, and she looked at him, startled. "For me. I love you. I always have." He looked down at Bill. "Also, I'll sleep better knowing where that porch rail is. Christ, you really did a job on him. I think he gets it now."

Frank stopped in the middle of the Miranda and frowned at Katie. "Dog, if he can't hear me, he hasn't been warned." He stooped to pat Katie to calm her down, and she squatted and peed next to Bill's ear.

"Good," Quinn said, trying to get her breathing back to normal, still terrified for Katie. "That bastard *hurt my dog*."

"That was his first mistake," Nick said. "Come on, let's get you dressed and her to the vet."

Quinn took one last look at Bill, who met her eyes. No smugness there at all. *"Never again,"* she said and he turned his head away. "Come on, Katie," she said, and Katie limped over to her, panting from barking so hard, not shaking at all.

THE DRIVE-IN OPENED the first Saturday in June, and Quinn and Nick parked in the back row because Quinn had never gotten there in high school. "I always dated nice guys who wouldn't make a move," she told Nick, and he said, "Well, those days are over."

"I stopped by Mom's today," she said as the cartoon came on—a black and white Woody Woodpecker about a cement mixer—and she snuggled down next to his shoulder.

Nick offered her a box of popcorn and said, "What's new?"

"The cable company just added ESPN2 and the Golf Channel." Quinn took some popcorn while Katie did her best imitation of a starving dog. "Dad isn't seeing Barbara anymore because she was pushing for commitment, and he told her he's already committed to Mom. And Mom and Edie went to a garage sale."

Nick laughed.

"Which reminds me," Quinn said, sitting up. "I saw Barbara today, and I swear to God, she looks like Princess Diana. Do you suppose she's planning a trip to England? Should we warn Charles?"

"I don't know and I don't want to know." Nick reached for her and pulled her back. "Barbara is not a good memory."

"She is for some people. Lois threw Matthew out." Quinn relaxed against him, fat with contentment. "She said she liked it better without him, and she'd never have known if Barbara hadn't snagged him. She says she still hates her, but she's stopped calling her the Bank Slut."

"Nothing like a happy ending." Nick looked past her to Katie, who had given up on the popcorn to peer out the open passenger window, looking for approaching trouble but fairly calm about it, as if she knew Bill was locked up for at least her life span. "Don't let that dog jump out the window. We've paid for enough broken dog ribs this year."

Quinn patted Katie's rump. "She's not going anywhere."

Katie dropped from the window and turned her attention back to the popcorn. She took a limping step closer to them on the seat, whining pathetically.

"Have you noticed that dog only limps now when she wants something?" Nick said, and Quinn fed her a piece of popcorn and said, "Yes. Isn't she smart?"

"No," Nick said, and leaned over to open the glove compartment. "Popcorn's bad for dogs. Give her a dog biscuit."

"You keep dog biscuits in the glove compartment?"

"Don't start," Nick said and changed the subject back to something safer. "So how are Edie and your mom and dad really doing?"

"Well, as near as I could tell, Edie looks relieved, Mom looks smug, and Dad looks at the TV." Quinn grinned at him in the deepening dusk. "They're pretty happy, I think. It's like things are back to normal after a really nice vacation. Oh, and Edie said the school board voted this afternoon to hire Dennis Rule as the principal."

"Poor old BP," Nick said. "If Bill had just won that tournament—"

"It wouldn't have made a bit of difference." Quinn tried to keep the satisfaction out of her voice, but it was hard. "He screwed himself on that one. When the super put the hiring committee together, he picked people who knew how the school worked."

"So?"

"So he put Greta on the committee," Quinn said, not even trying not to grin. "I would have paid to have seen Bobby's face when he found out. Although I guess he wouldn't have had much expression with his jaw still wired together like that."

"So everybody's happy," Nick said. "Except for me."

Quinn sat up, her heart skipping for a minute. "You're not happy?"

He shook his head, but even in the twilight she could tell he was up to something.

"I was thinking we needed a change," he said.

"Are you crazy?" Quinn said. "Life is damn near perfect and you want—"

He leaned toward her. "Beds, couches, walls, the kitchen counter, the backyard, the station bathroom." He shook his head. "Same old, same old. We're getting stale."

His eyes were dark on her, and his body was hard and warm as he leaned closer, and he was exciting and dear and sure and everything she'd ever wanted. Quinn thought, *Damn, I'm a lucky woman*, but she kept her voice nonchalant as she said, "So what's your point?"

He slipped his hand under her sweater as he leaned over to whisper in her ear, and she shivered as every nerve she had came alive. "Ever had screaming naked sex in the front seat of a pickup at the drive-in while the whole town around you watches a really bad copy of *Bachelor Party* and your dog eats your popcorn?"

"It's time for a change," Quinn said, and took off her sweater.

All Pan Books are available at your local bookshop or newsagent, or can be ordered direct from the publisher. Indicate the number of copies required and fill in the form below.

Send to: Macmillan General Books C.S.
              Book Service By Post
              PO Box 29, Douglas I-O-M
              IM99 1BQ

or phone: 01624 675137, quoting title, author and credit card number.

or fax: 01624 670923, quoting title, author, and credit card number.

or Internet: http://www.bookpost.co.uk

Please enclose a remittance* to the value of the cover price plus 75 pence per book for post and packing. Overseas customers please allow £1.00 per copy for post and packing.

*Payment may be made in sterling by UK personal cheque, Eurocheque, postal order, sterling draft or international money order, made payable to Book Service By Post.

Alternatively by Access/Visa/MasterCard

Card No.

Expiry Date

Signature

Applicable only in the UK and BFPO addresses.

While every effort is made to keep prices low, it is sometimes necessary to increase prices at short notice. Pan Books reserve the right to show on covers and charge new retail prices which may differ from those advertised in the text or elsewhere.

NAME AND ADDRESS IN BLOCK CAPITAL LETTERS PLEASE

Name

Address

8/95

Please allow 28 days for delivery.
Please tick box if you do not wish to receive any additional information.